SUZANN LEDBETTER

EAST OF PECULIAR

MIRA®

ISBN 1-55166-597-2

EAST OF PECULIAR

Visit us at www.mirabooks.com

Printed in U.S.A.

Sheriff David Henderson maneuvered his copy of the citation into the shallow well at the back of the clipboard, keeping one ear cocked at the radio, waiting for dispatch to run "Garvey, Hannah M." through the computer.

He didn't anticipate any wants or warrants. Scofflaws didn't sass a sheriff when he pulled them over on a traffic stop unless they were stone-cold stupid, and Hannah didn't fit that bill. Too observant and too quick with a comeback.

Idly, David wondered where she was bound for. Dressy outfit, Chicago address, temporary tag, no luggage and a mess of groceries in the cargo bay? Odd combination. She could, he supposed, be visiting someone at Valhalla Springs.

Too late to ask, and he'd blown Officer Friendly out of the water with that "attitude adjustment" remark. Sounded like something out of a *Dirty Harry* movie.

He scowled at the unresponsive radio unit bolted to the floor. His men kidded him about going out on patrol. Set a bad precedent, they said. But he'd known every inch of the zone he'd patrolled in Tulsa for ten years, and most of the faces had names attached. The citizens of Kinderhook County deserved no less.

Adam-101.

Well, it's about time. He unhooked the microphone and thumbed the transmit button. "Go ahead."

No outstanding wants or warrants on your 10-43.

"10-4. Adam-101, 10-8, this location."

10-4, Sheriff...but in case you want to go 10-46, we've got pizza incoming, this location.

"10-4. Adam-101, 10-46." David paused, then added, "And there'd better be something besides crust left when I get there."

For the men and women who pin on a shield every day, knowing full well they're more likely to be cursed, than thanked for a job well-done.

ACKNOWLEDGMENT

My enormous and heartfelt thanks to Christian County (MO) Sheriff Steve Whitney, for his time, expertise and willingness to answer scads of questions; Tabor Medill, Lansing Correctional Facility, Lansing, KS; Eugene E. Andereck, Andereck, Evans, Milne, Peace & Baumhoer, Attorneys at Law, Springfield, MO; Patrol Officers Joshua Ledbetter and Laurel Burton, Tulsa Police Department; Zachary Ledbetter, 2-D Black Belt and U.S.T.F. certified instructor; Gary and Lynna Helvey, Missouri Tae Kwon Do Center, Springfield, MO; Ellen Wade, R.N.; Daniel R. Wilcox, who knows I'm the one who's east of peculiar, but loves me, anyhow; Paul W. Johns, first reader, plot assistant and whine target; Dusty Richards, second reader, glitch finder and secondary whine target; the Gatti's Pizza Gang, who ignored my every-Friday-noon whining; my parents, who constantly tell me they're proud of me; and last, but not least, Dianne Moggy, Martha Keenan and everyone at MIRA Books who gave this flight of fiction wings, and agent Robin Rue, Writers House, whose belief in her clients is extraordinary and unshakable.

1

Road rumble hummed in Hannah Garvey's thighs and feet as she pulled up outside Valhalla Springs's decorative wrought-iron gates. Beyond them lay an expanse of lush, freshly-mown grass and trees a bad poet would call stately. Robins twittered and doused for worms. Squirrels chased their tails and each other.

Bambi, Thumper and Flower must get Sundays off.

Peaceful, it was, and God knew, Hannah needed some. Over the past two days, she'd survived almost six hundred miles of congested interstates, two-lane county roads and truckers who took a "mine's bigger than yours" attitude to the extreme. No small accomplishment for a woman who hadn't driven the length of Illinois and halfway across Missouri in...well, never.

Coming here was the biggest mistake she'd ever made in her life.

Coming here was the most soul-satisfying thing she'd done since she spray-painted Kiss My Ass in huge, red letters on the railroad trestle in Effindale, Illinois, twenty-five years, two months and four days ago.

Hannah eyed the change heaped in one of the console's cup holders. A coin toss wouldn't prove anything. Too easy to cheat. Only time would tell whether she'd screwed up, or finally wised up.

Yesterday's impulsive detour to her hometown certainly hadn't bolstered her confidence. All it had netted was a flat tire on the rental trailer and not a single, recognizable face amid Effindale's current population.

Because no gratification came from flipping off total strangers, Hannah had stopped at what used to be Mutt's IGA, now Food-For-Less, bought several cellophane-wrapped cones of flowers from a cardboard dump-display, then turned down Macon Street to visit her mother and extended-family members.

Talking as she'd pulled up the Johnson grass obscuring their headstones, Hannah had divvied the flowers among the Garvey kin, reserving the least wilted, brightest blooms for her mother's grave, then told her, and the drab, draggled burg that had never produced a congressman, much less a president, goodbye for the last time. Again.

"Okay, so quitting my job and taking off cross-country isn't exactly grist for a *National Geographic Explorer* segment," Hannah informed the Blazer's dashboard. "But for me, it's—well, it's downright..."

Her mind conjured images of Princess Diana boogying with John Travolta; a Harley's full-throttle roar blistering a canyon's walls; a dab of musky perfume spritzed behind the bends of her knees.

"...impetuous," she finished, emphasizing the second syllable and drawing out the fourth's expressive hiss. Like a child's snowsuit bought at an April clearance sale, she knew she had some growing to do before the adjective fit.

What had brought her to Valhalla Springs, a central Missouri retirement village described as "East of Peculiar and the closest thing to paradise this side of Sanity,'' depended on who was asked.

Coffee-bar chatter at Chicago's Friedlich & Friedlich Agency attributed the veteran advertising-account executive's unexpected resignation to burnout with a side order of chronic love-gone-wrong.

The suits put their balding heads together, diagnosed acute menopause, congratulated themselves for being born male—thus hormonally unchallenged—then hopped into their respective red sports cars to drive home for dinner with second wives approximately the same age as their daughters.

Hannah never found out who gave the Betty Ford Clinic her unlisted home telephone number, but reality had nothing to do with depression, heartbreak, estrogen or substance abuse. She'd simply wakened one Saturday morning, eyeballed the double briefcase–load of work she'd lugged home every weekend for twenty-five friggin' years and admitted how much she'd come to hate Chicago, her ''career,'' her employers, most of her clients, Gloria Steinem and capitalism in general.

After frittering away a half day composing an eloquent letter of resignation, the final draft read:

Memo to: Thomas Friedlich, President
Robert Friedlich, Vice president
Dear Tom and Rob,
I quit.
Sincerely,
Hannah G.

The following Monday, Hannah phoned resort developer Jack Clancy at his Saint Louis office to tell him Trina DeSalvo would be taking over the Valhalla

Springs account. Jack responded to the news by offering to beat a raise out of the Friedlich brothers.

A momentary flirtation with siccing the former Saint Louis County Golden Gloves champ on the one-time Wizards of Wabash Avenue suffused Hannah's black heart. Clancy as a literal hit man had definite appeal, but she knew he wouldn't let her watch.

"Sorry, Jack, you'd enjoy it too much, and money really isn't the issue," she replied, giving not a rip that twenty-seven grand in tax-deferred CDs was her only hedge against a refresher course in the fine art of Dumpster diving.

Somewhere between growing up poor, striving for rich and settling for comfortable, she'd realized the American Dream too closely resembled a coma; a concept Jack would regard as treasonous.

Their relationship straddled the realm between business and boon companionship, but admitting she'd quit first and would figure out how to support herself later would bring a lecture, a loan offer or a referral to a reputable psychiatrist.

Jack's chuckle wended up from the earpiece. "Money is always an issue, sweetpea. The weight of whatever you're shoveling is directly proportional to how much you're paid to do it."

"Not anymore." Hannah grinned at her uncustomary devil-may-careness. It felt good. It felt *great*. "I've done a lot of thinking, and a bigger paycheck won't cure what ails me."

"Then what will? No offense to Ms. DeSalvo, but if you're jumping to another agency, the Valhalla Springs and Clancy Development accounts are going with you."

Hannah picked nonexistent lint from the hem of her

plum power suit's skirt. "I haven't decided anything yet. Thought I'd fall back, regroup, consider my options...."

"Footloose and fancy-free isn't your style, Ms. Garvey."

Oh, yeah? She stared at the telephone's base unit, willing a button to blink. She'd told her assistant to hold all calls, but it had never stopped him before.

"But since you are," Jack continued in a thinking-aloud tone, "what would you say to a job as Valhalla Springs's resident manager?"

"Thanks, but no thanks."

"Too fast. Give me one good reason why not."

God, how she hated that phrase. No one ever threw it at her when she *had* a good reason. "Aw, c'mon, Jack, I'm only forty-three, and—"

"I thought you were forty-seven."

She winced. "The fact remains, playing bingo in the boonies with the Metamucil generation isn't what I had in mind."

"Even at twenty-five thou a year, plus a furnished cottage overlooking the lake?" He droned on like a hypnotist, "No Friedlichs breathing down your neck. No neighbors cranking up sound systems until your walls vibrate. No gangstas or dopers on the prowl within a hundred miles. The beauty and serenity of the Ozarks, Hannah, that's what I'm offering you."

She slumped in her desk chair and closed her eyes. Photographs of the development clicked behind them like slides in a carousel. Think, kiddo. One good reason.

Tension drained from her shoulders as she envisioned spring-fed creeks, their pebbled courses shimmering silver-white in the sun. She heard leaves riffle on the wind; saw blue sky and stars stretching from horizon to horizon, not to mention, the horizon itself.

For the first time in her life, she'd have a house of her own, complete with a front porch; Jack's covenant required them. Come evening, she'd plop her heels on the railing and drink in great gulps of country air—the kind you can't see and don't have to chew.

Jeez Louise. She felt as if she were melting.

"Why me, Jack? I don't know anything about managing a retirement community."

"You're smart and I trust you. No sense lying, it's a twenty-four/seven commitment. You'll tour prospective leaseholders, oversee maintenance and services, do some bookkeeping—stuff like that."

Hannah's internal bullshit detector beeped a warning. "Stuff like what, exactly?"

"Three hundred and sixty-one widows, widowers and retired couples live in Valhalla Springs. It's like a small town and you'll be the mayor. Use your imagination."

Her visions of paradise unraveled at the edges. As the fatherless child of an only child, she'd felt like the resident alien in a clan of elder tribesmen. Instead of being pampered by her extended family, they'd regarded her as a noisy pain in the ass. Which she was, but conversations revolving around Great-Aunt Lurleen's gastroenteritis, The Bomb, and yellow-dog Republicans would make any red-blooded, American tomboy retaliate with armpit farts.

"Well, it does sound interesting, Jack, but I need a little time to think it over. What say I get back to you, oh, Friday at the latest?"

"Uh-uh, sweetpea. It's now or never."

His ultimatum was no idle threat. Gut instinct had

made Jack Clancy a multimillionaire perpetually on the brink of bankruptcy. He had no patience for sissies.

Resort-industry colleagues and competitors had howled with laughter at Jack's plan to build a self-sufficient retirement community "in the middle of *Missouri*, for Christ's sake." Slow headshakes of the type common to funerals met his idea of leasing cottages to healthy, relatively wealthy seniors wise enough to know shrouds don't come with pockets.

IdaClare Clancy, Jack's widowed mother, had said, "Stick to your guns, boy. I like four seasons, I can break a hip on sand as easy as snow, and if you think you're shipping my butt to Florida or Arizona, you've got another think comin'."

Putting a couple of million dollars where her mouth was sealed Jack's resolve, or doom, or reliance on antacids, depending on Valhalla Springs's latest profit-and-loss statement.

Feeling slightly bilious herself, Hannah selected a pink and a green Tums from the apothecary jar on her desk and popped them in her mouth. "If—and I do mean *if*—I take the job, when would I start?"

"Yesterday. Mother has been in charge since Owen McCutcheon left. She means well, but the same was said of Imelda Marcos. If I don't do something quick, I'll have the Midwest's answer to the Alamo on my hands."

Hannah made a face, not entirely caused by the cherry-lime chalk coating her tongue. "McCutcheon left? Why?"

Silence, then a hedged, "Nothing job-related."

"J-a-c-k...?"

"Owen was recommended by a friend of a friend,

okay? It never occurred to me to ask if he had a history of mental disorders.''

''Such as?''

''Obsessive-compulsive, latent schizophrenia and more phobias than you can shake a stick at. I repeat, none of it job-related. Satisfied?''

Not entirely, but it explained Jack's eagerness to hire a known entity. All things considered, McCutcheon probably wouldn't be too tough an act to follow.

''I have a client cooling his jets downstairs in the atrium,'' Jack said. ''What's the verdict, Hannah Marie?''

Staring through her Blazer's bug-splattered windshield at the development's entrance put a rhetorical spin on the question. ''Impetuous,'' she said again, threw back her head and laughed.

She clicked on the tape deck and sighed as Janis Joplin's whiskey-scorched voice growled the opening lines of ''Summertime.'' So what if it was only early April? Who says good vibes must coincide with the season?

An emotion akin to stage fright surged through her when the semicircle drive fronting a mellow brick cottage similar to a miniature plantation house came into view. A woodburned sign posted beside the flagstone walk identified it as the manager's office.

The original *Miracle on 34th Street* was her all-time favorite movie, though she'd always envied Natalie Wood *her* wish coming true. Jack Clancy in the Kris Kringle role didn't fit the script, but she half believed she'd find a hickory cane propped up in a corner, and was half-afraid she wouldn't.

Unwilling to rush pell-mell into a fantasy only to find out, once and for all, there really was no such thing as Santa Claus, she rationalized that a new operations manager should have a better idea of the operation she'd been hired to manage.

To her right, golfers of both genders flocked the fairways and greens. A portly fellow whose red slacks and diagonally striped shirt reminded her of a buoy at low tide swung through his tee-shot well before the *whap* of three-wood meeting ball reached her ears.

Farther on, and opposite the golf course, johnboats with fishing rods jutting from their gunwales like antennae bobbed atop an expanse of rippling blue water. The spring and creek-fed seventy-acre lake was too small for skiing, but it teemed with white bass, smallmouths, crappie and catfish.

At sunset, the view from the adjacent community center's wraparound veranda would be glorious.

The calendar lost a century at the boulevard's intersection with Main Street's commercial district. Tripleglobe gaslights and striped awnings shading the ruddybrick storefronts harkened back to an era when gentlemen tipped their derbies to ladies in ruffled bonnets and long dresses with leg-o'-mutton sleeves.

Most of the shops, cafés and the mercantile were annexes of larger concerns headquartered in Sanity, the county seat twenty-two miles away. Residents benefited from the convenience, merchants profited from a semicaptive customer base and prospective tenants were relieved to find out that real-estate listings combining "remote" and "Ozarks" didn't always mean "accessible by mule during drought years."

Hannah smiled at a tole-painted, handsaw-shaped signboard in the clinic's front window. Dr. John Pennington, the resident "sawbones," and his wife, Lois, a registered nurse, had sold their general medical practice in Des Moines when MBAs who didn't know a stethoscope from a gyroscope gave Pennington a seven-patients-per-hour quota to meet.

In exchange for a rent-free cottage and a monthly stipend, the Penningtons treated minor ailments at the clinic three mornings a week and were on call if emergencies arose. The seriously ill or injured were transported by ground or air ambulance to Sanity's Mercy Hospital.

Terracing upward on three sides of the commercial district, single-story brick, native stone and clapboard cottages graced curving, tree-canopied avenues. Their architecture ranged from châteaus to Cape Cods to English half-timbers; more-or-less uniformly sized, but in no way pricier editions of the fifties cookie-cutter tract housing.

"Valhalla Springs?" Hannah had queried when the development was still in the blueprint stage. "I'd go back to the drawing board on the name, Jack. It's hard to pronounce, harder to spell and doesn't sound at all Missouri-ish."

"For your information," he'd replied rather snootily, "Valhalla is a mythological place where heroes' souls are received. Don't ask why that seems appropriate. It just does."

And you were absolutely right, Hannah thought. Heaven on earth it is, and photographs don't do it justice. Film is too one-dimensional to capture its sense of place.

Main Street wyed onto Hawthorne Street. She took the right fork, circled back to Valhalla Boulevard on Persimmon Lane, then braked at the intersection. Guest cottages, a pool and a gazebo flanked the golf course's clubhouse. Like the entire development, it must have cost a mint to adapt amenities to the terrain rather than bulldoze the land into submission.

Surveying the acres upon acres of rolling, uncluttered greenspace, Hannah realized the "lost in the madding crowd" adage for which cities were famous didn't apply here, unless you were a tree. Even the chipmunk squatting on its haunches beside a forsythia bush regarded her as curiously as a Neighborhood Watch program's block captain.

As if the bewhiskered gendarme had somehow signaled for backup, a vintage Edsel with a hood wide enough to land fighter jets pulled up behind the rental trailer. A skinny codger in chartreuse plaid slacks, a tangerine sport shirt, yellow pancake cap, black socks and sandals emerged from the driver's-side door.

A widower, Hannah supposed. No self-respecting wife would let the old boy fetch the morning paper in that getup.

"Car trouble?" he asked as he sauntered past. "Pop the latch and I'll take a look at the engine."

She craned her head out the window. "Thanks, but there's nothing wrong with my truck. I just stopped to admire the scenery."

Disappointment pinched his leathery features. "Are you sure? I'm a pretty fair, shade-tree mechanic."

She clicked off the tape deck just as Ms. Joplin revved into the *nah-na-nah* chorus to "Me and Bobby McGee," and gunned the Blazer's perfectly functional engine.

Mr. Goodwrench frowned. "By golly, you do have a knock under there, young lady. Could be watery gas. Could be you need a valve job. If it were me, I'd have 'er checked before I hit the road again."

Her expression a picture of distressed damselhood,

Hannah teased, "Gee, mister, do you think I can make it a half mile or so?"

"You mean you're moving in? Here?" He whisked off his cap and scratched the snowy mane beneath it. "Honeylamb, if you're old enough to retire, I want your plastic surgeon's phone number."

"Hannah Garvey," she said, offering her hand, "the new resident manager."

"Well, I'll be a monkey's uncle." Bony fingers closed around hers, then he rotated her hand and kissed the knuckles. "Delbert Bisbee, U.S. Postal Service—retired."

She smiled at his courtliness. "It's a pleasure to meet you, Mr. Bisbee."

"Delbert, if it's all the same to you." His brow furrowed as he inspected the Blazer's interior. "Kind of a hefty set of wheels for a girl, isn't it? Hope you're not one of those femi-nazis."

"Excuse me?"

"Ever listen to Rush Limbaugh?"

"Not without a gun at my head."

"Aw, ol' Rush rambles on some, but you won't catch him sashaying around in a bra and panties like that hippie pervert with the dirty mouth."

The allusion to Howard Stern and mental images of Limbaugh in lingerie had a negative effect on the Happy Meal she'd wolfed down for lunch. Gratitude abounded when Delbert followed up with, "So, is it Ms. Garvey, Mrs. Garvey or Hannah, plain and simple?"

"Hannah, plain and simple." She grinned. "If it's all the same to you."

"That's the ticket." His laugh rattled like gravel in

a tin can. "There's enough bossy ol' broads around here as it is. Plays Billy Ned with democracy, lemme tell you."

Hannah shifted into drive. "Give me a few days to settle in, then stop by for a cup of coffee. I'm not much of a cook, but I'm a whiz with a percolator."

He jerked a thumb at the trailer. "Bet you could use some help with your housegoods and all."

At five-seven, she had at least four inches and a couple-or-ten pounds on the wiry Samaritan. Nor had she ever made good on her promise to learn CPR.

"Much as I appreciate the offer, I really don't have that much to unload. I sold almost everything I owned before I left Chicago."

Salvatore Rizzio, her apartment building's super, had warned her against burning bridges, but Hannah's highrise garage sale had been the most fun she'd had in ages. Co-workers and neighbors mined her closets, wrestled furniture into the elevators and nearly came to blows over who'd seen "those *darling* pottery lamps" first.

By midnight, they'd stripped the place of its southwestern motif, including the towering, phallic cacti that thrived on intentional neglect. After locking the door behind the last bargain hunter, Hannah had leaned against it, murmured, "Farewell, Santa Fe phase, and thank God and the neighbors you're gone."

Her original Chicago apartment, a bleak, fifth-floor walk-up, had been furnished like a dorm room: hot plate and vaultlike Amana, Salvation Army furniture, thumbtacked posters, milk-carton candles tinted with melted crayons, roaches, rats and a former alley cat who preferred catching his dinner on the paw to bowls of dry kibble.

Once again reduced to keepsakes and can't-part-with-them clothes, she realized the horrid flat she couldn't wait to move from had been home in ways its successor never achieved in twenty-some years' occupancy.

Its inaugural "Uptown Mod" phase's black Naugahyde furniture, chrome-and-glass accessories, requisite water bed and boyfriend named Dirk, had evolved to Charles and an ultraconservative "Urban Sears Roebuck Look," then to "I ♥ Country" starring Cody Wyrick, pine primitives and lots of pastel bunnies, duckies and gamboling lambs.

"English Manorhouse," Hannah's longest-lasting thematic environment, coincided with her love affair with Jarrod Amberley, a European antiques dealer. Over a decade passed before she admitted she lied whenever she agreed marriage was redundant to a committed, monogamous relationship.

Another year went by before she faced the fact that Jarrod was neither committed nor monogamous.

She'd fallen for the "Santa Fe look" on the rebound, like a bride left at the altar who elopes with the best man. After living like a nun doing penance at Taco Bell, Hannah couldn't care less how her new cottage was furnished as long as she didn't have to share it with anyone who peed standing up.

"I didn't figure you were hauling that trailer around for ballast," Delbert said, startling her from her reverie. He hunched a shoulder. "Just thought you might want some company, that's all."

A basset hound would look giddy by comparison.

He shuffled off, head bowed, as though she'd swatted him with a rolled-up newspaper for chewing up a new pair of Capezios.

Having been related to several, she'd always been a sucker for crotchety old geezers. Something told her this one might also be a fountain of information not covered in the official Valhalla Springs operations manual.

"Hey, Delbert."

He spun around so fast his cap tilted askew. "Huh?"

"If you really don't have any other plans..."

"Lemme see now." He planted an arm across his chest and rested an elbow on it. "Me and Lydia Wallace have dinner on Mondays and Thursdays. Tuesday's square dancing with Maxine McDougal. Carol Fogerty whips up some low-fat nastiness on Wednesdays, and most Saturdays, me and some other stags cruise to town to check out the local action."

He scratched a concave cheek. "No, best I remember, the slate's plumb devoid of activities today."

Hannah laughed. "You're a scoundrel, Delbert Bisbee."

"Naw. Just your run-of-the-mill Renaissance man."

"Well, then, what are you waiting for? Crank up that aircraft carrier of yours and lead the way."

He chafed his hands, muttered, "Hot-ziggity," and jitterbugged to his car. The cream-puff classic peeled around Hannah's rig as if its tailpipes were on fire.

The world-balanced-on-its-axis kind of anticipation that makes blue moons seem ordinary brought gooseflesh racing up her arms. Who needed Kris Kringle's hickory cane when she had Delbert Bisbee, U.S. Postal

Service, retired, and self-proclaimed Renaissance man in her corner?

The white-on-white bathroom shimmered with a soft amber light and filled with the bewitching scent of "Midsummer's Eve" as Hannah held a match to each of the pillar candle's three wicks.

"Speaking from experience, Ms. Garvey," she said, "how many Delberts does it take to screw in a light-bulb?"

"One," she answered, glancing up at the darkened ceiling. "The same number of Delberts it takes to short-out all the fixtures while he's at it."

Chuckling to herself, she opened the shower stall's door, turned the faux-crystal knob to "H" and retreated. It was impossible to fault the results of her newfound friend's good intentions. Delbert had, after all, apologized until she ordered him to stop, and insisted upon reassembling the kitchen cabinet's lazy Susan when it collapsed after his slight miscalculation with a screwdriver.

Hannah's eyes traveled down her mirrored reflection and she wondered how long it had been since she'd seen herself naked by candlelight; wondering further how long it had been since she'd seen herself *clothed* by candlelight.

Before a particular old flame, or several came to mind, she sucked in her tummy and turned to and fro, arranging her extremities into a variety of print-model poses.

It had certainly been long enough to forget how dim illumination washed her skin with a golden, toasty glow and brought out the auburn highlights in her hair;

the slimming effect shadows had on her waistline and hips, and how they erased any trace of cellulite from her thighs.

Best of all, if she scrunched her arms just so, a pair of 34-Bs could be mistaken for 36-Cs.

She suddenly saw Delbert's unhandiness in a new light, as it were. Bathing without virtue of electricity could be habit-forming, now that she was old enough to appreciate it, instead of shuddering at memories of unpaid utility bills, galvanized washtubs and rinse-resistant detergent granules her teachers mistook for head lice.

The cascade drumming the fiberglass enclosure beckoned her. Ingrid Bergman couldn't have made a more sweeping entrance had an in-the-buff Bogie been waiting inside, ready to cause a temporary delay in her departure from Casablanca.

Expecting a stinging stream of hot water, it took Hannah's brain a moment to register the icy deluge pelting her from head to toe.

The rippled-glass door banged the wall. She leaped from the shower, sputtering and gasping, arms flailing and legs pumping as if running in place. Her wet feet skidded out from under her and she landed butt first on the very cold, very hard, ceramic-tile floor.

Sitting spraddle-legged and stunned, Hannah listened to the peck of water droplets, keenly aware of her tailbone, which was presently located in the vicinity of her shoulder blades.

Why didn't I notice the mirror wasn't clouded over with steam? Why didn't I do the ol' wrist-test before taking the plunge?

Delbert's voice informing her he'd reset the water

heater's thermostat crackled in her mind as if transmitted by shortwave radio. Or Satan.

A family-size tissue box hurtled through the air like a rectangular hand grenade and banged off the bathroom door. "Why didn't I *strangle* that old fart when I had the chance?"

2

Mondays happen, even in paradise.

The bedside telephone's trill yanked Hannah from dreamland. She bolted upright, swimmy-headed and in the throes of the kidnapped-by-aliens disorientation peculiar to the newly moved.

Sunlight blazed through windows on the wrong side of the room. The walls were a gentle cream beige, not toilet-bowl aqua. Wadded jeans, a Chicago Bulls T-shirt and an empty packing box blinked into view. Ah-ha. She was in Missouri, not entering the "Twilight Zone."

Mystery solved, she snatched up the receiver in the middle of its third ring. "'Lo?"

"Good mornin', Hannah," a woman drawled. "This is IdaClare Clancy, dear. I surely do hope I didn't wake you up."

The alarm clock's jumbo red numerals said it was all of 8:17. "Oh, certainly *not,* Mrs. Clancy."

"Jack has talked about you so much, I feel as if we're already friends. Do call me IdaClare."

"Okay…" Except friends do *not* call friends at eight-friggin'-o'clock in the morning unless they're hemorrhaging.

"The girls and I are meeting for brunch at Nellie

Dunn's Café at eleven. Please join us. We're all *dying* to meet you and simply won't take no for answer.''

That pretty much scotched the one Hannah had in mind. She ran her fingers through clumps of pillow-dried hair. ''I appreciate the invitation, Mrs.—uh, IdaClare, but I'm afraid I can't today.''

Silence thundered along the telephone line. Hannah blurted, ''Not that I wouldn't love to meet everyone, but the rental trailer must be returned before noon, and I have several other errands to do while I'm in town.''

''I understand perfectly, dear. No problem at all. We'll just reserve a table for eleven-thirty, instead. See you then.''

Click. Dial tone.

Crap. Playing beat-the-clock was supposed to be part of her former life. Hannah slam-dunked the receiver, whipped back the covers and dashed to the bathroom. The light-switch toggle flipped up, but nothing happened. She whimpered and jiggled it three or four times, in case God was in the mood to take pity on her.

She stomped to the office nook and ran a finger down the laminated list of departmental telephone numbers. Finding the one she sought, her years in advertising automatically converted its digital sequence into words. The obscene sentiment derived from it echoed her attitude.

''Maintenance, Bob Davies.''

''This is Hannah Garvey, the—''

''Sorry, we're all out on service calls. At the beep, please leave your name, number and a brief description of the problem. We'll get back to you as soon as possible.''

She complied through gritted teeth.

At precisely 9:01, she sprinted out the door, still dewy from a warp-speed cold shower. If her hair frizzed as it dried au naturel, so be it. If white slacks, a white silk blouse and crimson blazer screamed "blood-drive volunteer," screw it. Glamour was impossible when breakfast consisted of crackers, tap water and a black cohosh capsule.

The empty trailer rattled and bonged as she negotiated county road VV. Rectangular green signs paced off the miles remaining to Sanity—the county seat, not her mental condition. The enumerations had the same effect on her nerves as the whirling hands on the Mad Hatter's pocket watch.

Concrete bridges built before the Louisiana Purchase had been striped for two lanes by a highway-department employee who'd habitually rooked a younger sibling when candy bars were divided. Each oncoming school bus, semi and motor home put a terrifying new twist on "meeting someone halfway."

Thirty-two minutes post-departure from Valhalla Springs, a bulbous water tower announced Home of the Sanity Tigers. Pastures, dense woods, and hobby farms gave way to fast-food franchises, a Wal-Mart, a Price-Slasher supermarket, Holiday Inn Express and strip shopping centers; their order of appearance in any midwestern town as unique as Monopoly board properties.

A rectangular, orange-and-white U-Haul sign brought a sigh of relief. Hannah whipped into Bear Creek Rentals—"If We Don't Have It, You Don't Need It"—missing by inches a bisected whiskey barrel full of frost-nipped geraniums.

A young man in coveralls ambled from a concrete-block building painted like olive-drab camouflage.

Mike was embroidered on an oval patch above his left breast. "What can I do ya for, ma'am?"

"I need to turn in this trailer and hitch."

Mike's eyes skimmed the rental contract. "Illinois, huh? Don't get many from there. Now, California? Different story altogether. Appears them earthquakes, floods and whatnot is scarin' the sun-bunnies outta their holes."

"That's very interesting," Hannah lied, "but I am in kind of a hurry."

"Well, why didn't you say so?" He slicked back his bangs, then crammed on a Bass Pro Shops cap, bill-frontward; at his age, the mark of a nonconformist. "Lemme grab a wrench and a pair o' pliers, and I'll have you on your way in a jiffy."

By the dashboard clock, an Ozarks' jiffy constituted twenty-six minutes.

Hannah found the post office despite Mike's convoluted directions. The single-story, flat-roofed brick building, located in a primarily residential neighborhood, typified the postwar era's bunker mentality, in that government edifices built during that period resembled bomb shelters with flagpoles in front of them.

"My brother, he took himself off to Chicago, long 'bout eight, nine year ago," the clerk informed her. As if to help jog Hannah's memory, he went on, "Name's Buck Massey. Husky fella, with red hair and a beard? Loads baggage out to the airport."

Hannah shook her head, suppressing a grin. "Sorry."

"Hmmph." His gaze lowered to scrutinize the form he held between index fingers and thumbs. "That's cities for ya. Nobody knows nothin' about nobody. Wouldn't live in one for all the tea in China."

Hannah let the comment slide. Buck-the-baggage-handler, and Chicago's other three million souls didn't need her to defend them.

By 10:23, she was empowered to collect mail at Valhalla Springs's substation box number two. It came as no surprise that IdaClare Clancy had dibbies on number one.

Tiffany Meade, the new-accounts representative at the First National Bank, couldn't have been a day over twelve, had a flawless complexion, a cute set of dimples and wicked, red-enameled talons. While she tapped vital statistics into a computer, Hannah wondered how the girl managed trips to the powder room without maiming herself.

Presently, the printer spewed out sheaves of forms requiring Hannah's signature. Jack, bless his heart, had the clout and foresight to arrange myriad authorizations in advance and by telephone.

Her penmanship flagged as the responsibilities of her new job began to feel more like trip wires than challenges. Whoever coined the phrase "Ignorance is bliss" might well have been the same doofus who originated, "Sticks and stones may break your bones, but words will never harm you."

She'd been so safe, so sheltered at Friedlich & Friedlich. Known exactly what was expected of her, how to dress, how to act and react, her territorial boundaries.

Cool it, she told herself, before you have to ask Tiffany for a paper sack to breathe into. What did you know about the advertising business when you started? A helluva lot less than you led Tom and Rob to believe.

And weren't you the idiot who sat on a park bench and cried because you turned the wrong way at a street corner and didn't know how to get home?

You're spoiled, not stupid. You'll screw up like you always have, and learn from it. *Duc, sequere aut de via decede.* Lead, follow or get out of the way.

Once the business accounts were in order, the efficient accounts rep went to work on a batch of new-customer paperwork. Hannah's attention drifted to the drop-dead gorgeous cowboy on the beggar's side of an adjacent desk flirting his way into a car loan and, quite possibly, a nooner.

"Here's a book of counter checks to tide you over," Tiffany said, right when the neighboring conversation verged on a climax, so to speak. "Let me know if your custom-printed ones don't arrive in a week, or ten days."

"Will do."

Sliding a small card across the desk, Tiffany whispered, "This is your personal identification number— PIN code—for our automated teller machine at Valhalla Springs. Memorize it, then destroy the card. Never give your code to anyone—" she winked "—except maybe your husband or something."

Hannah stifled the impulse to add, whether you choose to accept this mission, this card will self-destruct in five seconds. "Thanks for the warning, but I don't have a husband, much less, an 'or something.'"

Tiffany's thumb massaged the diamond-chip and gold band on her left ring finger as if it were a miniature Aladdin's lamp. "Oh, gosh, I'm so sorry."

Hannah made a hasty exit before the starry-eyed bride thought of an eligible bachelor who specialized in putting horny spinsters out of their misery.

Her step faltered as Price-Slasher's pneumatic doors parted in welcome. Ten neighborhood markets the size of Brancusi's in Chicago would fit inside this blindingly fluorescent Godzilla of grocery stores, not counting the square footage devoted to liquor, flowers, video rentals, film developing and a branch bank.

Dodging around fiberglass archipelagoes heaped with fresh vegetables and produce, freestanding displays, children playing hide-and-seek, T-shirt racks and moonlighting grandmothers in aprons stationed behind card tables, handing out food samples, Hannah caught herself mentally filling in the lyrics to the Neil Diamond Muzak.

Somewhere between "Cracklin' Rosie" and "I Am…I Said," her heart leaped at the sight of an open-topped freezer case as long as a subway car, situated like a median between the stainless-steel-and-glass, cabinet-style sidewalls.

Frozen-Food Heaven. She shoved her shopping cart with the jammed back wheel up one side and down the other twice before admitting the microwavable, multi-ethnic cuisine that had anchored her daily caloric intake for a quarter century was also a part of her former life.

Oh, there were products with names that might sound foreign to the uninitiated, but Hannah had been in the advertising business too long to fall for "Chicken Terriyakki" manufactured in Wichita, Kansas. She also knew better than to select nationally branded entrées by virtue of the food photos on their cartons, but hey, a girl's gotta eat.

At 11:04, she was snarling "C'mon…c'mon," at the veritable convoy creeping along First Avenue. Each two car-length gap dared a launch into traffic and promised a fender bender.

A delivery van's driver slowed and waved Hannah into the lane. She blew him a kiss and hauled asphalt.

Without the trailer bobbing behind it, the Blazer lived up to its model name.

Twenty-two miles to Valhalla Springs. Five minutes—ten, maximum—to unload the perishables, which had better be sacked together, or the kid who packed them was not destined to ever celebrate Father's Day. By eleven forty-five, she should be shaking hands with IdaClare Clancy and The Girls, though they probably considered fashionably late to be ten minutes early.

As she topped a hill, Hannah glimpsed a cruiser's light bar in her rearview mirror. Then she glanced at her speedometer needle. It ticktocked between sixty-five and seventy.

"I am a figment of your imagination," she chanted. "You've already met April's ticket quota. You let Delbert fix your radar gun."

Flashing red white and blue brightened the horizon like a patriotic halo. A Crown Victoria loomed above her side mirror's "Objects may be closer than they appear."

"Now you tell me," she grumbled, edging her truck onto the shoulder. She thumbed the window button, cut the ignition, crossed her arms and pouted.

John Law braked to a stop a few yards behind her. Bright blue lettering spelled out SHERIFF on the cruiser's white hood. Its occupant spoke into a corded microphone, then stepped out, settling a black Stetson on his head.

Even without the haberdashery, the man was six-three or better, and an easy two hundred and thirty pounds, sans the Kevlar vest outlined by his navy blue uniform shirt. If convention prevailed, Mrs. County Mountie wore a junior-petite, size zero.

To his credit, he wasn't swinging a whomp-ass stick like Effindale's chief of police, Vic Brummit. The chief, who fancied himself a ladies' man, preyed on the poor, the powerless and, consequently, the Garveys. His style of law enforcement mimicked Buford Pusser's as portrayed by Joe Don Baker in *Walking Tall*, except Brummit broke bones for fun and profit. Fair or not, he'd tainted Hannah's attitude toward any man with a shield pinned on his chest.

"Mornin', ma'am." The sheriff propped a metal notebook on the window frame. "Taking those curves kinda fast, weren't you?"

Smart enough to neither confess nor argue, she handed him the license she'd taken from her wallet, noting the D. Hendrickson nameplate on his pocket flap.

"Chicago, eh?" He stepped back to examine the Blazer, presumably to check for evidence of any recent hit-and-runs. Hannah seized the opportunity to conduct a vertical reconnaissance: mid-thirties, aquiline nose, square jaw, no wedding ring, no telltale line where one should be, an oblong stain on his trouser leg above the right knee. Doughnut grease?

"Nice rig you bought, what—" he nodded at the temporary tag in the back window "—a week ago? In pretty fair shape, too, for a '96."

"Even better, for a '94." Hannah smiled sweetly. "The title and registration are in the glove compartment, if you want to see them."

"No need. You don't look much like a car thief." He consulted her license photograph. "Don't look much like this picture, either."

She wasn't sure the remark was intended as a compliment, but gave him the benefit of the doubt. The

Illinois Department of Motor Vehicles could turn Sandra Bullock into a bona fide barker.

"I clocked you at sixty-seven in a forty-five, Miz Garvey. Mighty risky, especially for a flatlander."

Flatlander? She repressed obscenities longing to be free. "The sign said the speed limit is sixty on this road, Sheriff."

"It is, save the dozen or so places it's posted slower on account of the hills and curves." His smile was as counterfeit as hers had been. "The highway department's real generous with them along this stretch. Fatalities put kind of a damper on the tourist trade, don't you know."

A pickup held together by duct tape and Bondo sputtered over the hill. The goateed driver wolf-whistled, then yelled, "Yee-oww! Need any help friskin' her, Sheriff?"

Hendrickson answered with a "Get outta here" wave.

"Relative of yours?" Hannah inquired, and instantly regretted it. On a scale of ten, the day had scored a solid zip, so why not frost the sheriff and sink it to negative numbers? Just think how impressed IdaClare would be when Hannah used her jailhouse phone call to tender her regrets.

"If I cared to, I could nail you for careless and imprudent, *and* speeding, ma'am." He took a pen from his pocket, then flipped open the citation book. "Fact is, if you weren't a lady, I'd be inclined to haul you out of there for a little attitude adjustment."

A small voice at the back of her mind warned, *Don't, Hannah. Don't, don't—* "Well, we wouldn't want to be guilty of discrimination, would we? Go ahead, haul away so I can slap you with the biggest police-brutality suit this county's ever seen."

He chuckled. ''I reckon you're just the type that'd do it, too.'' Reversing the citation book, he balanced it on the window ledge for her signature.

''You bet your—'' Hannah's lips compressed. No, she wasn't the type at all. She'd faked it a zillion times, to the extent the Friedlichs and her co-workers believed she'd burned her bra without removing it, first.

It was all an act, as phony as ''Chicken Terriyakki.'' She was the quintessential Monday-morning quarterback who never called a play, but critiqued every fumble, penalty and failure-to-score in twenty-twenty retrospect.

Hendrickson shrugged. ''A hundred in court costs and twenty bucks a mile over the limit ought to take the lead out of your foot.''

He handed her the ticket, a pre-addressed mailer and her license, but didn't release them. ''My advice won't cost you a dime.'' His gray-blue eyes bored into her brown ones. ''Call me everything but an American when I'm out of earshot, but don't let that temper get the best of you. Peeling pretty faces off windshields is part of my job, too, ma'am. I don't want the next one to be yours.''

With that, he tipped his hat and strode back to the cruiser. Hannah took a deep breath, letting it leak out slowly. He had a point. Being late for brunch wasn't worth reconstructive surgery.

However, self-reproach didn't diminish the hope that somehow the sheriff's holster got stuck in that proverbial place where the sun don't shine.

David maneuvered his copy of the citation into the shallow well at the back of the clipboard, keeping one ear cocked at the radio, waiting for dispatch to run "Garvey, Hannah M." through the computer.

He didn't anticipate any wants or warrants. Scofflaws didn't sass a sheriff when he pulled them over on a traffic stop unless they were stone-cold stupid, and she didn't fit that bill. Too observant and too quick with a comeback. Probably had his nameplate memorized before he opened his mouth.

A red glow appeared in his windshield. The Blazer's exhaust kicked up grit and dry grass. Its taillights flicked clear, then red, then the left signal blinked as the vehicle accelerated into the northbound lane.

Good for her. She'd let herself simmer down, maybe even think about what he'd said before hitting the road again. Most just threw their vehicles into gear and took off, cussing and whining and making excuses, instead of watching where they were going.

Idly, David wondered where she was bound for. Dressy outfit, Chicago address, temporary tag, no luggage and a mess of groceries in the cargo bay? Odd combination. She could, he supposed, be visiting somebody. Guests weren't expected to supply food in exchange for a couple of nights on a sofa bed, but it was good manners to do so.

Too late to ask, and he'd blown Officer Friendly out of the water with that "attitude adjustment" remark. Sounded like something out of a *Dirty Harry* movie, for Christ's sweet sake.

He scowled at the unresponsive radio unit bolted to the floor hump, then wedged the clipboard into the space between the driver's seat and console. His men kidded him about going out on patrol. Set a bad precedent, they said. Sheriffs parked their feet on their desks and administrated.

Paperwork. There'd be a ton of it to shuffle, whether he stayed in the office or not. Familiarizing himself with the county's back roads, box holders, corner posts and landmarks was his goal. He'd known every inch of the zone he'd patrolled in Tulsa for ten years, and most of the faces had names attached. The citizens of Kinderhook County deserved no less, though he suspected some of his deputies thought he was just checking up on them.

David chuckled. Nothin' wrong with killing two birds with one rock, was there?

Adam–101.

Well, it's about damn time. He unhooked the microphone and thumbed the transmit button. "Go ahead."

No outstanding wants or warrants on your 10–43.

"10–4. Adam–101, 10–8, this location."

10–4, Sheriff…but in case you want to go 10–46, we've got pizza incoming, this location.

David's chin rumpled. He didn't need the dashboard clock to tell him it was almost noon. "10–4. Adam–101, 10–46." He paused, then added. "And there'd better be something besides crust left when I get there."

"Well, David Hendrickson has put an end to most of the hellraising this county used to be famous for," IdaClare allowed, then paused to dab a speck of salsa from the corner of her mouth. "The governor could have done worse than appoint him sheriff when Larry Beauford had his stroke last year, but he's a cocky son of a gun, all the same."

Marge Rosenbaum chuckled. "Not to mention, as handsome as the day is long."

No argument here, Hannah mused, if good looks, a

bodybuilder's physique and a touch of "aw, shucks," make your motor run.

"He's single, too," Velma Billingsly chirped. "Dixie Jo Gage at the Curl Up and Dye said his wife left him about the time he quit the Tulsa Police Department. No children. Just as well, if you ask me."

Rosemary Marchetti nudged Hannah's shoulder. "Breaks your heart, doesn't it, to think of all that testosterone going to waste."

A mouthful of huevos rancheros averted Hannah's reply, which probably wouldn't have been heard, anyway. Had she been blindfolded, she'd have sworn she was sitting with a sorority's movers and shakers during rush week.

Benevolent scrutiny. No sweat. A far, far better thing than the business world's agenda-fraught meal-taking, where restaurant selection, table placement and what one ordered held greater significance than, say, China's emergence as a nuclear power.

IdaClare was unquestionably the ringleader, with Rosemary, her aide-de-camp. Marge was a good soldier, who'd defend the others to the death, but didn't hesitate to speak her mind. Velma, the only non-widow, was the peacemaker.

"A hot and heavy romance would sure liven things up around here," Marge said. "The Every-Other-Tuesday Bridge Club has gotten so dull, we're playing for score."

Rosemary crooked a finger at her lips and squinted through her bifocals. "I think the sheriff and our new manager would make a darling couple, don't you, IdaClare?"

"Not especially."

Hannah aimed a greasy smile at her savior. She'd

known the feisty matron with the cloud of pink champagne-tinted hair was Jack's mother before introductions were exchanged. Whatever Clancy, Senior, might have contributed to the gene pool, Jack's stocky build, pug nose and cornflower-blue eyes matched IdaClare's to a T.

Ropy veins and liver spots blemished hands not many years removed from a ranch wife's chores. Swinging a scythe and a golf club were essentially the same, as IdaClare's lock on Valhalla Springs's Ladies' Division Championship demonstrated. She still wore her wedding band, although Jack's father had passed away years ago. Apparently his widow viewed "Till death do us part" as a trial separation, not termination of the contract.

"Have you ever been married, Hannah?" Marge inquired.

She shook her head. "Veteran bridesmaid, never the bride. Saves a bundle on attorney fees."

Marge's graven face became rapturous as if acknowledging she was in the presence of the only middle-aged virgin in North America. Hannah didn't bother to correct the assumption. For all she knew, long-term celibacy induced some sort of gynecological recidivism.

"There's no harm in waiting for Mr. Right to come along," Velma said. "As long as you know him when you see him across a crowded room, or—"

"Along the side of the highway," Rosemary finished.

"Oh, for heaven's sake," IdaClare said, "will y'all stop prattling like Auntie Mame? Hannah has more important things to do than chase after David Hendrickson."

Watching her toenails grow ranked higher on Hannah's priority list than robbing the cradle in reverse, yet she detected an ominous note in IdaClare's remark. The sheets of tablet paper Jack's mother wrested from her handbag confirmed the suspicion.

Judging by the conversational lull, the bell was about to ring on the brunch's main event. Hannah drained her wineglass, then aimed a rueful look at the empty carafe. Would it be gauche to signal the waiter for a refill? And a straw?

IdaClare began. "As anyone who knows me would tell you, I think my son hung the moon and stars." She heaved a long-suffering mother's sigh. "But sometimes that boy really pisses me off."

"She didn't want to turn our party into a gripe session," Velma explained, "and wouldn't, if Jack hadn't ignored everything she told him while she was interim manager."

Rosemary chimed in, "We tried to talk to Owen before that, but he was too distracted by those voices in his head to listen."

"Owen-schmowen," Marge said with a sniff. "All Jack ever does is complain about being busy, and how he should have stuck to building resorts for investors instead of trying to own one."

IdaClare warned, "Y'all are wading into muddy water. There's a difference between me sniping at my son and anybody else drawing a bead on him."

Like goodwill ambassadors in aprons and satin bow ties, two busboys swooped in to clear the table. Leaning back in deference to their tidying, Hannah replayed Jack's reference to the Alamo. History wasn't her forte, but as she recalled, none of the good guys lived to tell about it.

When the staff retreated, she adopted her business persona: bent elbows braced on the table, hands steepled under her chin, a trust-me smile. "I haven't memorized Valhalla Springs's zip code yet, but give me some specifics and I'll see what I can do."

"We knew you'd be on our side," IdaClare crooned.

Hannah looked from one triumphant face to another. Obviously her hosts didn't know from corporate spinmeistering and she'd almost forgotten the ancient art of straightforward communication.

"First and foremost," IdaClare continued, "something must be done about Zerelda Sue Connor."

"Who?"

"The community center's physical fitness director," Marge clarified.

IdaClare's eyes narrowed. "She's a Nazi."

"She's a retired army drill instructor," Velma corrected, "with the personality of a Nazi."

"Oh, she was sweeter than honey on a biscuit when Owen hired her last fall," IdaClare drawled.

"But no sooner had those nice young men from the hospital taken him away," Rosemary said, "than Zee had us doing aerobics to John Philip Sousa marches."

IdaClare chuffed. "Hell's bells, at our age Mantovani could give us a coronary."

"Then last week," Velma said, "she started banging the side of the pool with a baton when we swam laps. 'Stroke, stroke,' she yells." Velma shuddered. "We want to stay in shape, not qualify for the Olympics."

Hannah fought the grin tugging at her lips. "I'll speak to Ms. Connor—"

"The time for talk is past, dear," IdaClare said, "unless it's something like 'Don't let the door bang you in the butt on the way out.'"

"That bad, huh?"

"Worse," was the unanimous response.

Wonderful. Hannah's first official duty would be to fire an exercise freak who specialized in elder abuse. She knew she should have ordered a double-fudge something with chocolate sauce for dessert.

IdaClare and The Girls proceeded with a string of grievances including the Workowskis' operatic beagle, potholes in Sassafras Lane, thistles growing in the golf course's roughs, the peephole drilled in the clubhouse's ladies'-room wall and Hubert Montague's habit of sitting on his porch in nothing but boxer shorts and Supp-Hose.

Forty-five minutes later, Hannah was on her way to the community center with IdaClare's list in her pocket and her cheeks smudged with four shades of red lipstick.

A pessimistic *What have I gotten myself into* wrestled with an optimistic *Buck up, kiddo. Bob Davies will have repaired the damage Delbert hath wrought, the sheriff didn't shoot you and IdaClare and The Girls didn't eat you alive. The worst is over.*

Wheeling into the center's parking lot, she muttered, "Well, most of the worst, anyhow."

3

Hannah gnawed her lower lip as she subtracted democracy's share of a part-time caddy's wages. A double check of her calculations tallied to the penny.

"Tripp, my friend, I'm doing you proud," she crowed.

Tripp Irving, the local accountant Jack Clancy kept on retainer, had couriered a "welcome aboard" cover letter, sheets of payroll checks, tax tables and four pages of instructions that read like a math wonk's term paper.

Her assignment was to complete the payroll, fax photocopies of the results for his approval, then deliver the checks to the respective departmental supervisors.

Simple, Tripp said, capturing her arithmetical essence in a single word. At supermarket math, she excelled: deducing whether ten-ounce cans of green beans priced three for a dollar were bargains compared to fourteen-ouncers at fifty-eight cents each was a snap. Foist larger increments, fractions or percentages upon her, and the abacus in her brain popped its beads.

After last night's dream of numerals armed with machetes chasing her through the jungle, Hannah called Irving's office in Sanity to inquire, "If I make a mistake, who goes to prison? Me? Or you?"

The CPA sounded like Big Bird, which was

strangely reassuring. "Relax, Ms. Garvey. I'll correct any discrepancies that may occur."

She hesitated before confessing a minor fault guaranteed to make bean counters curl into fetal positions and babble incoherently. "It seems only fair to warn you, reconciling my checking account fell into the life's-too-short category in about 1978."

"Oh?" A pencil *rat-a-tatted* in the background. "How good are you at keeping a secret, Ms. Garvey?"

Hannah held out the receiver, blinked at it, then returned it to her ear. "Somewhere between a priest and the Pentagon. Why?"

Irving either laughed, or suffered a bronchial spasm. "Because I don't reconcile mine, either."

"You don't?" She wondered what friend-of-a-friend had recommended the CPA to Jack Clancy.

"Don't get me wrong," he continued, "I crunch clients' numbers until they scream, but a bank is more likely to nickel-and-dime customers to death with service charges than misappropriate debits and credits."

"That's always been my excuse," she admitted, "but I never expected a pro to agree."

"Any other questions?" he asked.

The obvious one was why a nice girl like her had to play amateur CPA. "No, not at the moment."

"I'm as close as the phone if you need me," Irving assured. "And do stop by the office next time you're in town."

Hannah promised she would, broke the connection, then yipped when the telephone rang before she'd retracted her hand.

Go away, I'm premenstrual, she thought, then cleared her throat. "Valhalla Springs, Hannah Garvey speaking."

"Is this the lady of the house?"

"Wrong on both counts," she snapped, and cradled the receiver.

Adjusting a couple of switches silenced the phone's ringer and the answering machine. Math was enough of a challenge without telemarketers badgering her to buy lifetime siding, discount long-distance service and family portraits.

Hannah took a swig of lukewarm coffee, then cupped the mug in her hands and leaned back in her desk chair. After four days in residence, her great-uncle Mort would say she was as happy as a dead hog in the sunshine, which translated to mean elated and content, for reasons Hannah never understood.

Still, feeling less like a house sitter and more like a permanent resident hadn't completely dispelled her "mirage syndrome," and the cottage's decor and furnishings were major contributors to it.

Everything suited her perfectly, yet she wouldn't have chosen a single piece of her own accord. In combination, those facts were discomfiting. It was as if her subconscious had kept its own counsel for decades, then arbitrarily decided to clue her in.

Book spines striped the built-in shelves flanking the native-stone fireplace. An antique trunk anchored the sitting area's tufted, maroon leather sofa, love seat and paired club chairs. Winter was months away, but Hannah could hardly wait to curl up in front of a crackling fire to watch the flames dance and shape-shift.

Much as she thought she detested paisley, the fringed area rug's rich navy, gold, scarlet and kelly-green teardrop pattern was a mellow foil for the oak plank floors. From the raftered ceiling's paddle fan to the pedestal table that could serve six for dinner or as a conference table, the only flaw she found was with herself for waiting until midlife to have a midlife crisis.

Her gaze slid to the desktop. A Pop's Malt Shoppe hot-fudge sundae rode on finishing the payroll as promised. Some made deals with the devil. She bargained with Willy Wonka and had the thighs to prove it.

Setting the mug on its coaster, she exhaled a martyr's sigh, picked up her pen and upped the ante to a banana split with nuts, whipped cream, and sprinkles, but she'd make herself walk to Pop's to get it.

A siren wailed in the distance. A car wreck on VV, she supposed, having heard others, intermittently, over the last hour. It was doubtful she'd know anyone involved, but it was human nature to wince at the mournful howl. Even in the city, where incessant clamor was reduced to white noise, a siren caused necks to crane.

The keening halted midcrescendo. Moments later, she heard the rumble of a rapidly accelerating engine. A white blur streaked past the cottage's open, front windows.

In two strides, Hannah rounded the bannister between the office nook and living area, but the car had disappeared by the time she reached the porch. She was deliberating what to do next, when Delbert's golf cart careened into the circle drive.

"Get in," he yelled.

"What's wrong?" She grabbed the roof's support pole and dropped into the seat. Delbert's pallor frightened her. The odor of raw sweat permeated the open cart like a fog.

He tromped the gas pedal and cranked the steering wheel. The souped-up Cushman jounced over landscape timbers. Cedar chips arced from the rear tires.

The squatty vehicle shuddered, then shot up Valhalla Springs Boulevard.

Delbert peered straight ahead, his knuckles an ivory ridge atop the steering wheel. "Kathleen Osborn is dead. Me and Marge Rosenbaum found her about an hour ago."

"Oh, no..." Hannah clasped his forearm. "Was it a heart attack?"

He shook his head. "Looked like somebody beat her to death."

Hannah couldn't breathe, much less force out the questions stacking up in her throat.

"I had sense enough to go next door to use the phone." A mirthless chuckle burst from his lips. "Then what'd I do? Told 'em to send an ambulance. Like Kathleen wasn't way beyond needing one."

He glanced sideward. "Tried to call you, too. Kept getting that damned machine."

She groaned. "I turned off the phone, so I could—"

"Don't. Better to tell you something like this in person, anyhow. I'd have been here sooner but I hung around till the cavalry started to arrive."

Hannah's body swayed with the cart's motion. She hadn't met Ms. Osborn—or was it Mrs.? She felt guilty for not knowing that much about the poor woman. Surely Delbert was mistaken. It must have been a terrible shock finding her dead, but murder? In Valhalla Springs?

She clenched, then flexed her fingers; a public speaker's trick to channel and relieve tension. Speculation was useless. The facts would be known soon enough.

Another siren sounded from the highway. Again, the

yelps ceased outside the gate as if the development's blissful illusion must be maintained at all cost.

Delbert whipped the cart into the grass beside the road. A deputy's patrol car cruised by, exceeding the development's twenty-mile-per-hour speed limit.

The Cushman skirted the out-of-bounds and zig-zagged between trees. Golf clubs in the bag strapped to the rear deck clattered like aggies in a hustler's pouch. Delbert had been a fighter pilot during World War II. By the way he negotiated ground hazards, the top-gun mentality was still present and accounted for.

They bounced back onto the pavement, then veered onto Dogwood Lane. Sheriff Hendrickson's Crown Vic sat angled away from the curb, midway up the hill. A battered, gray sedan and two patrol cars were parked nearby.

Residents bustled across the street to join those already congregated in the yard. Fingers pointed. Arms wrapped shoulders in reassuring hugs. Hands cradled cheeks in despair and disbelief. All eyes were trained on a clapboard house with yellow shutters and green, gingerbread trim.

"Damned rubberneckers," Delbert said. "Where the hell was everybody when that son of a bitch attacked Kathleen?" He wove through a maze of pedestrian and vehicular traffic, motioning gangway and cursing anyone slow to respond.

Two paramedics watched from the shade cast by their ambulance. Hannah knew they didn't transport the deceased. Even when vital signs stopped before a hospital was reached, the patient was declared dead on arrival, not en route.

A deputy was questioning a group of bystanders. Two plainclothes officers photographed the house and grounds. A third uniformed officer catercornered from the side yard, his arms raised and waving. "All right, folks, unless you have something to report, go on about your business and let us tend to ours."

A few gawkers retreated, only to regroup on the sidewalk. The majority surrounded the deputy, demanding to know how Kathleen was killed, and when, and for God's sake, why.

A hearse and a second unmarked car commandeered the driveway. The ever-resourceful Delbert maneuvered the Cushman up the narrow strip of grass beside them without pruning a leaf off a waist-high hedge.

Switching off the ignition, he donned his cap and slid from beneath the wheel, his purple windbreaker whipping behind him. He hesitated, then gave several yellow, tent-shaped markers dotting the lawn a wide berth.

"Delbert?" Hannah hopped out of the cart. "Where are you going?"

He didn't break stride. "Where's it look like I'm going?"

She latched onto his arm. "You can't barge into the middle of a homicide investigation."

"The hell I can't." His tone matched the pain and defiance in his eyes. "I loved her, Hannah. She pushed me away with both hands, but I've got a right to know what's being done to find who killed her."

Hannah's arm fell to her side. The pale, stoop-shouldered old man was not the same Delbert who'd helped her move into her cottage and told the worst jokes she'd ever heard.

She didn't remember Kathleen Osborn's name among those in Delbert's "harem." Unrequited love left deeper scars than the mutual kind that blossomed, then gradually, inevitably, withered. Age didn't soften the blow. She wasn't so sure it didn't worsen it.

He started when she reached in front of him for the screen door's handle, which was sealed in plastic. She murmured, "I figured you might want some company, that's all."

His wan smile wrenched her heart. "'Preciate the thought, ladybug, but it's ugly in there."

Opening the screen served as her response. He drew himself up to his full five foot three, clasped his cap to his chest and marched inside.

Hannah's resolve wavered when she stepped into the herringbone-brick entry. Death wasn't something she handled well and she'd never been an ex post facto witness to a violent one.

No law enforcement personnel were visible, but muffled, male voices testified to their presence. Delbert hung a left into the dining room. Every instinct told Hannah to about-face and run for her quiet little house near the gate.

The windows' lined, muslin draperies blocked all natural light, just as the plush, ivory carpeting absorbed their footfalls. The stench of death and human excrement grew stronger; the house's stuffiness, more oppressive. Hannah focused on her sneakers' toes, battling her gag reflex.

"End of the line, mister..." Sheriff Hendrickson's baritone trailed away. Recovery added a decibel to its volume. "What in Sam Hill are you doing here, Miz Harvey?"

His size had been imposing in uniform. Wearing a black sports shirt, jeans, boots, latex gloves and a scowl, the man looming in the archway was downright intimidating.

"It—it's Garvey," she stammered. "Hannah Garvey."

"Beg pardon. Now answer my question."

"I'm Valhalla Springs's resident manager."

"Since when?"

Nerves and nausea writhed behind her breastbone. She gritted her teeth. "Since the day before you stopped me on the highway."

His expression hardened as he processed the information. "Funny, you didn't mention it then."

"You didn't ask."

Hendrickson's eyes flicked to Delbert. Hannah scored one for her side. Staring contests were like two hot-rodders playing chicken: he who swerves first, loses.

"Why would I," Hendrickson challenged, anger edging his tone, "with an Illinois license and temporary tag?"

"Back off, Sheriff," Delbert warned. "She doesn't deserve the third degree."

Light flashed behind Hendrickson. He turned, allowing an unobstructed view of the kitchen. A glass bowl of blackberries and a baking dish rested on the countertop beside the sink. The ball of pie dough atop a built-in marble pastry board was dried; yellowed like celluloid.

Rusty splatters streaked the white-enameled cabinet doors, the backsplash, the refrigerator. Their downward progression enlarged and elongated, guiding the eye to the dull pool on the floor. A woman with short white hair, clad in a faded housedress, lay sprawled, facedown, arms bloody, hands encased in plastic, one leg bent at the knee, the calf and bare foot mottled and bluish.

Bile scalded Hannah's throat. She retched and staggered backward. Delbert grabbed her around the waist to steady her.

"Let's take this outside," Hendrickson said, stripping off his gloves. He grabbed a clipboard off the dining-room table. His other hand closed around Hannah's arm firmly but gently.

As he steered her to the porch, fresh air and faint traces of bath soap, fabric softener and Aqua Velva cleared her head like smelling salts. She looked up, intending to tell Hendrickson she didn't need his assistance, but his smoky eyes met hers and telegraphed an apology. She interpreted it as regret for being an asshole.

At least they agreed on something.

Delbert joined Hannah on the swing, patting her knee as he sat down. Forsythia bushes, growing lush and fountain-like, as nature intended, partially screened the porch from the yard and Dogwood Lane. The ambulance was gone. Deputies had shooed away most of the curious, but Hannah knew watchers lurked behind every neighboring window.

The sheriff ignored a painted, metal lawn chair, choosing to slouch against one of the porch's supporting columns instead. Nonchalance failed to disguise his genuine anguish.

Laying the clipboard on the railing, he removed a notebook from his pocket and flipped through pages without appearing to read them. Intuition told Hannah he needed time to regather his wits as much as she and Delbert did.

Maybe the woman lying dead in her kitchen wasn't merely a statistic, a new case number for his files. She recalled his remark about peeling faces off windshields.

Could it be he sincerely gave a damn about the people he'd sworn to protect and serve?

Her mental tote board posted eighty-twenty odds in Hendrickson's favor. It further advised her not to discount the man himself. She admitted a mild curiosity about what he was like when he wasn't wearing a badge.

As if reading her mind, Hendrickson regarded her thoughtfully, then added a line to his notes.

Probably remindin' hisself to call his mama, you bein' nigh her age, and all, cackled a voice very similar to Hannah's maternal grandmother's. *Spring chicken, you ain't, Hannah Marie. What would a fine lookin' fella like him see in the likes of you?*

Up yours, you old bat, Hannah thought. The nicest thing Maybelline Garvey had ever said to her was that her teeth weren't as bucked as her mother's. Doubly insulting, since Caroline Garvey's sunny smile was one of her best features.

The sheriff stated, "You're Delbert Bisbee."

"I am."

"Detective Andrik has been looking high and low for you, mister."

"Well, I'm here, aren't I?"

Hannah groaned inwardly, knowing how little Hendrickson appreciated snippiness.

"You called 911?" he asked.

"I did."

"Where from?"

"I've read enough Mickey Spillane to know better than to use Kathleen's phone. I went next door to the Liebermeyers."

Hendrickson scribbled a note. "Do you remember touching anything while you were here?"

"We rang the doorbell two or three times, knocked, then tried the knob. It was unlocked, so we let ourselves in."

"We? Meaning you and Miz Garvey?"

Delbert snorted. "If you can't come up with a slicker banana peel than that, son, don't bother."

A corner of Hendrickson's mouth crumpled. "For the record, would you confirm that Margaret Rosenbaum came here with you at approximately 9:45 a.m.?"

"'Twas vicey-versy. I was on my way to pick up Leo Schnur for a round of golf when Marge flagged me down. She and Kathleen were supposed to go shopping in Sanity today. Marge called Kathleen several times before she came over, but nobody answered."

Delbert went on, "Every cottage has a panic button in the john, the bedroom and kitchen that trips an alarm and the intercom at Doc Pennington's. Marge was afraid Kathleen had slipped in the shower or something and couldn't reach it."

The sheriff prompted, "Once you were inside—"

"I knew Kathleen was dead before we found her body." Delbert's voice flattened, his gaze fixed at a spot beyond Hendrickson's cocked hip. "I smelled death during the war. Ain't likely to ever forget it."

Hendrickson nodded, respect evident in his eyes.

"I told Marge to stay outside," Delbert went on. "Being female, she didn't listen. Shoved right on past me, smack into the middle of things."

He twisted his cap in his hands. A wistful smile appeared. "The radio was on. Kathleen couldn't carry a tune in a bucket, but she liked to sing when she cooked. 'Chances Are' was playing. One of her favorites."

The melody and lyrics wended through Hannah's

mind. She and Jarrod had danced to it, made love to it, listened to it while sipping wine and pretending everything was just ducky between them.

Great. Johnny Mathis would own her mental jukebox for days. Seldom did songs associated with good times strike up the band in her head. But annoying jingles and tunes that fostered bad memories... They booted up out of nowhere and played over and over until fading of their own volition.

Hendrickson asked, "How well did you know the deceased, Mr. Bisbee?"

Delbert's mouth puckered, then made a kissing noise. "Better than most, and as well as she'd let me. She wasn't a hermit, but she didn't socialize much, either."

"Kind of a homebody, eh?"

"Oh, she stayed busy. Always puttering at one thing or another. She filled in at bridge once in a while, but not often. Kept her own self company too long, I guess."

Contrary to popular opinion, living alone isn't the worst way to go, Hannah thought. Better than being with someone and still being lonely.

Hendrickson said, "So, she and Miz Rosenbaum were supposed to go shopping today."

"Same as they did every Thursday," Delbert answered. "Kathleen didn't drive, and didn't like the development's bus service. Various ones of us jitneyed her around as much as we could."

"The Thursday shopping trip was a regular outing, then," the sheriff said. "Something Miz Osborn counted on, probably planned her week around."

Delbert shot him an I-know-you're-getting-at-something-but-can't-figure-out-what look.

"So, if they'd gone today," Hendrickson speculated, "she'd have stocked up on groceries, maybe refilled a prescription, gone to Wal-Mart, the bank...?"

"That's about the size of it." Delbert hesitated. "Well, except for the bank. The first of the month was last week. Kathleen would have cashed her pension check then."

"Cashed it?"

"She didn't trust banks." Delbert chuckled. "Didn't trust checks, either. She thought as long as her money was in hand, nobody could monkey with a computer and make it disappear."

Hendrickson's eyebrows almost met his hairline. "You're saying, without fail Miz Osborn cashed her pension check the first of every month."

"Yes, but it ain't like it took her, Marge and a burro to haul the money to the car. Kathleen had to squeeze six cents out of every nickel."

Hannah frowned. Did he mean she was frugal by necessity, or miserly? Expecting the sheriff's follow-up to provide clarification, she was miffed when he asked, "What about Miz Osborn's next of kin?"

"Didn't have any. Said her first and only love was teaching. She didn't need children of her own with twenty-some new ones to tuck under her wing every year."

Hendrickson's pen skittered across one page and midway down the next. Without glancing up, he inquired, "Any objections to being fingerprinted, Mr. Bisbee?"

"None."

Hannah received both gray-blue barrels. "How about you, ma'am? Any objections?"

"Me?" She fidgeted. God help her if she ever did

commit a crime. A felony, anyway. She'd spill her guts to the station-house janitor. "I guess not, but I don't understand why it's necessary."

"Exclusionary purposes. Once we rule out prints with reason to be here, we can concentrate on those that don't."

Gooseflesh crept up Hannah's arms like spiders on the run. I'm the newest, not to mention, youngest kid on the block, she thought. Ms. Osborn's lack of a spouse or children angling for an early inheritance makes me an automatic suspect.

"Hannah just got here Sunday afternoon," Delbert argued. "She didn't know Kathleen from Adam's off-ox."

"You moved here from Chicago?"

She nodded. "Until I quit two weeks ago, I was an advertising-account executive at the Friedlich & Friedlich Agency."

"Why did you quit?"

The obvious answer wasn't the one he sought. She groped for another that wouldn't sound suspicious, idiotic or Zen, then settled for honesty. "I spent a lot of years trying to be something I'm not. I decided the time had come to stop."

He eyed her as if she'd just stepped off the 11:05 shuttle from Mars. She didn't blame him.

"Any more questions?" Delbert asked.

"No, but Detective Andrik will have, later."

Delbert supplied his home address and phone number. "Damn shame murder isn't a hanging offense in Missouri anymore. I'd volunteer to knot the noose around the bastard's neck."

"I've felt that way myself a time or two, Bisbee."

Delbert clasped his fingers around a raised knee.

"So, how's about answering a couple of questions for me?"

Not *now,* Hannah pleaded silently. Take me home. Take me back to Chicago. Take me anywhere, as long as it's away from here.

"Depends on what they are."

Delbert shifted into Mike Hammer mode. "The perpetrator, or perpetra*tors,* beat Kathleen like a cur dog. Is that what killed her?"

Hendrickson looked from him to Hannah and back again. "We won't know until after the autopsy."

"Well, you dang well know whether she was shot or stabbed or somethin'."

"And you know I can't let details like that spread to hell and gone."

"Nothing you say will leave this porch. You have my word on it."

The sheriff graced Hannah with a contemplative expression.

"If you gentlemen will excuse me," she said, "I'll wait on the golf cart."

Delbert rose to his feet. Hendrickson made a noise similar to blowing one's nose without benefit of a tissue. "There you go again, Miz Garvey."

"What do you mean?"

"Assuming the worst. Didn't your daddy ever tell you cops are the good guys?"

"Never met the man." The tendency to blurt first and think later had served her well during brainstorming sessions. On a personal level, she often wished her mouth had come equipped with a zipper.

The sheriff hitched a thumb behind his belt. "I'll tell y'all this much—my guess is the deceased died from repeated blows to the head inflicted by a blunt instrument.''

"What, exactly?" Delbert asked.

"I'm not at liberty to say."

"That means you haven't found the murder weapon yet," Delbert guessed. "Any sign of a break-in?"

Hendrickson started to shake his head, stopping himself a few seconds too late. "No comment."

Delbert tapped his temple. "Then the killer had to be somebody Kathleen knew. Somebody she'd open her door to."

"Why do you say that?"

"We're supposed to tell the manager to look after things when we take a trip," Delbert explained, "but half of us have keys to the other half's cottages—except for Kathleen. In the year and a half she's lived here, she's done her share of watchdogging, but made it clear she didn't want anyone in her house when she wasn't."

By his frown, Hendrickson also discerned the basic flaw in Delbert's rationale. Just because Kathleen didn't hand out keys didn't mean the killer rang the doorbell. He could have obtained one somehow, or picked the lock. If she was singing along with the radio and intent on her baking, she might not have seen or heard an intruder until it was too late.

The office safe held master keys to every building in Valhalla Springs. Sheriff Hendrickson undoubtedly knew that. Bob Davies, the maintenance supervisor, also had a set.

It wasn't Davies, however, who'd been in the crosshairs of Hendrickson's peripheral vision for the last two or three millennia.

"How about—"

The sheriff held up a hand. "You've been a big help, Mr. Bisbee, but I've already said more than I should have. I'd appreciate it if you'd go home and write down everything you remember from when Marge Rosenbaum hailed you to now. Any personal information you can recollect about Miz Osborn would save us a lot of telephone time, too."

Reaching for the clipboard, he held it table-style and offered Hannah his pen. "Since you're the manager, I need your John Henry on this consent-to-search form."

"Consent to search what?" she asked.

"Beyond the crime scene's premises."

Delbert chimed in, "To look for the murder weapon, ladybug. If they get lucky, they might find footprints or a clue the perpetrator dropped whilst he fled the area. Right, Hendrickson?"

"Something like that. I also need photocopies of all records pertaining to the deceased. I'll stop by the office and pick them up after we finish here."

"Is there anything else I can do in the meantime?" she asked.

"No, ma'am. Not at the moment, anyhow."

As she and Delbert turned to leave, Hendrickson said, "Miz—uh, Hannah?" He motioned toward the door. "I know I came down pretty hard on you in there…"

"You're the county sheriff. It's your job." Realizing this might be another lame attempt at an apology, she added, "From what I saw, if you hadn't lost a little of your cool, I'd have wondered what it took to do it."

4

David watched Hannah walk across the lawn; her no-nonsense stride geared for heavy pedestrian traffic, not spongy grass in need of a trim.

She wasn't beautiful in a movie-star sense, but several notches above attractive. Intelligent and street-smart. Self-assured? Not entirely, but you had to look quick to see glimmers of uncertainty in her eyes.

Her jean-clad backside invited a double take. A younger woman, eager for attention, would have bought a size smaller. Probably shrunk the peach sweater accidentally-on-purpose, too. Hannah let the soft fabric imply slender contours, leaving the specifics to an admirer's imagination.

David's filled in a few of those gaps before he caught himself. Dream on, brother. She's way out of your league, and she doesn't cotton to cops.

No, he conceded, it wasn't dislike he'd seen in her eyes during the traffic stop or today. She radiated wariness; the kind that creeps from nape to ankles when you hear footsteps behind you, only to turn around and find no one there.

Bisbee's golf cart cut a tight one-eighty and cleaved the gap between David's Crown Vic and Marlin Andrik's junkmobile. Hannah had the presence of mind to grip the roof support, but she stared straight ahead, her expression pensive.

David reentered the cottage, reminding himself that curiosity and suspicion weren't the same things.

Lizzie Borden took an ax and gave her father forty whacks. When she saw what she had done, she gave her mother forty-one.

Mighty grisly for a rope-skipping rhyme, yet women were known to bludgeon victims beyond recognition. Like a long-smoldering fuse, overkill exploded in a blind rage fueled by fear of a counterattack and an exultant sense of power.

Except a man had killed Kathleen Osborn. David would stake his pension on it. Nor had Hannah Garvey conspired to commit, then gulled Bisbee into bringing her back to the scene to check her accomplice's handiwork. Scenarios like that only happened in old *Columbo* episodes.

Can't rule her out, either, he warned himself.

"Oh, Sheriff," a female voice trilled.

David whirled just as the screen door slapped shut behind IdaClare Clancy. She peered into the living room, tried to look past him, then said, "I know you're busy, but I have something I think might be of help to you." A red-enameled fingernail tapped the spiral notebook hugged to her bosom.

A few hundred voters lived in her son's retirement village, and the Queen Bee wasn't without influence. Much as David despised politicking, he'd known from day one that sheriffing was half beauty contest and half law enforcement. Too often, the split was nearer seventy/thirty. Much as he wanted to, he couldn't give Miss Marple the bum's rush.

"Well, ma'am, if you'd excuse me for a second, I'll be happy to give a listen."

He smacked the screen's wooden frame with an open palm and stepped out on the porch. "Hey, Vaughn! Front and center!"

While the deputy jogged toward him, David craned his neck and said, "Miz Clancy, I'd consider it a personal favor if you'd get yourself back where you were, and stayed there."

From the shadowy interior, rubber soles yipped across the brick foyer. Mothers of young children weren't the only ones who had eyes in the backs of their heads.

"Whatcha need, Sheriff?" Vaughn panted. "I'm about done taping off the perimeter."

"Is that a fact?" David kept his voice low enough for the deputy to hear, but not the nosy parker inside with her ear peeled to the door. He surveyed the yellow streamer warning Police Line—Do Not Cross now enclosing the Osborn property. "Want to explain how the hell-much good it'll do with everybody and their dog traipsing in and out of the house?"

"Huh?" Vaughn glanced around as if a ghost had tapped him on the shoulder. "I ain't seen anybody go in there, sir. Honest." His brow knitted. "Ozzie Duckworth did, but his brother being the coroner and all, I figured that was copacetic."

"Copa—what?"

"Copacetic. It means—"

"I *know* what it means. Been studying Increase Your Word Power in *Reader's Digest* again, haven't you?"

"Yes, sir. I mean, what else is there to do when you're 10–6?"

David's temper cooled as fast as it had boiled. A

contaminated crime scene was manna from heaven for a defense attorney, but Eugene Vaughn was so fresh from the academy, his utility belt creaked when he breathed.

"Did you rope off the backyard first?"

"Double rows, just like you said."

David nodded. He figured the killer had exited through the glass patio doors. Securing that portion of the scene was crucial. "All right, then. Soon as you're finished out here, tell dispatch you're 10–8."

The deputy's boyish features crumpled. "Are you sure? I was hoping I'd get to—"

"That's the breaks, rookie. Somebody has to be out patrolling the rest of the county."

"Yeah, I know. Rank has privilege."

Sure it does, kid, David thought. It's a pure-de-privilege to draw sketches, take reams of notes, collect every particle of evidence, pray you don't miss anything important and be gut certain you will.

He ducked through the door. Not to mention, give little old ladies a chance to natter at you because you put a rookie on guard duty.

"Sorry for the interruption, Miz Clancy. I believe you said you had some information for me?"

"I most assuredly do." Her chin thrust forward, mouth flattening to a scarlet slash.

A vein at David's jawbone ticked like a stopwatch. "Well, uh, do you want to tell me what it is, or would you rather I guessed?"

IdaClare sniffed. "I'll thank you to keep a civil tongue in your head, young man."

"Look, Miz Clancy—"

A hand fluttered in midair. "I know I'm being a pill. Mama said I started this life full of starch and vinegar and I plan to leave it the same way.'' Her head bowed. ''God willing.''

David wrapped an arm around her shoulders. She leaned into him, the scent of hair spray and Estee Lauder filling his nostrils. Her ragged sigh felt warm and moist against his shirt.

He'd never forget the day she stomped into his office to report a puppy mill operating on a farm near Fristoe Bluff. In her opinion, the owner deserved an on-the-spot lethal injection. So did David, when he told her, as gently as he knew how, the all-volunteer Kinderhook County Humane Society had neither the means, facilities nor staff to care for fifty-seven bitches, stud males and puppies.

''Sheriff Hendrickson, if I find out one—*one*—of those poor dogs has been put to sleep,'' she'd said, ''so help me Jesus of Nazareth, I'll sic PETA, the ASPCA, the Civil Liberties Union, the AKC and everybody else I can think of on you!''

''Miz Clancy—''

''Don't you 'Miz Clancy' me, young man. Sit yourself down and call whoever's in charge at the humane society. Tell them an anonymous, twenty-thousand-dollar cash donation will be made by morning, and you'll deliver another in that amount in six months.''

David had sat down, all right. Hard. ''Are you serious?''

IdaClare had rested her knuckles on his desk and skewered him with the brightest blue, shrewdest eyes he'd seen in many a day. ''Do I look like I'm joking, Sheriff?''

Reaching for the phone had sufficed as his answer. Now, her voice muffled but no less outraged than she'd been the first time he met her, she said, "It's just that I'm so damned mad, I can't see straight."

"You have every right to be, Miz Clancy."

"He robbed us, you know."

"That, he did. You folks felt safe here. Now you'll jump at branches creaking in the wind long after he's caught, tried and convicted."

She eased away, surprised. "You really do understand, don't you?"

"My hide isn't as thick as I want people to think it is, either, ma'am." He grinned down at her. "But I won't tell anyone if you don't."

From the kitchen, a gravelly voice boomed, "Hey, don't bitch at me, Duckworth. Last I saw of him, he was taking down that redhead's phone number."

Detective Marlin Andrik barreled into the entry. His eyes met David's. "Aw, shi— I mean, Sheriff, the coroner wants to show you—" his gaze flicked to IdaClare "—something."

"Tell him I'll be right there."

IdaClare blanched. She handed off the notebook like a quarterback hearing a linesman's footsteps behind him. "I wrote down everything Marge Rosenbaum said after I took her home this morning. She wasn't talking to me as much as to herself, so it rambles a bit—especially after the toddies I fixed started to settle her nerves."

David riffled through the numerous handwritten pages. "Why, I may have to put you on the payroll, ma'am. If you don't mind, I'll come by later to find out what sort of questions you asked before I talk to Miz Rosenbaum again."

"Oh, dear." IdaClare twiddled her gold necklace. "I didn't ask Marge any questions. I thought it best to just let her talk. I don't think she even noticed I was writing everything down.''

"You did great. Better than great, as a matter of fact." He cupped her elbow to guide her toward the door. "Now, if it wouldn't be too much trouble for you to stay with Miz Rosenbaum a while longer, I'm sure she'll appreciate the company.''

"I'd already planned to do *that*. I'll have a nice lunch all ready when she wakes up from her little nap." Stepping onto the porch, she turned and asked, "Would you rather have chicken salad or tuna?"

"Beg pardon?"

"Well, a big man like you has to eat, and I don't think Marge will give a care what's on her plate.''

He smiled. "That's real kind of you, ma'am, but I doubt I'll be able to take time for lunch.''

"You young people—always in a rush, rush, rush." She waggled a finger at him. "I'll tell you, the same as I tell my Jack, no need to fret about Social Security going broke before you're sixty-five. At the rate you burn the candle at both ends, you'll be lucky to see fifty.''

Fifty, hell, David thought, when he slid behind the Crown Vic's wheel at four that afternoon. The way he felt, he was already nudging fourscore and seven.

He, Marlin Andrik, Cletus Orr and Chief Deputy Jimmy Wayne McBride had busted their tails for hours. Among other things, David knew what Bisbee had eaten for breakfast, that Marge Rosenbaum pitied Kathleen Osborn more than she liked her, that the majority of Osborn's neighbors had picked a lousy time to be out of town and that all of it amounted to nothing much to go on.

Andrik and Orr had collected piles of forensic evidence, but analysis would take time, and it was usually more useful for scaring the truth out of a known suspect than identifying an unknown one.

While the detectives had applied their expertise, David had poked around the deceased's personal effects— a task he didn't enjoy. Those who screamed about invasion of privacy better pray they died in a hospital, or of natural causes in a physician's care. Homicide left few secrets to take to the grave.

Two hundred and ninety-three dollars in cash had been hidden in an empty, frozen-waffle carton in Osborn's freezer compartment, but he'd found no billfold, or purse other than the empty ones in her closet. From the looks of it, a robbery culminated in murder, and the killer hadn't netted more than a few bucks and change—the victim's carrying-around money.

David recalled Bisbee's remark about lynching. Whatever sentence this dirtbag received, it wasn't going to feel like justice. And they had to collar the son of a bitch first.

He rolled down the cruiser's window. Over the throaty, big-block engine and the air conditioner's fan, he heard birds chirp in the trees. One street over, a lawn mower bellowed. Nail guns spat in cadence on the roof of new cottages under construction.

That was the problem with peace and quiet. It amplified sounds and carried them a goodly distance. In a city like Tulsa, a man couldn't hear himself think over the subtle, inescapable drone created by a quarter of a million people occupying a hundred-and-ninety-one-point-five square miles. Until he'd lived there a while, he didn't believe it possible to hear everything, and nothing, at the same time.

Valhalla Springs wasn't noiseproof, but the residential area's topography bowled like an amphitheater, and houses weren't jammed so tightly together their rooflines resembled an upturned egg carton.

Junior Duckworth said Osborn's seventy-six-degree body temperature indicated she'd died between 10:00 p.m. and midnight. The third-generation mortician and two-term county coroner wasn't a medical examiner, and was a mite funny-turned for having played hide-and-seek in an embalming room as a child, but his guesses were correct more often than not.

At that hour, the development should have been as peaceful as a church house on Tuesday. Osborn had struggled with her assailant. Contrary to the interviews he'd done, somebody *must* have heard something twelve hours before Marge Rosenbaum ran screaming from the cottage.

David keyed his radio's microphone. "Adam–101."

A familiar drawl responded, *Go ahead, Sheriff*. Senior dispatcher Claudina Burkholz was as wide as she was short, had the personality of a Doberman if patronized, but her voice was as silky as a late-night deejay's.

"10–18?"

Negative. The bad guys must have taken today off to work on their tans.

It was warm for early April, though winter's last gasp was sure to blow in eventually. A sunny, calm Thursday also forecast the yahoos resting up to cut their wolves loose on Friday night. "Then I reckon you've had time to check disturbance calls 10–20 Valhalla Springs in the past month."

Roger, Claudina assured. *Short list, too*. Switching the mike to his left hand, David pulled a clipboard from the passenger seat's paper mountain. "Any on Dogwood Lane, Sassafras Lane or Redbud Lane?"

10–4. Need dates and times?

"Negative on the dates."

A peace disturbance on Sassafras—she snickered— loud party complaint at oh-niner-forty-two-hundred from a Herschel Payton. Two calls on Dogwood. Barking dogs, complainant, Harvey Liebermeyer.

"Same date on both?" David asked, suspecting the standard five-minute interval between calls.

Eight— No, nine days apart. Also a prowler call from Liebermeyer, last Saturday at oh-three-twelve-hundred.

Interesting. The Liebermeyers were Osborn's see-no-evil, hear-no-evil next-door neighbors. "That it?"

Roger, those specific 10–20s.

"I'm going to need the responding officers' reports on them."

Will do. Anything else?

"I'll be 10–24 in about an hour. A fresh pot of coffee for the boss will get you a gold star."

Roger on your ETA, Adam–101, Claudina purred. *10–30 on the java.*

David laughed at her Does Not Conform To Regulations response as he wheeled away from the curb. If the county paid Claudina what she was worth, she wouldn't have to wait tables part-time at the Short Stack Café to keep her three kids fed and clothed.

She reamed David a new one when he left tips that smelled like charity, but let him spring for pizzas and movie tickets now and then.

In Lana, Jeremy and Polly Burkholz's estimation, the sheriff was Santa Claus, their father was a photograph on the wall, and their mother was…well, she was just their mother.

David drove past the lake, surveying the tree-lined fisherman's paradise from bank to bank. Handy spot to ditch a murder weapon. Too obvious to be smart, but if lowlifes' IQs were bigger than their shoe sizes, they wouldn't be stacked in prison cells like cordwood.

He refused to consider the cost of bringing in divers. Ground searches weren't cheap, but Bisbee had volunteered himself and his buddies to help deputies and reserve officers. If a weapon didn't turn up soon, civilian assistance might be necessary, despite the consequences of contaminated evidence.

A prosecuting attorney with no "smoking gun" had to rely on expert testimony riddled with *probablys* and *usuallys* and had nothing to wave in front of a jury; in the minds of most, an automatic shadow of a doubt.

At the moment, however, David had a prearranged appointment and amends to make, if there was anything to the third-time-being-the-charm business.

Exiting the car, a discreet whiff at his shirt brought a muttered "Ugh." A splash of the aftershave stowed in the glove compartment would mask the wet-goat smell, except Hannah was waiting for him at the door.

"I expected to be here sooner," he explained as he strode across the threshold. "Hope I didn't inconvenience you any."

She removed a sticky note from the door's glass panel and held it up. "I'd forgotten I left this for you."

Sheriff,
I am not a fugitive from justice. Must deliver the payroll by 3. Back a.s.a.p.

Hannah G.

David teased, "Well, now, I might have taken that as a ruse to give yourself a head start."

"Come to think of it, you probably would have." Her eyes smiled when she did—a favorable sign. "I was on my way to the kitchen for a beer when I saw you pull up." Pink tinged her cheekbones. "Not that I'm much of a drinker. It's just…you know…"

Lord above. In two seconds, she'd gone from friendly to skittish. "Sounds like a great idea. If I wasn't on duty, I'd join you."

"Then how about a soft drink? Or a glass of iced tea?" The smile returned. "Okay, so I come from a family who force-fed the Avon lady."

"So do I. We had the fattest mailman, paperboy and propane delivery guy in two counties." He chuckled. "Surprised to hear that kind of hospitality extends to a big city like Chicago, though."

"You couldn't prove it by me. I grew up way downstate, in Effindale."

"Never heard of it."

"Trust me, 'Effin' was used more as a stand-alone adjective than two-thirds of the town's name." She motioned toward a club chair. "Are you a purist, or do you take sugar in your tea?"

He hesitated. "Much as I hate to decline, I'd better not. I told my dispatcher I was heading into the office."

"Oh." Her gaze slid sideward. She shifted her weight. "Well, it's already brewed and everything. It wouldn't take a minute to pour you a glass."

"I'm sure it wouldn't. Except whether my whistle gets wet or not, you're still going to have to tell me what you're trying so hard not to."

"That obvious, huh?" She grimaced. "You aren't going to like it."

"I already guessed that, ma'am."

Her frown deepened. "Would you mind dropping the 'ma'am'? Every time you say it, I feel like your mo—" She flipped a strand of hair from her face. "Just call me Hannah, okay? Or 'Hey, you' in a pinch."

David scratched a rib that didn't itch. "If it bothers you that much…" His hand found his hip. "No, by gum, if there's anything this world's losing faster than common sense, it's common courtesy, so you might as well get used to my brand of it, 'cause I'm not likely to change."

"Awfully young to be set in your ways, aren't you?"

"Sounds like the pot calling the kettle black to me."

"Nice try, Sir Walter Raleigh," she countered. "Except we both know whose pot is more seasoned."

David uttered a silent *Gotcha.* "Yeah, well, that ties into something I've been real curious about."

Her breezy, alpha-gal demeanor foundered. "Which is?"

"Why a woman who looks thirty-five, and couldn't be more than forty, has a driver's license saying she's three years shy of fifty."

"I—uh—" She shrugged. "The last time I renewed it, the clerk at the license bureau screwed up the date. Correcting it wasn't worth the hassle."

His tongue buffed his teeth. "I've never understood why folks who know they can't lie their way out of a paper bag don't just give up."

Anger, resentment and distrust animated her expression, as if she were playing a private round of charades. Hesitantly, she said, "All right, Sheriff, if it's off the record, I'll tell you why."

David nodded. Nothing told to a law enforcement officer was off the record. He knew it. She knew it.

"My mother was an alcoholic," she began, her tone detached, like someone commenting on the weather. "Pink-collar trailer trash, unwed mother and hopeless romantic with an unerring eye for Mr. Couldn't-Be-More-Wrong. I loved her as fiercely as she loved me."

She inhaled, her chin quivering as it rose. "Mama died of cirrhosis—one of those long illnesses with the bills to match. To pay them, I needed a better job than I was qualified to get, so I doctored my résumé, aged myself a little and went to Chicago where no one knew me as 'one of those goddamned good-for-nothin' Garveys.'"

That morning, she'd told him, *I spent too many years being something I'm not. I decided the time had come to stop.* At the time, David thought she'd gazed at her navel too long. Now he realized she hadn't joined the herd clamoring after the guru-of-the-hour, but had struck out on her own road, and a lonely one at that.

The civilian side of him wanted to tell her he knew what it was to move on, promising yourself not to look back, yet wondering whether the right thing wasn't self-righteousness in disguise.

The sheriff side warned, *Not now. Later. Soon.* "Like they say, birthdays are just for scorekeeping."

Hannah's smile expressed gratitude for letting the explanation stand and, if he wasn't mistaken, a speck of trust. "Which means, whether actual or inflated, I win, sonny-boy."

"Appears you need more'n one kind of attitude adjustment, Miz Garvey." He jerked a thumb toward the corner of the room equipped as an office. "What say we work on it when I'm not quite so pressed for time."

"I suppose that's my cue to hand over the records?"

"Yep."

She crooked a finger, indicating he follow her, then pointed at a built-in credenza behind her desk. "I sincerely hate to tell you this, but somebody ransacked the file cabinets. I sorted them out, but Kathleen Osborn's records are gone."

"You *what?* Why in holy he—" He clamped his mouth shut. The woman moves into his county five days ago, and Valhalla Springs's crime rate jumps from zip to a homicide and a burglary. "Why didn't you call my office and have me paged? We might been able to raise some prints."

She knuckled her hips. "Because I'm not a cop. Never been related to one, friends with one or dated one, so believe it or not, I don't think 'fingerprints' when I see a couple of messy file drawers."

David yanked his notebook from his pocket. Oh, you thought of it, all right, after you handled those files six ways of Sunday. God forbid you'd admit it.

"While you were *sorting,* did you check the other folders, in case Osborn's paperwork was misfiled?"

"I did, and it wasn't."

"Then I reckon you don't know anything about her living trust naming the operations manager as her estate's personal representative."

"Oh, puh-lease." Hannah laughed. "What hat did you pull that rabbit from? I never met Kathleen Osborn. Never even heard of her until this morning."

David removed a thin, business-size envelope from his back pocket. "Read it yourself."

The parchment sheets trembled in her hands. She shook her head, then gawked at him. "I don't know what to say. This is *insane.* Why would she want whoever happened to be operations manager when she died to handle her estate?''

''I asked Doc Pennington—he and his wife witnessed the trust—that very question. He said its terms are irrevocable, and Miz Osborn thought the person who had to dispose of her personal effects should be paid the three percent compensation prescribed by law.''

Hannah ran her fingers through her hair. ''Great. Wonderful. A woman I never laid eyes on set me up with a motive for her murder.''

''We're not talking a million-dollar fee here. A couple of thousand, tops, and you'll have to earn it.''

''I already am earning it. The ulcer I didn't have a minute ago is doing fifty squat-thrusts a second.''

He swiped a palm over his mouth to hide a grin. Wait till she found the page with instructions for Osborn's funeral arrangements.

''Back to this burglary,'' he said. ''Any broken windows or door locks?''

''Not that I noticed, but Valhalla Springs hasn't had an official on-site manager for weeks. I'm guessing whoever made off with Ms. Osborn's file did it before I arrived.''

David agreed, adding, ''You still should have reported it.'' He leveraged his pen in a drawer handle and opened it. ''Anything else missing?''

''I don't think so.'' She turned toward the desk. ''When I spoke to Jack earlier—''

''Jack Clancy?''

Her gaze transmitted a Who else? ''Jack has been— correction—*was* one of my clients for eons. When I told him about Ms. Osborn's death and asked whether he had duplicate files at his office, he thought I meant the computer files had been erased.''

Her arm swept over the desktop. ''As you can see, there is no computer. My predecessor, Owen McCutcheon, may have chucked it in the trash, or more likely, the lake. According to Jack, McCutcheon thought computers were electronic mind-control devices programmed by aliens.''

David laughed. ''Who knows? He might be right.''

''Except those data files sleeping with the fishes and no hard copies means no Osborn records anywhere. And no idea who took them, or why, thanks to me screwing up by not calling you.''

He kneed the drawer shut. ''The burglar probably wore gloves, but since one of my detectives will be coming by to print you, he may as well throw some dust around.''

She stiffened. Her face scrunched as if she were in pain, her eyes locked on the credenza.

''Hannah?''

She pushed at the air with her hand. ''Shut up for a minute.''

David cocked his head in astonishment. '''Shut *up?* Where do *you* get off telling *me* to shut up?''

''Have you found the murder weapon?''

''What's that got to do—''

''Yes? Or no?''

''No.''

''Would it help if you knew what to look for?''

''The coroner says a baseball bat.''

''Typical.'' She grinned like a kid with a new puppy. ''The coroner is male, right?''

In David's experience, two kinds of questions didn't

require answers: Smart-ass and rhetorical. Hers was both.

"Maybe I'm crazy," she said, having read his mind, "but 'dust' made something click in my head."

She started pacing. He backpedaled, as if spontaneous dementia were contagious.

"I didn't get a good look at the kitchen," she said. "I didn't *want* a good look at the kitchen, but I remember bowls, utensils and flour scattered on the counter, like white *dust*."

"Yeah. So what?"

She whirled. "Don't you see, David? Kathleen never finished rolling out her piecrust. The dough ball was flat on one side, not the other."

The sudden promotion to David distracted him a second. He flipped through his notebook, running a finger up and down several pages.

She was right. He'd missed it. *All* of them had missed it. The three basic rules of evidence collection are to look for what's there, what's there that shouldn't be and what isn't there but should be. Osborn's purse fit the third. So did the friggin' murder weapon.

"Cat got your tongue, Sheriff?"

He crossed his arms at his chest. "Maybe she'd already put the rolling pin in the dishwasher." The machine was empty, but Hannah needn't know that.

"Uh-uh. She wasn't finished with the dough, and a woman who baked enough to have a built-in pastry board wouldn't put her rolling pin in the dishwasher, regardless."

"Why not?"

"Heck if I know." She grinned. "But I'll bet twenty bucks it isn't there."

"Think you're pretty smart, don't you? Too smart,

maybe. If I was anywhere near the son of a bitch you
think I am, I'd run you into town for questioning."

"No, you wouldn't."

"Want to bet on that?"

She shook her head, laughing. "You'd lose again."

"What makes you so sure?"

"Because you'd realize somewhere between here
and your office that I'd blab about who pegged the
murder weapon to everyone. Your ego couldn't take
it."

David struggled to keep his expression impassive.
All kidding aside, his inexperience in homicide investigation had sucker punched him when he'd walked
into Osborn's house.

He'd been a patrolman in Tulsa, not a member of
the detective division. He'd secured countless crime
scenes, but street cops don't stay with cases from body
bag to the jury's verdict.

Fortunately, he had good men like Andrik, Orr and
McBride behind him, but he was the sheriff, the one
who'd catch the glory or blame depending on the case's
outcome.

In the meantime, the county commissioners, the *Sanity Examiner's* editor, and just plain folks would peck
at him, demanding to know what he was doing, why
he wasn't doing it faster and why he'd let an elderly
woman be killed in cold blood in the first place.

Hannah laid a hand on his forearm. "Hey, I got carried away playing one of the Hardy Boys, and—"

"The Hardy Boys? What about Nancy Drew?"

She rolled her eyes. "No insights into the male psy-
che—girls named George don't count—and I'm trying
to apologize here, if you don't mind."

"For what?"

"Like I said, I got carried away playing detective, I've never thought you were a son of a bitch, and I'm sorry if I insulted you."

"You didn't." His pulse quickened at her touch. Grinning down at her, he added, "Ma'am."

5

"**N**ew boyfriend, huh?"

The teenager who'd slunk up beside Hannah in the health-and-beauty aids aisle hoovered a bubble into her mouth, then popped it between her teeth. Purple gum webbed her nose ring, attesting to less successful implosions.

Ah, youth. With luck, she'd survive it.

The girl smirked at the tai chi video, replenishing cream, body lotion, aromatherapy candles and box of Twinkies in Hannah's shopping cart. "My old lady does a makeover when she gets the hots for a guy, too."

"I buy these things all the time," Hannah countered, unsure why she was defending herself to a tattooed, raccoon-eyed MTV wannabe.

"Uh-huh, sure." Ms. Worldly-Wise-and-Wearied-by-It snatched a box of hair coloring off the shelf. "This is better stuff. It's like, more natural, ya know? That junk you've got will fry your hair."

"It will?" Funny, the manufacturer's promotions executive had never mentioned side effects. Then again, anyone who believed supermodels used the products they endorsed believed bunnies laid decorated, hard-boiled eggs under bushes one Sunday, every spring.

"Thanks." Hannah returned the carton to the shelf. "Not that I was going to buy it, or anything."

The girl stretched on tiptoe to examine Hannah's scalp. "You're not, like, *majorly* gray yet. Mom's got *tons* more'n you."

Oh, I'll bet she does, Hannah thought. Along with high blood pressure, migraines and chronic acid reflux.

The volunteer cosmetologist lobbed her product recommendation into Hannah's cart. "Knock yourself out, girlfriend. I mean, like, you know, whaddaya got to lose?"

She skulked away, hips thrust forward, shoulders pulled back and swinging. In Hannah's day, that strut would have brought a summons from the school nurse for an emergency scoliosis screening.

In the next aisle, an unseen child screamed for a toy, endangering all glassware in a twenty-foot radius. Toxic herbicide fumes drifted in from the lawn-and-garden area. If this were a movie, cellos would be sawing gloom-and-doom chords, instead of an amplified, adenoidal voice demanding customer assistance in the shoe department.

The antsiness Hannah had come to Sanity to escape had returned with a vengeance. Sheriff's-department vehicles had paraded by the cottage all day, but she'd heard nothing from David Hendrickson since her brilliant deduction and excessive gloating.

However, Detective Andrik had dropped by unannounced that morning, leaving her office a powdery mess, her hands ink-stained and insinuations that her name topped his list of suspects.

Andrik reiterated all of David's questions and freelanced a thousand more beginning with, "I understand that you—", "Is it true you—" and "Are you sure—"

All were delivered in a monotone rife with feigned boredom. All circled the same topical ground, chipping at it from myriad angles, like a sculptor searching for the Madonna inside a block of marble.

The disconcerting feeling that her answers lacked consistency kindled memories of her high-school principal accusing her of stealing ten dollars from Debbie Katzenback's purse during gym class. Andrik's probing eyes transported Hannah back to the day her nails dug into the edge of a hard, wooden chair, fully aware that a cheerleader's allegation outweighed a Garvey's sworn innocence. Two weeks' detention and the shame of spending it picking up contraband cigarette butts and trash from school property had proven it.

Principal Willingham had apologized when the gym teacher caught Maggie Sue Smith with her sticky fingers in another girl's purse, but the "Thief" branded on Hannah's forehead was as indelible as her surname.

Growling softly, she stared at her shopping list, thinking, life will go on whether you buy the rest of this crap or not. Why don't you go home, where you should have stayed?

In addition to Andrik's interrogation, she'd made nice to a nosy probate-court clerk who also couldn't imagine why Kathleen Osborn wanted a stranger in charge of her estate, and had disabused Tripp Irving of having 'cocktails' with him, like, you know—*ever*.

If that wasn't enough aggravation for one afternoon, she could always call Delbert and ask him to come fix something. Poor old guy. What she should do is invite him to her cottage for a cup of coffee. He was, after all, mourning the loss of a dear friend.

Flashlights on the checkout lane's end-cap display inspired an impulse purchase. With or without Delbert, a leisurely stroll along the lake might put the "Thank God" back in "It's Friday."

Absently, she wondered what David Hendrickson did to chase away the willies. Probably shot at things. Tin cans. Tree branches. Small, furry woodland creatures.

A few minutes later and forty-eight-dollars-and-change poorer, she pushed through the discount store's doors only to be blinded by the sun hovering just at the horizon. Striking off in the Blazer's general direction, she peeked through her eyelids at its bent radio antennae to maintain her bearings.

As she rounded the front fender, a voice boomed, "Hey, *you.*"

Unable to concentrate on not swallowing a few molars, while simultaneously retaining control of her purse, her bladder and four plastic shopping bags, one sack smacked the asphalt, its contents spewing out between her truck and the station wagon parked beside it.

"Gosh, I'm sorry." David Hendrickson knelt down and scooped up a box of Tampax, two of panty liners, a roll of paper towels and her Twinkies. "I didn't mean to scare you."

Hannah plucked the merchandise from his arms, her face burning with embarrassment. At least he knew she hadn't hit menopause yet, for whatever that was worth. "The sun was in my eyes. I couldn't have seen King Kong."

He thunked the brim of his Stetson. "Maybe you ought to get one of these."

"I stopped dreaming of becoming the next Annie Oakley when I was six."

Oh, nice one, Hannah, she thought, her keys jingling

free of her shoulder bag. Do insult the man every chance you get.

"Need any help?"

She smiled, hoping he didn't mean the professional kind. "Thanks, but fifty bucks doesn't buy what it once did."

Hiking the sacks over on the passenger seat, she half expected his next words to be, "You have the right to remain silent." Why else would he have been polishing her truck's quarter-panel with his perfect buns of steel while she was inside, staving off a minor nervous breakdown?

She straightened, rested an arm on the window ledge and a foot on the running board. "Do you believe in coincidence, Sheriff?"

"Nope."

"Neither do I."

"Then I reckon you know my being here isn't one."

"Yep." Maybe she hadn't completely outgrown good ol' Annie's influence.

"I was passing through and saw your vehicle," he said. "Thought you might want to walk over to Ruby's for coffee and a bite to eat."

Hannah followed his nod to the storefront café across the parking lot. Scoping out the arched window lettering, gingham half curtains and steaming cinnamon roll painted on the glass between them gave her a moment to play mind games.

Was this a leaf from the "good cop" playbook? A bona fide dinner invitation, aka a date? Was Hendrickson after her winsome company, her body or a murder confession?

"Okay," she said, adding with a touch more enthusiasm, "I'm not very hungry, but a cup of coffee sounds good."

With his hand grazing the small of her back, they wove through the maze of parked cars, pausing to let vehicles scouting for a vacancy pass by.

Drivers acknowledged the sheriff with waves, or mouthed "How ya doin's?" Each noted David's escorting arm and eyed the woman receiving it. Hannah had never felt so self-conscious in her life.

Only a few of the café's tables were occupied. David indicated one midway along the far wall, then slid a chair out for her. "If you don't mind, I don't like to sit with my back to the door."

Hannah sat down, then peered over her shoulder at the entrance, feeling suddenly and intensely paranoid. She'd never given a moment's thought to her position in relation to a restaurant's door. Something told her she'd never *not* give a moment's thought to it again.

To distract herself from visions of armed terrorists bursting in for a little human target practice, she surveyed local artisans' overpriced paintings of wildlife on the wing and hoof hanging above the wood-paneled wainscoting. Ivy, philodendron and wandering Jew spilled from hanging baskets and the waist-high planter symbolically dividing smokers from nonsmokers.

Mingled aromas of roast beef, buttered corn, fresh strawberries and yeast reminded Hannah of Grandma Garvey's monthly Sunday feasts. Sometime between the prayer and the tapioca pudding, either Maybelline, or her sister-in-law, Lurleen, would take exception to a remark and try to stab the other with a fork. Advanced age and cataracts had affected their aim, so blood was rarely drawn, but reaching for the pepper shaker at the wrong time invited collateral damage.

Hannah started when a middle-aged man dressed in a filthy sweatshirt, grease-stained overalls and a slouch hat brushed her elbow as he shuffled by to the next table. He slid into the chair behind David's as though fearful of being charged with assaulting an officer if he bumped the sheriff.

"Smells like Ruby just took a fresh pan of hot rolls out of the oven," David said, offering Hannah a typed, plastic-jacketed menu. "Sure you won't order something to wash down with that coffee?"

"This is entrapment, Hendrickson."

"Darned right it is." He planted his forearms on the table. "And it sure beats eating alone."

"Any port in a storm, huh?"

His lips curled upward and his eyes narrowed slightly. "Nope."

Before Hannah summoned the courage to ask what it was, a potbellied woman with a towering, coal-black beehive and spit curls materialized at the head of the table. "Hidey there, tall, dark and handsome."

She wiped a palm on her apron and held it out. "Ruby Amyx, and you must be Hannah from over to Valhalla Springs. Right nice to meet you."

Hannah clasped the woman's hand, stammering, "H-how did you know my name?"

David laughed. "A cow can't drop a calf in this county without Ruby knowing about it before its mama licks it clean."

"Ain't my fault folks make their business mine," Ruby said. "And it's a good thing they did, a time or two, now, ain't it?"

David explained, "Ruby received a commendation six months ago for helping us bust a chop-shop ring out near Cobbler's Knob."

"Bought me the purtiest new parlor set you ever did see with the reward money, too." Her shelflike bosom heaved with ecstasy. "Red velvet with gold tassels and trim on the cushions, and throw pillows to match."

She went on without losing a beat, but lowered her voice, "Been keeping my ears open, but nothin's abuzz 'bout that murder, 'cept everyone's just sick about it. What is this world acomin' to when an old woman gets herself killed with her own rollin' pin?"

Hannah's gaze shifted to David. His eyebrows met, signaling he'd explain later. "Well, now, Miz Amyx, I'm beginning to think it may take unnecessary force to get some coffee and a couple of chicken-fried steak dinners."

"You gonna let him order your food for ya, Miss Hannah?"

"As long as he does it right, he can."

After oversize mugs of coffee were served and Ruby bustled off to the kitchen, David said, "You didn't know about the rolling pin?"

"I don't think Detective Andrik believes in 'better to give than to receive,' and I was away from the office all afternoon."

"A golfer found it buried in a sand trap near the fourth green. Andrik faxed a photograph of it to me while I was in Columbia witnessing the autopsy. The medical examiner says it fits the deceased's head wounds."

Hannah grimaced. "That's part of the job, too? A front-row seat at postmortems?"

"Not often, thank the Lord." He ran his knuckles along his stubbled jaw. "It helps to remember the spirit is in a finer place. What's left behind is key to nailing a killer."

"Or maybe ruling out a suspect?"

His smile deepened the shadows beneath his eyes and the creases at the corners. Hannah could only guess what a homicide investigation entailed, much less a sheriff's regular duties, but he looked a decade older than he had yesterday.

If only he were...

"You were never really a serious suspect," he said. "Sure, there's an element of everyone being a candidate at the get-go, only—" his index finger rimmed the mug "—call it a sixth sense, a hunch, whatever you will, but the scene conjured a man in my mind. A good-size jake, hot-tempered or desperate enough to grab what was handy when he didn't get what he wanted."

"Which was?" Hannah asked.

"Money." David shrugged. "Though other than whittling down the field of suspects, the whydunit isn't as important as the whodunit."

Hannah disagreed. Whenever a crime grabbed the national media by the collective throat—Oklahoma City, O.J., the Unibomber, and sadly, the rash of schoolyard killings—the "why" provoked a morbid fascination centering on what motivates people to act beyond the bounds of normal behavior. Ironically, when the "who" was identified, the villain never seemed equal to the deed.

"This hunch of yours," she said, "is it kosher to ask if any leads are bearing it out?"

"Too early to say. A lot depends on the forensic evidence, the M.E.'s final report, fieldwork...and luck."

Ruby swooped in, a heaping, oval plate in each hand. "Lighten up, Wyatt Earp. I won't have you talking ugly over my vittles."

A napkin-lined basket of hot rolls, butter and honey accompanied the meal. "Save room for a slice of banana cream pie," she said, refilling their cups. "It ain't good for bidness if y'all leave here hungry."

Hannah ogled the gravy-smothered meat, real mashed potatoes, a mound of green beans and stewed apples. "She's kidding, right?"

"Nope. Ruby isn't satisfied unless her customers are swollen up fatter than ticks on a prize bull."

"Lovely analogy for the dinner table, Sheriff."

"Dinner is at noon, city slicker. This is supper. Now dig in before Ruby's feelins get hurt."

They fell to their food, losing themselves in the unadulterated pleasure of porking out on bad cholesterol, more sodium than the Great Salt Lake, refined sugar and white flour.

Her zipper on the brink of a blowout, Hannah leaned back, drowsy, sated and jealous of David's larger digestive capacity. The Almighty was definitely male, and he'd always liked Adam best.

"Please, tell me you don't eat like this every day," she moaned. "Or if you do, lie to me."

He laughed. "I did when I played football, and at the Academy." Regarding his slick-clean plate, he smiled ruefully. "Reckon I still can, but I don't, except—"

His pause and inscrutable expression piqued her curiosity. "Except for what? Lent?"

"Weight watching isn't exclusive to females, you know. I like my belly to stay where I have to look down to see it."

"So, when do you treat yourself to Ruby's blue-plate specials?"

"When I need a tension reliever. That's why the Red

Cross gives out doughnuts and sandwiches during disasters and blood drives. Carbohydrates take the edge off stress.'' He wagged a finger. ''Not my theory—proven, scientific fact.''

''One of the few worth knowing, in my opinion.'' Hannah took a sip of coffee. ''IdaClare told me you were a police officer in Tulsa before you came here. Did you grow up in Oklahoma?''

He shook his head. ''Native Missourian. Dad started out with a pharmacy in St. Joseph, then bought seven others in surrounding towns.'' He grinned. ''Before you accuse me of being a city kid, we lived on a farm a couple of miles from town. It wasn't the Ponderosa, but there were plenty of chores to keep me and my three little brothers out of trouble.''

Hannah listened to him describe the kind of Ozzie-and-Harriet life-style she never had, envying him most for the father he spoke of with abiding respect and affection.

''I know Mom and Dad planned on me coming back to St. Joe after college,'' he said, ''and for sure, one of us taking over the family business. When it didn't happen, they sold the farm, sold the stores to a chain operation and are making up for all the vacations they never had time to take before.''

Their eyes met and held, then David chuckled and slumped in his chair. ''Bet you're wishing you'd saved one of those rolls to stuff in my mouth.''

''Not even close,'' Hannah teased. ''At risk of it going to your head, I was thinking how much I—''

A burst of static preceded a male voice blatting, *Adam–101.*

David's expression changed from tired but relaxed,

to solemn. He yanked a portable radio from its belt holster and held it close to his mouth. "Go ahead."

What's your –20?

"10–46 at Ruby's. What's up, Tony?"

A 10–91 at Fair Meadows Trailer Park. Charlie–203 requesting backup, that location.

Reaching for his wallet with his free hand, he said, "Roger on that 10–61. Clear."

10–4, Adam–101. Clear.

David kicked back his chair, then apologized to the man still seated behind him. Cash fluttered to the table. Radio resecured and Stetson in hand, he said, "Sorry, Hannah. You can stay and have another cup of coffee, if you'd rather."

"No way." She grabbed her purse and jacket, waved at Ruby and hurried from the café; David so close behind her, his breath ruffled her hair.

At the sidewalk, he took her hand, holding up the other to stop traffic circling past the shops anchored by Wal-Mart and Price-Slasher. Hannah looked down at their entwined fingers. Maybe he didn't trust her to cross the parking lot without getting run over by a soccer mom. Nothing meant by it. It's almost dark, after all. Safety first.

"That's the second piece of pie the Hewlitts have cost me this month," he grumbled. "Banana cream's my favorite, too, damn their hides."

"What's happening?" Hannah said, trotting to keep pace with his long-legged stride. "A drug bust? A holdup?"

He smiled at her as if she were a pigtailed ten-year-old. "Assistance needed on a domestic. They can be the most dangerous calls to respond to, but these two lovebirds come out swinging pretty regular."

A silver Mercedes bore down on them, its driver chattering into a cell phone. David angled his body in front of Hannah, then banged the vehicle's fender with his fist. Tires squalled. The car nosedived to a halt inches from the sheriff's thigh.

He stalked to the driver's side, pulling Hannah along behind him like a dinghy. The Mercedes's window oozed down, revealing an unseasonably tanned, white-haired gent with a comb-over starting at his sideburns.

"Raleigh, if I see you with that dadgummed cell phone clapped upside your skull *one more time,* I'll hail-Mary that thing so far, folks'll think it's a UFO. Do you understand me?"

"Yes, Sheriff. Yes, sir, I do." The receiver bounced off the car's back glass. "No more chatting when I'm driving, I swear."

"No more warnings, either." David inched backward. "Now, why don't you show me how slow this fine automobile will go with both hands on the wheel?"

The window glass ascended. The car purred forward, brake lights as bright as twin rubies. David cursed under his breath and started away.

"I don't get it," Hannah said, her hand still clasped in David's, but not nearly as keen on the idea.

"Get what?" David looked at her, puzzled. "What if we'd been a couple of kids cutting across the lot? Raleigh can't scratch and swallow at the same time, let alone talk on the phone and steer."

"That isn't what I meant. Why read the riot act to *him,* but do little or nothing to a guy who uses his wife for a punching bag?"

"You have the wrong—"

"Any jerk who lays a finger on a woman ought to

be arrested, thrown under the jail, and...well, the Supreme Court wouldn't allow other deterrents I could mention."

Before Hannah realized what was happening, David had her back pressed against the Blazer's door. He loomed over her, his eyes mischievous and more blue than gray. "I never saw a gal who truly was prettier when she's madder than a scalded cat."

She stared up at him, every nerve in her body tingling. Vows of celibacy were a real bitch at times like these.

"For the record, it's Neva Ann Hewlitt who has the sorry habit of conking her dearly beloved with a skillet if he doesn't hand over his paycheck fast enough. Until ol' Verlis has the balls to sign a complaint against the three-ton, pug-ugly she-bear he married, all me and my deputies can do is keep adding frying pans to the stack at the courthouse."

"Oh." Hannah giggled, a genuine, utterly ridiculous, uncontrollable, Shirley Temple-style giggle. "That's a 10–4, uh, Adam–101."

His lips brushed hers, a kiss so fleeting as to be disbelieved, if not for the physical jolt it left in its wake.

"And *that's* a 10–39," he drawled, then tipped his hat and strolled to the cruiser parked behind her.

Hannah slumped against her truck. Her shoulder bag's strap slithered down her arm. Why was the county's ten-foot-tall and bulletproof sheriff doing his best to cast a spell on her? Just to prove he could?

Reeling in her purse, she pawed inside it for her keys. Uh-*huh*. Another notch in the ol' pistol, eh? Well, include me out, buster. Not interested in a "Slam-bam, thank you, *ma'am*."

The seat belt's nylon edge stung the tender skin at her neck. "Cool your jets, oh horny one. If that was a kiss, Timmy Yates planted a better one on you in the cloakroom in first grade."

Pulling from the parking space, she didn't bother looking back to see if his car was still there. *That'd* teach him.

Night closed in early along highway VV's tree-lined rights-of-way. Hannah concentrated on the road, curbing her speed on downhill slopes and curves; their snakiness was exaggerated by decreased visibility and the bright white line at the pavement's edge.

Her headlights framed a possum waddling into her lane. The animal froze, its beady eyes blood-red and fixed. She swerved, tensing for the awful *thump* she feared couldn't be avoided.

Silence. She checked the rearview mirror. No animal, alive or dead, but she did notice a single headlight about twenty yards behind her. The same vehicle had followed her at the same distance since she left Sanity.

Hannah eased up on the accelerator. The lone beam neared for an instant, retreated, then held steady at the twenty-yard position. A slight increase in speed had the same result.

Her stomach muscles tightened. She sat up straighter, pressed down on the automatic door-lock button and blew out a breath. "Who said anything about a carjacker? This is Mayberry, not Chicago's South Side. The guy's just being cautious. Using your lights to compensate for his broken one. Perfectly reasonable explanation."

Oncoming vehicles held her attention for several miles. The Blazer auto-shifted into overdrive to climb a steep hill. Darkness loomed behind her. "See? He's gone. Turned off. Now, don't you feel stu—"

A single, white lancet skittered across the brushy fenceline beyond the southbound lane. The steering wheel slickened with sweat. Hannah gripped it tighter. Don't panic. You don't know the road well enough, haven't driven it at night. Putting the pedal to the metal is the dumbest thing you could do.

The light hurtled closer, the beam jouncing at the increase in speed. Her eyes flicked between the solid yellow centerline and the mirror. She glimpsed a tan pickup's hood. Dual high-beams exploded in the mirror.

"You son of a bitch!" Hunched forward, she squinted against the glare and her own shadow reflected on the windshield. The pickup nosed her bumper as if attached to a tow-bar.

Ahead, a pair of headlights bumbled around a curve like ghostly feelers testing the asphalt for soundness. The pickup backed off, and...disappeared?

Hannah could just make out the truck's receding silhouette, running with *no* lights. "What in the—"

A horn blared. She wrenched the steering wheel hard right, barely missing the oncoming sedan. The Blazer fishtailed and rocked around the curve, then settled onto a straightaway.

Amber coachlights atop Valhalla Springs's gate shone like beacons offering safe harbor from a dense, potentially deadly fog. Hannah whipped into the broad, aproned driveway, stopping short of the entrance. Pulse pounding like congas in her ears, she smoothed her clammy hair from her face. "Okay, asshole, come and get me. Lights or no lights, I can see well enough from here to give David a pretty good description of your pickup.''

A whippoorwill whistled its eponymous tune from a nearby branch. Across the valley, coyotes yipped and howled like puppies shut up in a dark garage until their bladders could be trusted. The brisk, dampish air was as soothing as Prozac and twice as effective.

A subcompact, then a Jeep, cruised by on the highway, headed toward Sanity. Hannah's fingertips drummed the window ledge. ''No guts, no glory, nimrod.''

A southbound motor home pulling a pontoon boat confirmed her suspicions. ''Ducked and ran down a back road, didn't you?'' She fisted the steering wheel. ''I hope you break both axles.''

Moments later, she recoiled, blinking like a desert nomad would at a lemonade stand. IdaClare's Lincoln, Delbert's Edsel, Rosemary Marchetti's moped and a car she didn't recognize were circled in her driveway as if to fend off an enemy attack.

I don't need this. She jabbed the button on the garage door opener clipped to the visor. *I don't know what's going on, but I don't need it.*

Rather than bother unlocking the cottage's back door, she marched along the side porch and entered through the front.

''Where in the world have you been?'' IdaClare exclaimed. ''We've been waiting for nearly two hours.''

Hannah lofted the shopping bags. ''I'm sorry I kept you—'' She shook her head. ''Whoa, cancel that. How did you get in here?''

''Well, with a key, of course.'' IdaClare grinned at her own rapier wit. ''I already had one, and made copies for everyone this afternoon. Except Velma. Stuart won't let her go anywhere after dark.''

Hannah counted backward from a hundred as she set her plunder on the desk and took off her jacket. Pivoting on one heel, she clenched the railing instead of her teeth. ''*You* had *keys* made to *my house?*''

Delbert patted a sofa cushion. ''Oh, get yourself over here, ladybug. I want you to meet my buddy, Leo Schnur, and then we'll fill you in.''

A bald, portly man sprawled in a club chair wriggled around and saluted. The thick, black-framed glasses, brush mustache and prominent nose seemed vaguely familiar. Character actor? Taxi driver?

Ohmygod. Delbert's best friend and golfing partner was Mr. Potato Head.

All four eager, crinkled faces beamed at Hannah as if Ed McMahon and the Prize Patrol were due any second. Be calm. Be cool. If worse comes to worst, close your eyes and think of England.

She shook Leo's doughy hand, then plopped down next to Delbert. The magazines, bookmarked novel and heirloom S.S. Kresge candy dish, formerly arranged on the trunk, had migrated to the hearth, replaced by chocolate-smeared plates, forks, cups, balled-up papers and a cardboard box.

The blaze-orange, quilted coveralls Rosemary wore for visibility when she rode her moped at night rested on the love seat beside her like a phantom deer-hunter. Reduced to gold lamé stirrup pants and a sweatshirt sloganned I'm A Senior Citizen, Give Me My Discount, she poured coffee from the carafe to Hannah's coffeemaker into a cup from her cabinet and served it with a smile. ''Ralph at the mercantile donated a pound of decaf to our cause.'' Her tongue clucked a reproof.

"We wouldn't have slept a wink tonight if we'd brewed that imported stuff in your cupboard."

"This is decaf?" Hannah asked, her tone indicating she'd prefer hemlock.

"See, I told you not to tell her," Delbert said. "She'd have never known the difference."

The heck I wouldn't, Hannah fumed.

"Well, these are made from genuine Swiss chocolate," IdaClare informed her, placing a napkin and two iced brownies on Hannah's knee. "Now, can I get you anything else, dear? Cream? Sugar?"

Not trusting herself to be civil, Hannah shook her head.

"How 'bout we get this show on the road," Delbert said. "*Friday Night Fights* comes on at ten."

Rosemary sneered, "I'll remember that next time you call a residents' board meeting during *As the World Turns*."

"That's enough, y'all," IdaClare said, taking the vacant club chair. She'd worn a rose wool pantsuit to brunch. Tonight's slacks and sweater were the same shade of pink as her hair. Strange, unless Jack's mother once sold cosmetics door-to-door.

Delbert muttered, "Bossy ol' broad," but if IdaClare heard him, she ignored it. "Hannah, you know how upsetting Kathleen's death was to us."

Hannah nodded.

"Well, the four of us started talking this morning, then one thing led to another and we decided something must be done, and who better to do it than her friends?"

Anticipating that a committee to help with Kathleen's funeral arrangements had been formed, the iron spike supporting Hannah's head began to feel like a neck again.

"Something, hell," Delbert said. "We're going to catch us a killer. Got a bunch of questions, a list of people to buttonhole, and that's just for starters."

Coffee whooshed into Hannah's windpipe. Over her respiratory distress, Leo added, "Gumshoes we will be. We watch. We listen. We use our noggins. Very hush-hush."

Delbert said, "That's why we're confiscating your place for our headquarters. If we traipse back and forth between each other's houses too much, somebody'll guess what we're up to."

"Then our cover," Leo said, "it would be blown."

"You're so lucky to have this much privacy," Rosemary said, looking around the room. "We can come here anytime we want and no one will think a thing about it."

"Anyone want to know what *I* think about it?" Hannah asked, barely disguising the snarl in her voice.

IdaClare raised a hand. "There's no need to thank us, dear. The police want our help, and if we'd gotten involved sooner, this meeting wouldn't have been necessary."

"Sheriff Hendrickson asked you to do this?"

"No, but…oh—what's his name?" Rosemary snapped her fingers. "It's Mc-something…"

"Chief Deputy McBride?" Hannah suggested.

"No, no, it's McGruff." Leo buckled his chins, thrust out a pudgy finger and growled, "Help take a bite out of the crime." His dentures clacked for emphasis.

"He's so cute," Rosemary said.

"Hear that, Leo?" Delbert teased. "She thinks you're cute."

"Not him, the *dog*, you old fool. He's right, too. McGruff, I mean. If we'd kept our eyes and ears open, Kathleen would still be with us."

The quartet exchanged sorrowful glances. Hannah waffled between knowing precisely how Custer felt at the Last Stand, and compassion.

Turning her home into IdaClare and Company's clubhouse gave her cold chills, but it would allow her to supervise their "investigation." And honestly, if it made them feel useful, what harm could four elderly Sherlocks do?

During dinner, she had sensed David was homing in on a suspect but still lacked sufficient evidence. The remark about forensics, the medical examiner's report and fieldwork sounded like press-release patter. The luck? She knew by the tiny shift in his expression that he anticipated Dame Fortune to smile in the near future.

When an arrest was made, the four senior sleuths would swap their deerstalkers and briar pipes for golf clubs, fishing gear and tournament bridge again. In the meantime, if tonight was any indication, either Rosemary or IdaClare would bake a gooey, homemade dessert for every meeting. Virtue might be its own reward, but refreshments were a nice touch.

"This is no fly-by-night operation, either," Delbert said. He opened the box on the trunk and removed a device encased in black plastic. Its oblong face had a numbered keypad, like a calculator. An array of buttons and knobs surrounded a small LED screen. The bow-tied cord dangling from the back was reassuring. Hannah was relatively sure a bomb didn't need to be plugged in to an electrical outlet.

"What we have here, ladybug, is a deluxe, 800MHz, twelve-band radio scanner. Set it on the right frequency, and it'll pick up the sheriff department's radio chatter."

He rubbed the case as one would a beloved house cat. "With this little baby, the cops can't pass wind without us knowing about it."

"Delbert bought one for each of us," IdaClare said. "Wasn't that sweet of him?"

"I suppose, but..." Hannah eyed the scanner dubiously. "Is it legal?"

"Well, if it wasn't, do you think I'd have bought five of 'em? T'ain't me I'm wanting to put in the hoosegow for life."

He handed her two typewritten sheets. "These are the ten codes cops and dispatchers use to talk to one another. It's confusing at first, but you'll get the hang of it."

"10-44," Rosemary and IdaClare chirped in unison.

Leo's brow furrowed, then he punched the air with his fist. "Message received by all—yes?"

"Correct-a-mundo," Delbert said.

Hannah remembered David murmuring, "That's a 10-39," after he kissed her—for lack of a better term—in the parking lot. Her finger traveled down the columns.

A fluttery sensation batted at her ribs. *Message delivered.*

6

David's eyelids fluttered open. Sunlight striped his desktop. He brought his watch up almost to his nose, the face and numerals blurry, gradually coming into focus, like the bottom line of letters during an optometric exam.

Almost seven? How long had he been asleep in his chair? The crick in his neck said a couple of hours at least. Sore muscles everywhere else said not long enough.

Muffled office clatter beyond the pebble-glass door indicated a verbal "Do not disturb" had been ordered. Closing the manila folder spread across his lap, he swung his feet off the desk, wincing at the needles shooting up his legs, careful not to let his boots thud to the floor. Better to allow the blood to find his brain before everyone realized he'd risen from the near dead.

The boot-cut khakis and white polo shirt he'd exchanged for his uniform the night before still looked presentable. He slid open the bottom drawer, took out a shaving kit and laid it on the desk. Five minutes in the men's room and he'd be good as...well, as good as could be expected.

Dozens of photographs, some gruesome, others of no interest to anyone not involved in law enforcement, were scattered across the blotter. "Don't let yourself turn into RoboCop," he recalled his Tulsa field-training officer telling him. "But don't let the shit people do to each other get to you, either, or it'll eat you alive."

"Right, Sarge," David muttered, scrubbing his face with his hands. "Except nobody's ever figured out how to keep it from getting to you."

Kids and old folks were the worst. Same vulnerability. Same bone-deep certainty you'd failed them when they needed your protection the most.

If only Kathleen Osborn had known the danger she'd put herself in by distrusting banks, paying cash for everything and adhering to a routine. Her age, gender and habits had made her a victim just waiting to happen.

"Profiling" was a hot-button issue for law enforcement these days. David had known and despised the few cops who'd thought of their badges as human hunting permits. The majority based probable cause on the sense "something doesn't feel right," similar to the old saw about what constitutes pornography: "I can't explain what it is, but I know it when I see it."

Criminals knew easy marks when they saw them, too, though it wasn't called "profiling" when a thief looked for, and set his sights on, a pigeon like Kathleen Osborn.

As a rule, senior citizens carried more cash than those in their forties or younger, who relied on credit cards and checkbooks for transactions. If given the choice, a purse snatcher would hit an elderly woman over a thirty-something female, just as pickpockets preyed on older men. Not because advanced age meant the victims were less likely to give chase, but for the same reason Willie "The Actor" Sutton robbed banks: That's where the money is.

Kathleen Osborn lived alone in an upscale retirement community, only patronized her bank the first week of the month, then shopped and paid bills like clockwork on succeeding Thursdays. From that alone, any halfway intelligent eight-year-old could divine the optimum time for a robbery—between her go-to-the-bank Thursday and the next regularly scheduled trip to town.

David shook his head. "Except it wasn't an eight-year-old who beat her to death Wednesday night."

He and Marlin Andrik had compared interview notes and instincts regarding Harvey and Miriam Liebermeyer, Osborn's next-door neighbors. The couple knew more than they were saying, no doubt about it.

Maybe the right questions hadn't been asked. Maybe they had, but in the wrong way. Rapport wasn't as easy to establish with some as with others, and older people were sometimes intimidated by authority figures.

Cletus Orr would pay a call on the Liebermeyers later that morning. Like Marlin, David didn't think they'd spill any beans to Orr, either, but it was worth a shot.

Five Valhalla Springs employees hadn't reported for work on Thursday. The same five, plus two others, skipped out Friday.

Of the first group, one had the flu and another stayed home to care for an asthmatic child. Two of the remaining three had general delivery addresses and hadn't been located yet. The last, and two of her male co-workers, had taken advantage of the warm weather to get a jump on the weekend.

Of the pair David lacked physical addresses for, both had rap sheets. Neither hailed from Kinderhook County. Neither had been charged with anything since they'd blown into his jurisdiction, but that didn't mean they'd found Jesus.

One of Andrik's snitches had told him, "this guy," an unnamed drifter he'd had a few beers with from time to time, expected to make a "score" big enough to set him up for life, but "it tanked, and this guy, he's in a world o' hurt, man. A real world o' hurt. He was already in to his dealer for the crank he used 'stead of mulin' it, and now there ain't no money to pay it off with."

Translation: "This guy" was a methamphetamine addict who'd tried to support his habit by selling the drug, but ended up shooting, snorting or smoking the inventory.

Gee, David mused, you just can't trust a junkie to be a good, commission salesman.

The informant swore "this guy" hadn't said how he'd planned to score or why he hadn't. It was even-odds his tip was twenty bucks' worth of hooraw, too, but the freebies IdaClare Clancy had been phoning in weren't worth squat, either.

David raked his fingers through his hair. The prints Andrik had lifted off the rolling pin's handle had been photographed, scanned into the computer and the points of identification enumerated, then transmitted to the National Crime Information Center. In less time than detectives would have believed possible a decade ago, NCIC's Automated Fingerprint Identification System's database would process the information and provide up to ten candidates for preliminary comparison.

One by one, Andrik would examine the candidate prints displayed on the computer screen alongside the unidentified latent. If a definitive comparison could be made, "this guy" might not remain nameless forever.

David stood and stretched, sucking air through his teeth, then yawned so hard tears rimmed his eyes. He was in for a long day of waiting for something to happen. And there was no guarantee anything would.

Hannah's gloved hand closed around a plastic, pointy-tipped bottle. Raising it, she licked her lips in anticipation, then aimed the nozzle at the top of her head.

A stream of cold, purple goo seeped through her scalp. Purple? She retrieved the empty box from the wastebasket. Medium reddish-brown. Okay, but...

What if the manufacturer had screwed up? Since that tiny fiasco with a client's do-it-yourself trimmer, she'd put her hair in Henri of Chicago's ungodly expensive, professional hands. Shouldn't something as critical as hair coloring be done in a salon?

Hannah made a face at the mirror. "Like, for instance, Sanity's premier parlor of poof, the Curl Up and Dye?"

Gamely, she squeezed out another squirt, and another. Ammonia fumes literally took her breath away. She flipped on the exhaust fan. Flyaway, goo-coated hair left trails of brownish freckles on her forehead, jawline and neck.

Brownish is good. Freckles are not.

The empty bottle pitter-pattered in the sink. She massaged in the noxious stuff, then slicked her hair up against her skull, as directed by the kit's instruction sheet.

Then, no sooner had she grabbed a towel for emergency freckle removal, than her hair came unglued from its moorings. Hannah watched in horrified fascination as layers succumbed to gravitational pull, fan-

ning downward in wide, winglike sections. Purplish-
brownish drizzles began meandering down her
forehead, neck, and into her ears.

Stripping off the gloves, she bent at the waist and
wrapped the slimy mess formerly known as her hair in
a towel. "Little Miss Nose Ring, I'm going to hunt
you down like a dog, and..."

The threat faded to a whimper. Splotches stained her
arms from elbows to wrists. Her neck looked like the
winning entry in a hickey contest.

"Shit-oh-shit-oh-shit!" Spatters dappled the once
virginal white switchplate, the vanity top, basin, splash-
back, commode, linen cabinet doors, the floor— "Four
ounces of purple goop did all this?"

Snatching a can of bathroom cleaner from the sink
cabinet, she wielded it like a flamethrower, foaming the
perimeter; its pine scent meshing, probably lethally,
with the lingering ammonia. Bubbles billowed and
hissed as she scrubbed and scrubbed at the stains, an
arm crooked over her mouth and nose.

At a glimpse of her Nefertiti headgear in the mirror,
she shrieked, "Oh, no, I was supposed to rinse the
gunk out in fifteen minutes." She snatched her watch
from a basket of hand towels. "Ye gods, what time did
I start?"

An hour and a half later, dressed in tan slacks and a
navy shell, makeup in place and aspirin beginning to
take effect, Hannah pondered her reflection, determined
to make lemonade from lemons.

Collateral damage included a nightshirt, two towels,
a washcloth and a hand towel. The adhesive bandage
holding a bleach-soaked cotton ball to the countertop?
Well, if the stain beneath it didn't disappear, she'd dash
off an S.O.S. to Heloise.

Her hair smelled like a combination fertilizer factory and Marshall Field's first-level perfumery. All seventeen of the gray ones, however, had vanished. Her natural wave was bouncier, too, and seemed thicker, softer. "And redder. Much, much redder."

A halo shimmered up from her crown, like the aura around Jesus's head in religious paintings. Unlike his, which denoted purity and divinity, at certain angles hers looked as if her head were on fire.

Hendrickson would surely make some remark to that effect. If he did, she'd laugh in a cheery, self-deprecating manner, toss off a witty comeback, then kick him in the *cojones*.

The wicked, nether regions of her mind word-associated to another facet of masculine genitalia, specifically David's, and whether a man's shoe size indicated anything besides big feet. Jarrod Amberley's were small and narrow, almost dainty.

Hmm.

The telephone interrupted her idle, lascivious speculation. She answered, smiled and sat down on the bed.

"Just wanted you to know," Jack Clancy said, "the computer I promised should be there by the first of the week. Top-of-the-line CPU and whatchamacallits—peripherals. Lots of peripherals."

"And a tech-in-the-box to show me how to use it?"

"It's supposed to be plug-and-play."

"'Hope springs eternal in the human breast,'" she recited. "'Man never is, but always to be, blest.'"

"Well, don't hurt yourself thanking me, sweetpea. I live for Saturdays when I can screw off the whole morning on crap like this."

Her palm dusted the top of the nightstand. Iced, double-fudge-brownie crumbs tumbled to the carpet. "We know each other pretty well, wouldn't you say?"

The shift in tone and subject matter induced a hesitant, "Sure. Of course we do."

"Then how about telling me what's really biting you in the boxers."

Stammered protests fizzled. She envisioned his knuckles kneading his temple. "For openers, Chase Wingate called a while ago."

"Who's he?"

"Owner/editor of the *Sanity Examiner*. He wanted my thoughts on the murder."

"Did you tell him you were opposed to it?"

"Easy for you to be flip. You don't have a thirty-some million-dollar house of cards shaking in the wind."

She bit her tongue, wishing she'd done so a few seconds sooner. "C'mon, Jack. Don't you think you might be overreacting just a little?"

"Every retirement development in the country has a golf course, a lake, swimming pools, activities—part and parcel with the 'endless vacation' shtick," he argued. "A rural setting and peace of mind are Valhalla's strongest selling points. Both fly like ruptured ducks when a tenant—especially a woman—dies of extremely unnatural causes. That kind of publicity I need like an IRS audit."

"I understand, but how much damage can a story in a county weekly—"

"The *Sanity Examiner* doesn't worry me. A wire service picking it up, and a tabloid-TV stringer thinking, 'Focus on the Heartland angle and gore and this'll scare the bejesus out of our over-fifty audience'... *That* concerns me."

Clancy's fears weren't unfounded. So-called reality television hungered for murders most foul in small towns; the smaller, the tastier. The underlying "Violence is everywhere. You could be next" theme exploited fear and called it entertainment.

"I expect Wingate will call you, too," Jack warned.

"What do you want me to tell him?"

"Just be honest. Bob Bernstein, he isn't. It wouldn't hurt to throw a bone to the sheriff's department. Say you have every confidence they'll catch the person responsible, yada-yada."

"If it's any consolation," Hannah said, "I do have every confidence in Sheriff Hendrickson. He's smart, Jack. From what I've seen, he won't let up until an arrest is made."

"Good to hear, but it can't come soon enough for me. Whoever murdered Ms. Osborn should be bludgeoned the same way she was, only a helluva lot slower."

Hannah nodded. "Ditto."

Paper rattled in the background. "But the fact remains, we'll have ten new units ready for occupancy by mid-May, plus another ten framed, and seventeen vacancies."

"I know," she said, realizing his "we" was of the royal persuasion, meaning her.

Developments like Valhalla Springs were two-stroke engines fueled by the "takes money to make money" philosophy. Planned growth drove one piston: the bigger the bandwagon, the more eager people were to jump on it.

Steady capitalization fired the other. A small percentage of vacancies ensured availability for new tenants. Too many was like a busload of unemployed relatives. They devoured assets without contributing a nickel to their upkeep.

This wasn't the time to tell Jack she had no tour appointments scheduled that weekend. Although many prospects liked to drive through first and ask questions later, bookings indicated a higher level of interest.

"I have about forty info requests to mail this afternoon," she said, "and another dozen or so packets to put together this afternoon."

"Demographics?"

"Mostly Midwest, a few California and Nevada, one New Hampshire, two Pennsylvanias and a New York State—Buffalo, I think."

"So, what do you need a computer for, sweetpea? You're a human database."

"Not enough RAM for the long haul. And if you're toying with the idea of canceling mine to save a buck, logging addresses by hand for follow-ups is a pain in the butt."

"Owen never complained."

She rolled her eyes. "Yeah, and before he went completely around the bend, he covered the windows with aluminum foil to deflect particle beams, too."

Hearty laughter burst from the telephone receiver that was music to Hannah's ear. If she could get signatures on a half-dozen lease agreements in the very near future, she still might have a job come the Fourth of July.

She asked, "Besides mail-outs and charming the drive-bys, what else can I do at this end?"

Jack paused, she assumed, for thought. "Light a fire under that sheriff and hold his feet to it," he said, anxiety again sharpening his tone. "Smart and diligent is fine, but I want *results.*"

* * *

Hannah skimmed the block-printed information on the boilerplate application. The young man seated in the chair beside her desk had a pleasant face, an infectious grin and the annoying habit of sucking on a water bottle as if he hadn't been weaned properly.

Willard Johnson was twenty-six, divorced and had a B.S. in English from Southwest Missouri State University in Springfield. For the past two years, he'd worked as a freelance copy editor for several New York publishers.

Terrific. Expertise on noun/verb agreement and sentence structure were precisely what she needed in a physical fitness instructor.

So far, the Efficient Employment Agency in Sanity had sent her a retired football coach who'd have IdaClare and The Girls begging for Zerelda Sue Connor's return, a bored housewife interested in earning "pin money" and a grossly obese nurse's aide who collected celebrity-workout videos.

Stop being so snappish, Hannah lectured herself. You're just irked because you look like Bozo's worst hair day and your tenure as operations manager might be numbered in weeks instead of projected life expectancy.

"Your résumé is impressive, Mr. Johnson."

"Only you're not in the market for an English major who writes paperback sci-fi novels in his spare time."

Ten points for perceptiveness. "Not at the moment."

"How about an upstanding guy who has a second-degree black belt in tae kwon do, is a volunteer youth-activities minister at Christ the Redeemer Church and a Red Cross certified lifeguard?"

Hannah's eyes didn't leave his as her head cocked

slightly, unwilling to believe salvation was so near. "Exercise equipment. Any experience?"

The wily grin reappeared. "While I was in college, I worked part-time at Gold's Gym."

Her arms flew up as if he'd kicked a field goal. "Why didn't you put any of that on the application?"

"Where? In the margins?"

A valid defense. Questions concerning prior convictions, workmen's comp claims, union affiliations and current permits commanded three-quarters of the agency's form. She particularly admired the "Have you ever been convicted of a felony?" inquiry, as if anyone who *had* would blithely check the "yes" box, secure in the knowledge it would have no effect on employability.

"Are you sure you can live on twenty-five or thirty hours a week at eight-fifty per?" she asked.

"I can, unless my parents evict me from the apartment over their garage."

He parked the water bottle on the corner of her desk, freeing his hands to join the conversation. "It's enough to convince Pop I'm not a bum, the hours won't interfere with my writing schedule, and I won't have any more excuses to skip workouts. It doesn't get any better than that."

"Well, if you're happy, I'm thrilled, and the Efficient Employment Agency isn't as guilty of false advertising as I thought."

His jaw slackened. "You mean I have the job? Just like that?"

"This makes it official." She held out a file folder. "Tax forms, employee info sheet, activities schedule, participants' list, et al. You can drop off the returnables on your way to work Monday morning."

"I won't let you down, Ms. Garvey."

"Hannah." She smiled and rose to her feet. "Since I need to go up to the community center anyway, why don't you ride along? It'll give you a chance to see the layout and meet some people."

On their way out the back door, she pushed the button to open the smaller garage door at the lower end of the cat-slide roofed garage. "Give me a sec to back out. I parked too close to the wall last time."

Expecting to be self-immolated à la Wile E. Coyote, she gritted her teeth and unhooked the battery-charger cables from the Yamaha golf cart at her disposal for jaunts around the development. Delbert had cackled like a mad scientist when he'd demonstrated why the charger must be turned off when attaching or detaching the cables.

"Watch what happens when the gripper ends touch," he'd said. Miniature orange lightning bolts shot in every direction. "Yow-ser!"

"I get it, I get it," Hannah had yelled over the *zzzzts* that obviously delighted him even more than his home-made meteor shower.

"Whatever you do, ladybug, *don't* stick the negative cable on the battery's positive post or vicey-versey."

Few phrases arouse curiosity faster than "Whatever you do," buttressed by a *don't*. It begged a "Why?" just as Wet Paint signs beg a confirming finger.

Delbert's graphic description of explosions fraught with shrapnel and flying battery acid had made her triply careful, as well as wish her arms were longer.

Sliding into the cart's passenger side, Willard said, "I don't suppose the physical fitness instructor gets one of these buggies, too, does he?"

"No, you have to jog everywhere. Set a good example for the residents."

They putt-putted up the boulevard, the Yamaha's motor not having been modified by Daytona Delbert Bisbee. Willard looked around, nodding appreciation and approval.

Wild-cherry trees, phlox, dogwoods and redbuds added splashes of color; a minor phenomenon, as their blooming cycles didn't usually coincide. Scavenger birds tidying the shoreline had the lake to themselves; another rarity, especially on a sunny, sixty-plus-degree afternoon.

Willard patted his jacket pockets, frowned and started playing patty-cake with himself. His clothing's faint acrid odor alluded to a recent ex-smoker. The fidgets said he'd sell his soul for a nicotine hit right now.

Forgot your water bottle, didn't you, Hannah thought, sympathizing with the misery quitters suffered during withdrawal. She considered returning to the cottage, but they were already late, their destination was in sight and his craving would pass in another five or ten years.

"What's going on over there?" he asked, indicating the community center and its full parking lot.

"That's where you'll report for duty, Monday. The indoor pool, exercise rooms, weight equipment, etcetera, are in the basement. This afternoon, on the main floor, the residents' board is sponsoring a 'Get Acquainted' coffee."

Shortcutting across the lawn, she aimed the cart at a gap between two budding forsythias. "I'm the guest of honor." She glanced sideward. "You're the surprise announcement."

His eyes widened. "This is what you meant by meeting some people?"

"Hey, I've only been here a few days, myself. I figured we rookies ought to stick together."

He joined her on the steps, his hands jammed in his trouser pockets like a small boy forced to attend his sister's piano recital. "Now I know why Mama told me to never get in a car with a stranger."

Hannah grinned. "Okay, I snookered you. You'll thank me for it, later."

"Uh-huh. Heard that one before, too."

Laughter and conversation rushed the doors like water through floodgates. Sunshine glazing the glass wall overlooking the lake reduced those milling about the multipurpose room to faceless silhouettes. Thirty-cup percolators exhaled steam and a scorched-grounds smell, thickening air already smogged by perfume, cologne and wind gusts clocked at a hundred mouths a minute.

Hannah waded in, murmuring greetings and introducing herself, then Willard, by name only. Amplified caterwauls sent hands scrambling for delicate ears.

"I told you the volume was too high, Walt," blasted from ceiling-hung speakers like a wrathful god whose voice bore an uncanny resemblance to Delbert's.

Attired in a red-striped shirt and madras pants, the chairman of the board didn't need the raised platform to stand out from the crowd. He thumped the microphone. "Can you folks hear me all right?"

Folks at home in Sanity had heard him all right.

A Lincolnesque man clomped across the stage and whispered in Delbert's ear. "Okay, okay," Delbert said. "I'll tone it down. Now go twiddle your knobs and let me master these ceremonies."

Delbert embraced the podium and surveyed his audience. "While our new operations manager makes her way up here—" Delbert began, "I want to thank everyone for being here when you could be out enjoying yourselves."

He paused, confused by the chuckling response to his remark, then said, "Now, if nobody objects, let's have us a moment of silence in our friend and neighbor Kathleen Osborn's memory."

The woman standing beside Hannah bowed her head and quietly recited the Twenty-third Psalm. Hannah sensed it was as much in honor of Kathleen as a personal declaration: I will fear no evil. Except the woman did, just as everyone in the room feared the killer still at large.

Delbert cleared his throat. "Allowing just enough further ado for our guest of honor to hike her fanny up here..."

Hannah stepped onto the platform, pulling Willard along by his sleeve as he hadn't thought to slip out of his jacket, or had the good graces not to.

Delbert winked at Hannah, nodded at Willard, turned back to the microphone, then frowned and did a slow double take.

"What in the hell have you done to your hair?" echoed off the walls like an Alpine mountaineer's yodel.

The audience exploded with laughter. Hannah looked daggers at the master of ceremonies prostrated across the podium, winged her arms, did a soft-shoe and took a bow.

Applause and whistles burst forth. Striding to the microphone, she butted Delbert aside with a hip, and none too gently. "Mr. Bisbee, it's safe to say I've never been introduced quite like that before."

Neither Leo Schnur nor any of the brunch bunch were in attendance. Hannah tried not to think about what IdaClare and Company might be doing as she rattled off remarks revolving around the beauty of Valhalla Springs and how much she looked forward to becoming acquainted with everyone.

"Last, but not at all least, and knowing you've all been wondering who the guest I brought with me might be, it's my pleasure to introduce our new physical fitness instructor, Willard Johnson."

At the group's enthusiastic applause, he grinned ear-to-ear, waving his arms like an incumbent politician at a fund-raising picnic.

Hannah whispered, "Would you like to say something?"

Without altering his expression, he whispered back, "No thanks."

"All community center activities will reconvene beginning at nine, Monday morning," Hannah said, "and for those who've expressed interest in the martial arts, Willard is a tae kwon do black belt, and will be happy to talk with you about adding a class to the schedule."

In a voice too soft to be picked up by the microphone, he pleaded, "Please, Ms. Garvey, have mercy on me."

"Thank you, everyone, for making Willard and me feel so welcome. Now, take it away, Delbert."

The chairman stood gazing off into space a moment, then started and hastened to the podium she'd abandoned. "Any other announcements? No? Okay, Walt, pull the plug so's we can get on with the socializing."

Hannah nudged Willard with an elbow. "See? That wasn't so bad, was it?"

"It could have been worse. I was scared to death the next hat trick you were going to pull was a creative-writing class, or something."

She gasped. "Willard, you are a genius."

He slapped his forehead, uttering sounds a drowning victim makes before going down for the third time. "Me and my big mouth."

"The expenses would be negligible. We can have flyers printed—post them all over town, too. Charge nonresidents a small fee, which might add up into a nice bonus for you."

She snapped her fingers. "What about an annual writers' retreat? That would be a terrific hook to attract prospective tenants. Different angle, different demographic, different advertising venue. I love it."

Delbert inserted himself between her and the horrified physical fitness instructor. "The gym and stuff are downstairs. How's about while she's talking to herself, I show you—"

"Hold on, Delbert. Willard and I are discussing his concept for—"

"*My* concept? All I said—"

"Take it easy, young fella," Delbert soothed, steering Willard away. "She'll be fine as soon as that hair dye gets out of her bloodstream. Why, my third wife— No, 'twas the second—Ruth, I think her name was. She bleached hers and *wham*. Went loco in the cabana so fast…"

Hannah stared after them, her whole body shaking with laughter. No wonder she'd been irritable. She was a walking biohazard.

"Ms. Garvey?" The tall man who'd been in charge

of the public address system edged nearer, his elbows pressed to his ribs and hands dangling like a bashful Tyrannosaurus Rex.

"It's Hannah, and you're Walt, right?"

"Walt Wagonner, yes. One G, two N's. W-a-g-o-n-n-e-r."

O-k-a-y. "Nice to meet you, Walt. How long have you lived in Valhalla Springs?"

"Twenty-three months, next Tuesday." His head jerked to one side, to her, to the side and back again. "Outside. A deputy. He asked me to find you."

Walt's mouth spasmed a smile. He turned and lumbered away, a round-shouldered wraith in spit-polished wing tips.

Assuming he'd accidentally demoted David in rank, Hannah started for the door, then stopped, grabbed a hank of hair and held it where she could see it.

In direct sunlight, her head was going to glow like a supernova. David would take one look at her and start staggering around, laughing and snorting and slavering all over himself, but God wouldn't let her just shrivel up and die on the spot because he wasn't known for giving vain, chemically impaired, mortified women a break when they needed it most.

Walt One G, Two N's Wagonner skulked into her peripheral vision, peering at her as if she were demented. Which, by only a slight fault of her own, she apparently was. Having no choice other than destroying what remained of her self-esteem, Hannah palmed the door's metal frame.

You are surprised, not disappointed, she told herself, when Chief Deputy McBride, a lanky, mustached fellow with a Jim Carrey grin, rose from an ornamental, concrete bench. They hadn't met formally, but Hannah had seen him the morning of the murder.

David Hendrickson is a nice guy, she admitted further, *but it isn't as though you've lost any sleep over him.*

McBride said, "Sorry to pull you away from the party."

Unable to stifle a yawn, she patted her lips, then excused herself.

"The sheriff wanted you to know we're taking down the tape and releasing the Osborn property, and that he took the liberty of hiring Ti Li to clean up the inside."

Hannah grimaced. "A job I wouldn't wish on anyone, including myself."

"Ti's been a housekeeper around here longer than I am old. She doesn't speak English real good, but she's fast, and as trustworthy as they come."

"How do I reach her to make an appointment?"

"Oh, she's already at the house," McBride said. "She'll want her seventy-five dollars—cash—when she's done, too. The sheriff hoped that wouldn't be a problem."

Uh-oh. Her purse and ATM card were at the office, and she'd hidden the top-secret, mandatory PIN code there, too...in a safe place...somewhere.

Wait. It's Saturday—Delbert's night to trip the light fantastic in town. He'd be good for a loan, could take Willard back to his car and had a key to let him in to collect his water bottle. If Delbert wasn't in the mood for favors, she'd alert him to the profound psychological distress his remarks about her hair had caused her.

To McBride, Hannah said, "I can meet you over there in—oh, ten minutes?"

"Good enough." He tipped his campaign hat; a courtesy not exclusive to his boss. "If me and Vaughn should get a call, I'll leave the keys where you can find them."

"Fine, but before you go, are there any updates on the case you can tell me about? In confidence, of course."

"The sheriff hasn't called you yet?"

She shook her head.

"He will. I'd go as far as to say you can count on it."

The gleam in the chief deputy's green eyes and sardonic smirk implied locker-room style banter Hannah wasn't privy to, but had a starring role in. Nor did she need three guesses to figure out *who* had kissed and told.

"If things go down the way they should this afternoon, he'll have reason to get in touch," McBride went on, oblivious to the vengeful flush creeping up her neck. "If they don't, I suspect he'll think of one."

7

On this, the second consecutive warm, sunny Saturday in April, the Short Stack Café on the square was about as lively as the county library.

David had hoped Claudina Burkholz would be working. Heber Pollock, the owner, said she wasn't due in until six.

David's chin had rested on the heel of his hand so long, the left side of his face was numb. His finger clinked the table's salt and pepper shakers together like a white knight and a black one squaring off in the world's slowest joust.

Every time he'd called Valhalla Springs, he'd gotten that infernal answering machine. He'd left one message. A second and third try confirmed Hannah was out of the office, not ducking him. Didn't it?

Maybe he shouldn't have kissed her.

Maybe he should have kissed her the way he wanted to.

Maybe the electricity between them was wishful thinking on his part.

Maybe. He hadn't liked the word when he was a kid, and it damn-sure hadn't improved with age.

He ought to be fishing. It was the kind of afternoon when a creek bank soothed a man's soul, and he wouldn't care if he caught anything or not. Truth be known, a smallmouth taking the bait would screw up a fine nap.

So would a summons to the courthouse. David grinned. Judge Messerschmidt would raise Cain at having to tear back to Sanity from his cabin on Jinks Creek to sign bench warrants. Messerschmidt was decent enough, as judges went, but hadn't yet grasped the literal meaning of "public servant."

A brown porcelain mug skirred across the table. Jessup Knox pulled out the chair opposite David and mounted it as if stirrups dangled from the seat. "Looks like you could use some company, Dave."

Like a boar hog needs teats. "I'm just waiting for my beeper to go off. Ought to, any minute." David added silently, Oh, Lord, hear my prayer.

"I didn't expect you'd be hanging around the café with a killer on the loose."

"Yeah, well, the wheels of justice turn slowly sometimes. Seeing as how you're running against me in August, I'd advise you to practice up on patience." David's lips stretched into a tight smile. "In the off chance you'll ever need any."

The owner of Fort Knox Security Service, who featured himself a dead-ringer for Elvis, appeared wounded by the remark. "Hey, now, filing for the primary was the farthest thing from my mind till folks told me I should, to—you know—keep things honest."

David's jaw throbbed from the pressure exerted on it. "Mind explaining what you mean by that?"

Being elected by popular vote put any sheriff in the unique position of sitting duck for accusations of cronyism, graft, extortion; the list was longer than a woman's memory. There were some who made the criminals they arrested look like crackerjack citizens by comparison, but clean or dirty, no sheriff was immune to innuendo or outright slander.

Worse, any Tom, Dick or Harriet who'd lived in the county one year prior to a primary election's filing date could get his or her name on the ballot. No law enforcement training required; no proof needed that the candidate had the sense God gave a goose.

"Kinda edgy today, aren't you, Dave?" Knox said. "You know all I aim to do is give you some friendly competition." He splayed his hands. "Small as this county is, it happens pretty regular, but I don't believe anybody should run for office unopposed."

David sipped his coffee. He agreed, but wouldn't admit Jessup Knox was right about the time of day. His gaze flicked to the salesman's wafer-thin timepiece. Yep. Three minutes fast.

"But, politics aside," Knox went on, "I surely wouldn't want to lose a friend in the process."

David snorted. "You won't."

"Whoo-ee, am I ever glad to hear you say that." A ham fist gaveled the table. "May the best man win, right, ol' buddy?"

A phantom fingernail clicked down David's spine. The best man didn't always receive the majority of the votes.

Jessup Knox's extended family could fill one side of the Sanity High School's bleachers, even if those born on the wrong side of the blanket stayed home to watch *Dukes of Hazzard* reruns on cable. Of Kinderhook County's six commissioners, one was a cousin twice removed and another married Knox's mother's sister-in-law. A fair percentage of the clan hated Knox's guts, but blood is thicker than water.

"How you coming along on that old gal's murder?" Knox's face went mournful. He wagged his head. "Terrible thing to have happen. Reflects bad on the whole county, if you ask me. Why, before you know it, we're gonna have gangs taking over, home invasions, carjackin's—"

"Not as long as I wear this badge, we won't," David said.

"Oh, it's coming, Dave. Worst mistake you can make is turnin' your back and hopin' it goes away. Why, my bidness is up thirteen percent over last year and the first quarter ain't over yet. Don't think folks haven't noticed the rise in burglaries, vandalism, car theft—you name it—'cause they *have*."

Intentional or not, his opponent had given away his campaign platform. Trust an alarm salesman to paint the town blood-red. Statistics showed a decrease in crime, but who the hell believed statistics?

David sat back. "Did you know our dinky little Wal-Mart just set a fishing-gear sales record for a store its size?"

"Huh?"

"Using your style of cause and effect, I reckon that means I'll snag a short-ton of bass the next time I go fishing."

Knox reached for a paper napkin and swiped it across his mouth. "With all due respect, Dave, this ain't no joking matter. 'Specially not after a crippled old lady was raped, sodomized and had her throat slit right in her own kitchen.

I tell people they're still as safe as a bug in a rug,

but…well, they say that Osmond woman probably thought she was, too.''

David's level stare should have dropped the café's air temperature fifty degrees. ''The only facts you're telling straight are the victim's gender and location of the murder.''

He slid from the booth and planted his knuckles on the table. ''Five of Kathleen Os*born*'s fingers, both collarbones and an arm were broken trying to fend off her assailant.''

David leaned closer, his eyes boring into Knox's skittery ones. ''Isn't what she did suffer enough to scare up more *bidness,* ol' buddy?''

David whisked his Stetson off the table. The crown clipped Knox's cup. Coffee splashed the stammering security salesman's custom-tailored shirtfront.

Waste of a good accident, David thought, striding from the café. The danged coffee was barely lukewarm.

He paused at the curb, allowing a Volvo station wagon the right-of-way. Texas plate. Registration sticker, current. Rock-kiss on the windshield, probably from tailgating a gravel truck. Cargo area crammed with cast-off junk. Amazing how far people drove and would pay to clean out a stranger's attic for them.

The sixyish couple inside reciprocated David's nodded ''hello.'' He hoped the *tick* he heard was a pebble caught in their hubcap, not a wheel bearing going bad.

Catercornered across the square, Eli Cree slumped on the bench outside his barbershop, waiting for time to turn back a few decades. Like the witch hazel he swabbed on customers' necks, Eli's stories about the good old days were part of the service.

His cracked voice mended when he spoke of Saturdays, when people flocked to Sanity's square. Nickels doled out to children for the picture show were the small price parents paid for the freedom to shop and socialize.

Matrons clustered on sidewalks, telling each other who was ailing, who'd given birth and who they expected after church for Sunday dinner. Men propped boots on vehicle bumpers nosed into the curb and jawed about the weather, politics, baseball, politics, livestock and politics.

Teenage boys with a pound of slick'em on their cowlicks cruised round-and-round in their daddies' cars. As a rule, if a girl smiled back at a boy twice, she was interested.

Just a few days ago, David had sat in the antique chrome-and-leather barber chair, listening for the umpteenth time to the tale of Eli and Jane Ellen Adley's courtship.

"That sweet young thing didn't want no part of me," Eli said, "'cept water wears down limestone if it drips long enough. We got to be friends—just conversated, like regular folks, then she took to grinning huge when I circled the square. Been fifty-two years since she did me the honor of becoming my bride, and it don't matter if her day has been sour, sweet or middlin'. My Janey still looks happy to see me when I walks through the door, come evenin'."

Eli and Jane Ellen had the one thing everyone sought and few found. Love was part of it, but as the saying went, love wasn't enough. Like biscuits made from an heirloom recipe that never quite taste like Grandma's, you either have the knack or you don't.

Had Cynthia ever smiled like that at David when she

saw him? He supposed, during their first years together. The last three or four, his wife had been happier to see him leave, and he'd been glad to go. She'd taken a lover. His job was his mistress. All they'd had in common was guilt.

David considered detouring to waken Eli, but decided against it. The wizened old barber had snoozed on the bench, or in his chair, every Saturday afternoon since he marched home from World War II with a chestful of medals and a trade learned in the trenches. Why tamper with the square's last remaining tradition?

The pager clipped to David's pocket settled the matter. The 10–47 on the LED translated to "Call home"—his cue that Judge Messerschmidt had finally arrived. David lengthened his stride, mindful of the sidewalk's cracks and heaves.

Time and tree roots had buckled the walks leading to the courthouse's compass-point entrances. Every spring, Sanity's street department threatened to chain-saw the mammoth oaks to end the thankless chore of patching and repouring new concrete. David sympathized, but the gnarled giants camouflaged the courthouse's pure-de-ugliness.

Rather than a dignified granite edifice with marble columns, pediments and cornices, the century-old Kinderhook County Courthouse was a three-story, half-red, half-yellow brick box.

Air conditioners jutted from some of the windows like moss-blackened tongues. Steel bars striped windows at the top floor's northwest corner, affording prisoners a crow's nest from which to hurl wolf whistles, obscenities and, on occasion, excrement.

On weekends and after office hours, access was limited to one door equipped with an electronic lock and key-card system. David bounded up the empty building's central spiral staircase's steps two at a time.

Gasping like fireplace bellows before he reached the second floor's landing, he soldiered on, the theme song from *Rocky* trumpeting in his head. The endorphin high needed to shake off exhaustion and the mental cooties from parlaying with Jessup Knox flooded David's body midway to the top floor. He swerved around the banister and followed the curving corridor, listening for the buzzer indicating the department's steel-framed, bulletproof glass door had been unlocked electronically.

The front office was a rat's nest of salvaged furniture, equipment shoved where it fit, heavy-duty extension cords strung from here to yonder, and paperwork, files and manuals stacked up like sandbag levees.

Twenty-two people contributed to and worked from that pile system. By some miracle, any one of them could lay hands on needed material in minutes.

Chief Deputy McBride pushed away from the high counter dividing a two-chair visitors' section from the office, proper. He gave David the once-over and drawled, "Gee, boss, what took you so long?"

David bent over and clasped his knees, sucking wind. His Stetson landed like a wide-rimmed bowl between his boots. Much as he appreciated the offer, if he puked, it wouldn't be into a hundred-and-twenty-seven-dollar, 5X beaver hat.

"Your forty-five-degree jogging is gonna kill you one of these days," McBride warned. "You're pushing thirty-seven, ol' buddy, not seventeen."

"Stick it, Jimmy Wayne," David wheezed. "Where's Messerschmidt?"

"The Fuehrer has already been and gone. Rode the elevator down while you were shaking the whole courthouse comin' up."

"God help you if you ever slip and call him 'the Fuehrer' to his face."

"Might could." The deputy grinned. "Andrik started it, but seeing Hizzoner's frog-eyed, screamin' hissy fit would almost be worth it."

David straightened and blew out a deep breath. Sweat plastered his shirt and Jockey shorts to his skin. If the arrest went as planned, he'd race home for a shower before paying an official visit to the lovely Miz Hannah Garvey.

Thoughts of it becoming unofficial had an immediate tourniquet effect on his underwear. While actresses and centerfolds could stalk a man's dreams, it had been a long time since a woman's eyes shimmered unbidden into waking moments, arousing him physically, stirring up emotions that had nothing to do with sex.

He stared at the governor's portrait hanging on the opposite wall. Imagining Missouri's chief executive tarted up like a drag queen eased the pressure at his groin and swept romantic notions from his mind. Nice to know career politicians were good for something.

Bending over to pick up his hat proved a bit premature, but he managed without inflicting permanent damage. "Did the judge issue the warrants we need?"

"As fast as he could sign them," Jimmy Wayne said. "Then he told me to tell you, he was locking his cell phone in the trunk until Monday morning."

"He's bluffing. Five will get you ten, he stays in

town tonight, so he's handy if we need him. How about Andrik? Heard anything from him?''

"I gave him a holler before I paged you. No one in or out since he began surveillance at about fourteen-thirty hours.''

"How close has he gotten to the trailer?''

Jimmy Wayne shrugged. ''The cover's too sparse to window-peek. Marlin doesn't want to spook the guy.''

Not the answer David would have preferred, but the detective was playing it smart. "Might as well have dispatch tell him we're on our way.''

"Will do.''

David stepped into his office and took his utility belt from a desk drawer. Some constituents thought it odd the sheriff didn't "pack heat" twenty-four hours a day, but because there hadn't been a draw-down shoot-out on the square since 1874, David assumed he could make it across the street to the café and back without being loaded for bear.

Walking while he buckled the thirteen-pound belt around his waist, he called, "Anything for me before I head out again?''

"Nothin' majors," and "10–19s" rang out from various corners and cubicles. None of the message slips on his desk had Hannah's name on them, either. Maybe she *was* ducking him.

Get your head where it needs to be and keep it there, he warned himself. Settling his Stetson on his head, he said, "All right, McBride. Let's go.''

Thanks to traffic and no justification for lights or siren, a full forty-five minutes passed before David turned off Highway VV onto Fox Fire Road toward a remote gouge of real estate locals called Cracker-neck

Junction. As a crow flew, Kinderhook County's version of a drug-infested ghetto was less than three miles from Valhalla Springs.

He rolled down the side windows. Ether didn't dissipate very quickly. Methamphetamine cooks knew it, but too much fast, easy cash could be made off poor man's cocaine to sweat the details.

The Crown Vic slumped into ruts carved in the dirt track by erosion and neglect. Beer cans, mattresses, discarded appliances, ruptured garbage bags, dried-up Christmas trees with tinsel clinging to their branches, bald tires and litter too diverse and disgusting to itemize mounded both shoulders.

Breaks in the elongated junkyard led to travel trailers, shacks and mobile homes that might never have seen better days. His passage flushed chickens, scrawny kittens and dirty-faced kids from behind junked cars and bushes. Porch dogs raised their heads. One had the gumption to streak after the cruiser, snarling and nipping at its tires.

David closed the passenger window as he pulled up alongside Andrik's gunmetal-gray Chevy. "Anything?"

"Nope." The detective scratched his five o'clock shadow, usually in evidence by noon. "Either the dirtbag is passed out cold, or I've been baby-sitting an empty tin palace for four freakin' hours."

McBride's unit braked to a stop behind David's. "You need to stretch before we move in?"

"Uh-uh." Marlin switched on the ignition. "I watered the flowers a few minutes ago."

"That's indecent exposure, Detective. Public nudity, lewd and lascivious—"

Marlin twanged, "Why, 'twern't no such a thang, Sheriff. Swear to goodness, I didn't pull out no more'n I needed to. Left mosta my hose adroopin' down arounst my knee."

David threw his head back and laughed. It felt good. Real good, as a matter of fact. There hadn't been many opportunities for a belly-shaker, of late. Andrik, being stoic by nature and a detective by profession, didn't crack a smile.

"Okay, lady-killer," David said, "after McBride goes by, drive down a ways and swing around to block the road. He'll cut off the pass at the other end."

"The road peters out to nothing a couple of hundred yards farther."

"I know it does. I also know I pursued a stolen SUV another two miles up the old logging road branching off it a month or so ago."

"Hey, I'm not arguing," Marlin argued, "but there's no tan pickup on the premises. No vehicle of any description."

"Better safe than sorry."

"I hear ya. So, me and McBride are to close in on foot from either side?"

"That's the plan."

"While you do the *High Noon* thing?"

Rhetorical and smart-ass, but David answered it anyway. "Yep." Shutting his window on Marlin's shouted "Then where the hell's your *vest*, Hendrickson?" David muttered, "It's ridin' shotgun, Mother dear."

He knew his men respected him, but sometimes wondered how long it would be before he earned their trust. Not that he blamed them. Former sheriff Larry Beauford kissed the right babies and behinds to win at the ballot box. All David had to do was prove he was a law enforcement officer first, a politician second, *and* win the August primary and general election in November.

His heart rate and respiration kicked up a notch as his car neared the rust-streaked, ten-by-sixty, no-longer-mobile home jacked up on crumbling concrete blocks. From the swaybacked couch, folding chairs, barbecue grill, two cannibalized motorcycles, scrap lumber, engine parts and assorted paraphernalia, it looked as though no one had gotten around to cleaning up after last year's yard sale.

Andrik had been wise not to venture closer. The trailer was situated on a barren, bald knob and its jalousie windows would act like baffles, funneling every sound inside.

David put the cruiser in park. It was awkward as all get-out poking head and arms through their respective openings in a thirty-some-pound Kevlar vest while in a seated position, but he had no intention of letting Jessup Knox run for office, unopposed, either.

McBride's radio call notified dispatch and all units to their position. The three second-shift deputies would stay tuned in case backup was needed.

David wheeled his vehicle into the yard, grimacing at the crunches and pops of God-only-knew-what his tires were rolling over. He stopped about fifteen feet from the trailer and killed the engine. No silhouettes were backlit in the windows; no curtains over them to hide an interested observer. He frowned at the trailer's pocked, metal door. Ought to be a law against them opening out.

Fire regulations did require mobile homes to have a

second door, typically on the opposite side near the back end, which afforded a convenient escape hatch to a fleeing felon. If this one tried it, McBride and Andrik would be on him like bluetick hounds on a raccoon.

David swung the car door open and rested a boot on the ground. All quiet, but for the *swish* of the other two officers' approach parting the weeds. McBride's hand rested on the butt of his service revolver. Andrik's right arm crossed his midsection, his hand and shoulder holster hidden by his sport coat's flap.

Exiting the cruiser, David repressed the possibility their suspect had bailed. That kind of assumption could get a man shot. He sauntered around the front bumper, his manner casual, his senses alert.

Andrik halted to the right of the trailer's door, his Glock in a two-handed grip. McBride took the same stance, away from its double windows.

David pounded the door. Stepping back a swing's width and slightly sideward, he shouted, "Sheriff's Department. Open up."

Robins catapulted skyward. Unseen critters rustled the brushy ground cover. Silence. Hinky as all hell. David pulled his service revolver. The slide snapped loud, disturbing the uneasy peace.

He started when McBride coughed, then cursed. "Eau de corpse, gentlemen. A ripe one, too."

"Hear anything inside?" David asked softly.

McBride grinned. "Quiet as a tomb."

David reached and tried the doorknob. Unlocked. He nodded at McBride, who crouched and crab-walked under the windows. He repositioned himself behind and beside Andrik.

David turned the knob. Feeling the bolt clear the

jamb, he murmured, "One...two..." The door's piano hinge squealed. Andrik leaped in front of David, eyes darting in all directions.

Face contorting at the stench, the detective mounted the block step, then entered the trailer, his Glock swinging left-to-right. McBride followed, then David.

The interior reeked of death, rotting food and filth. None gave more than a cursory look at the dead man sprawled half on, half off a threadbare couch. A close-range gunshot wound just above the bridge of his nose, maggots feasting on the remains and beetles feasting on the maggots left no doubt about mortality.

David's gut twisted. Countless man-hours. Eyestrain. Legwork. Waiting, praying, hoping, and all the while, the son of a bitch they'd come to arrest had been lying here deader'n a damned doornail.

The gomer wasn't going anywhere. Question was, was he alone? They fanned out to check the kitchen, bedroom and bath for bodies, breathing or otherwise. Finding none, they regrouped outside.

"He matches the physical description," McBride said. "Near as you can tell."

David clamped his hands on his hips. "We'll need a positive ID, but I'd say it's him. Weird, but I'd swear I saw him somewhere in the last day or two. Can't place it, though."

"I didn't expect to clear the Osborn case with a shiny new homicide to work," Marlin grumbled. He looked up at David. "You willing to listen to a suggestion?"

"Such as?"

"Let us handle things from here. Jimmy Wayne and

I slept in this morning. I'm told you never went home last night."

"I'm okay." David chafed his face. "I caught a few zzz's at my desk."

McBride clapped him on the shoulder. "No lie, David, we'll need you bright-eyed and bushy-tailed in the morning a helluva lot worse than we need your ass in the way now."

David chuckled, neither his heart nor any mirth in it. "If we were on the high seas, this would be mutiny."

"If this were the high seas," Marlin shot back, "we'd have already tossed you overboard."

David looked from one to the other. The high-pitched whine between his ears said he was running on caffeine, nerves and the last vestiges of adrenaline. He was too wired to sleep, too dog-tired to think straight. That spelled mistakes waiting to happen. He sighed in resignation.

"All right, then," Marlin said, starting away. "Get your unit out of my parking place and point it toward Sanity. I'm not hiking my equipment back and forth from the road."

McBride trotted toward his unit. "I'll have dispatch send the meat wagon," he called to Andrik. "We need anybody besides Orr?"

"Phelps had a date with Judy Wilson tonight. Tell Tony to page him, too. Wouldn't want the kid to miss out on the fun."

David watched them, swallowing his pride, tasting its bitterness, fighting the impulse to remind them he was the sheriff, by God and gubernatorial appointment.

Throwing open the Crown Vic's door, he shrugged

out of the vest. It clunked against the passenger side and tumbled onto the floorboard. Maturity in action, Hendrickson. A tad harder or higher and it would have busted out the window.

"Hey, McBride," he yelled.

"What?" The chief deputy whirled. "You still here?"

"I want another APB on that pickup."

"Will do. Now, *scram* . . . sir."

8

Hannah leaned against the kitchen counter, arms crossed at her chest, staring at the microwave clock's reverse countdown. A pan of frozen lasagna she didn't want revolved on the oven's carousel like an auto show's pick of the model year.

She hadn't eaten since morning, but hunger wasn't the same as appetite. The past four hours had been a roller-coaster ride. She needed grounding.

David.

"Huh? You've known the guy less than a week, and you've got a Vulcan mind-meld thing going?" She appealed to the refrigerator, "Let us not confuse lust with trust. Or, in keeping with family tradition, confuse horny with anything besides hormones tooting reveille."

Besides, other than venting to a human instead of major appliances, what good would it do to drop the day's baggage in David's lap? One gratingly familiar, "You're all upset over nothing," would bespeak the end of some incredibly scintillating fantasies. Why blow it, so to speak?

Her frown deepened. The hours following the reception had begun innocuously enough. By the time she'd tracked down Willard and Delbert, secured a loan from the latter and told the former she'd see him Monday, McBride had decamped from the Osborn cottage.

As promised, the crime-scene streamers were gone, yet neighboring homes seemed to shrink from the cheery, yellow house as if a quarantine notice were tacked to its door. Sidewalk strollers would give it side-long glances and hasten past the property lines for weeks, if not months to come.

Hannah made a mental note to call Bob Davies about repainting the exterior. A pearl gray with white trim might trick the eye and dull the memory. When Jack screamed about the expense, she'd tell him she'd pay for it. With martyrdom being the second-most powerful weapon in a woman's arsenal, he'd relent before he knew what hit him.

Due to the language barrier, she'd affected a true nodding acquaintance with Ti Li, housekeeper extraor-dinaire and owner of the snazzy, gold-trimmed Lexus monopolizing the driveway. The dour little woman's irritation at Hannah's interruption needed no transla-tion. While Ti Li scurried back to her grisly chores, Hannah pondered the difference between a snoop and an estate's personal representative.

In accordance with the probate court and Kathleen Osborn's wishes, an inventory must be made and the cottage's contents boxed and readied for charitable do-nation or disposal. Not a pleasant task, but unlike sift-ing through the annals of her mother's and elder rela-tives' lives, never having known the deceased would spare Hannah waves of grief, nostalgia and forever un-resolved "what-ifs" and "if-onlys" that often plague surviving family members.

Which made her a snoop with a purpose, she de-cided, feeling neither vindicated nor heartened by it.

A rich, loamy smell greeted her entrance to the living room. Groupings of palm trees, ferns, ficus and yuccas appeared random, but their varied heights, shapes and shadings complemented and contrasted too artistically to be accidental. Needlepoint ivy cascaded from glazed wall pockets. A massive philodendron draped a console TV like an English barrister's wig.

Painted wicker furnishings with floral cushions were in keeping with the indoor-garden theme. Hannah opened the curtains, then raised the windows a few inches, telling herself it was the plants who needed light and air.

A creased, paperback romance novel lay on a side table. The bookmark from Page Turners, New & Used hinted that Kathleen also delayed finishing a good story by saving the last chapters for a grand finale. Medieval settings were not Hannah's favorite, but Kathleen's death had left too many things unfinished. She tucked *Lancelot's Lady* into the crook of her arm.

A Victorian, twisted-wire plant stand occupied the corner between the living room and breakfast nook. Instead of begonias or African violets, its mesh shelves held life-like ceramic, wooden and stone turtles, from thumbnail-to platter-size. A few craned their necks as though sniffing the breeze. Most huddled in their shells, only the tips of their wedged noses visible.

"If ever you see a turtle atop a fence post," Hannah's Great-uncle Mort always said, "it's a good bet he didn't get there by hisself."

Mortimer Xavier Garvey froze to death in a tree years before Hannah understood the wisdom in his goofy turns-of-phrase. Had he been standing beside her, he'd spout an obtuse but razor-sharp perception relating turtles to the type of woman who'd collect them, rather than spoons, or thimbles, or Kewpie dolls. If Hannah thought long and hard, she might have eventually figured out what he'd meant by it.

Herbs and flowering plants she couldn't identify because she'd never watered them to death, thrived in Kathleen's breakfast room. A less nosy visitor would never guess four mismatched, metal folding chairs and a round card table supported the dinette's striped-ticking slipcovers.

Ti Li was on her knees scrubbing the floor when Hannah peeked into the kitchen. Brownish lather trailed from the housekeeper's stiff-bristled brush, but the cabinet fronts glistened and the countertops shone like white patent leather.

Yes, Sheriff David Hendrickson really was a nice guy. Hannah couldn't have sloughed off the cleanup on Maintenance any more than she could have done it herself. Being hurl-prone was one of many crosses she must bear.

Outside, the deck's corners angled around fat, clay pots of geranium cuttings. Folded, plastic bags were tucked under the saucers to cover them, she assumed, in the event of frost. A garden hose caddy stood at ready beside the steps; a pair of canvas slip-ons had been toed off on a mat outside the sliding glass door. Kathleen's preference for the front porch's seclusion extended to not owning a stick of patio furniture.

Two raised beds had been constructed along the back property line; a recent project, as per the landscape timbers' greenish cast. Hannah wondered what Kathleen would have planted in them. Vegetables? Flowers?

Both, she imagined. Scarlet cannas at the back, then irises—no, gladioli. Then, in descending order, Roma tomatoes, Calypso green peppers, leaf lettuce and a marigold border to repel insects.

Hannah's breath hitched. She clutched the novel to her chest like a shield. What was a Calypso green pepper, as opposed to a—a green-green pepper? Why gladioli over irises? Garveys were renowned for raising hell, public assistance budgets and auto insurance premiums, not food or flowers.

Had all the gardening-magazine ad copy she'd written joined hands and leaped from her subconscious? Were flashes of botanical genius symptomatic of repressed Martha Stewart envy? Either explanation was more reasonable and rational than the alternative, which could make her the star of a psychic hotline infomercial.

Hearing voices, as though from a great distance— such as another world—scared her stiff until she realized they originated from the portion of the golf course visible to the east. Jack's obsession with maintaining the land's beauty and integrity extended to a groundskeepers' shed, whose rough-cedar siding blended with the surrounding trees.

A woman knelt to remove her ball from the cup, while another hoisted the flag to reset in the hole. The white cloth waving on the breeze was emblazoned with a large numeral four.

Tensing, Hannah shaded her eyes, spotting almost immediately a deep, kidney-shaped sand trap poised to annoy duffers who put too much chutzpah on their approach shots. Or act as a burial site for a murder weapon.

Hannah moved to the deck's far corner. She hadn't had time to tour the entire course, but the fourth hole's green and fifth's tee box were a manicured inlet bordered by dense woods. Other than an asphalt cart path and a dirt service road leading to the groundskeepers' shed, that section of the course was inaccessible, except on foot.

"So, why did the killer run that way?" Houses blocked her view of Valhalla Springs Boulevard and the entrance gate, but she turned in that direction. "If *I'd* just killed somebody, I wouldn't take off cross-country, unless..."

She spun around. "Unless I knew about that service road. A strange car parked on the street might be noticed, but none of the residents would be out wandering the golf course that late at night."

The Liebermeyers told Delbert they hadn't heard or seen anything the night of the murder. Mr. Vande-Camp, next door to the right, had been transferred to a nursing home in Sanity the Thursday before Hannah arrived.

The Birchfields, who lived directly behind Kathleen, were in Minneapolis celebrating the birth of a grand-child. The cottage to their right had been leased, but the tenants wouldn't move in until mid-June.

Hannah's eyes traced a path from the deck, through the unfenced yards, to the equipment shed. "Even if somebody's dog had a barking fit," she speculated, "the killer could have melted into the shadows before Fido's owner looked out a window."

Common sense saved her the embarrassment of calling David to announce yet another brilliant deduction, which was surely old news to IdaClare and Company, as well. It irked Hannah to no end, but life was at least consistent.

The nearest she'd ever come to first-to-know status was when a Kimberly-Clark research and development wonk asked her opinion of adding "wings" to maxi-pads. Said wonk hung up in a huff when Hannah asked if they'd be fore or aft of the cockpit.

The whiny roar of a vacuum cleaner erupted from inside the cottage. Considering it wiser to stay out of the Asian dynamo's way, Hannah hiked a hip onto the deck rail to think and deduce more stuff everyone else already knew.

Assuming the killer used the service road to enter and exit Valhalla Springs, he hadn't done so on a whim. If burglary was his intent, why didn't he target the Birchfields or others who weren't home last Thursday night? If he had no qualms about committing robbery, why not pick a wealthier victim?

Kathleen's talent for rejuvenating castoffs was borne of thrift not miserliness. Her trust fund's $72,000 balance might be a windfall to the Beatrice, Nebraska, school system's special projects fund, which she'd named as beneficiary, but her lease took an annual $28,000 bite out of the principal.

Her teacher's pension covered day-to-day expenses, with few dollars to spare. Not that Hannah would wish Kathleen's fate on anyone, but IdaClare, Rosemary, Marge—virtually every woman in the development—were more lucrative candidates for a heist.

David envisioned the killer as a big man with a hair-trigger temper. Okay, but what induced his rage? Equally mystifying was why Kathleen had let a homicidal Incredible Hulk into her house.

Delbert insisted she'd known her murderer well enough to open the door to him. If Hannah's "service road theory" was valid, the killer also had foreknowledge of its proximity to the cottage. That meant premeditation not happenstance. Was robbery secondary?

A red herring? Could he have had a reason to want Kathleen dead? If so, there were lots of quieter, neater ways to kill—

"Missa Gah-vay!"

Lancelot's Lady flew from Hannah's grasp and *thwacked* the clapboard wall. Swiveling off the deck rail, she yelped when a splinter the size of Excalibur stabbed her left glute.

Ti Li's expression registered neither amusement, surprise, nor concern. She held out a palm, which also required no translation.

Figuring an inspection would be taken as an insult, Hannah pulled the hundred-dollar bill she'd borrowed from Delbert from the pocket of her slacks. "Thank you, Ti Li."

The housekeeper snapped the banknote, held it to the light, then flipped it over to examine the back. Satisfied it was genuine legal tender, she crammed it into a bulging coin purse. "I go now," she said, whirled and vanished inside.

In the sixty seconds it took for Hannah to check her punctured buttock for arterial bleeding, retrieve the book and follow Ti Li inside, the housekeeper was scuttling out the front door, unhindered by a canister vacuum, five-gallon bucket, cleaner caddy and tote bag clanking with sundry tools of her trade.

A few minutes later, the housekeeper barreled away as if to a fire, or having had just set one, only the top of her head showing above the Lexus's window ledge.

Hannah stood in the foyer and looked down the hall. The bedroom at the end was a gloomy cave, its curtains closed and as opaque as those in the dining and living rooms. The refrigerator's compressor whirred into its defrost cycle. A cloud of ammonia, pine and chlorine wafted from the kitchen. Somewhere, a clock ticked like a metronome.

Her sandals slapped loud on the kitchen's pristine linoleum. She swept the key ring and McBride's business card from the counter. The breakfast room's glass door slid smoothly on its track, the lock and security bar engaging with minimal effort.

She was not a lily-livered ninny. She was not afraid to be in the cottage alone. She'd come to pay Ti Li and lock up after her. Mission accomplished. Now there were other priorities to consider. She'd know what they were as soon as she got back to the office.

The smallest key on the ring unlocked the detached garage's side door. The building was empty except for wire tomato cages and other gardening-related items. Hannah pulled the door shut but didn't relock it.

Ralph, whose last name seemed to be At-the-Mercantile, had promised to drop off a load of empty boxes after he closed for the evening. If Kathleen's cabinets and closets were as spartan as her decor, Hannah wouldn't need many.

As she strode to the golf cart, a televised chorus chanted, *"Wheel...of...Fortune,"* then screamed like born-again teenagers at a Rolling Stones concert. Hannah looked up at the Liebermeyers' roof, expecting to see the shingles vibrating.

Laying the key ring and *Lancelot's Lady* on the cart's floorboard, she sidled through a break in the hedge. No time like the present to introduce herself to Kathleen's neighbors.

She thumbed the doorbell. The cottage's interior racket burped like automatic-weapon fire. X-ray vision wasn't needed to know Mr. Liebermeyer was an avid channel-surfer.

The door opened enough for a glimpse of a plump, kindly face marred by thick-lensed glasses and poodle-permed hair tinted the same shade as Hannah's. Egad—future shock.

"Yes?"

Hannah stated her name and title. Mrs. Liebermeyer shook her head, said, "Just a moment, please," then turned and yelled, "Turn it down, Harve."

"What? You going to town?"

Mrs. Liebermeyer aimed an apologetic look at Hannah, then vanished. Presently, Pat Sajak's game-show patter ceased. Harve Liebermeyer shouted, "Hey! Gimme that back, Miriam."

The lady of the house reappeared holding a remote control. "Won't you come in, Ms. Garvey?"

Hannah declined her offer of refreshments, citing lack of time. Mrs. Liebermeyer didn't insist, but disappointment wilted her smile, implying the doorbell was one of the cottage's least-used appliances.

While the cottage's floor plan mirrored Kathleen's, all similarities between the homes ended there. A riot of enormous, intricately carved antiques and bric-a-brac glutted the Liebermeyers' dining and living rooms. Gilt-framed mirrors and oil paintings scaled the walls. Family photographs filled the spaces between them, as well as every flat surface, including the top of the big-screen television angled in a corner of the living room.

A hideous, orange-and-brown-striped recliner centered the area like a raft amid a fleet of barges. "Harve," Miriam said, the remote hidden behind her back, "say hello to Ms. Hannah Garvey, the new manager."

A scowling man in need of a shave and a haircut

glowered around the side of the chair. Milky blue eyes took inventory of her person, then narrowed. "Who are you?"

Hannah repeated her name and job title, and lied about what a pleasure it was to make his acquaintance. Harve regarded his wife, who again repeated the entire spiel.

"Manager, eh?" he barked. "You'd better fix those ruts in my yard, or I'm calling my lawyer." He shook a fist at her. "I should have sicced him on that Osborn woman, instead of waiting for her to make good on her promise, the lying old bag of bones."

"Now, Harve," Miriam said. "I'm sure Ms. Garvey—"

"Who? No, I don't want nothing from Arby's." He disappeared into the depths of the recliner. "You girls go on to town and leave me be."

An arm shot out. Miriam sighed, and laid the remote in his hand. Audio blasted from the television speakers before visuals burst across the screen.

Walking Hannah to the door, Miriam said, "When Harve is having one of his bad days, there's no getting along with him. Most of the time, he's the sweetest man you'd ever want to meet."

The man's features mapped a life of petulance, self-pity and vindictiveness, but who was Hannah to argue? "What about the ruts he's so angry about? Did Kathleen do something to damage your yard?"

"Oh, that." Miriam waved a dismissal. "I should be as picky about the house as Harve is about his lawn."

Hannah smiled, but said nothing.

"Retirement is harder on men than women," Miriam said. "Harve never was the type to socialize much, didn't have any hobbies…just work, work, work. Then one day he didn't have that anymore.''

''He needed a reason to get out of bed in the morning,'' Hannah suggested.

Miriam looked surprised. ''He stills spends far too much time in front of the television, but yes. The yard is his *job*. If Harve was able to do it himself, he wouldn't let the man from Grounds & Greens mow and trim the grass.''

Hannah imagined Harve stalking the poor workman, pointing out every missed or miscut blade.

''Harve is a perfectionist,'' Miriam allowed. ''Always has been. He plants flowers just so and goes wild at the sight of an aphid, but this feud between him and Kathleen…''

She shook her head. ''I was embarrassed to tears when he stormed over there and threatened to sue *her*. And over what, I ask you?''

Hannah's raised eyebrows expressed, I haven't a clue, but do tell.

''The man she hired to build her garden beds left a few wheelbarrow tracks in our lawn. For that, you yell and curse at a neighbor? A friend?''

''No…'' Hannah surveyed the woman's cluttered, immaculate domain. Perfectionism wasn't exclusive to Harve. ''But if someone came in here and left a mess for you to clean up, wouldn't you be angry?''

''After four children and being married to Harve for forty-three years?'' Her hand flew to her lips, as if she'd confessed to a mortal sin. ''What good would it do to swear and shout? The mess would still be mine to clean.''

And Harve's underwear is yours to pick up off the floor, Hannah mused, his towels yours to hang on the rod and his dishes yours to wash. "Well, those ruts are my responsibility now. This man Kathleen hired, do you know the name of the landscaping company he worked for?"

"Oh, he didn't work for—" Miriam frowned, then looked away. "There's been enough trouble already. I won't have Earl fired for doing odd jobs on the side."

Hannah's mind raced. Valhalla Springs' employees were prohibited from moonlighting inside the development. She couldn't remember last names or which department, but two Earls were on the payroll.

Stay cool. Don't force the issue. Wrapping a comforting arm around the older woman's waist, she said, "I understand your reluctance, Miriam, especially after what you've been through the past few days."

Head lowered and voice soft but strained, she said, "A living hell it's been. Deputies in and out at all hours, asking the same questions over and over." She kneaded her hands. "And Harve, he's—well, you saw him. He's moody, always has been, but nothing like this."

Hannah bit back questions she knew better than to ask. "Men are raised to be knights in armor, here to protect us fair maidens. I think my dad would have reacted the same way if something so unthinkable had happened to one of our neighbors."

And if that load of fertilizer didn't grow roses, nothing would.

Miriam looked up, eyes glistening with tears, then bowed her head again. "If only it were that simple. Harve feels guilty, all right, but it's my fault he does."

Hannah leaned closer, straining to hear over that damnable television.

"We went to bed before the news came on. I'd

helped Harve outside all afternoon, and we were both worn out, except he was up again, I don't know, maybe an hour later. Couldn't sleep, he said. On went the TV.''

Her hands spread apart, then clasped. "He won't wear a hearing aid most of the time, or use closed captioning. Says if he wants to read, he'll buy a book. That's why I thought the screams came from the television—a movie, or something. I—I covered my head with the pillow and went back to sleep.

"The next morning, when Delbert told us...I felt sick. I lashed out at Harve—said it was his fault Kathleen was dead. That with all his racket, how was I to know the screams came from next door?''

Hannah stroked her arm. "You didn't tell the sheriff any of this, did you?''

Miriam gasped. "Oh, no. I—I just *couldn't*. Like Harve said, if whoever killed her found out, he might—'' She turned a stricken face toward Hannah. "He jokes about tuning me out, but it's frightening not to be able to hear a smoke alarm, or a phone ring, much less the person on the other end. He's never sure until I signal him that the car is running.''

Her chin jutted upward. "Humiliating my husband in front of the sheriff won't bring Kathleen back.''

Protecting Harve's pride came from the heart, but Hannah sensed the reasoning behind it did not. Earlier, Miriam had said Harve's feelings of guilt were her fault.

"Even if you or Harve had known what was happening next door," Hannah said, "you couldn't have saved Kathleen.''

"But if the TV hadn't been so loud, if I'd gotten up...if we'd known to call the police—''

"They wouldn't have made it here in time," Hannah finished. She didn't know that for a fact, but what harm was there in easing the woman's conscience?

Miriam clasped Hannah's hands. "Thank you, Ms. Garvey. I feel so much better, just for having told someone."

That made one of them. Then again, cops must constantly manipulate nice people in the pursuit of truth, justice and the American way—a thought Hannah wished she hadn't thought.

On her way home, the air curling around the cart's windshield had descended to brisk, on the verge of nippy. Shivering, Hannah floored the accelerator, the electric motor rising to the challenge by putting along at precisely the same rate of speed.

Willard's car was gone. No IdaClare and Company vehicles circled the drive. Hooray. Hannah zipped into the open shed, but didn't connect the cart to the charger. Delbert would use her indebtedness as an excuse to drop by later—as if he needed one. Let Ol' Lightning Bolt give it a transfusion. He enjoyed staring death by electrocution in the eye.

The answering machine's message light was winking frantically. Murphy's Law. Had she been at her desk all afternoon, she'd have been lonelier than the Maytag guy.

She grabbed a pencil and notepad, punched Replay and hoped for a rash of wrong numbers.

Newspaper editor Chase Wingate asked her to return his call, and dictated his business and home telephone numbers.

Junior Duckworth needed to speak with her regarding the arrangements for Kathleen Osborn. According to Duckworth's records, the deceased had a small, prepaid funeral policy, but...well, he'd prefer discussing the matter with Hannah, personally.

She drew an arrow from Duckworth's number and wrote *IdaClare, Delbert,* then, *Help!*

Hoarseness roughened David's voice. He was sorry he'd missed her and would try again later. In the meantime, he'd appreciate it if she'd tell Delbert and Leo that impersonating law enforcement officers was a felony.

When had the old fart and Mr. Potato Head had time to commit one? Dumb question. Even on decaf, IdaClare and Company had more energy than Hannah did.

Then a man's muffled voice said, *If ever I see that black boy in Valhalla Springs again, he'd better be carrying a tray and have a napkin over his arm.*

Her mouth fell open. The machine beeped. IdaClare trilled, *I'm sorry I missed the reception, dear, but we simply lost track of the time.* Then she giggled. *Just wait till you see what the girls and I have been up to!*

For a moment, Hannah thought IdaClare had left a postscript, when a woman's voice drawled, *Ms. Garvey, it's only fair to warn you, the residents are circulatin' a petition callin' for your resignation. Nothin' personal, and bygones will be bygones if you change your mind about hirin' that—well, surely you know who we mean. His kind don't belong here.*

Disbelief and anger packed a double emotional punch. Hannah glared at the machine as if it were the source not the messenger.

Another beep. She stiffened. *Chase Wingate again. I can be reached at my home number all evening. Please do return my call at your earliest convenience.*

The device clicked, then whirred as the tape rewound. Too infuriated to sit still, Hannah bolted from the chair. "Lousy slimeball bigots. Petition, my ass. If you don't have the guts to identify yourself, fat chance you'll put your names on a petition."

Which of the friendly smiles and handshakes at the reception were fraudulent? Or was Willard the grapevine's man of the hour? "Damn it! Damn *you*. If this backwater burg had Caller ID, I'd be on your doorsteps…"

She whirled and snatched up the receiver. Star–67's *dah-dee-dah* teedled, then the automated redial sequence.

One ring…two… A voice Hannah recognized as Chase Wingate's recited, *The* Sanity Examiner's *office hours are from eight to—*

Shit. So much for the marvels of modern technology. God, how she needed to yell at someone. Someone who'd sit back and let her rip until she ran out of steam, then hand her a tub of butter-brickle ice cream and a spoon.

Gradually, reason nudged anger aside. It was better not to know who'd left those vile messages. Confronting them wouldn't solve anything. Not confronting them, but knowing who they were, would affect her attitude toward them in the future.

Doing nothing sucked.

The microwave's buzzer jolted her back to the present in a most annoying manner. Index finger zeroing in on the door latch, Hannah noticed the clock-timer read one minute, fifty-eight seconds and counting.

"Since when do you give a two-minute warning?" she inquired, as if expecting the appliance to explain itself.

Settling back against the counter, she inhaled oreg-

9

David was turning to leave when the cottage door flew open. Hannah blinked up at him, her expression befuddled, then surprised, then…

She smiled. Not an Oh, it's just you, or a Hello, Sheriff, but a bona fide Jane Ellen Cree–style Gosh, am I ever glad to see you.

"Hi," he said, and swallowed hard. Nice going, fool. That ought to sweep her right off her feet.

"Hi, yourself." She leaned to look past him and whistled. "Cool pickup, but do you think it's red enough?"

"For all that I drive it, I don't worry much about sun fade." Yep, smoother by the minute.

She stepped back. "Come on in."

The kitchen's fluorescent glare overwhelmed the soft, track lights illuminating the stone fireplace wall. David's eyes roamed across architectural features and furnishings he'd been too preoccupied to notice during his earlier visit.

An eerie exhilaration flowed through him when he realized he was standing in the room he'd envisioned since he was a teenager, dreaming of the home he'd build with his own two hands someday. He'd shown Cynthia the folder stuffed with blueprints sketched on graph paper. She'd laughed, said they were soul mates, then fetched a fat spiral notebook with pictures cut from magazines.

He should have known as he flipped through page after page of china patterns, marshmallowy furniture upholstered in flowery fabrics, crystal geegaws and linens trimmed in ribbon and lace that she was Scarlett O'Hara to his Daniel Boone.

Cooking smells whooshed straight from David's nose to his midsection, which rumbled greedily. "Did I interrupt your supper?"

"Your timing is perfect," Hannah said, then added, "that is, if you don't mind the cook looking like a slob, you're hungry and you like lasagna."

"You don't, and I like it fine, but I didn't come here to mooch a meal."

"The few who have, lived to regret it." Her eyebrow arched—the feminine equivalent of a radar antenna. "Official business could have been taken care of with a phone call."

"Yep."

"And something has happened you want to tell me about."

"Right again."

He should have anticipated a soft-spoken, direct "Then, why did you drive all the way out here?" but didn't, and it blindsided him.

"I don't know." He shrugged. "Yeah, I do. I'm nine-tenths addlepated from no sleep and too much coffee, but truth is, I enjoyed the heck out of talking to you at Ruby's."

"So did I." Her eyes searched his for a long moment. "So, how's this for a plan? A little lasagna, a bottle of wine—which you're going to help me drink, on-duty or not—and maybe we can squeeze in a few words edgewise.''

David grinned. ''Sounds good to me.''

Her bare feet squeaked on the wood floor as she turned. Slob? Lord have mercy, the woman had no idea what she did to a pair of drawstring sweatpants and a cropped, fleece shirt. She wouldn't believe him if he told her, either.

''What can I do to help?'' he asked.

She pointed at the wall beside him. ''How about cranking down the rheostat? It's so bright in here, I feel like a lab rat.''

David dimmed the ceiling panels to a hazy glow. ''Better?''

''Much.''

''Now what?''

''Park yourself on a bar stool and look confident.'' She chuckled. ''One of us should be.''

She assembled salad makings, a knife and cutting board on the counter. Nerves strung as taut as barbed wire slackened with the mindless pleasure of watching her tear lettuce into bite-size pieces.

Despite her remark, Hannah looked as much at home in the kitchen as David felt. The knife blade's rhythmic tap as she sliced and diced a tomato took him back to a time when supper was the best part of the day. Three hundred and sixty-two of them, anyway. Halloween, Christmas and the morning of his birthday being the exceptions.

''Earth to David.'' Her lips curved into a sympathetic smile. ''You really are exhausted, aren't you?''

''No more than you are.'' He held up a hand. ''No insult intended, I swear.''

''The bathroom mirror already told me I wasn't the

fairest of them all when I got out of the shower.'' She rummaged in a drawer for a corkscrew, then an upper cabinet for two glasses. "Some wear their hearts on their sleeves, I wear my angst on mine." The refrigerator yielded a chilled bottle of sangria.

"Italian food just doesn't taste right without wine, even if it's cheap and Spanish," she said defensively, as she'd been a couple of days earlier when she'd stated her intentions to have a beer.

Don't, David wanted to say. I've been there, girl. Straddled the line between social drinking and abuse, then jumped back before I crossed it. Someday we might swap "Oh but for the grace of God" stories, but not tonight.

She slid the bottle and corkscrew toward him. "You do the honors while I bitch. House rules."

"Do I get a turn?"

"Probably. I've already given you fifty points for not saying anything snotty about my hair."

The bottle's wire bale had been invented by Houdini. Through gritted teeth, he said, "A death wish isn't among my many flaws."

"Oh, yeah?" The knife guillotined the vine end of a cucumber. The woman had a vicious sense of humor.

"So, maybe I do," he said, actually wishing she'd bought screw-top wine, "but why did you tamper with perfection?"

"Bonus points for flattery." She pushed a strand away with the back of her hand. "New job, new life, new house, new…everything, and old hair? De-ah boy, it simply isn't done."

He slid a glass toward her and lofted his. They

clinked rims in a silent toast, but she hesitated before taking a sip. "Does it really look that bad?"

"Women." David shook his head. "It's a little different—kind of redder, that's all. Go platinum blond or shave it off? *That* would be bad."

The sweetish, fruity wine slid down his throat like velvet, unlike the horsewater his ex-wife and her friends had raved about and guzzled like soda pop.

"Straight-from-the-hip Hendrickson never bullshits, does he?"

"In the line of duty, you betcha, but I'll never lie to you. When I tell you something, I mean it."

Their two-beat visual deadlock confirmed she'd read between the lines. "Smart answer. No way will I ever ask you if my jeans make my butt look big."

Proof her derriere was above reproach flashed before him as she engaged the microwave's reheat function, then flittered about gathering salad bowls, plates, silverware, place mats and napkins.

The phone rang. Her head wrenched sideward and she glared at the wall unit. At the third ring, he asked, "Want me to get that?"

"No." Dishes clattered on impact with the counter. "I'd better go listen to the machine, though, in case it's important."

As she jogged to her desk, he grabbed the abandoned place settings. A table had rarely been laid with greater stealth, except distance and the microwave's fan squelched all hope of eavesdroping. The timer's beep coincided with her return to the kitchen.

"Everything okay?" he inquired.

"Yeah. Wrong number."

He caught her arm. "Your pants are on fire."

She looked up at him defiantly. "Let 'em burn. Supper is ready."

They completed the preliminaries in tandem, as if putting the finishing touches on a meal were an everyday occurrence. David pulled out a bentwood chair for her, seating himself across from her. A face in profile told, at most, half a story.

Raising his glass, he said, "My compliments to the chef."

She managed a closed-mouth smile. "I'll take credit for the salad. Stouffer's gets the rest."

The breakfast room was almost spartan, but the round, braided rug under the pub table added color and warmth. French doors opened onto a spacious wooden deck. Beyond the trees, a sliver of the lake sparkled in the twilight.

He'd visited a similar place countless times, but only in his mind. To be there in person was at once disorienting and comforting.

Hannah appeared to be hypnotized by her plate. "If you don't start talking," he warned, "you lose your turn." He gave her a No Arguments look. "That's sheriff's rules, and my jurisdiction is bigger."

"You don't miss much, do you?"

"Same can be said of you." He wiggled his fork. "Out with it."

"Nothing major, really." She blew out a resigned sigh. "The physical fitness instructor I hired this afternoon didn't meet with everyone's approval, that's all."

As concisely as a textbook police report, she related Willard Johnson's bio, a summary of the reception and the threatening messages left on her answering machine.

"That's why I overreacted when the phone rang," she said. "My great-uncle Mort told me to never let an idiot make me mad. Except, who but the idiots of the world make anyone mad?"

"What are you going to do about it?"

"Nothing I can do, besides hope Jack Clancy wasn't a branch of their nasty little telephone tree." Her fork stabbed a bite of pasta. "My short career as manager is several levels below illustrious already."

David glanced at his watch. Marlin and Cletus Orr were probably midway through processing the second homicide's scene. Alerting Hannah to the victim's identity would dump more weight on her shoulders. It'd keep a while longer.

"The phone company could monitor your calls," he suggested.

"I considered that, but then what? Prosecute a couple of tenants for harassment?" She shook her head. "Doesn't strike me as the best way to promote racial harmony."

"True, but Sit Back and Do Nothing doesn't sound like your family motto, either."

"No, that would be Life Sucks, Then You Die." She shrugged. "Maybe the subtle approach would be worth a try. Gather everyone together to light candles and sing 'We Are The World,' or something."

David laughed. "It couldn't hurt."

She popped a cucumber chunk into her mouth. "I think the shock value is wearing off. Of course, if I hadn't bought into my own Ozarks Paradise campaign, I wouldn't have been so shocked."

"I don't know about that..."

"The people living here come from all parts of the

country and all walks of life—the upper-middle strata of it, anyway. They packed their attitudes and prejudices in the ol' kit bag and changed their address, but not who they are. Statistically speaking, some of them have to be assholes—pardon my French.''

''I suppose that applies to just about anywhere,'' David said around his last bite of pasta. ''The finest folks you'll ever meet live in Kinderhook County, slap upside some Grade-A ornery cusses, aka assholes.''

''Oh, really?'' Her head angled sideward. ''Encounter any especially ornery cusses lately?''

''I reckon that means it's my turn to bitch.''

''Uh-huh.''

He looked from his empty plate to hers. ''It can wait until after I help with the dishes.''

''No, David.'' She settled back in her chair. ''It's the dishes that can wait.''

''Yeah, well, then how's this for a plan? We split what's left of the wine, carry our glasses into the other room and give my back a break before it does.''

''No objections here. I'd already decided these chairs were designed by a chiropractor.''

The couch exhaled a whispery sigh as David sat down. Its leather upholstery was cool to the touch, warming as it wicked heat from his body. Laying his head back against the soft, padded crest, he let his knees splay wide. ''This is the nearest I've been to relaxed since...I can't remember when.''

Hannah settled on the cushion beside him, instead of the corner, as he expected. She tucked her long legs under her, took a sip of wine and sighed. ''Not bad...only wouldn't you'd be more comfortable with your feet up on the trunk?''

"Probably, but the minute they land, I'll hear my mother holler, 'Get those dirty clodhoppers off the furniture.'" He chuckled. "Besides, a man can only take so much comfort before he...starts...snoring."

She nudged his shoulder. "Not even a decent effort. C'mon, John Law. Let's have that official business."

His thoughts had already strayed well into unofficial territory, but fair was fair. Yanking himself back to reality, he said, "I guess it's sort of a nonissue, but the medical examiner says Kathleen Osborn was in stage three of chronic lymphomatic leukemia. Depending on how fast her health declined, she only had six months or so to live."

"Sad," Hannah said. "But it helps explain why she moved here, even though her trust fund was relatively small."

"And why some of the people I interviewed described her as tighter than bark on a tree. A couple thought maybe she was an eccentric, like you read about in the paper. The type who pinch pennies, then donate a million or ten to charity."

"Vultures. Weren't they ever taught not to speak ill of the dead?"

David rubbed his palm along his thigh. "Once upon a time, back in Tulsa, I was the first officer on the scene of a shooting. Neighbors on both sides told me the usual hoorah—the victim was a great guy, never caused any trouble, always waved and said hello.

"Then the ol' codger from across the street piped up, and brother, did he have a hate on for the dead man. His gripe session gave the detectives a half-dozen leads. One paid off with a second-degree murder conviction."

Hannah's mouth hiked at one corner. "A windy way of making a point, but I get it. Just don't tell me somebody saying mean things about Kathleen is doing likewise."

"Well, no, not exactly." He planted an ankle on his knee. "A nifty, computerized link to the National Crime Information Center tattled loud and clear. Its fingerprint classification system identified our suspect in less than twenty-four hours."

"Damn you, Hendrickson." She jostled around like a tigress about to pounce. "If you have the killer in custody and waited this long to tell me, I'll—I'll...I don't know what I'll do, but you won't like it."

He winged an elbow to protect himself and his glass. "Heel, woman. The individual isn't in custody, or I'd have said so when I walked in."

"Oh." She sank back, then stiffened. "But if you know who he is, why isn't he in jail?"

"Because he's probably en route to Columbia for an autopsy about now." He paused. "His prints matched those on the rolling pin and at the scene, but somebody parted his eyebrows with a bullet before we could arrest him."

Hannah fingercombed the hair off her face, gripping it at her crown. "Jeez, Louise." She took a deep breath, exhaled, then sipped her wine. In a low, quavering voice, she said, "Now we'll never know why he killed her."

David took her glass and set it next to his on the trunk. Sliding sideward, he laid his hand over her small, cold one. "The guy was scum—a meth-head with a string of priors. Nothing since he moved here six months ago, but 'reform' wasn't in his vocabulary.

"Our guess is he needed money for dope, Kathleen refused to give him any and he went ballistic. We found her purse in his trailer. Looked like he'd taken a chainsaw to it."

Hannah shook her head, her eyes boring into his. "I don't buy it. A wigged-out addict sees Valhalla Springs as the mother lode, then tries to rob the poorest tenant here? Uh-uh. Even stupid and desperate have their limitations."

"It wasn't quite that random," David said. Here we go. Bombshell time. "The dead man was one of your greenskeepers."

"Earl Barton."

He started. "How did you know? Who told you?"

"Miriam Liebermeyer, in a roundabout way. She said a man named Earl did yard work for Kathleen. Miriam wouldn't give me a last name for fear I'd fire him for moonlighting on development property.

"I checked the payroll," Hannah went on. "Earl Weiss is a maintenance department employee. Earl Barton, Grounds & Greens. Bingo."

David scowled. Orr's interview with the Liebermeyers had been Stonewall City, too. Husband belligerent and deaf as a post, wife scared of her own shadow.

If they'd had a name to go on the day of Osborn's murder, it might have saved Barton's life, David and his men a couple of sleepless nights and the county the cost of a second homicide investigation.

"I called your office," Hannah said. "Whoever answered didn't exactly blow me off, but I got the impression my tip about Barton was worthless."

"Depending on the time, we were probably already at the scene."

"Of another murder. *Jesus.*" She eased back her hand, opened her fingers and slid them between David's. Her eyes telegraphed a need for an anchor.

David studied their joined hands—his big and blocky, scarred by helping his dad and uncles string new fence, an opposing lineman's granite jaw and a K-9 dog who missed its intended target. Hers was flawless and graceful, but as strong and dexterous as a musician's.

He'd almost forgotten the simple wonder of a hand to hold, and resisted the impulse to tighten his grip, for fear of losing it.

"Do you know who shot him?" she asked.

David shook his head. "Meth buy gone sour, most likely. Barton's trailer was a landfill on wheels. Makes gathering forensic evidence a nightmare."

He added, "There's a chance the shooter stole Barton's pickup. With luck, and we're overdue for some, it won't turn out he just loaned his vehicle to somebody."

Hannah recoiled. The color drained from her cheeks. "Barton drove a pickup? What kind? What did it look like?"

The short hairs at the back of David's neck bristled. "'82 Dodge, long-bed. White or light brown, we aren't sure which."

"Oh my God." Her eyes widened, then narrowed to slits. "Want to bet the right headlight is burned out? The low beam?" A growl percolated in her throat. "It must have been Barton who tried to run me off the road the other night—or at least scare the crap out of me. He rode my bumper like a maniac, then hit his brights. I caught a glimpse of a pickup's grill and a light-colored hood just before he blinded me.''

"When did *this* happen? And where?''

"The night you ki—er, Friday, after we left the café. I noticed Cyclops behind me a few miles from town. He hung back a while, then was on me like ugly on an ape. He turned off somewhere, not far from the gate.''

Fox Fire Road. Barton got his jollies, then headed for home. But why go after Hannah?

That's where he'd seen Barton before—at Ruby's. Barton came in after them and sat at the next table. If he caught a fraction of their conversation, no wonder he got hinky. Sure as the world, he thought Hannah would interpret the careless-and-imprudent routine as a warning.

"Miz Garvey," he drawled, "why didn't you tell me this before now?''

"I didn't know from Earl Barton at the time, Sheriff.'' Sarcasm laced her tone. "Let alone that he'd killed Kathleen Osborn.''

She tried to tug her hand away. He stopped that nonsense with a gentle squeeze. She chuckled under her breath, squeezed back and relaxed.

"Any other secrets you're keeping from me?'' he asked.

"None I'm willing to divulge. What I would like to know is why you're hanging around here when there's another homicide to investigate.''

"Is this a hint that I've worn out my welcome?''

"Subtlety, thy name is not Hannah. It just seems odd for a workaholic like you not to be hip deep in Earl Barton's trashy trailer.''

He shrugged. "Much as I've enjoyed every second

of being here, truth is McBride and Andrik pulled rank they don't have and ordered me to catch up on some sleep. Yeah, I was stumbling around Barton's like a poleaxed mule, but after I got home, I was still too keyed up to hit the pillow.''

A bemused smile had crawled across her face partway through his explanation. ''And I suppose there wasn't anything on TV worth watching.''

''Nope.'' David's arm curled around her shoulder. ''I can't get cable out where I live.''

Too many women associated sensuality with cleavage, a fancy haircut and perfect makeup. Hannah's tousled hair, natural complexion and dark, intelligent eyes defined it for him.

She allowed herself to be drawn into his embrace, her body neither resistant nor submissive. ''You could buy a satellite dish.''

David lowered his head until his lips hovered an inch from hers. ''Waste of money.''

The tip of her tongue glided from a corner of her mouth to the other, leaving a glistening trail in its wake. He felt her heartbeat accelerate against his chest; her breath fan warm and moist on his skin; his belly swirl with the giddy, glorious sensation of falling through thin air.

Their fingers slipped apart, her hand skimming up his arm, his eager to explore the curve of her waist, exposed and inviting his touch.

With anticipation and desire peaking almost beyond endurance, David closed his eyes, brushed his lips against hers, then claimed them tenderly, reveling in the soft sweetness he'd known he'd find there....

The front door burst open. A raspy voice bellowed, "Front and center, ladybug. Hell's a-poppin'."

Delbert Bisbee stopped in his tracks. IdaClare Clancy, Rosemary Marchetti, Marge Rosenbaum and Leo Schnur piled up behind him like a chain-reaction car wreck.

10

Hannah and David jolted apart as if a bomb had detonated in their laps. She seconded every curse he muttered, adding a few of her own.

"Well, hel-*lo-o*, Sheriff," IdaClare cooed, her penciled brows rising midway to her hairline.

Delbert scowled at David. "Should have known that cowboy Cadillac in the driveway was yours."

"Don't they make a darling couple?" Marge said, a hand at her bosom as if about to pledge allegiance.

Rosemary harrumphed. "When I said that very same thing at brunch, IdaClare bit my head off."

"We have the devil's food cake," Leo said, hoisting a lidded basket. "So good, it will bring the tears to your eyes, I promise you."

"I suspect *he* had a different kind of dessert in mind," Delbert sneered.

David aimed a sidelong glare at Hannah. "Good thing my service revolver is locked in the truck."

"Who would you shoot?" she whispered. "Them? Or me?"

"It's a toss-up."

"Let's put the coffee on," Rosemary suggested. "The sooner we have refreshments, the sooner we can share our information with the sheriff."

IdaClare sniffed. "We wouldn't need to if he ever returned his telephone calls."

Leo and the female contingent trooped into the kitchen, voicing dismay at its messy condition.

Delbert didn't budge an inch, his bony little body practically vibrating with fury. "Hannah, go fold a napkin or something. Me and Hendrickson are gonna have us a mano-a-mano on the porch."

"Suits me just fine, Bisbee." David rocketed from the couch looking grim, wrathful and about twenty-seven feet tall.

Before the door slammed behind them, Hannah was duckwalking to the office nook. The night air was too cool for open windows, but she crouched at the sill, primed for what was sure to be a fascinating discussion.

"I don't know what put the burr under your saddle," David said, "but the only reason I came out here with you was to spare Hannah more embarrassment than you've already caused."

"Oh, yeah?"

Atta boy, Delbert, Hannah thought. Assert yourself.

"Fact is, I'd like to know where you get off barging into *her* house and giving *me* the evil eye for being here."

"Because I care about her," Delbert shot back. "She's special. Knew it the minute I met her."

"I reckon that makes two of us, pard."

Hannah grinned into the darkness. It withered when Delbert said, "Except *I'm* not the one with the reputation for boinkin' everything in a skirt."

David's throaty chuckle was long on menacing and devoid of humor. "No, Bisbee, you're the one with the reputation for *boinkin'* everything in Supp-Hose."

"That's a damned dirty lie."

"Yep," David said. "It is."

"So, you're saying you're a choirboy, eh?"

"I'm saying the difference between truth and rumor depends on who's doing the talking, and who's doing the listening."

A lengthy silence was broken when Delbert begrudged, "Okay, so I thought I was over it, but maybe I kind of always wanted a daughter to look out for."

"You don't have any children?"

"Five wives, but no youngsters of my own." Delbert snorted. "Not for lack of trying, believe you me."

"I hope you know, Hannah is mighty fond of you, too. Pretty obvious that morning on Miz Osborn's porch."

"Well, if I was a shade younger, I'd be giving you some serious competition." Delbert cackled. "Hell, I might anyhow."

"I'll consider that fair warning." David added, "Which I'd appreciate having the next time you're inclined to drop by."

If Delbert answered, Hannah didn't hear it. She could, however, imagine his expression registering a "Maybe, maybe not, bucko."

Floorboards creaked. David said, "Now that we appear to have things squared between us—"

"Not quite. I've got one other bone to pick with you."

"Like what?"

"I want to know why you aren't working that 10–18 on Fox Fire Road." The buzz saw returned to Delbert's voice. "My taxes pay your salary, bub, and it didn't set well finding you here, instead of investigating a 'dead at the scene.'"

Hannah flinched. Ye gods, Delbert, haven't you ever

heard of quitting while you're ahead? As in, before you get knocked on your behind?

"*My* taxes pay my salary, Bisbee, along with everyone else's in the department."

"Hmmph. Guess that's right, now that you mention it. Only it doesn't answer my question."

"I do my job the best I know how, but I'm no superhero, any more than you, Miz Clancy and the others are the Mod Squad. If my best isn't good enough for you, vote for somebody else this fall."

"Kathleen was our friend. All we're trying to do is see justice done."

"I respect that," David said. "Trouble is, you and Schnur interrogating people, monitoring radio traffic, and the ladies calling my office twenty times a day *impedes* justice."

"All right, I'll have a little talk with the girls," Delbert offered. "But you know how women are. There's no reasoning with 'em once they got bees in their bonnets."

David muttered something, probably obscene. "Anything else you care to discuss with me?"

The screen door's hinges yipped, then the interior one rattled open. Hannah froze, heart thumping wildly. If either man saw her, she'd hold her breath until she suffocated. Death before dishonor.

John Law Hendrickson and Barney Fife Bisbee stomped to the kitchen. Hannah peeked over the railing, then sprinted for the couch, praying the sink clatter and conversation muffled the slap of bare feet on wood.

In the midst of an airborne leap, she swept *Lancelot's Lady* off the trunk, gasped when it bumped a wineglass, then landed on her back on the couch. Not a four-pointer, but a definite three-point-one.

Boots thudded on the oak floor. Hannah whipped open the novel and looked innocent.

"What the—" David knuckled his hips. "You weren't here when I walked by thirty seconds ago."

She blinked, as if bringing him into focus. "Oh, was that you? I was so engrossed in my book, I didn't notice."

He reached over the back of the couch, turned the paperback right side up and replaced it in her hands. "You'd be lousy at undercover work, Garvey."

"Think so?" She tossed the novel on the trunk and flounced to her feet. "Pity you'll never know for sure."

The gleam in his eyes was positively lecherous. "Never say never, sugar."

Her face flushed hotter than it had when IdaClare and Company made their entrance. Uncontrollable blushing had always been an aggravation, but it had worsened of late. Maybe Delbert was right about hair dye seeping into the pores.

"I'm turning for home," David said. "Just wanted to thank you for the finest evening I've spent in a coon's age."

"Mod Squad and all?"

"Yeah. They're too nutty to stay mad at for long. But I meant it when I told Delbert to cease and desist."

"Oh, dear. What have they done now?"

"I know you were listening at the window, and I'm not joking around. If a town cop hadn't gone by Mother Truckers this afternoon, Delbert and Leo would have had pool cues for tails. The clientele doesn't take kindly to the real thing, let alone a couple of geezers playing Holmes and Watson."

Hannah clapped a hand over her mouth to keep from laughing out loud. "I-I'm sorry," she stammered. "I know it isn't funny, but Leo and Delbert? In a place called Mother Truckers?"

"It ain't the V.F.W. on bingo night, I assure you." He started for the door.

"I really will try to discourage them," she said, falling in beside him, "but there's no telling what they'll do when they hear about Barton."

David paused. "I'd rather they didn't yet. We have some loose ends to knot before saying positively that Barton killed Kathleen Osborn."

Hannah made a tick-a-lock motion and an "umm-um-ummm" sound to demonstrate her lips were sealed.

He rolled his eyes, then planted a chaste kiss on her cheek. "I'll call you tomorrow."

"I'll be at Kathleen's cottage all day. I have to start on the inventory and disposing of her…things."

David chucked her under the chin. "Keep that up, sugar, okay?" Leaning down, he glanced at the kitchen, frowned and straightened again. "Better go put dibs on a piece of cake before Leo licks the plate clean."

Hannah closed the door behind him, feeling as swoony as a teenager after a first date. Her hopscotch-style about-face foundered. IdaClare and Company were lined up along the half-wall divider like a senior citizens' bowling league team photo.

"Got an itch you can't scratch?" Delbert's palm shot up. "Don't answer that, just get your tush in here."

The kitchen was spotless and fragrant with Hannah's favorite scents—fresh-perked coffee and chocolate. Cups, forks, napkins and six huge slices of cake encircled the pub table. An equal number of thick file folders were labeled Code name—Alpha, above the respective gumshoe's name.

"Code name Alpha?"

"Delbert's idea, it was," Leo said. "Instead of a case number. Everyone uses *those*."

"I designed the labels and printed them," IdaClare said.

Hannah's eyes widened. "You have a computer?"

"Oh, yes. Owen gave it to me before they took him to the hospital. Wasn't that sweet of him?"

Wait till Jack hears about this. On second thought… If I tattle on his mother, the new one he ordered for me is history.

"You ought to see IdaClare play Mortal Kombat," Rosemary said. "She kicks butt."

Delbert clinked a spoon on his coffee cup. "I'm calling this meeting to order."

"All *right*." IdaClare gave Hannah a mother-of-the-bride smile. "Do you have more chairs, dear?"

Hannah volunteered to hold down a bar stool, leaving the table to the now-five gumshoes. While Leo fetched her desk chair for Marge, IdaClare insisted they all sit at the table, which was, after all, laid for six. Marge apologized for skewing the seating, which prompted Rosemary to end the Great Chair Debate by reminding everyone whose house they'd commandeered and that their host had the right to sit wherever she pleased.

Hannah hadn't seen Marge since they'd met at brunch, but was glad she'd joined the group and told her so. Not that Hannah was glad there *was* a group, but a four-female to two-male parliamentary edge could prove fortuitous, despite IdaClare's tendency toward bossiness.

"Where's the scanner I bought you, ladybug?" Delbert mumbled past a mouthful of cake.

"In my bedroom."

The answer did not please him. She also knew the essence of what was running through his naughty little mind, but he refrained from going public with it.

IdaClare flipped open her folder and removed a stapled batch of papers. "Pass this one to Hannah, would you, Leo?" further explaining, "It's your copy of the dossier on Kathleen."

"For hours, she worked on it," Leo said. "Impressive it is. Very impressive."

As Hannah speed-read the top sheet, Rosemary commented, "Can you imagine anyone in this day and age not having a single credit card?"

"Maybe she applied and was turned down," Delbert said.

"Why?" Marge argued. "She had income from a living trust, a pension, a lovely home—"

"And no bank account," IdaClare broke in, "no driver's license, and she leased her house. It wouldn't have counted as an asset."

Rosemary frowned. "Yes, but they're given out to college kids like pizza coupons. I read somewhere a man filled out an application in his cat's name, and the company issued it a card with a two-thousand-dollar limit."

Leo contended, "A true story, I am sure, but why Kathleen did not have a credit card is not important."

While they debated the state of Kathleen's finances, Hannah reviewed the documentation, formatted like a résumé. Vital statistics such as date of birth, age, height and approximate weight included a reference to Kathleen's health as being "average."

Had IdaClare chosen not to disclose that Kathleen had been diagnosed with leukemia? Minutiae such as "K.O. allergic to aloe vera, peanuts and MSG," and "K.O. deathly afraid of dogs" indicated her cancer wasn't common knowledge.

The only doctors' names on a list of health-care professionals were an osteopath in Sanity and Dr. Pennington. Impossible. Kathleen must have been receiving treatment from one or more specialists. But who? Where? And how did a nondriver get to and from appointments in secret?

Memories of her mother's slow, agonizing death and the indignities Caroline Garvey endured pushed at the door of the mental vault where heartaches were stored. Hannah slammed and bolted it before they could escape.

A Work History section noted Kathleen had taught every elementary grade level within the Beatrice, Nebraska school system. Nothing unusual there.

Information under the subheading Leisure Activities was, in Hannah's opinion, a misnomer. Besides gardening and reading, Kathleen baked cheese bread for The Flour Shoppe and did alterations for a dry cleaner. The extra money bought supplies for the stuffed work-sock monkeys she sewed for seriously ill children in Sanity General Hospital's pediatric ward.

Flaws in her saintly image appeared under Personal/Anecdotal. Unnamed sources called Kathleen snobbish for not participating in social activities and thought her closed curtains and locked doors meant she imbibed sherry more often than she cooked with it. Her most unpardonable sin, according to the backstabbers, was refusing to share her recipes with anyone.

My heavens. How selfish can one be?

The final paragraph related Kathleen's tale of playing the female lead in a mid-forties film entitled *Kansas City Killers*. That claim to fame was the only bit of personal history she ever divulged, but divulge she did, like a parrot with a one-phrase grasp of the English language.

Hannah tossed the report aside. "Three pages to summarize a person's entire life."

Naturally, her remark thunked into a conversational lull. Judging by IdaClare's pouty expression, she'd taken it as a criticism of her handiwork.

"You did a wonderful job on the dossier," Hannah averred. "It's just sad to think Kathleen's biography is so short."

"It is how she chose to live," Leo said over his shoulder. "Kind and good, she was, but, oh, so independent."

"I gathered that, except how independent can anyone be without a driver's license or a car?"

Delbert said, "I took her wherever she needed to go."

"You did *not!*" Marge exclaimed. "I drove her into town every Thursday."

Rosemary and IdaClare belabored their chauffeur duties, while Delbert stared into space, his chin rumpled, his lips pressed together in a manner common to men whose fathers took pride in never having shed a tear.

Hannah should have guessed Kathleen had confided in him. Delbert had taken her to those unknown doctors' appointments, done whatever was needed to help her, and her secret remained safe with him.

The morning Marge flagged him down, he must have been afraid Kathleen was near death or already gone, only to find her brutally murdered. No wonder "cruel" preceded "twist of fate" more often than other adjectives.

Sliding off the bar stool, Hannah squeezed between chairs to Delbert's side. She laid her hands on his shoulders, bent down and whispered, "You're a sweetheart, Delbert Bisbee."

He cocked his head, his rigid features relaxing into a sly grin. "Well, hell, don't say it where anybody 'cept me can hear it."

"I won't. The shock would be too much for everyone."

She straightened, stretched and groaned at its agony and ecstasy.

"If you're tired, dear, don't mind us," IdaClare said. "Toddle on off to bed. We'll lock up when we leave."

Telling David she didn't drop hints wasn't entirely true. The IdaClares of the world simply never took them.

"We've wasted too much time on junk we already knew," Delbert grumbled, "which isn't doing a thing to advance our investigation."

"That is true," Leo said.

"What about—" Delbert pointed at the bar stool "—hie back over there, baby doll. I'm getting a crick in my neck talking at your belly button."

Marge gasped. "Delbert!"

"Don't 'Delbert,' me. I calls 'em likes I sees 'em, and that's what I was a-seein'."

"Well, if I had her girlish figure," Rosemary said, "I'd show it off, too."

Delbert drawled, "You didn't have one when you were one, Rosie."

She raised from her chair, a fist drawing back in ready position.

"You're the voluptuous, Sophia Loren type," Delbert continued, "and Hannah's nearer to Audrey Hepburn. Or maybe it's Katharine Hepburn. Never could keep those two straight."

Great save, Hannah thought, admittedly enamored by the Hepburn comparison, despite the fact one was deceased and the other was old. More like ancient.

As for Rosemary, tack on six vertical inches, knock off a decade and a hundred-some pounds horizontally, and you'd have…Marlon Brando as Don Corleone in drag.

"You are the babe, Rosemary," Leo blurted, then his jowls flushed beet red.

"For the love of Pete," IdaClare said. "Sit down, Rosemary, and stop batting your lashes at Leo. As for you, Delbert, get things moving or I'll adjourn this meeting faster than you can say Jack Robinson."

"Since when are you in charge?" Delbert huffed.

"Since y'all decided to carpool." She lanced a key ring with her pencil and jingled it.

Delbert grunted, then leaned back, crossing his arms at his chest. "Okay, Hannah, under new business, let's start with you filling us in on the corpse Hendrickson found on Fox Fire Road."

Her head snapped up. "What makes you think I know anything about it?"

He grinned. "I didn't, till just now. Like anybody in the P.I. biz knows, you'd have said, 'What dead body?' if you hadn't known about it."

Wily old fart. "David mentioned it in passing, but they aren't sure who the…person is."

"Male or female?" Delbert prodded.

Sheesh. "Male."

"Cause of death?"

Any regular C-Span watcher knows pleading the Fifth is the world's crummiest defense strategy. "He was shot, I think."

Tongue-clucks chorused around the table. "They're right when they say guns don't kill people," Marge said. "People with guns kill people."

Delbert asked, "How did Hendrickson find out about the dead guy?"

"I don't know," Hannah answered truthfully, which was the best lead-in for a whopper. "I'll bet you picked up more information from the scanner than David told me. Homicide wasn't something I wanted to discuss over dinner."

"Of course not, dear," IdaClare agreed. "A terrible pall to cast over a romantic evening."

Well, given time, it might have turned into one. Then again, it was better it hadn't. Probably.

"What David did say is, the calls to his office have to stop. Not that he doesn't appreciate your help and your concern, but, well..." She spluttered to a halt. Diplomat, she was not.

Delbert nodded at IdaClare. "I told her those hot tips of hers weren't so hot."

Before another squabble erupted, Hannah said, "He also mentioned yours and Leo's escapade this afternoon. As in how close you came to starting a brawl."

"Comes with the territory," Delbert countered. "Right, Leo?"

"Ah, um, er...I suppose."

An affirmation need not be enthusiastic, but shouldn't sound as though it was delivered breech.

"No, it does not come with territory, Delbert. You and Leo don't have a territory. None of you do."

Five puppies who'd just been swatted for piddling on the carpet would not have looked more woebegone. Hannah couldn't see Leo's face, but would swear the hairs sprouting from his ears were drooping.

"Aw, c'mon, you guys. If any of you got hurt—" Hannah's voice cracked. "Want to talk risks? Well, that's one I don't care to even think about."

Clamping her hands on her thighs, she plowed on. "There's a lot you can do without interfering in the sheriff's investigation, or hanging out in biker bars."

"Like what, for instance?" Delbert sneered.

"Think about it," she said, doing so herself, having committed to suggesting alternatives without actually having any. "You do have one big advantage. Everyone in the county knows the sheriff and his deputies. Instead of asking questions, why not try just listening?"

"You're not making a lick of sense," IdaClare grumbled.

"People talk—constantly. In cafés, beauty shops, standing in checkout lines. And they pay no attention to who might overhear, unless that 'who' is wearing a badge."

Delbert tapped a finger on his lips. "She may be on to something. Spying instead of P.I.-ing."

"The Curl Up and Dye," IdaClare chirped. "You need a trim, Marge. See if Dixie Jo can work you in, Monday."

"Okay, and Rosemary can go, too, and eavesdrop at Ruby's while she's waiting."

"Leo, let's me and you deploy at the cafeteria after church tomorrow." Delbert nudged IdaClare. "You, too, Jeeves. I'm driving, but we need a plant in the ladies' room.''

"Why can't we all go?" Marge asked. "IdaClare can't trot to the rest room every five minutes. You know what people think when a woman our age does that.''

Delbert shook his head. "It won't work, unless we take separate tables. Walk in together and they'll stick us in the family section with the rug rats.'' He shuddered.

Rosemary said to Marge, "While they're in town, we'll make a list of the good spying places. That way, we won't meet each other coming and going.''

Hallelujah. The new plan had not only met with unanimous approval, it had given them a second wind. Chair legs hobbled across the rug as they hurried to gather their belongings.

Hannah asked, "Might I make one more teensy suggestion?''

"Fire away, honeylamb.''

She whisked the dossier from the counter. "If you'd combine your, er, notes and print them out like this, I'll make sure Sheriff Hendrickson gets a copy.''

"I already thought of that," Delbert said.

Well, of course. How silly of me.

After offering to wash the dishes, which Hannah refused, the gumshoe crew repaired from headquarters as noisily and swiftly as they'd barged in.

Dealing plates into the dishwasher's rack, Hannah heard a motor idling in the side driveway. She crept through the utility room and peered through the back door's mini blind. With the help of IdaClare's headlights, Delbert was hooking the battery charger to Hannah's golf cart. God love him, not a bolt of 220-volt lightning sparked in the process.

Jaw-cracking yawns punctuated the ritual lock-checking and light-dousing. It had been a Walt Disney World day: Daffy, Goofy and Mickey Mouse, with a touch of bibbidy-bobbidy-boo.

Tomorrow? She'd think about tomorrow, tomorrow. Setting the alarm for 6:00 a.m. was punishment enough.

Off with the bra without removing the T-shirt; a minor feat of contortion, but grand is the satisfaction in recycling grub wear into pj's in one easy strip.

Disjointed thoughts flashed through her mind as her head sank into the pillow.

I forgot to repay Delbert.

I forgot to return what's-his-name, the mortician and Chase Wingate's calls.

Who shot Earl Barton?

Buy paper plates and plastic forks before the next squad meeting. Tacky, but lugging trash bags is easier than washing dishes. The environment gets screwed either way.

Kathleen's and Barton's murders are connected.

How? Heck if I know. Yet.

David thinks too much like a cop. Too linear.

I couldn't be linear with a ruler.

David doesn't kiss like a cop. Not like anyone. Ever.

Shouldn't have kissed him.

Won't happen again.

Can't happen again. He's just…too…*wrong*.

Damn.

Afternoon sunlight waxed and waned as an armada
of cumulus clouds sailed by, their passage noticeably
cooling the air angling through the open windows of
Kathleen Osborn's cottage.

Not once had the expected, dreaded feeling of intru-
siveness crept over Hannah like a shadow. Hunkered
on the breakfast room's floor nibbling an Eskimo Pie,
she mentally checked her progress against the unfinished balance.

Kitchen and both bathrooms' drawers and cupboards
were now empty, their contents boxed for charity or
pitched in the Dumpster alongside the deck. Refrigerator, ditto, other than two cans of soda she'd brought
with her. A third load of linens and slipcovers swished
in the washing machine. The curtains, which looked
recently laundered, would be taken down and packed
last.

The chronological plan of attack had hit a snag at
the dining room. The china cabinet and sideboard must
wait. The turtle collection, everyday dishes and bake-
ware had used up the stack of old newspapers Hannah
found in the garage. That left the entry closet, linen
cabinet and the bedroom to sort, divide and conquer.

"And the plants." Her cheeks puffed as she blew

out a breath. "What the devil am I going to do with them?"

The smaller ones were wilting, but she could no more just toss them in the trash than she could the pampered, leafy monsters in the living room.

The probate clerk had given her a mimeographed donor information sheet from the county's Council of Churches' Neighbor-Helping-Neighbor program. Its smudgy, purple print and inky odor reminded Hannah of junior-high pop quizzes and indicated the nonde-nominational organization's office equipment was nearer museum quality than her own.

The sheet contained not a single "Do," which seemed vaguely significant. Had Moses been commanded to deliver the list of "Shalt nots," he'd have never made it down the mountain.

No sooner than she'd rationalized that rule number twelve's "No perishables" might not apply to house-plants, number twenty-three's "No items that must be watered, fed or housebroken" nixed all hope of palm-ing off six-foot palms as charitable contributions.

"Too bad there's no such thing as a quality used-plant lot," she grumbled. "Or a Houseplant Humane Society."

Her tongue paused midway around the last gooey, ice-creamy corner. What if she conned a maintenance guy into hauling them to her front porch, then asked IdaClare to tell everyone they needed good homes?

Hannah balled the ice-cream wrapper and scored a trash bag, no-net, two-pointer. "Yes-s-s." Cosmic af-firmation.

Like a locomotive pulling its cars, she dragged nested boxes down the hallway and into the bedroom.

Muffled race-car engines identified Harve Liebermeyer's choice of Sunday-afternoon entertainment.

"The man has a wheel fetish." She cranked in the windows, leaving the curtains open for light. A shiver rippled through her from the crisp, dampish air and a tummyful of ice cream. The thermostat, set at sixty-eight degrees, would stave off hypothermia. So would doing something besides chafing her arms and telling herself she was cold.

The stripped, mismatched mattress and box spring looked shabby compared to the carved, quarter-sawn oak headboard and footboard. A swell-front dresser with suspended glove boxes flanking a beveled mirror and a four-drawer bureau completed the suite.

Jarrod would loft his patrician nose and call them "late nineteenth-century, catalog crap." Would she ever be able to look at a piece of furniture without hearing his phantom appraisal?

A past relationship's inevitable flotsam was another good reason to put the brakes on starting one with David Hendrickson. His eventual need for more space, time to find himself, or a roll in the hay with a buxom, blond wood-nymph would leave Hannah reluctant to sit with her back to restaurant doors and seeing suspects instead of faces for the rest of her life.

The garbage bag rustled as it plumped with Kathleen's undergarments. Wasteful, perhaps, but altruism had its limits. Hannah smiled when her fingers nudged a velveteen jewelry box buried under a layer of panties. Caroline Garvey also ascribed to the idea that thieves wouldn't paw through a woman's unmentionables searching for loot.

Kathleen's dime-store-grade, Sarah Coventry and tarnished silver- and gold-plated baubles resembled her mother's trove. Hannah never had the heart to tell her the family jewels were as safe on top of her dresser as inside it.

One drawer held nothing but scarves, plastic rain bonnets and winter gloves. Christmas gifts, she surmised, envisioning children presenting beribboned, heavily adhesive-taped bundles to their teacher with a gleeful and unnecessary "I wrapped it all by myself, Miss Osborn."

Hannah grabbed her clipboard and flipped to a clean sheet. "There you go again," she said, "skipping down memory lane with a stranger."

Years ago, an expedition with Jarrod through a multivendor flea market left Hannah feeling as if her childhood had been shot from a cannon, the pieces scattering like confetti and coming to ground in this booth, that one, and another over there.

A similar, gentler nostalgia tugged at her when she found Jade-ite dishes just like Great-aunt Lurleen's in Kathleen's kitchen cabinet, the bubble-blowing, pink ceramic fish on the bathroom wall and the unfinished work-sock monkey in her sewing basket.

One exactly like it, named Bojangles, had absorbed Hannah's little-girl tears and listened to her secrets, worries, wishes and dreams. Stained, musty-smelling and minus an arm, Bojangles's crooked smile still greeted her from a shelf in her closet.

"But you aren't here to take sentimental journeys," Hannah reminded herself as she emptied the last bureau drawer. "Kathleen gave you a job to do. Stick with the program."

The precept of volume expanding to fill a void applied less to the double-doored walk-in closet than the rest of the cottage. Kathleen's Sunday dresses, house-dresses, robes, blouses and skirts hung in a single, abbreviated row.

A wide-brimmed straw hat and a black bowler were stored in zippered, clear plastic bags on the shelf. Purses in navy, black, brown and white were bookended by shoe boxes labeled with corresponding colors.

Without looking, Hannah knew the white pair's soles weren't as scuffed as the rest. Even she couldn't bring herself to wear hers before Easter or after Labor Day, and noticed when other women did.

Adjustable shelving sections along the opposite wall and at the back held storage bins, fabric, portable file boxes and a sack of used paperbacks Kathleen had likely intended to trade for a new batch.

Hannah gasped when she removed the largest storage bin's lid. Having unearthed not a single photograph, scrapbook or memento of any kind, the jumble of class pictures, dried corsages preserved in zip-top bags and crayon-and-construction paper mash notes were like plucking gold nuggets from a gravel bar.

Studying a glossy black-and-white photo dated 1959, she said, "Delbert was right. Kathleen was a knockout."

The slender young woman standing in semiprofile at the back row reminded Hannah of Lauren Bacall in her heyday; sloe eyes, prominent cheekbones and a sleek pageboy with rolled bangs softening a wide forehead and slashed eyebrows.

Kathleen wasn't in about half of the shots, yet the Dorian-Gray-in-reverse effect was fascinating. As the years progressed, her hairdos shortened, the color faded to white and the style took on a self-trimmed raggedyness. God-awful horn-rimmed glasses appeared in

1964, changing gradually to silver-framed bifocals; an improvement on the clunky ones, but not at all flattering.

Propping the photographs on the shelf, Hannah stepped back and compared them. Kathleen was always in the back row, by virtue of height, if nothing else, but whether she stood on the right, left or at center, she never faced the camera.

Which defied the law of averages. Which meant it was intentional. No hooray-for-the-PTA smiles, either, but a stoic "Can we just get this over with?" expression, like men have when coerced into posing for a family reunion's group picture.

But why?

Other bins and file boxes held paperwork archives—receipts, tax records, insurance policies. There were no personal letters or greeting cards, not even a wish-you-were-here postcard from the Grand Canyon's gift shop.

Hannah knuckled her hips. "What's the scoop, Kathleen? Didn't you have a friend in the world? Why were three-year-old utility bills more important than a single, solitary keepsake from that movie you bragged about to everyone?"

Frustrated, she whirled and yanked a stack of shoe boxes from the shelf, then yipped when the topmost bashed her nose, sending the whole bunch toppling to the floor.

"Enigmas are a pain," she muttered, cramming shoes back into their boxes, and boxes into a packing carton. "Darned gutsy to put me in charge of your estate, but God forbid I should get a clue about who you were, or why you're dead."

After duly noting "dress shoes/5; handbags/4" on the inventory, she checked inside each purse. Her own were time capsules full of ticket stubs, old lists, pen caps and loose change. Naturally, not so much as a lint-fuzzy breath mint stuck to the linings of Kathleen's.

While packing the paragons of neatness, Hannah realized there was no beige pocketbook to match Kathleen's stack-heeled pumps. Oh, well. Maybe she carried the brown one when she wore those shoes.

Two minutes later, she was holding a cold soda can in one hand and the kitchen telephone's receiver in the other. To the man who answered, she said, "Sheriff Hendrickson, please."

"Sorry, he's out of the office."

Hannah frowned. "Is Chief Deputy McBride available?"

"Not at the moment. Is this an emergency?"

"No, but—" In desperation, Hannah tried the only other name she could think of. "How about Detective Andrik?"

A sharp click preceded a lengthy hum, then a, "Yo— Andrik speaking."

Hannah introduced herself, ignored his chuff of recognition and said, "I understand Kathleen Osborn's purse was found in Earl Barton's trailer last night."

Andrik hesitated. "No harm in confirming that, I suppose."

"Was it beige-colored, or maybe off-white?"

"Yeah-h-h," he answered, his voice climbing to a questioning pitch. "Was that a real lucky guess, Ms. Garvey?"

"Closer to an educated one." Hannah explained why she was inventorying Kathleen's effects—though he'd surely read the trust's fine print—and the reasoning behind her question.

"First the rolling pin, now matching handbags and

shoes." He made a noise that could have been a chuckle. "Maybe the sheriff is right about needing a female deputy or two around here."

Hannah grinned into the receiver. Coming from him, a backhanded compliment was a coup. "I suppose you have to keep the purse for evidence?"

"For the time being, but trust me, Osborn's billfold and handbag are too far gone for duct tape, if you get my drift."

"Why would Barton do something like that?"

"Because he was a nutcase."

The mental image of a killer running across the golf course carrying a bloody rolling pin and a purse was the stuff of Monty Python. If Barton wanted cash, why not pocket Kathleen's billfold instead of fooling with her purse? Or, heck, why not simply steal the money?

"You still there?"

"Sorry, Detective. I'm just trying to figure out why Barton would ditch the murder weapon and take Kathleen's purse home with him."

She could almost hear his eyes roll up in their sockets. "Most of our customers aren't Rhodes scholars, ma'am, and methamphetamines fry what brains an individual has left. Makes him hyper, paranoid, delusional—off the friggin' wall, basically."

"I know I'm pushing my luck here," Hannah said, "but do you think the Barton and Osborn murders are connected?"

"No." A ringing phone and garbled voices filled the dead air. "Look, you didn't hear this from me, but Barton was shot execution-style. Drug dealers don't operate on credit. One bullet, no muss, no fuss, and a deadbeat junkie becomes a dead-meat example of what happens when you don't pay for your fun."

"Shoot first, then rip off your truck later?"

"Possible, if that's all you have that's worth two cents on the dollar."

She shook her head. "So, Al Capone is alive and well and hijacking beat-up old pickups in central Missouri."

Andrik shot back, "I'd take bathtub gin over drug cookers any day, and our fair state happens to be the ice capital of the country right now."

"I'm not doubting you, Detective. Just trying to make sense out of a tenant and an employee being murdered within days of each other."

Patiently, he replied, "I understand where you're coming from, but there is no sense to be made out of wrong place, wrong time and coincidence. Stuff happens—you know?"

Yeah. Whatever. "I won't keep you any longer, Detective, but I do appreciate your answering my questions."

"No problem, and, uh—" he sort of chuckled, again "—I'll be sure and tell the sheriff you called."

The dial tone interrupted Hannah's response. Or would have, if she'd had one. Rhodes-level intelligence wasn't needed to know the entire department was gossiping about David and his new main squeeze, Miss Marple.

Peachy, freakin' keen.

She hoisted her soda for a long, temper-drowning pull. The dryer buzzed like an airhorn. Carbonated water scorched her throat, all eight sinus cavities, and gushed out her nose. The can thudded to the floor, tipped over and gurgled out what appeared to be five gallons of brown, foamy fluid.

Choking and sputtering, she fumbled for the roll of

paper towels she couldn't see through watery, stinging eyes. Mopping her face, then the linoleum, she chanted a tai chi mantra, which was as soothing as reading the list of ingredients off the soda can.

"That's it. I'm tired, hungry and furious at everyone both living and dead—present company included. One more load in the washer and it's happy trails to me."

A warm, fabric softener–perfumed quilt and the dinette's slipcovers joined the unfolded heap on the wicker love seat. With another load revolving in the dryer's enameled maw, Hannah stomped down the hall to fetch Kathleen's eyelet-lace bed skirt.

Grunting choice words the delicate, buttercup walls had probably never heard, she hiked the mattress over the footboard until it drooped half-on, half-off the bed. The skirt's platform top ruched backward. A manila file folder lay between it and the box spring's muslin cover.

Hannah knew what it was before she saw Kathleen Osborn's name typed on the label. "But why?" She thumbed through the paperwork it contained. "Why would she steal her own tenant file?"

"What a lovely surprise," IdaClare said. "Come in, dear. Come in."

Hannah did two or three steps' worth of "in" before halting, blinking, then goggling at the living room's decor. Carnivorous-looking wallpaper peonies in every imaginable shade of pink trellised the walls and ceiling. Ropes of white, gauzy fabric spangled with twinkle lights hung in swags, festooned the bay window and trailed down the curtains' folds.

The white wing chairs and a U-shaped sectional that could seat twenty of IdaClare's closest friends looked conservative in comparison to the pink-enameled bombay chests, side tables and baby grand piano in one corner.

"It's a sin to be house-proud," IdaClare cooed, "but I've dreamed of a room like this since I was knee-high to a grasshopper. Patrick, God rest him, simply never understood my vision."

"It's, uh—striking, all right. I can't say I've ever seen anything quite like it."

"Do tell my son that, next time you talk to him." IdaClare tossed her head. "If Jack calls it a blind madam's whorehouse one more time, I'll show him I'm not too old to tan his hide, good and plenty."

"I'll just bet you could," Hannah said, laughing.

Blue eyes sparkling with anticipation, IdaClare asked, "Has the sheriff arrested Earl Barton's killer? Who is it? Not another Valhalla Springs employee, I hope."

"Sorry to disappoint you, but I haven't talked to the sheriff since last night."

"Don't worry, dear." IdaClare patted Hannah's arm. "I'm sure it's only because he's terribly busy right now."

If anyone else expressed interest in micromanaging her personal life, Hannah would have season tickets printed.

IdaClare motioned toward the sectional. "Make yourself at home while I rustle up a snack. You truly are a mite thin, dear."

"Don't tempt me, please, because I really can't stay. What I need is a favor and answers to a couple of questions."

Had IdaClare been a horse, her ears would have

swiveled and cocked forward. "I'll do anything I can to help, you know that."

"The favor first, then. As soon as I have Kathleen's plants moved to my porch, would you pass the word they're free for the taking? I honestly don't know what else to do with them, and can't just throw them away."

"Certainly *not*, and people traipsing through her cottage simply would not do. Except, if you don't mind, may I have the starts in the breakfast room? Most of them are cuttings from my plants, anyway."

"I didn't know you had a herb garden."

IdaClare's shoulders scrunched. "Well, it has to stay our little secret, but I had the most divine greenhouse built onto my deck a month or so ago."

"Meaning, Jack doesn't know about it yet," Hannah stated, rather than asked.

IdaClare flapped a hand. "Oh, you know how he is. He'd have gone on and on about easements and covenants and such until he ruined the whole thing for me."

Jack's gored-bull roar when he sees Mama's divine addition will be audible clear to my cottage, too, Hannah thought. "Built onto the deck, eh? I'd love to see it."

IdaClare started. "See it? Oh, dear—no. I can't show it to anyone. I have exotics from…er, Borneo." She tittered. "Persnickety things. They have to have twelve hours of darkness every day or they won't bloom."

Hannah cocked an eyebrow. "But it isn't dark yet."

"Window shades—I have window shades and they're down, and I can't turn the lights on, or it'll interfere with their cycle."

Hannah recalled David's remark about bad liars, but

surrendered as graciously as he had. "Another time, then."

"After they bloom."

"Right." Shrugging off her bullshit detector's alarm, Hannah said, "Besides asking you to help me farm out Kathleen's plants, the other reason I came by is because I'm curious about this movie she starred in."

IdaClare looked surprised, then irked. "I almost didn't include that in the dossier. We don't think there ever was a movie. That it was just her way of...well, adding a touch of glamour to her life." She sighed. "To gild a very dull lily, sad as it is to say."

Hannah didn't ask who the "we" included, assuming it extended well beyond the Mod Squad. "What did she tell you, though? Any details, like what year it was filmed or anything?"

IdaClare frowned. "In late 1944—not long before World War II ended, if I remember right. She said it was made in Kansas City because sets would be too expensive to build in Hollywood, or some such nonsense."

"What was the story line?"

"Oh, one of those silly Bonnie and Clyde shoot-'em-ups, except it had two Clydes—brothers. Kathleen played the Bonnie part—a gun moll, which would take more than a spoonful of corn syrup for *me* to swallow."

"And the male leads? Do you remember who played them?"

IdaClare twitched and clucked a moment. "Ward Bond? Yes, I do believe he was the younger one, and...what's his name, William, um—Frawley. That's it. He was the older Clyde. Kathleen's paramour, or whatever you call it."

Hannah made a face. "William Frawley? Wasn't he Fred Mertz on *I Love Lucy?*"

"Oh, dear. Now that you mention it, he was, wasn't he?"

In unison, they crinkled their noses and did a Lucille Ball signature, "Eee-yew."

Hannah smiled when she saw Henry Don Tucker behind his desk in the Grounds & Greens department's office. "I didn't really expect to find anyone here on a Sunday evening."

The paunchy supervisor with an arrow-pierced heart and an anchor tattooed on his respective biceps rose to his feet. "Well, I'm here most every Sunday evening making out the next week's work schedule."

"On your own time?"

A ham-sized hand invited her to take a chair. "It's this, or hear Reverend Lang pound the pulpit twice in one day. Me and Pinky kinda spell each other, but my daughter volunteered him to help in the nursery. He'll get out of it by and by."

Pinky Dobbs, Henry Don's son-in-law, assisted him in the thankless job of maintaining the golf course, residential areas and undeveloped grounds. Their crew expanded fourfold during spring, summer and fall, but winter in the Ozarks, a season notorious for dumping hip-deep snow followed by shirtsleeve temperatures, gave few opportunities for slacking.

"Bet I know what brought you here," Henry Don said. "Seems everybody and their cousin Charlie is asking after Earl Barton."

"Oh?" Hannah folded her hands in her lap. "Who else besides the sheriff's department?"

He leaned back and winged his arms behind his

head. ''Them, mostly, but rumors is hopping from lips to ears like bunnies in a carrot patch. That damned— beg pardon—ol' Bisbee, the resident board's president? He's pestered my men like there's no tomorrow. Come by here once, and it don't trouble me to say, I told him and that Leo fella to scat.''

Hannah grinned. ''Delbert can be insistent, but his heart is in the right place.''

The supervisor's dour expression spoke volumes better left unsaid. He nodded at a folder at the corner of his desk. ''That's Barton's particulars, if you care to look at 'em.''

Hannah feigned nonchalance as she reviewed the application. Mental subtraction put Earl G. Barton's age at fifty-two, two or three decades older than she'd presumed. High-school dropout. Divorced. Most recent prior employment included a chicken-processing plant in Arkansas, a machine shop in Iowa and over-the-road trucking for a company in Joplin, Missouri—all within the last five years.

Barton answered, ''Have you ever been convicted of a crime?'' truthfully, although the form didn't allow much space for specifics. Why Henry Don had hired an ex-con was clarified by the letter of recommendation stapled to the application.

''Your minister vouched for Barton?'' Hannah asked.

''The Son of man hath power on earth to forgive sins,'' Henry Don quoted, then shook his head. ''Reverend Lang was driving home from a seminar up in Kansas City and spied Earl hitchhiking and nigh froze to death. 'Twas a week before Christmas, Brother Homer was singin' 'Wayfaring Stranger' to the radio and a-tremblin' with Christian charity, so he took it for Providence.

"Earl's uncle had ripped him off, then knocked the whey out of him, and Earl was bound for Saint Louis to find work. That didn't make Homer no nevermind. He's a fine man, but fervent, if you know what I mean."

"Yes, I do." Effindale's Pastor John Warren was cut from the same devout cloth; a man of God who genuinely believed no living soul is beyond salvation.

"Right after New Year's, an ice storm whistled in," Henry Don continued. "Irrigation pipes froze, trees shattered, branches snapped like shotguns. I needed help like nobody's business. The wife and Reverend Lang had faith in Earl. Didn't reckon it'd hurt to give him a chance."

Hannah said, "He must have done his job, or you'd have fired him a long time ago."

"Didn't expect he'd last a week. Eager beaver he wasn't, but he did what he was told and did it right."

Henry Don sucked at his teeth. "Can't say I ever liked him, though. He didn't talk much, and bathed less. Showed up every Monday hungover as all get-out, but on time and ready to work."

Hannah's fingertips pressed her temple. "In his condition, that had to hurt."

"Woulda killed me outright, but guys like Earl can't recollect when they didn't wake up feelin' rode hard and put away wet."

Her gaze shifted to the cheesecake calendar on the bulletin board. I knew the feeling once, too, she mused. Sins of the mother temporarily visited on her arrogant, self-made daughter, who should have known better.

"Did Earl's personality or habits change recently?" she asked.

"Well, I'll be." Henry Don shifted to a forearms-on-desk position. "Jimmy Wayne McBride asked me the very same thing."

"And?"

"'Long about Tuesday, the chip on Earl's shoulder slid down to his backside, if you know what I mean. He was jumpy as frog legs in hot grease. Spooky-actin'. Said his ship was comin' in, and he wouldn't have to take orders from nobody no more.

"When he didn't show Thursday or Friday, me and Pinky didn't think nothing of it. Stayin' as long as he did was a bigger surprise than him quittin' without notice."

Henry Don stared down at the coffee-ringed blotter. "I suppose I could have guessed Earl would come to a bad end, but I sure never figured him for a murderer."

After trying to assuage Tucker's apparent guilt about hiring Barton, Hannah drove home wondering how Reverend Lang was dealing with his wayfaring stranger being both a killer and a homicide victim.

Little did she know, the answer was as close as her cottage.

12

Reverend Homer Lang's resonant speaking voice suggested he tackled "Amazing Grace's" chord progressions with aplomb. His message was a gracious offer to conduct Kathleen's funeral service, as he'd been told she had no "church home."

"The Lord works in mysterious ways," he said, "and at times, his tests of faith must be met with a bowed back, as well as a bowed head."

Hannah smiled, and noted Lang's telephone number.

There were three messages from David; one after his ever-faithful detective apprised him of his and Hannah's earlier conversation. She arbitrarily decided not to play telephone tag with the county sheriff.

The bigots had either given up, were waiting to see if Willard Johnson made an appearance tomorrow, had qualms about making threats on the Sabbath or had gotten a life.

Duckworth's Funeral Home could wait until morning. Delbert could wait in perpetuity. Chase Wingate's patience would be rewarded.

The newspaper editor was polite but frosty when his wife called him to the phone. Hannah apologized for the delay and gave no excuses for it. He'd recognize them for what they were, and she was in no mood to grovel.

Wingate was, however, a shrewd interviewer, double-checking Kathleen's age, and other basic facts like a dogcatcher feeding treats to a stray mutt to gain its confidence.

A smooth shift to the nitty and gritty began with, "How would you describe the residents' reactions to Ms. Osborn's murder, and now, Earl Barton's?"

"In Ms. Osborn's case, they're saddened by the loss of a friend and neighbor. I don't know how many are aware of Earl Barton's death."

"Or that Barton allegedly killed Kathleen Osborn?"

Hannah paused. "I've received no official notification from the sheriff's department to that effect."

"How about unoffically?"

"Really, Mr. Wingate. Does the *Sanity Examiner* print unsubstantiated rumors?"

"There's a difference between rumor and information conveyed to a property manager-slash-employer in the course of an investigation, Ms. Garvey."

Careful, kiddo. Don't put your butt or David's in a bind. "To the best of my knowledge, evidence that could link Barton to the Osborn murder is being analyzed, but no definite connection has yet been established."

A two-beat silence preceded Wingate's, "Oh, you're good. Ever consider running for office?"

"I'm not that good, Mr. Wingate."

"What about security at Valhalla Springs? Any plans to increase it in light of the recent homicides?"

"None that I know of." Hannah wriggled in her chair.

"Interesting, since many retirement communities are gated or have guards to ensure the safety and security of their residents."

She pursed her lips. Pitch me curves, spitballs, sliders, whatever you like. I don't have to swing at them.

"All right, then," he demurred, "did you know about Mr. Barton's arrest record when he was hired, and will applicants be screened more closely in the future?"

Ouch. This guy didn't miss a trick. Other than the supervisory level, departmental hires and fires weren't her responsibility, but saying so was the same as passing the buck and the blame to Henry Don Tucker, who deserved neither.

"As I'm sure you know, Mr. Wingate, I have only been resident manager for a week, which has not allowed sufficient time to review policies and procedures affecting all facets of operation."

"You didn't answer either question, Ms. Garvey."

"I believe I did."

He cleared his throat. "Off the record—and I mean that—I hope you understand it's my job to ask these kinds of questions. Nothing personal, and I sincerely appreciate your cooperation."

"Such as it was?"

He laughed. "Hey, Jack told me you were smart."

"Can I quote you on that?"

The interview ended on an up note, but Hannah rotated her head and rolled her shoulders as if she'd just survived a date with Mike Tyson. The nicest thing she'd done for herself all day was snork an Eskimo Pie. Time for a little self-indulgence. More than a little.

Two baloney, mustard and crushed potato-chip sandwiches fed the inner woman and comforted the inner child, as they had since the day desperation inspired their invention.

A cup of strong, black coffee revived her.

A long, hot shower relaxed her.

Standing stark naked, staring at a package of taupe, silk panty hose atop pairs of balled crew socks in the drawer scared the living hell out of her.

She must be mistaken. She'd dressed in a hurry that morning…maybe the panty hose were there then.

On wobbly knees, she scurried to the bathroom to wrap herself in a towel. The solid wooden door and its lock fostered thoughts of peanut butter, crackers, bottled water and voluntary incarceration until Valhalla Springs's crime rate returned to normal.

"First, I'll call David, then I'll lock myself in the bathroom," she decided, only to yank her hand back from the phone. "And just what do you propose to tell him? Hit the lights and siren and haul ass, cowboy. My panty hose have migrated from the bottom of the dresser drawer to the top."

She snorted. "Oh, and by the way, Sheriff, I'm naked."

Temper told fear to take a hike and stay there. She surveyed the room for other signs of disturbance. The closet door was propped by yesterday's shirt, sweats and underwear. Check. The bed looked like the aftermath of a Roman orgy. Yeah, well, in my dreams. Check. A fine layer of dust glazed the bureau, mirrored dresser and bedside chests.

She snapped her fingers. "Checkmate."

Overhead fixture extinguished and the flashlight from the utility room in hand, she knelt beside the dresser and shone the beam down its length. Smudges, swipes and broad, splayed lines in series of threes and fours indicated the intruder had worn gloves. "Or else his fingers were webbed, like a duck."

Needing a complete return to the status quo to banish

her heebie-jeebies, she donned a clean pair of jeans, fisherman-knit sweater and suede loafers, brushed on mascara and blusher, then moved her still-too-red hair around with the blow-dryer.

All the while, two thoughts refused to budge from the forefront of her mind: Kathleen stole her own residency file for reasons unknown, but it wasn't her nature to leave drawers in disarray. Earl Barton may have rifled the file cabinets in vain before Hannah moved in, but dead guys don't burgle.

Further inspection yielded numerous things the unknown intruder might have, and probably did shift around, but memory laced with paranoia wasn't the most reliable consultant. The fact none of the door locks appeared to have been jimmied would have her wedging chairs under the knobs until Maintenance changed them. Again.

She poured another cup of coffee; a magical beverage with the ability to jazz one up or calm one down, depending on the need of the moment, such as an extended, cozy brood on the couch.

Objectively, if that were possible, the break-in should strengthen her resolve, not weaken it. Which was good, because it had. Whether David, Marlin Andrik or anyone else believed a connection between Kathleen's and Barton's murders existed, she did.

No doubt, Barton killed Kathleen and robbery had been his motive. Beyond that, Hannah wasn't sure of anything, other than that the official "why" explanations were about as satisfying as dreaming of an orgasm as opposed to having one.

Drugs or no drugs, could a man gain access to a home, either by invitation, key or lock-pick, then go psycho and beat a woman to death with a kitchen tool, then snap back to reality long enough to bury the murder weapon and drive home, then whip up a second, insane rage and slash his victim's purse to ribbons, then hang around his trailer for a couple of days, whereupon his dope dealer, annoyed the killer was a lousy credit risk, put him out of his misery?

"Only in the movies," Hannah said.

Striding to the office nook, she flipped on the desk lamp and reached for the phone.

"Yeh?" rasped a three-pack-a-day Camel snarl.

"Has absence made your heart grow fonder?"

"Hannah! Christ Almighty, how are ya, sweetheart? How's t'ings goin' down there in Hooterville?"

Salvatore Rizzio, apartment-building superintendent par excellence, devoted Bears fan and walking cinematic encyclopedia believed Chicago was the epicenter of the universe.

"I miss you," she said, "but I'm doing fine. Valhalla Springs is gorgeous. A hundred times prettier than any of my brochures."

"Seen any cowboys yet?"

She laughed. "You never give up, do you, Sal?"

"May have to, kid. Mrs. Delvecchio's nephew and his partner are interested in your ol' crib. Want I should stall 'em a coupla days? In case you wise up and come back where ya belong."

Hannah paused to allow regrets to assert themselves. "No, Sal. I think I'm already there."

Guttural noises, like one makes when a toe stubs a bedpost in the middle of the night, purveyed his dissenting opinion.

"As soon as you finish the hog impersonation," she teased, "I'll tell you why I called."

"Good to know ya ain't lost the lip. Wha'sup?"

Hannah told her premeditated fib about surprising a tenant on her birthday with a piece of memorabilia, or better yet, a video reproduction of the movie she starred in during her teens.

Sal's response was instantaneous. "The old girl's pulling your leg."

"Are you sure? It may have been very low-budget, with limited distribution."

"Ya wanna listen or ya wanna argue? It didn't happen. William Frawley made *Flame of the Barbary Coast* in '45 for Joseph Kane. Ward Bond would've been wrapping up *Dakota,* another Joe Kane flicker, or reporting to John Ford to start *They Were Expendable.*

"Frawley was a boozer, a troublemaker and no box-draw," Sal went on, "so the studio might've let him to pick up a few bucks on the side, 'cept he didn't make a movie by that title—ever. And Ward Bond? No way, no how. Duke Wayne was Bond's meal ticket. He didn't need the money, and wouldn't fool with a fly-by-nighter if he did. The studio would've swung him from a flagpole by his balls for a stunt like that."

"No doubt in your mind?" Hannah asked.

"Abso-tively posi-lutely none. Granny Garbo is doing a number on ya."

"Thanks, Sal."

His gravelly voice softened. "Take care of yourself, sweetheart. Ya hear me?"

After hanging up, Hannah gnawed on a knuckle. Sal knew his stuff. IdaClare's belief that Kathleen fantasized the whole movie scenario was looking more like fact than opinion.

Not inclined toward recusing himself from a mental debate, Hannah's inner devil's advocate chimed in with the reminder: hundreds, if not thousands, of films had deteriorated to dust, burned up in fires, been misplaced, mishandled or lost, for varied reasons. No knowledge of a movie titled *Kansas City Killers* being made didn't guarantee it had not.

Still, Kathleen's yarn was awfully detailed for a figment of imagination. That she'd also been consistent, rather than gradually enlarging upon it, was like a fisherman's prize catch never gaining an ounce.

A human information operator transferred Hannah to an electronic drone who enunciated the requested number in a mechanical monotone. A follow-up call to Kansas City and a well-told lie provided a name and phone number.

IdaClare answered her telephone on the second ring. No, she wasn't busy, television was a bust, and she'd love some company.

"I'm in a rush as usual," Hannah warned, "so don't you dare put a tea party together."

"Oh, all right, dear," IdaClare said with a sigh.

Hannah bolted from her office under the influence of an adrenaline spike. Hindsight could put the fear of God and federal indictments in her later.

The smallish matter of someone other than a Mod Squad member having a key to her cottage stopped her cold as she entered the utility room. She could do the chair thing to the front and deck doors, but not the one she'd leave by.

Hannah shrugged, took a step, then halted. Almost every light inside and outside the house was blazing away. Traffic was lighter after nine on a Sunday evening, but a burglar would have to be crazy to risk being spotted.

"Comforting thought. Crazy is a given."

Refusing to give in to neurosis, she dropped her

purse and keys on the washing machine's lid and marched back to the office. Picturing Delbert's thumbs-up approval for the alarm she rigged didn't send her confidence soaring into the stratosphere, but as Great-uncle Mort decreed, "Somethin's better'n nothin'."

She paused outside the utility room's door to scrutinize the scrap of paper lodged in the crack between the edge and the stile. The other two doors had been flagged likewise. Theoretically, if anyone gained entry while she was out, the paper trail would alert her to it.

Eat your heart out, Mike Hammer.

A skunk toddling across Valhalla Springs Boulevard and a glimpse of a larger animal, probably a deer, were the only signs of life Hannah encountered en route. The proliferation of porch and yardlights shining along the side streets looked like a trick-or-treater's El Dorado.

Turning onto Sumac Drive, she cruised its curving length to 2404, the white Victorian with fuschia balconets, gable trim and gingerbread, second from the corner. Whether by accident or design, the neighboring homes' sedate chocolate-over-ivory and natural cedar exteriors muted IdaClare's Hansel-and-Gretel-meet-Barbie's-Dream-House effect, especially after dark.

True to her word, a velvet-robed, feather-mule-shod IdaClare clopped straight to a kitchen alcove where the expropriated computer and peripherals rested on a built-in desk.

Faint, bluish light slivered through the closed, vertical patio-door blinds. IdaClare's "exotics" must be fluorescently tanning their tootsies.

Forget it, Hannah thought. You aren't here for a crash course in botany. She chafed her hands, seated herself and began the boot-up process.

"Do you mind if I watch?" IdaClare asked. "Rosemary brags on me all the time, but I'm not as technified as she'd have everyone believe.''

Hannah caught her tongue between her teeth. Could IdaClare be trusted to keep her mouth shut? Did donkeys fly?

She swiveled in her chair. ''Here's the deal. Since I promised not to tell Jack about the greenhouse, you have to promise to keep what I'm about to do a secret, too.''

''I won't tell a soul, dear. I swear.'' A fingertip etched a cross above her bosom for emphasis. ''Oh, this is so exciting! What are we going to do?''

''Conspire to commit a felony.'' Hannah chuckled. ''But like you said, there's nothing on TV anyway.''

With IdaClare huddled beside her, Hannah scanned the directory, then frowned. None of the software programs listed were appropriate for record-keeping.

''Did you install these games yourself?'' she asked.

''Heavens, no. After Owen gave me the computer, Roscoe Hocking, next door, came over and erased things he said I didn't need cluttering up the machine and showed me what buttons to push. Wasn't that sweet of him?''

Hannah moaned, ''Ummhmm,'' in effigy for the deleted tenant records and archived business files. A computer wonk might be able to retrieve them, but it would cost a fortune. She didn't have the courage to ask if Owen McCutcheon had passed along any disks. A wise woman didn't ask questions whose answers might make her bang her head, repeatedly, against the nearest wall.

Thankfully, Roscoe Hocking's purge didn't include a basic desktop publishing program. Keystrokes tapped a merry rhythm as a letterhead format appeared on the monitor.

"Well, isn't that something," IdaClare said, gasping. "Except...the sheriff's department doesn't have a substation in Valhalla Springs, dear."

At the left margin, Hannah typed *Major H. M. Garvey, Unit Commander.* On the right, she slugged in the number for the manager's office's fax machine. A double space below a bold dividing line, she centered *Information Request: Priority Status.*

From the corner of her eye, she saw IdaClare gawk at the screen like a child watching a magician pull doves from his pocket. Hannah issued a silent prayer that Bryant L. Smythe, whom her telephone inquiry had identified as the *Kansas City Star*'s archivist, would be similarly impressed.

She titled and saved the bogus dispatch in the program's memory. The laser printer whirred, clacked, then set to the task of producing Exhibit A.

IdaClare rested a hand on Hannah's thigh. "Why are you asking for news items about bank robberies in 1944 and '45?"

"Because a friend in Chicago says there is no movie like the one Kathleen described."

"Well, I already told you we didn't believe there was."

Hannah nodded. "I'm probably way off-base, but I have a hunch there was some truth to her story. Fabricating the whole thing to make herself seem more interesting just doesn't make sense to me."

IdaClare favored her with an indulgent smile. "If you'd been acquainted with Kathleen, you'd know her being a real-life Bonnie Parker is more ridiculous than her being a movie star."

"I agree, but what if she based her story on a real heist? What if she knew, or was related to, the robbers?" Hannah initiated the keyboard commands to shut down the computer. "I guess it can't hurt to try and find out."

"Oh, Hannah..." IdaClare made mother-hen noises. "What if the newspaper calls the sheriff's office for verification or something?" She gasped. "Lord above, what if somebody calls and asks for Major H. M. Garvey?"

Hannah stood and hugged her worried co-conspirator. "Then I'll have a lot of explaining to do to David Hendrickson."

IdaClare's eyes twinkled. "Careful, young lady. That boy's brag-dog handsome when he's mad."

"Hey, what happened to, and I quote, 'Hannah has more important things to do than chase after David Hendrickson'?"

"My mind hasn't changed one iota, and from what I hear, you aren't the one who's in—" she frowned and waggled a fist "—oh, fiddlesticks, what do they call it?"

"Heat" might have filled the blank, but Hannah refrained from suggesting it.

IdaClare's finger slashed the air. "He's in *hot pursuit*. That's a 10–63 in cop-talk."

"Well, I'm 10–outta here." Hannah paused and waved the fax. "This little caper stays between us, right?"

Again, IdaClare crossed her heart. Considering the lateness of the hour, Hannah figured it'd be nine, nine-thirty tomorrow morning before the rest of the gumshoes were told and duly sworn to secrecy, and midafternoon before everyone in Valhalla Springs knew the scoop.

As she backed from the driveway, a turquoise Edsel prowled by the intersection of Sumac Drive and Valhalla Springs Boulevard. Wondering why Delbert was out cruising segued into no desire to explain her own moonlight ride.

She hooked a right from Sumac onto Hawthorne Street, avoiding Sassafras Lane, in case he was taking the long way home and spotted her before she diverted onto the boulevard.

No mile-wide headlights appeared in the mirror as Hannah turned onto Dogwood Lane. Unless Delbert had doubled back on the boulevard for some reason, she'd outfoxed him.

At the top of the hill, she glanced at Kathleen's cottage. Her foot depressed the brake pedal, slowing the Blazer to a crawl. Eyes roaming left to right, she surveyed the clapboard facade. Her tires yipped the pavement. A walnut tree cast deceptive shadows on the bedroom and dining-room windows, but the living-room curtains she was sure she'd left open were definitely closed.

She shifted into reverse, the truck sweeping backward a few feet, then cut toward the curb. Leaving the engine running and the door open, she skulked around the side of the cottage. If the patio drapes were closed, she'd tear out for Delbert's house and speed-dial 911.

A murky, bush-flanked tunnel middled the adjacent residences; the grassy, shallow slough protected from lunar and man-made illumination.

Snatching the penlight from the glove compartment would have prevented her from swallowing a scream when she blundered into a spiderweb. Scrubbing at the

tickling remnants with her coat sleeve, she willed herself not to contemplate the whereabouts of the giant,
fanged spider who'd spun it, or its attitude regarding
the destruction of its masterpiece.

Hannah rejoiced when the deck rail loomed from the
gloom. She jogged around its corner, pulling up just in
time to avoid a collision with the Dumpster. Hastening
past it, she squinted up at the patio doors. The curtains
were closed. The slider itself was open.

An arm lashed across her throat. Yanked backward,
Hannah struggled, clawing at the choke hold crushing
her windpipe. Pressure at the right side of her neck sent
pain needling along her jaw. Another arm crooked her
chin like a vise. A knuckle dug in hard—*harder* beneath her left ear.

She hurtled, helpless, into a bottomless, black abyss.

13

"Who's— That you, Hendrickson?" Delbert shouted. "Get on your squawk box. See what's keeping that ambulance."

There was a burst of static, then David's voice, loud and stern. "Adam–101. What's the twenty on the ambulance for Valhalla Springs?"

Static. *ETA, five minutes, 101. The Pike's Grove unit is already out on a call.*

David barked, "Tell 'em to by-God step on it."

Roger, 101. Clear.

Hannah squinted through her lashes into a high-powered flashlight's indirect beam. She blinked up at twin Delberts, both of them grim. Looming over her from the opposite side, duplicates of David's stony face ratcheted down to one.

"Hey, sugar. Lie still. Help will be here in a second."

She rolled over and raised up on her elbow. Her pulse throbbed in her skull. Sneaky son of a bitch. There was no honor in being felled by an assailant's thumb and finger. Five hundred bucks' worth of self-defense classes for nothing. She didn't so much as kick the sucker in the shin.

Delbert clasped her shoulder. "You don't mind real well, do you?"

"I'm not hurt." Physically, anyway. She pushed herself into a sitting position. The ground heaved. Her stomach followed suit before both settled into an even keel. "Some creep jumped me from behind and put me in a choke hold, that's all."

"Can you describe him?" David asked.

"Cancel the ambulance, then I'll talk."

"But—"

"*Do* it, David. Please?"

His eyes flicked to Delbert and back again. "You going to let me take you home?"

"No, but if you insist, you can follow me."

"Christ, you're stubborn." David keyed the mike and transmitted a string of 10–codes, one of which Hannah recognized as a request for backup.

"No lights, no sirens," she warned. "I won't have everyone scared out of their wits again."

David glared at her, but instructed the dispatcher accordingly. "Any other orders, before I sign off?"

She grinned. "A large pepperoni with extra cheese, if you can swing it."

Delbert held out his hands. "Before he 10–4s, show us you can stand up and stay that way."

Uh-oh. The price of smug. She should have known her saviors would tag-team the damsel in distress.

Hannah clenched her teeth and grasped Delbert's cool, sinewy hands. Vital organs did swan dives as she rose. She staggered a bit, head lolling as though her brain cavity had been pumped full of helium. A deep breath and slow exhale stifled the urge to throw up on Delbert's Hush Puppies.

"You okay?" he asked, sliding an arm behind her.

"Yeah." His eyes denoted skepticism. "Honest, I am. Other than being seriously pissed at myself."

"I reckon that makes two of us," David said.

"Where did you guys come from, anyway?"

Delbert replied, "I'm on the eleven-to-one shift, and saw your truck—"

"Say again?" she inquired.

"Mobile neighborhood watch. Me, Leo, Walt Wagonner and Harve Liebermeyer put it together this afternoon."

David groaned, "Oh, Lord."

"Harve Liebermeyer is in on it?" Hannah asked.

"Walt's idea. Him and Harve fish together sometimes."

Walt didn't talk. Harve couldn't hear. Not as strange a pairing as one might think.

Delbert hitched a shoulder. "Coulda knocked me over with a feather when Harve volunteered, but he's gung ho about it."

Compensation, Hannah mused. Guilt works in mysterious ways, too.

Delbert went on, "He clocked out early, though. Said Miriam's bran muffins always tear him up. Just as well he's with us, though, since I used his phone to call in the cavalry, again."

"I'd just left your cottage and was heading this way when dispatch relayed it," David said. "I thought you were working late on the inventory."

Hannah recognized the leading quality of his remark. She attributed her drive through the development to antsiness, then explained the curtain discrepancy. It didn't satisfy him in the least, but he didn't press.

A notebook and pen materialized. "I want everything you can remember from the time you bailed from your vehicle."

The debriefing took a maximum of fifteen seconds.

Her description of the assailant was of a man, four to five inches taller than her with dragon breath who reeked of body odor and cigarette smoke.

"He must have been crouched in front of the Dumpster," she said. "I was looking up at the sliding glass doors and he had me by the throat so fast, I didn't know what hit me, much less who."

David grunted. "Why don't you scope out the Big Dipper for a second." He leaned in and shone the flashlight on her neck. "Now, turn your head the other— Bisbee, back off a step, will ya?"

"I'm just trying to see if she's bruised or anything."

David's response was unintelligible, but guessable.

"Am I?" Hannah's voice sounded like Lily Tomlin doing her Edith Ann character.

"Not yet, but you may be by morning," David said. "Whoever knocked you colder than a mackerel knew what he was doing. Carotid submission can be deadly if it's done wrong."

The world heaved anew as her head straightened. She lusted after the bottle of extra-strength aspirin in her purse.

"Bisbee, if you want to make yourself useful, take the keys out of Hannah's ignition, then wait there for the burglary detail. Give the keys to one of them when they arrive."

Delbert's eyes narrowed. "Sending me on a goose-chase, huh? What are you going to do while I'm at it?"

"If Hannah's up to it, we'll check inside." The flashlight's beam whisked the ground around them. "Tell the deputy to come in the front. We've tromped around back here quite a bit, but still might find some prints."

He paused, issuing a level gaze at Delbert. "I'm not thrilled about you and your buddies cruising around this late, but I'm glad you did tonight."

David consulted his watch. "After you hand off Hannah's keys, I'd advise you to finish up your, uh, shift. The less said about this incident the better, too."

Delbert's whole body sagged. Hannah reached around his shoulders and hugged him. "I'd have been too scared to breathe if you hadn't been here when the fog lifted." She smooched his temple. "Thanks, Delbert."

Even in dim light, his complexion glowed with a sudden, rosy hue. "Anytime, honeylamb."

He started off, then about-faced to circle the cottage on the opposite side Hannah had used.

"Pretty smart ol' codger," David said. "Hope I'm half as sharp as he is when I'm his age."

Hannah thought, I hope I'm still *alive* when you're his age.

In a soft yet businesslike tone, David asked, "Are you sure you're okay?"

Before she answered, he'd stuck the flashlight in his back pocket and gathered her into his arms. She wrapped hers around him, nestling her cheek against his chest. He was so big, and warm, and strong... My hero. Ummmmm.

"I reckon I could keep this up for a week, maybe ten days," he murmured.

Promise?

"But," he said with a sigh, "that's something else we're going to have to wait till later to find out."

Taking that as a hint for her to detach her aching, horny self from his obviously, equally horny, magnificent self, she shivered. The night air seemed to have cooled in a measly few seconds.

David winced, shifted his weight, then did a sneak-adjustment with one hand, while the other disappeared behind his back to retrieve the flashlight. "I, uh, didn't want to ask with Bisbee here, but the assailant, was he Caucasian?"

Hannah frowned. Sheesh. Talk about abrupt changes in subject. "It was pitch-dark. He could have been green, with orange stripes."

"Nothing else you can recall?"

Bowing her head, a hand at her brow like an awning, she thought back to the seconds before the world went black. "He was wearing long sleeves, a jacket, I think. Not a windbreaker—the fabric was coarse, scratchy." She dropped her arm. "That's it. That's all I can remember."

David nodded. His pen made a checkmark motion on the notebook.

"Why did you play the race card?"

His cop face would fit in well with those at Mount Rushmore. "The better the description, the better chance—"

"There was more to it than that, or you wouldn't have waited until Delbert left."

He hesitated. Apparently remembering that her curiosity, when aroused, was like an octopus reeling in a squid, he answered, "Carotid suppression is common to the military, law enforcement and the martial arts. You said the new physical fitness instructor has a black belt, so—"

"Oh, puh-leeze, Hendrickson, just because Willard..." Her voice trailed away into a chuckle. "By golly, character assassination aside, that's a pretty slick two-plus-two-equals-four.''

"Why, thank you, ma'am. I was right fond of it myself.'' He turned and started for the deck.

Following him up the steps, she said, "Except I don't believe it for a second," without as much conviction as she'd liked to have felt, since Willard was about the right height, and was an ex-smoker.

David looked back over his shoulder. "Let me go in and scout around first.'' Shoving back his denim jacket, he unsnapped the holster guard, batted the curtain aside with the flashlight and disappeared behind its folds.

Hannah slipped her hands into the back pockets of her jeans to warm them. Leaves rustling, toad serenades and the ever-baying coyotes broke the quietude. Looking around, she rocked on her heels, as if awaiting the crosstown bus. Anyone watching from the shadows could see she hadn't a care or worry in the world. She'd have whistled a happy tune if she'd been able to think of one.

She was so abrim with false confidence, she almost peed her pants when David said, "Looks like a tornado hit the place.'' He held the curtain aside for her. "You know the drill. Don't touch anything.''

Blinking against the interior light and assuming he'd exaggerated the mess she'd made while inventorying, the wholesale wreckage brought a cry of anguish.

Her eyes skittered from plants ripped from their pots, to upended, emptied boxes, to slashed cushions and pillows, the cuts leaking tufts of foam and batting.

In the dining room, the china cabinet's shelves had been swept clean. Shards of broken dishes littered the carpet. The sideboard's drawers had been pulled out, dumped and pillaged.

Speechless, Hannah followed David down the hall, stepping over bed and bath linens jumbled like a barricade in front of the storage closet. The destruction seemed worse, more violating, in Kathleen's bedroom. The mattress and box spring had been dissected. Clothing, photographs and papers covered the carpet. The intruder had even slit the lining of every coat and jacket.

Tears welled in Hannah's eyes as she reached for a crumpled class photograph. David stayed her hand. "I don't expect we'll find much to go on, but leave things be for now."

She looked up at him. "Why would anyone do something so—so *vicious?*"

"It isn't vandalism, sugar. At least, property destruction wasn't the prime objective. Whoever you surprised in the act was searching for something."

Hannah turned on a heel to hide her reaction. What awaited her when she got home? Nothing like this, she reasoned. Ransacking on such a grand scale took hours.

"You're holding out on me again," David said.

"I am not, and I'm damned tired of you accusing me of it."

He nudged her around to face him. "What you're tired of is me knowing you too well, too fast. Your deflector shield doesn't work where I'm concerned, and it bugs you."

The laser glare she aimed at his shirt placket should have vaporized the fabric and any essential anatomical components in its vicinity.

He slipped a finger under her chin. "Hard as it is to separate the professional from the personal with you, Sheriff Hendrickson expects answers to his questions."

"Oh, does he now?"

"Yes, ma'am. He does."

"All right, then, *Sheriff*." She stepped back and tossed her head. "I think my cottage was searched while I was here today. Not vandalized—just the opposite. Laugh if you want, but if I hadn't found a pair of panty hose where they didn't belong, I'd never have noticed."

David made notes. "You didn't report it."

"No."

"What's your excuse this time?"

"Whoever did it wore gloves. I haven't dusted since I moved in, and the marks on the furniture were too clean for bare hands to make."

"Forcible entry?"

"No." She rolled her eyes, irritated by the curt, Sergeant Friday routine. "How about here?"

"Looks like he wedged a chisel or a crowbar into the sliding glass door's frame and popped the lock."

"But I put the security bar down before I left."

"Yeah, well, it's about as flimsy as your excuse for not reporting another B and E."

Footsteps scraped across the porch. Seconds later, a tenor voice called out from the entry. David responded, then said to Hannah, "C'mon. Time to take you home."

"Follow me home, you mean."

"Whatever."

Deputy Bill Eustace, a pudgy, bespectacled veteran, was likely nicknamed "Pop" whether he answered to it or not. Josh Phelps, a sandy-haired detective with a Wyatt Earp mustache that neither aged nor complemented his roundish face held out Hannah's key ring.

"The old guy outside said these were yours." Phelps

grinned. "I wish they fit that Edsel. Sweetest set of wheels I've seen in a while."

David briefed his men, then told them he'd be back in a few minutes.

"No rush, Sheriff," Eustace said and winked.

Hannah kept her mouth firmly shut, even when David opened the Blazer's door for her.

"When we get there, I'm doing a walk-through," he stated.

She nodded, at once relieved and annoyed by his guardianship. Pulling away from the curb, she steered with one hand and folded the incriminating fax into thirds with the other. Before stowing it in her purse, she mined the purse's depths for a barrel-shaped bottle of aspirin.

Without taking her eyes off the road, she thumbed the lid, extricated three tablets and swallowed them. Great-aunt Lurleen, for whom prescriptions and over-the-counter medications comprised a fifth food group, had taught Hannah well.

Like toilet training by moon phases and planting lettuce on Valentine's Day, Lurleen Garvey's wives'-tale wisdom said corn syrup as a pill propellant must cease before a child's sixth birthday. Using Red Hots as teaching aids was effective due to the incendiary scald cinnamon pellets have on tender throat tissue if allowed to lodge there until they dissolve.

The lessons kiboshed Hannah's love of cinnamon-flavored candy, gum and oil-dipped toothpicks, but she sincerely believed she could gulp down an English walnut, whole.

Her downhill approach to the cottage found it shining as brightly as a UFO in a soybean field. In her heart of hearts, Hannah was grateful for the candy-apple red, chrome-intensive pickup hovering behind her like a caboose.

The garage door yawned open. The Blazer's headlights assisted the ceiling fixture in confirming no boogeymen lurked in the wings.

David met her at the deck steps and held out a hand for her keys. His cop face was still firmly affixed. Hannah was glad—mostly.

He examined the dead bolt above the knob before inserting the key. "No scratches."

"I know. I checked."

"How many keys are floating around?"

Hannah bit her lip. "Five, maybe six. I don't know how IdaClare latched on to a dupe to fit the new locks Maintenance installed last week, but she doesn't take no for an answer, either."

"Fancy that." David strode into the utility room, head swiveling, left arm ramrodded behind him, commanding her not to tailgate. Beneath the hem of his jacket, his holster's security strap dangled free.

Anxiety washed over her like a chill. Guns scared her. His readiness to use one scared her more. She wondered if he'd ever shot anyone in the line of duty.

They entered the kitchen, then the breakfast room. Hannah matched David step for step, like Robin following Batman into the Penguin's hideout. The cottage was quiet but for the clock in the kitchen, the beat of its second hand not quite keeping time with her heart.

She almost swallowed her tongue when David howled, "What the *hell* is that?"

"What's what? Where?"

Laughing, he pointed at the notepaper sticking out between the French doors' seam.

"I—uh, well— Where the heck did that come from?"

Between chortles, he said, "I suspect there was one in the back door, and—" he leaned back "—yep, the front's hog-tight and goose-proof, too."

Heat flumed upward to her hairline. "Okay, so what was I supposed to do? Waltz in and hope the intruder was too tired from tossing the joint this **aft**ernoon to make a return trip?"

Grinning like the idiot he was, he pressed his fingertips above the bridge of his nose. "Swami see chairs jammed under doorknobs. Tin cans stacked in front of them like the Great Pyramids of Egypt."

She seriously considered clouting him with her purse.

"It's just a minor technicality, Miz Garvey, but if you'll notice, the deck doors swing *out,* not in."

"I hate you, Hendrickson."

She must have looked like she meant it. He sobered so fast, the appearance of a KA-POW balloon above his head would have been redundant.

"For Christ's sweet sake, woman. You and the Hardy Boys' great-grampa are about to drive me nuts. We haven't even discussed you reconnoitering the Osborn house all by your lonesome *because you thought somebody had broken in.*"

Her keys and purse clunked on the pub table. Right again, damn him for living. She blew out a disgusted sigh. "Okay, so we've established my antennae doesn't pick up all the channels sometimes. Satisfied?"

"Hold that thought," he said, "while I finish poking around."

Hannah waved a dismissal, envisioning a burglar cowering in the closet having overheard David's megaphonic reproach. If the intruder had any sense, he'd grab the sheriff's gun and shoot himself.

"You were right about no prints," he said, breezing through from the bedroom en route to the living room, "and the dust."

Boots drummed the hardwood floor, the dirge interrupted by pauses, becoming louder as he backtracked. Hannah sent up silent regards to Dr. Felix Hoffman for recognizing aspirin's pain-relieving qualities and steeled herself for the inevitable lecture.

David strode into the breakfast room, said, "I'm sorry I hollered at you," then took her by the hand and led her to the couch where he seated her on his left, in deference to the weaponry on his opposite hip.

"Look at me," he said.

Cocking back her head for a sidelong perspective incurred the wrath of sore neck muscles and tendons. She grudgingly wriggled around to face him.

The cop expression was still present, contradicted by the large, warm hand resting atop her cold one. "When dispatch transmitted that assault call, I knew Bisbee had phoned it in, you were the victim, and the location. That's all. It was my job as responding officer to find out whether you'd been shot, stabbed...whether you were dead or alive.

"Finding your truck with the door hanging open added rape to the possibles. That's how cops think, Hannah. Always prepare for the worst. In that regard, a victim's identity, or the lack of it, doesn't matter."

David hesitated. His brows peaked. "Seeing you sprawled on the ground like a broken doll... Well, that mattered a helluva lot. It's something I don't ever want to see again."

Hannah felt an inch tall, precious, defensive and

ashamed all at the same time. The negatives could be dealt with easily enough. Suppressing the need to be held, to hold, to let herself care and be cared for above and beyond friendship was like bailing the *Titanic* with a ladle.

David leaned nearer. Lightning shot through her, tingling, humming, throbbing at its flashpoint. Her lips parted. Mmm, just one more kiss, then I'll tell him he's a great guy, but—

She pulled back from his embrace. Control had waged an inner battle with desire...and won.

"I'm moving too fast, aren't I?"

A nervous chuckle arose at the idea of consenting adults brushing lips once, and a single, sabotaged, toe-curling, holy-Moses kiss fitting anyone's definition of lechery. "No, it's the moving that's the problem, David."

He froze, then sat back, stunned. "Are you trying to tell me the attraction isn't mutual?"

The man possessed the discomfiting ability to monitor her pulse rate from across a room. Corny, and patently non-nineties though it might be, she also respected him too much to lie to him.

"The attraction is mutual. A 'damn the torpedoes, full speed ahead' attitude is not."

He studied her for a long, pensive moment. "Why." His tone posed a challenge, not a question.

"We're too different."

"Nope. Try again."

"I don't want to be hurt again. Ever."

"Now, that's unique. Most couples enter a relationship aching to have their guts torn out and stomped in the mud."

Hannah favored him with a wry look. "Smart-ass."

"Got any real bullets in your cylinder? Or are you fixing to wave the white hankie?"

"Don't, David."

"Don't *what?* Pester you until you say out loud what the voice of doom nags you about from dawn to dark?"

He laughed bitterly. "Do you think you're the only one who's conjured a dozen reasons to back off? To have sworn fifty times to abide by the Life Is Good, Don't Complicate It plan? Congratulated yourself for being so ding-damned wise, then caught yourself daydreaming?"

Hannah smiled, identifying with what he said, and charmed again by his open-floodgate style of expressing it.

"Okay, I get carried away hearing myself talk," he admitted, "but I'm not leaving until you tell me what's so blessed wrong with damning those torpedoes."

"Fine. Great. Take what little ego I have left and do a slice 'n dice on it. Will that make you happy?"

Flinching at her snide tone, he stammered random interjections and pronouns.

"How old are you, David?"

"Huh?" From an advertising perspective, the contortions his features underwent could launch a thousand antacid commercials. "I'll be thirty-seven in October—the eleventh. Why?"

Only the supremely secure and males in general projected their age, rather than mumble the actual number, or a lesser one. The gap wasn't as huge as she'd guessed, but she had been fully literate, permitted to cross the street alone and well into the first quarter of second grade before he'd left the womb.

"Don't you see?" she asked. "I'm too— You're too— It's like this. I saw the Kennedy assassination on

TV an hour after it happened. You read about it in a textbook. Ditto Martin Luther King, Apollo 13, Vietnam...I'll bet you've never even *heard* of Jim Croce, for crying out loud.''

David shook his head. ''I've not only heard of him, I own every album he ever made.''

''Yeah, well, you're a history buff. High-five.''

''Aw, c'mon, Hannah. So what if you're—if *I'm* a couple of years younger? You sure don't look—'' he groaned. ''Oops.''

''Oops? I feel a compliment on the wind, and you say oops?''

''Oh no you don't. I came an inch from painting myself into a corner and I'm dang-sure not going to let you shove me back into it.''

''Excuse me?''

His unfettered hand chafed his jaw. ''I was about to say you don't look your age, which would be a compliment if you'd take it as one, but you won't. Being female, you'll twist it around to mean I'd have run like a striped jackrabbit if you *looked* forty-three, but since you can 'pass' for a younger woman, what the hey. Might as well hang around until you start having hot flashes, or something.''

Hannah laughed until tears drenched her lashes. ''You are amazing, Hendrickson. Half chauvinist pig and half Prince of Enlightenment.''

That killer, crooked grin crawled across his face. '''Fess up, sugar. The way you figured it, all I wanted was to get laid.''

''David!''

''Because that simplifies things. My wanting to be with you because you're smart and funny and sassy and the sexiest woman I've ever met muddies water you're too chicken to wade.''

His soft, full lips descended on hers, gentle, hungry and sweet. He kissed her possessively, daring her to deny the passion roaring through her.

She curled her arms around his neck, lips parting, tongue exploring, demanding, dancing with his, her fingers sliding through his hair, then grasping, as if to anchor herself against a swirling pool of desire.

David eased away, leaving her gasping, her eyes hooded and lead-weighted. ''I don't know about you, sugar, but it ain't the voice of doom I'm hearing right now.''

He stood, adjusted his belt and holster.

''I'll lock up as I leave,'' he said, ''but someday, when the time is right for both of us, I'm gonna lock up and stay.''

14

Hannah drew a ten-gallon hat on another stickman doodle. The model for her creation kept trying to sneak into her thoughts, but she banished him, as business must come before pleasure—real or erotically imagined.

Instead, she absently wondered if Michelangelo would have finished the Sistine Chapel had telephones with hold buttons been around in his day. It would have also been a pain climbing up and down the scaffolding to answer one, which might explain why most of the great paintings were done before Alexander Graham Bell got inventive.

The Beatrice, Nebraska, superintendent of schools secretary had twice inquired whether Hannah was still holding, a faux courtesy to encourage the holdee to give up and leave a voice-mail message as originally suggested.

While at Friedlich & Friedlich, Hannah had conducted a private survey of how many incoming and outgoing electronic messages netted return calls. Finding eighty-two-point-three percent were ignored showed voice-mail for what it truly was: a high-tech smoke signal.

The ear not being cauliflowered by the receiver monitored the fax machine on the credenza behind her. Mr.

Smythe, the *Kansas City Star*'s archivist, had received her information request at 8:03. It was now 8:25. What part of "urgent" did he not understand?

Hannah added an enormous, phallic holster to her stickman's accoutrements. If Bob Davies was trying to reach her, which she doubted, his efforts had been rewarded by a busy signal for the past twenty-two minutes.

Earlier, a lengthy hum before the beep denoted the maintenance department answering machine's typical Monday-morning crush. Her message consisted of a call-back request. Whether paranoid or smart, ignorance of a killer on one departmental payroll, plus an unknown entity breaking and entering with abandon, fostered a general distrust.

"Grigsby Shrader."

The pencil lead snapped. Hannah bolted upright, startled by the authoritative voice ricocheting off her torpid eardrum. She introduced herself, then as gently as possible, imparted the news of Kathleen Osborn's death.

Sorrow was evident in Shrader's tone. "I was one of her students, more years ago than either of us would have admitted, and she taught two of my children, as well."

His prolonged sigh intimated a hand being positioned to cradle his brow. "I knew Kathleen was ill, of course, though she wouldn't confide any specifics."

Hannah didn't correct the assumption Kathleen had died of more or less natural causes. Why add horror to grief? "She was an extremely private person. I don't even know why she elected to move here, after living in Beatrice more than half her life."

"It surprised me as well," Shrader admitted. "Then

completely out of the blue, when I was driving her home from her retirement dinner, she said she'd been born and raised near Valhalla Springs. Going back was a sort of homecoming.''

"Did she still have relatives in the area?"

"None she laid claim to," he answered with a slight chuckle. "Again, Kathleen didn't say as much, but I guessed no chance of a reunion was a large part of the attraction."

Shrader promised to overnight-mail copies of Kathleen's employment file, and didn't question why a personal representative needed them to settle an estate. In return, Hannah said she would send the school photographs she'd found, and notify him of funeral arrangements once they were finalized.

Bob Davies didn't take advantage of her availability during a bathroom break, so she had no qualms about tying up the line again with a call to Duckworth's Funeral Home.

LaVeda Duckworth, the disconcertingly cheerful woman who answered with the mortuary's name and We're Here When You Need Us slogan, said her son, Junior, had two funerals and a visitation scheduled for the day, but she would tell him Hannah had called.

"In the meantime, if you could bring the clothes Miss Osborn would like to wear for her service, we can finish preparing her for viewing."

Hannah said, "It's my understanding she wanted to be cremated."

"Junior didn't mention the particulars, but surely her friends and family expect a memorial service of some kind. I wasn't acquainted with her, but she looks like such a nice person. A handsome woman, if you don't mind my saying so. I can just picture her in aqua, or soft lavender.''

Hannah recoiled at the dulcet, present-tense references, spoken as if Mrs. Duckworth traded fashion tips with a genuinely captive audience.

The memory of Great-uncle Mort reposed in a horse-head-print shirt, bolo tie and the Sunday-best overalls he'd reserved for special occasions such as weddings, other people's funerals and hardware-store grand openings progressed to the hideous, cabbage, rose-print dress Great-aunt Lurleen's Sunday-school class chose because God was certain to recognize it, and on to Mark Malone, F&F's comptroller, who looked so life-like in his starched white shirt, black suit and striped tie, Hannah felt as though she were being groped from the Great Beyond.

A burgundy wool suit and cream silk shirt with a lace-trimmed jabot shimmered behind her eyes. She'd bought the outfit—the classiest, most expensive one Caroline Garvey ever had—with the help of Delores Kirksey, a salesclerk at Effindale's Chic Boutique. Delores wrote up the transaction as a layaway, trusting Hannah to make the ten-dollar monthly payments on garments never to be seen again in this life.

Neither fine clothes, a wig, nor a mortician's skilled application of putty and cosmetics disguised the ravages disease, hard living and a hand-to-mouth existence had wrought on Caroline Angeline Garvey. All Hannah saw was her mother laughing at a bawdy joke, sunlight glinting off her long, auburn hair, and the dark, soulful eyes that always held love, even when clouded by anger, self-loathing or shame.

LaVeda Duckworth's patter wended from the earpiece. ''We have a second entrance marked Employees

Only if you happen by when a service is under way. Just ring the buzzer, and someone will answer."

As Hannah hung up the phone, she added another reason to track down Delbert. She'd rely on his judgment whether Kathleen would approve of a formal memorial service.

Crunching noises alerted her to a car rolling to a stop in the driveway. She skirted the railing, then grabbed the saucepan with teaspoons angled around its rim resting against the bottom of the door. Shoving the jerry-rigged burglar alarm in the rocker, under her mother's afghan, she beat Willard Johnson's knock by a nanosecond.

Dressed in navy parachute pants, a white T-shirt and zippered warm-up jacket, he looked like a physical fitness instructor straight out of central casting.

Hannah stepped out on the porch. Her eyes slid from Willard's hands to the muscled forearms and biceps outlined by the silky fabric. Had they caged her neck like a stanchion last night? Was a paycheck a secondary motivation for working at Valhalla Springs? Was she on the verge of taping aluminum foil over the cottage's windows to deflect particle beams?

"I'm running a little late," he said, holding out the folder she'd given him the previous Friday. "A wreck on the highway had traffic backed up."

"Late? The first class doesn't start for a half hour."

"I want to go over the aerobics routines again. Check equipment. Do some warm-ups." He spoke and gestured like a videotaped commercial's pitchman on fast-forward. "You know, loosen up, before people start coming in."

"As in, burn off some of that nervous energy?"

"Right on. The whites of my eyes are easy enough

to see as it is." He glanced over his shoulder, adding, "And it seems some tenants aren't as happy about your hiring me as we thought."

"Oh?" Her hands clenched behind her back. "What makes you say that?"

A wicked grin broke across his face. "Well, Sanity isn't very big, but there's a dozen Johnsons in the book, a third of them relatives. The phone in my apartment is an extension of my folks' number—" his grin widened "—listed as 'Johnson, Xavier P.'

"Whoever tried to scare the NAACP out of me Saturday night must have started with my cousin Ardel and talked trash to every Johnson in town. By the time they hit Xavier, Pop could tell their heart just wasn't in it."

Hannah forced a smile. "Sounds like you picked a good night to let him field the phone calls. Probably last night, too. Beautiful evening for a drive, wasn't it?"

Willard squinted and cocked his head as if listening for an echo. "I didn't leave my apartment except to gas up Mom's car for church, like I do every Saturday. I spent the whole weekend fighting the Brasniaks for control of the planet Fleer."

As alibis went, she couldn't fault its originality. "I, uh, guess that would keep a guy pretty well occupied, all right."

He grumbled, "If my books stayed on the stands as long as it took me to write them, I wouldn't need a day job."

Still ruminating his more bizarre remark, it took a moment to relate galactic warfare to his sci-fi novels.

His brow corduroyed. "I do have a day job, don't I?"

"Of course you do." She waved at a vehicular convoy passing by, all with right-turn signals blinking their directional intentions well in advance. One or two might even turn that way after reaching the gate.

"Then why do I have the feeling you're playing cat to my mouse?" Willard asked.

Because my interrogation technique is pathetic, she thought, but if you can't bedazzle 'em with brilliance, baffle 'em with bullshit.

"I have a thousand things on my mind, Willard. I'll try and drop by the community center later, and see how things are going."

Backpedaling, palms aloft, he said, "Okay, okay. You wanted the paperwork, you've got it. Sorry I bothered you."

Blue sky and mare's-tail clouds reflected in his car's window shuddered when he slammed the door. He started the engine, then paused before shifting from park, as if to transfer his grip on the steering wheel to his temper.

A foul taste invaded Hannah's mouth. Could Willard be the assailant? She was pretty sure he was too burly, too barrel-chested, too easy a circumstantial target. If only she could be sure...

Thirty minutes later, she whisked from the bedroom, determined to whittle her "To do" list to sticky-note size before noon. Peering over the room divider at the fax machine's empty bale dashed hopes patterned after the "A watched pot never boils" adage.

A *bang-bangety-bang* on the screen door sent her heart lurching into her throat. She crept through the living room, stuffing her key ring into her jeans pocket to muffle the jangle.

The minivan in the drive did nothing to help identify

who was using her door for soccer practice. Nor did reading This End Up through the clear glass portions of the door's oval insert.

She wasn't expecting any deliveries, she thought as her fingers closed around the doorknob. At the same time she was calling herself a fraidy cat, she pondered the wisdom in opening the door to a stranger she couldn't see.

His arms trembled from strain. The boxes weren't that heavy, but it was awkward holding them high enough to hide behind.

He shifted his weight and reared back a leg to give the screen another kick. The clack of a retracting dead bolt stopped his foot.

"Yes?"

Chin tucked to deepen his voice, he rasped, "Special delivery for Hannah Garvey."

"I'm Hannah Garvey," came the reply, though she didn't sound entirely certain of it.

"Where ya want I should put it, lady?"

Silence, then, "Anywhere you'd like, me boyo. After all, you own the joint."

Crushed as a six-year-old with a bowl of floating goldfish, Jack Clancy craned his neck around the cardboard barricade. "How did you know it was me?"

"Elementary, Watson." She stiff-armed the screen, flattening herself against the jamb. "Delivery guys don't wear four-hundred-dollar, custom-made, Italian loafers."

Jack squeezed past her and set the cartons on the floor alongside the office railing. Plucking at the voluminous khaki coveralls with "Arnold" on a patch above the pocket, he grumbled, "I went to a lot of trouble to borrow this monkey suit, and all you notice is my shoes.''

"Sorry if I spoiled your surprise." She snickered. "But do tell Mr. Schwarzenegger hello for me when you return his outfit."

"Okay, that's it." He slapped the sides of the topmost box. "I'm taking this computer to someone who'll appreciate it."

"Your mother already has one and all she drinks is decaf. I, on the other hand, can have a fresh pot of high-octane Colombian brewed in about two minutes flat."

"You've chugged a whole pot?" He consulted his watch, a platinum disc with numerals the middle-aged could read only after undergoing laser keratotomy. "Already?"

She shot him a scathing look. "It's Monday. I've been here a week, and you can count my accomplishments on your thumbs. Chances are, I'll speak fluent Spanish by this afternoon. *Comprendar, usted?*"

Jack backed off, literally and figuratively. "*Con su permiso,* I'll finish unloading the van."

"There's more?"

"Sí, señorita."

"Knock it off, Clancy."

"Hokay, but never let it be said I skimp on perks for my employees. I even popped for a flatbed scanner so you won't have to retype all the files."

"You wouldn't know a flatbed scanner if it bit you on the butt."

"Neither would you, but that's beside the point."

Her lips curved into a pensive smile. "Want to know the best thing about all these new toys? Besides you, whom I've adored from afar lo these many years, delivering them?''

The affection was mutual, rarely expressed and only acted upon once. In the process of accepting that the love of Jarrod Amberley's life was Jarrod Amberley, Hannah had received notification of Valhalla Springs's kickoff campaign's nomination for a CLEO—the advertising industry's equivalent of an Oscar.

Amberley couldn't attend the ceremony due to an estate auction in Frankfurt, Germany. Hannah had masked her disappointment with stoicism. Jack had alternated between thanking God for small favors and hoping a four-ton, Baroque cabinet fell on the jug-eared son of a bitch.

He'd always thought Hannah an attractive woman. Attired in a strapless, formfitting, midnight-blue velvet gown and matching long, matte-satin gloves, she was breathtaking the evening of the awards ceremony. An antique cameo pinned to a wide, ribbon choker showcased her elegant neck, her hair brushed her bare shoulders in soft, shiny waves, and she hadn't troweled on the makeup as some did for a special occasion.

When he recovered his voice, he'd told her she looked like a goddess. She'd blushed, complimented his tuxedo, socked him in the arm and twanged, ''I s'pose we clean up right good for a farm boy and a trailer-park princess.''

Miss Manners would have fainted. Jack understood, as only a by-the-bootstraps wheeler-dealer whose intestines kinked at tables laid with finger bowls, crystal and excess silverware could.

Throughout the ceremony, they'd whispered and laughed like high-school kids at the prom. A hot, new Los Angeles agency winning the award fazed neither of them; the outcome was as predictable as the emcee's jokes. When the interminable presentations ended, they'd repaired to Jack's hotel suite for a nightcap, both reluctant for the evening to end.

A tentative kiss escalated to a dreamlike shedding to bare skin…and the eventual, heartbreaking realization that love can't conquer all, not even for one night.

Forcing that magical, painful memory to the back of his mind where it belonged, Jack said, "Okay, so what *is* the best thing about your new toys?"

Hannah ran her fingers through her hair, as she always did when pondering, worried or slightly timorous. "I don't think even Generous Jack Clancy would throw in top-of-the-line computer components as part of a severance package."

His jaw dropped. "Are you serious?"

She hitched a shoulder.

"Lord above, Hannah, what kind of a jerk do you think I am?"

"Connecting my arrival to all hell breaking loose does not a jerk make. Factor in a dearth of prospective tenants beating paths to my door—springtime, and a roaring economy notwithstanding—and what do you get?"

"Hemorrhoids." He chuckled. "Which is what Valhalla Springs has been since I took leave of my senses and built it."

"Don't try snookering me. I heard the pitter-patter of little ulcers gnawing away when you called Saturday."

"That's right, sweetpea, and you recognized the gurgle because you've heard it eight million times. The difference is, you were on the outside looking in until last week."

"Maybe..."

"Look, we'll discuss your self-esteem problem after you go make like Mrs. Olsen. I have to be in Kansas City for a meeting by two."

By the time Jack emptied the rented van's cargo bay, a rich, mellow aroma was crooking an invisible, tantalizing finger under his nose. He shucked the coveralls, glanced around, then tossed them over a club chair.

A tug at his charcoal suit jacket, minor adjustment to his powder-blue silk tie, and smoothing his rapidly silvering hair brought a laugh from the vicinity of the kitchen.

"Delivery dude with great shoes to *Gentleman's Quarterly* cover hunk in the blink of an eye," Hannah teased.

"More like a Rotary Club life member, which I hate, and you know it." He gestured at the pillow and rumpled blanket on the couch. "What did you do? Lose an argument with yourself last night?"

Another shrug, and a flounce into the breakfast room. "I fell asleep reading a book."

Sure you did, Jack thought, seating himself at the pub table. Never let 'em see you sweat. He couldn't remember whether Tom or Rob Friedlich had nicknamed her "Balls to the Walls" Garvey. It fit the image she projected, not the genuine article.

"I like what you've done to the place," he said.

An eyebrow arced as she scanned the breakfast room. "I haven't done anything to it, besides move in."

"Exactly." He took a sip of coffee. "No thematic urges tells me you must be content, as is. I wasn't sure I'd live to see the day."

"In some ways, I am, I guess." Her fingertips twirled strands of the place mat's fringe. "Did you, um, stop by your mother's, or is this visit a secret?"

"I lucked into a hen party in progress. A little chit, a little chat, the usual yes-no-yes, then I flew the coop."

"Come again?"

"Yes, Mother, I work too hard. No, Mother, I can't do lunch. Yes, Mother, I will drive carefully, and call when I'm back in Saint Louis."

He ripped open a sweetener packet. "As for what you're really asking, Hannah, dear, yes, Mother brought me up to date on current events, including the attack on you last night."

"Attack is a bit strong for what happened," she corrected. "And don't bother lecturing me on being dumb. All I intended to do was snoop outside, then run for the nearest phone. The vandal caught me in the act, instead of the other way around."

She broke eye contact. "I'm obsessed with the why behind Kathleen Osborn's murder, Jack. Truth is, I've spent a lot more time trying to decipher the riddle than I have being operations manager."

"I knew it the second I drove through," he said. "Rack and ruin from one end to the other. Total devastation."

She smiled, sort of. "Well, you aren't paying me to skulk through the bushes at midnight."

"Come to think of it…" He slapped the tabletop. "Okay, Garvey, you're fired."

"You are such a doofus," she said, laughing.

"Uh-uh, sweetpea, that would be you. The one with the best job security in the world in her back pocket."

"Meaning?"

"IdaClare Belinda Clancy, the real ruler of this roost, thinks you're the greatest thing since waterproof mascara." He pointed an accusing finger at her. "Being nice to my mother wasn't enough, was it? Oh, no, you just had to tell her you *like* that pink monstrosity she lives in, didn't you?"

Hannah laughed until her breath came in wheezes. "What I said was that I'd never seen anything quite like it."

"The State Department should have such diplomats."

Jack topped off his cup from the thermal carafe; a last dose of caffeine for the road he'd regret drinking about midway to Kansas City.

The mantel clock chimed ten bells. He ought to get moving. A motor home waddling along the two-lane between here and I–70 could eat an hour's drive-time. As sure as it did, tractor-trailers would choke the interstate like a buffalo herd on wheels.

A crease formed above the bridge of Hannah's nose. She recrossed her legs as if bracing herself. "Since you've dinked around for almost an hour, isn't it time you told me why you did the delivery-guy thing? It isn't like you to blow a whole day driving from one side of Missouri to the other and back."

"Lambert International was socked in by fog this morning," he hedged. "Delays, cancellations, reroutes out the wazoo. I'll take a detour to see you over flying from Saint Louis to Kansas City via Atlanta, Dallas and Vancouver."

"Uh-huh."

Slowly, he slid the place mat out of the way and folded his arms on the table. "Okay, Karnak the Magnificent, it's like this: I'm hearing grandma noises again, and guess who Mother has chosen to bear my children.''

"Oh, Lord." Hannah rested her head between thumb and index finger as if stricken by an instant migraine. "What an historic moment for the Garvey gene pool—a first, actually."

"That's why her approval of you and your sheriff swings from pro to con, depending on how interested you seem to be."

"Hendrickson is not my sheriff. He belongs to the county. And to think I thought the dirty looks IdaClare hurled sometimes was because of our age difference."

"How much age difference?"

"Some."

"Two, three years?"

Her tongue capped an incisor, then retreated. "Seven."

"It's only a number, sweetpea. No hill for a climber, unless you let it be."

"Tell that to someone who didn't spend two and a half decades in the Youth Rules business. C'mon, Jack, you know as well as I do, a decrepit old fart squiring a debutante equals Venus-envy. A crone with her boy-toy is pitiful."

"Want to know the real definition of pitiful?" Anger edged his tone. "Anyone who puts other people's opinions above how they feel."

"Nice platitude, but I don't know how I feel. I like David, when I'm not tempted to knock him into the middle of next week. He makes me laugh, he makes me think—"

Jack grinned. "I saw the tablet on your desk."

"Okay, so, he makes me horny. Big deal."

"Apparently, it is."

She squeaked like a mouse with its tail in a trap. "If you ever tell a soul, I'll—I'll—"

"Temper, temper. Your secrets are as safe with me as mine are with you. Always have been, always will be."

She slumped back in her chair, glowering and smiling simultaneously as only she could do. "How did the topic under discussion derail to my track, anyway?"

Jack shrugged. "Easier to hassle you than talk about my situation."

"Does IdaClare know about, uh—"

"No, and she never will." Jack's palm tapped his elbow. "I'm not ashamed of it, and right or wrong, I can't say I regret it, other than the hurt it caused you." He chuffed. "Who am I kidding? The hurt it caused us both."

Their long-ago romantic interlude marked his last attempt at denying his homosexuality. Every gay man he'd ever known had tried more than once to be what society considered normal. Some married and fathered children, but eventually, the truth will out, just as it had the night he and Hannah tried—and failed—to make love.

Now, as then, her beautiful brown eyes mirrored a whisper of sadness, but no remorse. "For one fabulous, wondrous evening, I was Cinderella and you were my Prince Charming. As it turned out, the shoe didn't fit. So be it. What we have is more precious to me than what might have been."

"Same here," he said, forcing the words past the lump in his throat.

A lesser woman would have cursed him, ridiculed him, salvaged her ego by destroying his. Hannah had called him the next morning from her room to remind him he'd promised to take her to the zoo and buy her all the cotton candy and hot dogs she could eat. "Shower, shave and hit the lobby in fifteen minutes," she'd threatened, "or I'll sue for breach of contract."

Jack smiled at the memory. "My mother humming the go-forth-and-multiply song again is your fault. If you weren't so terrific, I could keep changing the subject when she blubbers about her friends waving their pictures of new grandbabies and all she has to show are Itsy's and Bitsy's."

"Itsy and whatsy?"

"Mother's teacup poodles. The apricot, nappy-yappy Fur Wads from Hell."

"I didn't see any dogs when I was over there yesterday."

"They were probably in their room," Jack sneered. "I bought them for her the last time she had delusions of grandmotherhood. Now I'm shelling out forty bucks a month for cable so the mutts can watch the Animal Channel."

"Small price to pay, if it had worked."

"Except it didn't."

Hannah's finger traced her cup's handle. "I thought IdaClare accepted your relationship with Stephen years ago."

"Callous as this may sound, she accepted him as my life-partner very much like she accepted Dad's cancer. Intellectually, yes. Emotionally, no."

Jack sat back in the chair. "Hope can be as cruel as it is kind, you know."

"Sure it can. Being an only child doesn't help. There's no one to divvy up all the dreams and expectations." Her voice gentled. "Would you like me to talk to IdaClare? I'm probably kidding myself, but maybe I can help her understand.''

He shook his head. ''You've already given me what I needed most, babe. Steve and I are as close as two people can be, but—well, now and then, the handiest shoulder to lean on isn't always the best one.''

He stood and held out his arms. ''Gotta go, or I'll have to glue wings to that van to make my appointment.''

Hannah sprang into his embrace and delivered a rib-cracking hug.

''If you haven't figured it out yet,'' he said, rocking her back and forth, ''part of the reason I hired you was pure selfishness. I couldn't handle losing you while you were out finding yourself.''

''Where did you get that idea?'' She stepped back. ''Have you been listening to that radio shrink again?''

He kissed the tip of her nose. ''If I've told you once, I've told you a hundred times, Hannah Marie. You're as transparent as glass to anyone who cares about you enough to look.''

16

"Miz Bumgartner, you can't call 911 for every little thing that goes wrong," David lectured into the telephone receiver. "I know you're upset, but fishing an earring out of a toilet is a plumber's job, not ours."

"Do you have any *idea* what plumbers charge these days?" The Macedonia Free Will Full Gospel Church's organist didn't need brass pipes to be heard for a country mile. "Forty dollars for a service call, plus twenty-five dollars an hour, and nary a one of them has a hurry bone in his whole, *entire* body."

"Ma'am, that's not my—"

"Well, you *are* the sheriff, aren't you? If it isn't a crime to steal god-fearin' people *blind* at every turn..."

Claudina Burkholz waved from the doorway to attract David's attention; an unnecessary gesture, since her orange muumuu streaked with squiggly black lines made her look like a giant traffic cone that had been plunked too near an asphalt spreader.

Plump face aglow with amusement, she hugged herself, puckered as if kissing the air, then pointed at his telephone.

David glanced from his senior dispatcher to the flashing button and back again. Gracing Claudina with a "two can play that game" leer, he said, "Beg pardon for interrupting, Miz Bumgartner, but let me transfer you back to Claudina. She helped you last week when your refrigerator was making that funny noise.''

Grinning triumphantly, he jabbed the hold button. "Gotcha!"

Claudina's fists disappeared in the vicinity of her hips. "This is the thanks I get for covering for Heather? I clocked out five minutes ago, and I'm not talking to that old bat for free!"

David attempted to look past her at the reception desk. During regular courthouse hours, Heather Gray, County Commissioner Paul Gray's daughter, answered the phone, dotted *i*'s on messages with smiley faces and flashed her orthodontic smile at visitors.

Her ambitions centered on becoming Miss Missouri, then Miss America, marrying a board-certified plastic surgeon, bearing two children whose gender didn't matter as long as they were healthy, then winning the Mrs. Missouri competition—pageantry's illusive and as-yet-unrealized Triple Crown.

"Where did Heather run off to this time?" David asked.

"The ladies',"' Claudina shot back. "Medical emergency."

"Is she sick?"

"Worse. Chipped a nail on a file drawer."

David gazed morosely at the pulsing hold buttons. "All right, tell Hannah I'll call her back sometime next year."

"World's smallest violin," Claudina teased, her forefinger sawing the top of her thumb. "But, lucky for you, I'm a sucker for romance. Go for it."

"I owe you one, big time."

"You owe me billions."

David hesitated, suddenly unsure which line was

Beauty and which was the Beast. He held his breath and punched two. "Hannah?"

Snores reverberated in his ear. "Aw, c'mon, you weren't on hold that long."

"Long enough. I've spent all day waiting on someone or another."

He twirled a pen on his desk blotter. "Anyone I know?"

She capsulized her earlier conversation with the school superintendent. "Interesting, Kathleen didn't tell any of her friends she was born and raised near here. Not even Delbert."

"I suspect her family moved around," David said. "Her social security number was issued in southern Mississippi."

"Really? How did you find that out?"

"I knew when I saw the number. The first three digits indicate the state of issue and the next two the region within the state."

"I had no idea social security numbers were sort of a code," she said, as if he'd just translated the Rosetta stone. Strange, the things that impressed this woman.

In an obvious attempt to change the subject from a cleared case, he asked, "No aftereffects from last night's tussle? With the assailant, I mean."

She responded with a throaty chuckle. "Would you believe, I'd forgotten all about last night until you mentioned it?"

"Uh-huh. Well, seeing as how you're feisty as ever, and it'll be suppertime pretty soon, how about I pick up some steaks, then you, and give you a taste of my home cooking?"

Silence burrowed a hollow in his midsection.

"I'd love to, David, honestly, I would, but I can't

tonight. IdaClare and the troops are coming over later for a strategy session.''

"So? Why do you have to be there?"

She laughed. "This isn't a self-governing group. Someone has to referee and make sure they don't get too ambitious. Most of all, by the time Jack left this morning, and—''

"Jack who?"

"Clancy," she replied in a "Who else?" tone of voice. "He dropped off a new computer for me on his way to Kansas City, and we—''

"Valhalla Springs isn't on the way to anywhere, Hannah, much less Kansas City." David's teeth snapped together like barn doors shutting after the horse is gone.

"I don't appreciate being interrupted, Hendrickson."

"Sorry. You were saying?"

"And I dislike the hint of green-eyed monster I heard more than I dislike being interrupted."

David's chuckle sounded bogus even to him. "Darlin', if I were the jealous type, I'd have known my ex-wife was cleavin' unto another a long time before I did."

He looked up at the grimy, punched-tin ceiling. "That's twice in two seconds I've shot my mouth off when I shouldn't have. Honest, I don't usually snipe at people I don't know, or at Cynthia. Leastwise, not out loud."

"I think maybe that's why God created Mondays," Hannah said. "An equal sin-and-repent opportunity."

"A poor excuse, but if it gets me off the hook, I'll take it. Now, go on. Tell me about Jack, the computer and what that has to do with turning down the best steak you've ever stuck a fork in."

She moaned. "The piña colada cake Rosemary is baking for the meeting pales in comparison," she admitted, then commenced rehashing her day.

The hen party Jack had crashed was a rallying of the development's garden club members. The ten who answered IdaClare's S.O.S. descended on Kathleen Osborn's cottage to clean, repot houseplants, rebox housegoods and complete the inventory, noting every item the intruder had damaged beyond repair.

"I was flabbergasted," Hannah said. "Still am. What those women did in three hours would have taken me three days. On top of that, I'd asked IdaClare about moving Kathleen's plants to my front porch, so tenants could—well, adopt them, like puppies from the humane society."

David marveled at her ingenuity. No wonder Delbert admired Hannah so much. In many ways, they were two peas in a pod.

"Maintenance couldn't spare anyone," she went on, "so IdaClare put Delbert in charge of a golf-cart wagon train." She laughed. "I'd give anything to have seen him and his buddies putt-putting along like a miniature Rose Bowl parade."

"You mean they pulled off the whole shebang without you even knowing about it?"

"They sure did. After Jack left, I cooled my heels in Bob Davies's office—who'd been sworn to secrecy—for over an hour waiting to talk to him about repairs to Kathleen's cottage and my new locks. By the time I got to Kathleen's, the place was spic-and-span, and empty of all life-forms."

David smiled at the image of a lolly-eyed Hannah wandering from room to room. "Which is why taking a powder tonight would make you feel like an ungrateful louse.''

''Bingo. And, to be completely honest, I'm also baby-sitting my fax machine.''

''Uh-huh.'' David knew he needn't ask why. The woman was fawnching to tell him.

After confirming he'd heard about Kathleen Osborn's supposed movie stardom, she told him her hunch the story was a cover for Kathleen's knowledge of, or involvement in, a real bank robbery.

A cinematic archive had seconded Hannah's movie-buff friend's opinion no film of that title existed, as had a quick Internet search, courtesy of her new, modem-equipped computer.

Before he left, Jack Clancy promised to use his friendship with the *Kansas City Star*'s editor-in-chief to speed up the response to Hannah's information request. No results yet, but, ''Jack has never failed me yet.''

David muttered, ''Like they say, it isn't what you know, it's who you know.''

''Bingo, again.''

''Yeah, well… Look, I'm not trying to put a damper on things, but have you given any thought to what happens if your hunch proves right?''

A moment passed. ''If that's a loaded question, which, coming from you, it must be, I'm not sure how to answer.''

David shifted in his chair. ''Just hear me out, okay? There's enough forensic evidence to confirm Barton killed Osborn to clear her case file. Now, I realize you've never accepted a botched robbery as Barton's motive, but whether it was or not, Miz Osborn is dead. If digging into her past brings up skeletons she spent her life burying, what good will it do you, her or anyone else?"

He mustered on, despite an ominous silence at the other end of the line. "I know the thrill of the chase— the rush when puzzle pieces begin to fit. Trouble is, the harder you concentrate on the puzzle, the easier it is to forget the *person* you're tearing apart and putting back together again."

Curling the receiver away from his mouth—which might have his foot, clean up to the knee, stuck in it— David pulled in a deep breath and let it out, taking heart in the fact she hadn't told him to go fly a kite in a thunderstorm. Or worse.

"In a way," she said, "I wish we'd had this conversation yesterday. But damn me for a grave robber, I still want to know."

David chuckled, as much with relief as at the distress in her voice. "Surprise, surprise. Question is, are you going to tell me what you find out?"

She laughed. "Absolutely."

"One other thing before somebody reminds me I'm the sheriff. About this steak dinner we aren't having tonight— Under special circumstances, I do give rain checks. Real short expiration dates on them, though."

"Same menu?"

"Yep."

"Tomorrow? Barring unforeseen circumstances either here or there."

"It's a date." He grinned. "Only, to make up for tonight, how about sticking back a piece of piña colada cake for me?"

"I may have to arm-wrestle Leo for it, but I think I can take him."

* * *

A sharp north wind buffeted David's sport coat as he descended the courthouse's steps. KJPP's Ken-doll weatherman had predicted temperatures would drop to the low fifties with intermittent showers tomorrow, possibly continuing into Wednesday.

Buttoning his coat as he walked, David wondered if meteorologists more accurately foretold crappy weather, or if it just seemed that way.

On the west side of the square, a narrow storefront's tinted glass door and plate window gave the appearance of vacancy. No gold-painted shield or signage designated it as the detective division of the Kinderhook County Sheriff's Department.

Leasing the eight-hundred-and-fifty-foot cave was the commissioners' solution to David's demand for more space, much like Sanity's school board conquered overcrowding by building two new elementary schools five miles apart; each, an additional three miles from the middle school and high school, respectively.

As a result, carpooling parents' odometers spun like slot-machine wheels, and the local petroleum distributor and his wife could now afford semiannual junkets to Europe, Mexico and "the Islands."

David inserted his plastic key card into the door's electronic lock, courtesy of Fort Knox Security. Jessup Knox's generosity extended to interior surveillance cameras, motion-sensitive lights and a silent alarm system. Money couldn't buy better advertising than the sheriff's department topping Knox's client list.

The green light above the slot winked permission for David to enter what Marlin Andrik dubbed "The Outhouse."

A mossy smell common to root cellars and century-old buildings and a Marlboro haze made David's nose wrinkle in self-defense. The interior's walnut paneling, dropped-ceiling and mud-brown carpet must have set the building's owner back fifty, maybe seventy-five bucks when he remodeled in '83.

Along the far wall, four metal desks were rowed like tombstones, facing the window. At the back, file cabinets were alcoved beside a tiny, not-at-all-soundproof interrogation room. Three spavined banquet tables lined the near wall, heaped with cartons, portable file boxes and the assorted junk that flat surfaces attract like a keg party attracts minors.

In deference to its all-male staff, the rest room's toilet seat saluted all who entered there. Beyond it, the steel, strap-hinged rear entrance had been welded shut, in violation of the city's fire code.

The halogen lamp on the hindmost desk carved jack-o'-lantern features on Marlin's stubbled face. The chief of detectives pushed back in his swivel chair. "Afternoon, boss. Out slumming?"

"Where is everybody?"

"Orr and Phelps are still interviewing dirtbags, aka, associates of our boy Barton." Marlin glared at the tidy desk nearest the window. "It was either send Reserve Officer Moody home to mama, or wring his neck. I took the high road."

"He is eager to please." David folded himself into a plastic lawn chair in front of the detective's desk.

"Rudolph the Brown-nosed Reindeer." Marlin snorted. "Can you imagine hating a baby enough to name him Rudy Moody? The kid probably got wedgied at every recess."

"He told me all he's ever wanted to be is a cop."

"Yeah, and I get hard chills thinking about how a

gomer like him finally slogged through the Academy. On the sixth try.''

"As long as I'm in office, he'll never be a full-fledged deputy.'' David shrugged. "There isn't much I can do about him working Reserve on his own time, for free.''

"Rudy Moody packing a side arm keeps me awake nights, boss.''

"I sympathize, but we've got enough trouble without borrowing any.''

"Tell me about it.'' Marlin nodded at a computer monitor. "From print matches and borderliners I'm working up, Barton was acquainted with a fair number of homeboys. Pettys, mostly, with two or three itching to graduate to felony whatever. A couple already have, but we don't have enough to charge them and make it stick.''

David pulled his arms out of his sleeves, letting the coat sprawl over the chair back for padding. "Man, I love a mile-long suspect list. Makes the job as easy as it looks on TV.''

"Oh, it gets better,'' Marlin said around a cigarette clamped in his lips; a violation of the state's Clean Air Act pertaining to government buildings. Dropping a lighter in his shirt pocket, he exhaled locomotive-style, instead of blasting his superior with secondhand smoke.

"My guys can't find anyone who gave a rat's ass whether Barton kept on breathing or not. Nobody particularly hated the guy. Nobody particularly liked him. The dude was a drone.''

David said, "Makes me real curious about the toxicology report. I'm assuming Barton was higher than the Goodyear blimp the night he killed Osborn. If he'd been aching for a hit, he'd have sooner offed himself than somebody else. Whether he was coming down or gaining altitude might be important."

Marlin stared at David, arms crossed, the lit end of his cigarette dangerously close to igniting his sleeve. If he were a dog, rabies would be suspected.

"By the look on your face, I don't know whether to restrain you or start CPR."

The detective's statuelike demeanor ended with a snarled, "Score another one for The Guppy."

His nickname for Heather Gray derived from her prominent eyes, vacuous expression and intelligence quotient, though Marlin admitted the sobriquet did fish a disservice.

"I intercommed The Guppy four hours ago and told *her* to tell *you* Jimmy Wayne had phoned in the preliminary tox on Barton."

"Shit."

Marlin's humorless chuckle echoed off the walls. "Jeepers, Wally. Is that the best you can do?"

"If I cut loose, I'll bust an artery." David's fist hammered the desktop. "It gripes my soul, there's nothing I can do about your being stuck in Siberia, but I'm gonna fire Miss America first thing tomorrow morning."

The detective shook his head. "You can't. Her adoring daddy would lead her to an attorney and file a sexual harassment suit against you by noon."

"I have never—"

"Not a viable defense, pard." Marlin stubbed out his cigarette, leaned forward and propped his chin on steepled fingers. "Even if it were, the court of public opinion would hang you, and not by the neck. Small counties, and small towns in small counties, are the best and worst places to live. Neighbors pitch in when you need 'em, and flock like chicken hawks to roadkill when the shit hits the fan.''

David glowered at him. "Well, aren't you Mr. Cool all of a sudden.''

"I've played the game longer. Oh, it gets to me— ask Beth about the loony tune she married, sometime— but like you corking the cussing, I roll with the punches the best I can.'' He smiled. "Want to ask me again why I wouldn't run for sheriff if it paid a million a year?''

"You and Jimmy Wayne, both.''

"Just goes to show how smart your main men are, now, don't it?''

David's anger drained away along with his energy. Whoever said "You can't fight city hall'' must have held an elected office.

"So, what's the verdict from Columbia?'' he asked with a weary sigh.

Marlin snared his reading glasses with one hand and a legal pad with the other. "Want to hear the message The Troll told Jimmy Wayne to relay, first?''

David shook his head. He couldn't recall Andrik ever referring to the medical examiner by his Christian name. "Do you have a nickname for everybody?''

"Pretty much.'' Marlin peered over his half-glasses. "Got two of them for you.''

"Oh, yeah? Such as?''

The detective sucked his teeth. "Nah, the mood isn't right. I'll tell you when the veins aren't standing out in your neck.''

His attention averted to his notes. "The Troll says you've maxed out on express postmortems for the year. I quote, third-hand from McBride, 'Kinderhook isn't the only county experiencing negative population growth. Tell Hendrickson he'll wait his turn in the future, unless he's in the body bag.'"

David grunted. "I am not amused."

"Jimmy Wayne was. Anyhow, the skinny on Barton is that he crossed the River Jordan between 10:00 p.m. Friday, and 1:00 a.m., Saturday."

That corresponded with witness reports, such as they were. A thirteen-year-old neighbor-kid had been outside at about 8:30 or 9:00 p.m., when Barton's truck went by with two men in the cab. No descriptions on either, but it was presumed Barton was driving.

Another witness who lived nearer Fox Fire Road's intersection with the highway heard Barton's vehicle roar past her trailer around midnight. She yelled out the window for him to slow down, but the truck had disappeared.

"Barton's blood-alcohol was 2.1," Marlin continued. "Brain tissue and organs indicate chronic methamphetamine usage. Meth present in his bloodstream, but levels suggest he hadn't ingested the drug for twelve hours, maybe longer."

"How ingested?" David asked.

"Orally. Evidence of snorting, and he likely smoked it, too, but didn't mainline."

David frowned. "An addict with an aversion to needles? Not the usual M.O."

"The Troll thinks Barton was off ice for relatively long periods, such as when he was in jail. Considering his age, he wasn't a walking skeleton like a constant user would be."

"A yo-yo junkie?"

Marlin made a "take it or leave it" gesture. "Sounds like Barton took the pledge, kept it a while, something or someone would push him off the wagon, then sooner or later he'd climb back on.''

"Old habits die hard." David eyed the terra-cotta plant saucer his detective used for an ashtray.

"A .45 slug installed in your frontal lobe is a sure cure.''

"What kind of condition was it in?"

"Decent. Clean enough lands, grooves and a left-twist to match it with the shooter's gun, if we find it.''

"Smith & Wesson, huh?" David said. "Not exactly a rarity around here.''

"Well, aren't you on your tippy-toes. Picked the wheat right from the chaff.''

David said, "Anybody who knows anything about guns knows S&W is the only manufacturer who puts a southpaw twist in the barrels.''

"Rudy Moody wouldn't know a gun-twist from an ice-cream cone.''

"That's why he's a glorified file clerk, and we get to play cops and robbers every day.''

Marlin's expression darkened as if an eclipse had occurred. "Chase Wingate says Rudy is doing free-lance night patrols again. Joked about giving Rudy a camera to take car-wreck pictures for the paper, since he's at the scene before Chase is, half the time.''

"You're just determined to make my day, aren't you, Andrik? When did you talk to Wingate?"

"About noon, when I took the initiative of phoning in a definite on Barton," Marlin answered smugly. "Said he was too close to putting the *Examiner* to bed to downsize his Elderly Woman Found Brutally Murdered headline, but swore he'd reformat the front page to slug in a smaller, but eye-catching Sheriff's Investigation Identifies Osborn Killer.''

According to physicians, hypertension has no discernible symptoms. The tamped-down, pressure-cooker sensation swelling within David's chest belied medical opinion. "Your call was the first Chase had heard of it, right?"

Marlin's lack of response shouted affirmative.

"I okayed a press release before the chamber of commerce breakfast this morning. Heather was told to fax it to Wingate, pronto."

"Sounds fishy as hell to me."

"Shit."

"Among so many other things." Marlin did a drumroll with his pen. "Wingate got his scoop, so don't sweat it. Just don't give The Guppy jobs too complicated for her to handle. She's already bustin' her gills divining the finer points of world peace and cultural harmony."

David laughed at the image of Heather in a glittery crown and sash addressing the United Nations' General Assembly. "Every department needs a comedian like you to keep it sane."

Marlin spread his hands and looked around the room. "Hey, it's what got me where I am today."

"You taking off pretty soon?"

"Uh-uh. Parent-teacher conference night. Beth has to suck up to all the mommies and daddies even though it's too late in the year for their little pinheads to pull their fat out of the fire."

David grasped the armrests to leverage his hips from the chair. "Want me to bring you something to eat from the Short Stack?"

"Thanks, but I had a late lunch."

David jerked a thumb toward the back of the building. "You okay on coffee and pop? The route guy stiffed us last week."

"What's with the Rudy Moody imper— No, wait." Marlin folded his hands on his stomach. "What we have here is a Beth Andrik impersonation. You're in the mood to rearrange the furniture, right?"

"Naw. No muscle needed for this favor, except the one between your ears."

"Shoot."

"You didn't run Osborn's prints through NCIC, did you?"

"No reason to."

"Would you mind checking when you have time? Just for curiosity's sake."

"I'll probably have something for you midday tomorrow."

"No rush." David put on his coat and started for the door, then turned. "What about those impressions Phelps took at Osborn's last night?"

"Josh was so proud of 'em, I hated to break his heart, but I don't think Kung Fu wore size fourteen shit-kickers."

David looked down at his feet. "Fourteen and a half."

"The tire tracks he found on the golf course," Marlin continued, ignoring the correction, "were A-plus. Except we both know how often they're worth the price of a bucket of dental stone."

"Well, one thing for sure, if Henry Don Tucker gets ahold of whoever drove across those greens, there won't be enough left of the guy to put cuffs on."

17

"The word on the street is 'serial killer,'" Rosemary stated.

Delbert sneered, "Well, that's just silly."

"Read my report and tell me how silly it is," she huffed. Her finger crawled down the typed page. "One, two, three...six different women at the Curl Up and Dye are scared to death a serial killer is on the loose."

Delbert harrumphed. "I rest my case."

"Oh, what do you know?" Marge said. "The young man at the Bagel Barn—such a nice boy, always gives me extra cream cheese and doesn't charge me for it—says the exact same thing."

IdaClare argued, "No, he doesn't. He told me he thinks Barton was one of Kathleen's students. That she failed him a time or two and he grew up hating her for ruining his life."

"The bagel boy said that?" Marge sat back in her chair. "Well, so much for my report. I should have known the little twit would change his tune."

"It is not such a bad guess," Leo said slowly, as though chewing the words along with his cake. "Better, I think, than a serial killer. A grudge, it can be a bad thing in the wrong hands."

Hannah, who'd been unanimously elected the evening's moderator, said, "Two problems with that one, gang. Barton could have been her student, but Kathleen taught elementary school. For him to carry a grudge from childhood into his fifties doesn't seem plausible.''

"Those are formative years," Delbert countered, "and kids are like wagon wheels. Warp 'em young, and they stay warped for life."

"Wagon wheels?" IdaClare's coffee cup clinked in the saucer. "Have you lost your mind entirely?"

"As I was saying," Hannah continued in a loud, hopefully authoritative voice, "even if we assume the student thing, it doesn't answer who killed Barton, and the vote was five-to-one their deaths are connected."

"The hell they are," Delbert grumbled.

Leo's bulbous head tick-tocked a few beats, then stopped. "Ahhhh. Maybe it was the suicide, not murder. Barton, he was so overcome by remorse, his own life he took."

"Horse apples," IdaClare said. "Everybody knows he was plugged smack-dab in the middle of his forehead."

She made a pistol from a thumb and index finger. Arm bent and contorting like a bird with a broken wing, she finally managed to stick the pretend gun barrel between her penciled eyebrows. "See? Barton would have given himself bursitis trying to pull the trigger."

"Too bad yours ain't loaded," Delbert said, sotto voce.

IdaClare disengaged the weapon from her forehead and drew a bead on his. "I couldn't agree more."

Delbert slapped his thighs and whipped two imaginary revolvers into firing position.

Ignoring the reenactment of the shoot-out at the OK Corral taking place at her elbow, Marge smiled at Hannah and said, "I move we drop the student-killer angle."

"All in favor?" Six "ayes" responded.

In a quest for democracy and to lessen the chance of hurt feelings, fisticuffs and delays keeping them from their favorite Monday-night television programs, IdaClare and Company had also decided to share their investigative findings and pet theories in round-robin order.

Which meant Delbert was next.

Hannah's groan at that realization was lost in Marge wielding the thermal carafe and pouring coffee refills.

"My turn," Delbert announced before Hannah could proceed parliamentarily. Realizing his gaffe, he winked at her and said, "If it's okay with you."

"You have the floor, Mr. Bisbee."

The old fart either took her literally, or wanted to dominate the minions, for he rose to his feet. "Me and Leo cooked up a couple of theories to present—"

Marge yelped, "That's not fair. 'Favorite' means one. You have to choose between them."

All eyes zipped to Hannah, with the exception of Leo's, whose back was toward her. Delbert's features arranged themselves into his patented basset-hound mien. "If that's true, I sure hope I never have to pick my favorite amongst you four lovely ladies."

The "aw-w-ws" the four lovely ladies uttered in unison proved again all rules have exceptions.

Delbert said, "All rightie, then, my first theory is a pip-a-roo and a half." He cleared his throat. "You know without me telling you, those damn fools and Democrats in Washington have borrowed money hand over fist from Social Security for years."

Oh, Lord, Hannah thought. He's been brainwashed by Limbaugh.

"At the same time," Delbert continued, "young folks are paying in through the nose thinking they're putting aside a nest egg for themselves and keeping us senior citizens from eating dog food for dinner.

"Except Congress can't borrow from Peter to pay Paul forever and they're not about to admit they're the foxes in the henhouse, so what's the next best thing to do?"

The table sitters and moderator exchanged mystified glances. IdaClare's shrug induced a chain reaction. When none of the women looked the least bit tempted to tender the obvious response, Leo-the-Shill prompted, "The next best thing, it is what?"

Delbert's mouth pulled back in a sly grin. "You knock some people off the payroll. As in permanently, if you get my drift."

IdaClare looked at him as if he'd just sprouted a second head. Or needed a replacement for the original. "You're about twelve cookies short of a dozen, you know that?"

She unloaded, machine-gun style. "In the first place, that's the stupidest notion I've ever heard in all my born days, and let me tell you, I've heard some dillies.

"In the second, Barton wasn't old enough for a pension, and you know darned good and well, Kathleen received a teacher's pension in lieu of Social Security."

"Oh." Delbert scratched at his neck. "Now that you mention it, that does kinda ring a bell." He thrust a hand in his tattersall-plaid trousers. "Well, my *other* theory—"

"Hannah, dear," IdaClare cooed, "would you kindly tell this lunatic to shut up and sit down?"

"C'mon, gimme a chance. I got carried away some on the conspiracy angle, but just 'cause I didn't hit a homer, don't bench me for trying."

Rosemary chuckled. "Let's not be too hard on the poor man. I think he was warped during his formative years."

IdaClare's hands clapped together, her whooping belly laugh infecting the others. Through teary eyes, Hannah saw Delbert join in, despite the joke being on him.

Presently, he tugged a handkerchief from his back pocket and waved it. "I surrender. No wind left in the flue. Defer to Leo." He collapsed in the chair, dabbing his beaded brow with the hankie.

"Are you all right?" Hannah asked.

"Fit as a fiddle," he wheezed, adding, "Nero's."

Because IdaClare and Rosemary were patting their respective bosoms due to mild respiratory distress, Hannah took him at his word. "Any objections to Leo taking over?"

"Yes," Leo said.

Delbert croaked, "You can't—"

"I can, and I do." Leo knuckled his hips. "The second theory stinks. Not as bad as yours, but stinks is stinks. IdaClare, it is your turn."

"Well, of all the..." Delbert's voice trailed away to garbled muttering.

IdaClare riffled the papers in front of her. Tapping them into a neat stack, she turned to look at Hannah, her smile as bright as a little girl awaiting permission to go out and play after cleaning her plate.

"You heard the man," Hannah said.

"Thank you, dear." She paused a moment, then warned, "Whether y'all like my theory or not, you must promise not a word of it leaves this room." A finger wagged for emphasis. "Strictly confidential."

Leo, Rosemary, Marge and Delbert crouched forward simultaneously, murmuring assent.

Not one to beat around bushes, IdaClare said, "I think Harve Liebermeyer did it."

After a few seconds of pin-drop silence, Rosemary whispered, "Did what?"

"I had to rearrange things a mite, since the sheriff is so all-fired sure Earl Barton murdered Kathleen," IdaClare allowed with a sniff. "But I do believe Harve killed Barton *and* wrecked Kathleen's house, *and* attacked Hannah the other night."

Frowning faces, including Hannah's, exchanged skeptical glances this time. The deepened creases in the back of Leo's bald head indicated unanimity.

"What did you think before you, er, rearranged things?" Hannah asked.

"That Harve killed Kathleen, too, of course." IdaClare heaved a sigh. "A crime of passion."

"Harve Liebermeyer?" Rosemary said. "Passion?"

"Oh, ick." Marge pinched the bridge of her nose. "If you don't mind, I'd rather not think about it."

"It's the most common motive for murder," IdaClare insisted. "And if you recall, Harve and Kathleen were very neighborly, then jiggledy-bang, they couldn't stand the sight of each other."

Hannah had sensed that the day she spoke to Miriam.

In a hushed voice, Rosemary asked, "Do you think they had an affair?"

Delbert bellowed, "Damned if I'll sit here and listen to you talk about Kathleen like she was a Jezebel."

IdaClare quickly laid her hand on his arm. "I'm sorry, Delbert. I don't mean to upset you, truly I don't."

He yanked from her grasp. "She was a good woman."

"Yes, she was. It's Harve I'm really accusing here. I think he fancied himself in love with her, and Kathleen told him to go to hell in a handbasket."

Delbert nodded. "By God, she would have, too."

"Why, then, would Harve do the other things?" Leo asked.

"The Liebermeyers know more about what happened that night than they'll admit," IdaClare answered. "I think Harve saw Barton run from the cottage, snuck over there, and saw—well, the aftermath."

"Is possible," Leo said, speaking for Hannah and the others. "Is very possible."

IdaClare went on, "Harve could tell Kathleen was beyond help, but he panicked. He didn't know how to explain finding her body, or maybe right then, he was afraid of Barton—"

"Or," Delbert snarled, "didn't want to tell the sheriff he didn't lift a finger while Barton was killing her."

Marge shook her head. "I don't like Harve. I don't know anybody besides Miriam who does, and I'm not even sure about her, but—" her nose wrinkled "—isn't this becoming awfully *personal?*"

"I'm not comfortable with it, either," Rosemary said.

Hannah recalled David's remarks that afternoon. IdaClare and Company weren't as much exhuming buried skeletons as debating whether or not any bones existed. Still, it seemed ghoulish.

The principal accuser said, "Three points to ponder,

then I'll quit. What if Harve recovered his wits and killed Barton to avenge Kathleen's murder? What if Harve tore her cottage apart searching for love letters he wrote her, or for something he gave Kathleen, because he was afraid Hannah would find it and tell Miriam? When Hannah almost caught him, he didn't want to be seen and didn't want to hurt her, so he knocked her out long enough to make a getaway."

After mulling over the scenario, Hannah's second thought agreed with her first. IdaClare had hatched a darned good theory; a majority opinion, judging by the "Gee, why didn't I think of that?" expressions on the other gumshoes' faces.

Delbert said, "Pretty slick, IdaClare, except for the last part. When I found Hannah, I called the sheriff from Harve's house. He was kicked back in his recliner, same as always."

"So?" IdaClare challenged. "He'd been out earlier, supposedly on patrol. Tire tracks are all over the course near Kathleen's. He could have shortcut through there to circle back and head home on the boulevard, and—" IdaClare lobbed the ball into Hannah's court "—you didn't struggle with the attacker, right?"

"I hit the ground like a sack of potatoes."

"Then do you think Harve Liebermeyer could have done it?" Rosemary asked.

Hannah had never seen Harve vertical, so could only guess at his height. He wasn't as skinny as Delbert, but was hardly overweight. She closed her eyes and pictured herself in the Liebermeyer's living room. The odors she rekindled didn't include stale cigarettes.

"Neither of the Liebermeyers smoke, do they?" she asked no one in particular.

"Harve does," Marge said. "Miriam won't let him do it in the house, though. She's allergic."

Great. Hannah was relatively sure her job description didn't include slandering tenants, but even Leo had wiggled around in his chair, anticipating her answer.

"As fast as everything happened and no more than I saw, it could have been about any tall, medium-built, male smoker," she hedged.

IdaClare clasped her hands atop her report. "Which means," she concluded in a venomous monotone, "it could have been Harve Liebermeyer."

Delbert jutted an elbow at the cake pan Hannah was swaddling in plastic wrap. "Your hind end is gonna be as big as IdaClare's if you eat all that."

"Rosemary left it for David. Wasn't that sweet of her?"

Delbert grunted and turned back to the sink. "I'll hurry up with the dishes, then, if he's coming over."

Hannah stepped in beside him. "*He* isn't coming over tonight, and it was your idea to wash the dishes by hand."

Delbert shrugged. "I like bubbles. Machines don't blast off the lipstick smudges you gals leave, either."

"I don't wear lipstick anymore."

"Hmmph."

A cup joined the others in the rinse side of the sink. She flipped off the excess water and began drying it with a towel. "You're still mad at her, aren't you?"

"Who?"

"IdaClare."

"Nah. She's as fulla crap as a Christmas goose, but life's too short to stay mad at somebody for being addlepated."

"Even you admitted her theory had some merit," Hannah reminded.

Three saucers slid into the drink before he said, "If Harve saw Barton, or peeked into Kathleen's kitchen way before me and Marge found her, IdaClare and the others can pester him till the cows come home, but he'll never admit it."

"What do you think?"

"Between you, me and the bedpost, I'm ninety percent sure he didn't see Barton. 'Bout the same on Miriam hearing a ruckus and sending Harve to check on Kathleen."

"Unfortunately, I agree."

"When Detective Andrik interviewed me the second time, he pretty well said as much, too. If they hadn't homed in on Barton so fast, I suspect he'd have taken the Liebermeyers to Sanity for another little talk."

Delbert's rheumy blue eyes probed Hannah's. "You didn't find anything Harve might have given Kathleen when you went through her stuff, did you?"

"No."

His chin bobbed once. He reached for a stack of dessert plates.

"But," Hannah added hesitantly, "I'm not sure that means anything. Kathleen wasn't sentimental. At least, not the type who tucked away letters, or cards, or, well—mementos."

He rested his sudsy forearms on the sink's apron. "This is the long and short of it, missy. She tried to neighbor with the Liebermeyers. Miriam's never had a thought in her head to call her own. Harve is a crotchety old bastard—insufferable, was Kathleen's way of putting it. She got a bellyful, told him to keep to his side of the hedge, and he told her to do likewise."

Hannah ruminated the explanation, duly noting its basic flaw: Delbert's love for Kathleen biased him against giving any consideration to another man's attraction to her, let alone hers for another man.

Harve did not, by any stretch of the imagination, fit the Romeo image, but who knew how he perceived himself? At that moment, in karaoke bars across America, self-deluded dorks were belting out "Feelings" into microphones, believing to their very marrow their audiences were awestruck rather than soused to the earlobes.

Hannah acknowledged how much she wanted IdaClare to be right. The scenario wrapped everything into a tidy package, including why Hannah's cottage had been searched: Harve looking for those infamous love tokens. Accepting IdaClare's reasoning would also spare Hannah from asking an intimate, intrusive question of the adorable old gentleman who could answer it.

While she shelved the last of the dishes, Delbert gleefully used the sink sprayer to chase the remaining bubbles down the drain.

"Thanks for the volunteer KP duty," she said, offering him the towel to dry his hands.

"Glad to help, ladybug." He smiled, as one did at salesclerks who wished every customer a nice day. "Now, you want to tell me what's bothering you, or leave it go?"

Hannah started. "Ye gods, is everyone in this county part Gypsy?"

"You don't need a crystal ball when somebody's looked cockeyed at you all evening long."

"I—it—you'll get mad…"

"I might, but I'll be madder if you don't." He laid

the folded towel on the counter and ironed it with his palms. "I figure whatever's rattling around inside your pretty head isn't something you wanted the whole gang to pounce on. I haven't met many, but I admire a woman who can muzzle herself."

Leaning against the cabinets, he crossed his arms at his chest. Woolly, white eyebrows arched in a "So, what gives?" fashion.

"We'd be more comfortable in the living room."

"I'm doing the ten-to-midnight patrol. Traded an eight o'clock with Walt on account of the meeting."

The microwave clock read 9:37. Sheesh. Then again, maybe it would be less painful to rip into her scenario like one ripped off an adhesive bandage. Quick and dirty.

She paced, as she once did in her office in Chicago when deadlines required fast, out-loud thinking. "I've approached this from every possible angle. I know you don't believe Barton's death is related to Kathleen's. I'm also pretty sure you agree with David that Barton picked her at random."

"Mostly at random," Delbert corrected. "Barton worked in her yard a couple of days. Gave him time to size her up as an easy mark, then *whammo*."

Hannah pulled up short. "Why am I the only one who sees a huge glitch in that motive? It was obvious Kathleen didn't have any money. Homemade clothes, flea-market furniture— I'll bet she pinched every penny she could on the garden beds she hired Barton to build."

"She lived in Valhalla Springs, Hannah. Highest rent district in Kinderhook County."

"What difference does that make?"

"A helluva difference." Delbert shifted his weight

to his other foot. "Eavesdropping on folks in Sanity didn't give much to go on investigation-wise, but me and Leo picked up on some stuff we didn't expect."

"Such as?"

"Let's just say not all the locals have the warm fuzzies about Valhalla Springs. More'n a few resent us for being old and living high on the hog, while they sweat blood, get nowhere and don't have a hope in Hades of ever retiring to a place like this."

Hannah waved a dismissal. "That's ridiculous. Sure, it's a beautiful development, but Palm Springs, it isn't."

"It is to a working stiff earning five, six bucks an hour. There's some pricey subdivisions in and around town and a few farms I'd hate to pay taxes on, but Valhalla has the county's *only* golf course, and it's private. The *only* stocked fishing lake—private. Lighted tennis courts. Indoor and outdoor swimming pools. You name it, it's here, and it's off limits to the townies."

Have-nots envying the haves probably dated back to cavepeople. Hannah remembered despising Brenda Frake because she had pretty clothes and patent-leather Mary Janes to match. And whenever Jeffy Sturgis rode by the trailer park on his electric-blue Schwinn Spyder with handbrakes and a metallic banana seat, Hannah beaned him with chirt rocks.

She didn't, however, understand how the idea related to Barton murdering Kathleen for money she didn't have.

"Because she appeared to have it by living here," Delbert stressed. "Most of the residents thought Kathleen was well off, but tight with a buck."

He made a growling noise. "Truth is, she was planning to move somewhere cheaper. The doc in Nebraska said a year, eighteen months tops, for the cancer to take her. She worried if she lasted much longer, there'd be nothing left of her trust to give the school.''

Hannah didn't know what to say. Mere words couldn't lessen the horrible irony of it all.

"Oh, don't go all blubber-pussed on me," Delbert chided. "Kathleen loved children and was a devoted teacher, but a saint? No. It rankled her to depend on anyone, to feel beholden. Like those turtles she collected, she pulled herself into her private shell and shut everyone else out.''

Despite the bluntness of his words, no bitterness or anger tinged his voice. Frustration and sorrow, but no rancor.

"Then why did you care so much for her?" Hannah asked gently.

He gazed upward for a long moment. "I never knew why, but Kathleen held an abiding distrust of everyone." He shook his head. "I wanted her to trust me. Wanted to bust her out of her shell. Take a little joy in what time she had left.''

He inhaled deeply, held it, then exhaled in a rush. "Finally had to admit that was what I wanted for her, not what she wanted for herself. It was as if she was doing a penance, and nothing I said or did could change it.''

"I'm so sorry, Delbert.''

"Don't be, ladybug." He smiled. "Did anyone ever tell you there's nothing you could do to make them stop loving you?''

A knot welled in Hannah's throat. "My mother did. I told her that, too, all the time.''

"Well, either no one ever told Kathleen, or if it was said, it wasn't meant."

Hannah licked her lips. "I think I know who. In fact, I think I know why Barton killed her."

Delbert chuckled. "Does that mean you've decided to make me mad?"

"What I have to say very well could."

He shrugged. "If it does, I'll get over it."

"Promise?"

"Do I need to?"

Hannah fingercombed her hair off her face and made a fist atop her head. "While Barton was working on those garden beds, I think Kathleen told him the story she most loved to tell."

"What story? She didn't— Oh, that movie bush-wah?" He snorted. "Yeah, like as not, she did."

"What if Kathleen was mostly telling the truth, Delbert? What if she was involved in a bank robbery and made it the plot of her movie?"

Delbert cackled almost as energetically as he had earlier that evening. "Why didn't you toss that out at the meeting? Woulda made my Social Security scam look finer than frog's hair."

"What if," Hannah went on, "Barton recognized details in Kathleen's story—the brothers as ringleaders, or things pertaining to the robbery itself?

"What if Barton realized they sounded familiar be-cause he'd overheard gossip about his mother giving birth to him before or during her imprisonment for bank robbery? That she, the man who fathered him and his brother were members of the gang?"

Delbert cautioned, "That's about enough of—"

"Please, just listen. If I'm right, it explains why

Kathleen lost her ability to trust anyone, including you."

He nodded, his features rigid and wary. "What if Barton confronted Kathleen? Demanded money or he'd tell everyone she was an ex-convict and had abandoned her son in infancy. True or not, Kathleen would have been horrified by the threat to her precious privacy.

"The terms of her trust didn't allow cash withdrawals. Maybe she told Barton she didn't have long to live and tried to buy his silence with a promise to make him a beneficiary."

Delbert's arms fell to his sides; fingers clenched, the skin taut and pale.

Hannah looked away. "High on methamphetamines, Barton flew into a rage. He didn't mean to kill her, but couldn't control himself. When he saw what he'd done, he grabbed her purse and ran.

"Later, he ripped the purse apart, searching for cash, a safe-deposit box key—anything of value. He'd already bragged to his boss about his ship coming in. To buy time, I think he told his meth dealer about his long-lost, wealthy mother and his blackmail scheme.

"When the dealer came to collect the money Barton owed him, either he didn't believe Barton, or killed him as an example to other deadbeats, then ransacked Kathleen's cottage for the cash Barton said she'd stashed there."

Tension, as thick and oppressive as ozone, rived the air. Hannah sagged, as emotionally drained as Delbert appeared to be.

"That it?" he asked.

"Yes, and if—"

"Kathleen got sicker than a horse on some medication the oncologist in Sedalia gave her," Delbert said, his voice wooden. "Couldn't keep anything down. Soiled herself. I helped her to the tub and bathed her. Had to three or four times before the stuff was out of her system."

He glared at Hannah. "Her skin was like rice-paper. Every vein, every mark on it, showed. She hated me seeing her…raw and frail and helpless and, worst of all, naked."

His eyes never leaving hers, he pushed away from the counter. "There wasn't a stretch mark on her, Hannah, and she was too slender to have borne a child without them."

With that, he stalked from the kitchen. Seconds later, the front door banged behind him.

Hannah slumped against the refrigerator, rolling to one side against its chill, metal facade as if sleeping in an upright position. She felt ill, disgusted with herself and her obsessive need for someone, something to blame for Kathleen's death.

No next of kin. Not even an ex-husband to claim as a distant relative. Independent to a fault. Acquaintances, but few close friends. Work was her life; alone, her life-style.

If those clues were given to an old game show's celebrity panelists, half would write "Kathleen Osborn" on their answer slates. The rest would guess "Hannah Garvey."

She started at footsteps shuffling across the linoleum. Bundled in a leather bomber jacket, his face shadowed by the bill of a cap with Sexy Senior Citizen embroidered on the panel, Delbert clasped Hannah's wrist and led her through the cottage to the front door.

"Tried to lock up after myself," he said. "My key wouldn't fit. You had 'em changed again."

"Delbert, I'm—"

"Nuttier than a goddamned fruitcake factory. Now batten down the hatch after me, and get some sleep." He kissed her cheek. "Ladybug."

18

Hannah stood paralyzed, eyes squinted, hands atop her head, staring at the shower nozzle. Or more accurately, staring at the spot where she believed the shower nozzle would be, had she been able to see it, or locate it by virtue of water jetting from it.

Drips rat-a-tatted the fiberglass floor. She struggled to relate the sound to sudden pitch darkness, shampoo lather slithering down her back, gooseflesh rippling upward from her ankles.

Delbert. Last night's apparent forgiveness had been a ruse. In retaliation for her disparaging Kathleen, he'd sabotaged the utilities.

No, he only broke things when he fixed them. He probably didn't know how to break stuff on purpose.

Janet Leigh had been oblivious to shrieking violins warning her of Anthony Perkins's cutlery-intensive approach. Hearing a similar, albeit slow-paced *Ree-eep...Ree-eep,* Hannah dropped to a crouch, holding the last breath she might ever draw.

Ree-eep.

She slapped the shower door open, clipped the edge of the counter with a hipbone and groped for the bathroom door's handle. With two springing leaps, she dove headfirst into the bed, swaddled herself in the covers, then snagged the telephone receiver.

"Valhalla Sp-prings," she said through chattering teeth. "Hannah G-Garvey speaking."

"This is Hetta Caldwell at 3230 Hawthorne Street. I have no electricity or water. Do you *understand* me? No utilities whatsoever. Don't bother telling me to call Maintenance. I already have, twice, and no one answers."

Hannah forced herself to smile, hoping to lighten her tone. "Mine just went off, too, Mrs. Caldwell—"

"That may be true, but my brother and sister-in-law drove in from Duluth last night, and here we sit in the *dark,* with no way to bathe, no breakfast, and on top of that, it's too cold and rainy to play golf!"

Do tell. If I were you, I'd just give it up and make a suicide pact. Aloud, Hannah said, "My apologies for the inconvenience, but I'm sure service will be restored as soon as possible."

"It had better be," Mrs. Caldwell snapped, and hung up.

Hannah muttered to the dial tone, "Peace and love from my house to yours."

The instant the receiver depressed the disconnect button, the ringer *reeped* again. She abbreviated the standard greeting to, "Valhalla Springs."

A male voice drawled, "Say, uh, did you know the power's out?"

"Yes indeedy, I did, and it'll be back on before you know it. Thanks for calling!"

Hannah hung up, snarled at another immediate ring, and decided if Maintenance could ignore its phone, so too shall the operations manager.

A crackling noise in the vicinity of her ear reminded her of the shampoo basting her hair. She scurried to the closet for her ratty, warm, chenille robe and Tasmanian devil house shoes, vowing to have a bathtub installed, or forgo personal hygiene altogether since her shower was, no doubt, hexed.

Logic insisted that water doesn't clog in one section of a house's plumbing and flow freely in others. Hannah tried every faucet, anyway. Water spat from her bathroom tap and the kitchen's, but before she could position herself advantageously, both winnowed to a few fat drips. She pinned her hopes on the quarter-size, guest bath off the living room.

The sink's oval, scalloped basin didn't look large enough for a Malibu Barbie. Hannah considered her options, confirmed she had none, then wedged her head into the tight space under the faucet.

Squinching her eyes shut, she twisted both knobs simultaneously. Icy water shot directly into her ear. She wriggled sideward, just in time to catch the inevitable, final, futile last drops gravity pushed out the pipe.

Contrary to Mrs. Caldwell's snippy weather alert, it was not raining. If it were, Hannah would have shed her robe and let nature have its way with her stiffening hair and increasingly itchy scalp.

She stared out the French doors at the gray, gloomy sky, counted the phone's unanswered rings and mentally doused for a water source other than one she wasn't quite desperate enough yet to use.

Fist hammered palm. "Yes-s-s-s!"

Pots, pans and lids clattered in the cabinet as she rummaged for her never-used Dutch oven. A couple of well-aimed left jabs unstuck the ice maker's bin. Chuckling merrily, she dumped slices of frozen water into the stew pot, whipped the stove's knob to High and skipped off to her bathroom for a dry towel.

Midway through the bedroom, she stopped short,

whirled, then stomped back into the kitchen. The cold, unelectrified kitchen where a potful of ice sat on a cold, unelectrified stove burner.

An hour later, Hannah added her Blazer to the vehicles parked spoke-fashion around the development's waterworks facility. Beyond it were four tall standpipes painted dark green to blend with the landscape.

Bob Davies separated himself from a group of men huddled outside a cinder-block building and strode toward her. She noted his haggard expression, then her eyes locked on the steaming, foam cup he held.

She pointed to it and said, "Where'd you get that?"

He chuckled. "Take it. There's plenty more in the thermos over yonder."

"Bless your heart." She cradled the cup in both hands and sipped the nectar of the gods, known to mere mortals as strong, black coffee.

"Happy to oblige. First 'bless you' I've heard all morning."

"What caused the outage?" Hannah asked.

"The REA boys—"

"Whoa," she interrupted. "What's an REA?"

"It stands for Rural Electrification Administration, but to my dad it's the right hand of God. If not for the REA setting up a system to provide power through local co-ops, farmers might still be using coal oil lanterns to find their dairy barns."

That explained the logo and abbreviated REA lettering on a nearby midsize sedan's passenger door. The governmental agency's full name couldn't be spelled out on a stretch limo.

"Anyhow," Bob continued, "the co-op thinks our well pumps might have overloaded and blown out their transformers." He nodded toward a bearded man in coveralls and knee-high rubber boots. "Dick Wingo dug our wells and set the pumps, and he says a surge in voltage zapped the pump motors."

Hannah smiled. "And what does Bob Davies say?"

He laughed. "He doesn't know the front of this mule from its backside. I'm just a country boy who lucked into steady work."

Humbleness became his tanned, blond good looks. Davies's Construction, a company consisting of its namesake and twenty-six Mennonite day laborers, had built Valhalla Springs's main buildings and many of the original cottages. The opportunity to exchange a self-employed contractor's headaches and income fluctuation for a maintenance supervisor's salary had been a classic no-brainer.

"Okay, so what's the country boy's best guess?" she inquired.

Bob glanced at the men still talking among themselves. "Better for Clancy if the fault lies with the electric co-op. A fair argument could be made for them to replace our pumps, and those babies don't come cheap."

"Nothing critical to life as we know it ever does," she said. "But before your phone and mine ring their little bells off, I thought I'd drive around and—" she gestured as if waving a magic wand "—spread hope and reassurance throughout the land."

"It won't cut down on the complaints, but what the heck. Go for it."

"I'd rather hide in the woods with you," Hannah teased, "but since one of us has to go before the firing squad, any idea when the utilities will be back on?"

Bob reached up to adjust his MFA gimme-cap. "Optimistically, pessimistically or realistically?"

"All of the above. The merchants need realism, and the residents, optimism. A little pessimism factored in will cover both our butts."

"Spoken like a born contractor." After pondering a moment, Bob answered, "Dick should have the replacement pumps installed this afternoon. The rest depends on how fast the pole-jockeys can switch out the damaged transformers—if that's all it is."

Hannah tapped her foot on the floorboard, praying Dick-the-pump-guy worked faster than Bob talked.

"At best," he said, "early afternoon, and sometime tomorrow at worst. Most likely, by suppertime today."

"Can I quote you on that?" she asked.

"God, no. Lay it on the co-op. They're used to being scapegoats."

"One last thing, Bob." She wagged her empty cup. "Is that thermos you mentioned good for a free refill?"

Having purposely avoided the residential area by staying on the service roads, Hannah steeled herself for prevailing grumpiness with scattered showers of out-and-out hostility.

To lighten her own mood, she thought about the evening's dinner plans—the prospect of leaving Valhalla Springs and its problems behind for a few hours, savoring the advertised, fork-tender steak in the company of the man who'd cook it and an intriguing gamut of who-knew-what-else-might-happen possibilities.

"At the very least, I'll get a decent meal and a place to take a long hot shower out of it."

Her eyes flicked to the rearview mirror. The pair looking back narrowed to slits. "Jarrod couldn't have said it better, now, could he?"

She hadn't meant it that way, but... Dating isn't a hobby, it's an apprenticeship. She couldn't just like David, look forward to seeing him, have a few laughs, fit him into the holes in her life when they need filling and hold him at bay when they didn't.

In theory, that sounded like the perfect relationship. Autonomy, commitment and a side order of great sex. Otherwise, to each his or her own, from living spaces to laundry. Shame it didn't work worth a damn, in practice.

So what are you going to do, Hannah Marie?

Piano keys tinked a familiar intro in her mind. She pulled the plug on her mental jukebox before the do-dee-deedle-dee-dahs segued to ''Desperado'''s poignant lyrics.

Whatever happened between her and David, which included *nothing,* she needed a new, favorite song. A heavy-metal, kick-ass, kiss-mine tune with lots of attitude and F-words.

Uh-huh. Sure.

Hannah turned onto Main Street, which looked like a ghost town, except no tumbleweeds tumbled between the curbs. Seeing Ralph leaning against the doorframe of his mercantile, she did a U-turn at the intersection with Hawthorne Street, then pulled over and lowered the passenger window.

"You're more dependable than the post office," she called.

The store owner ambled over, his apron flapping at his shins and starched, white shirt still buttoned at the cuffs. "Imogene goes home when the power fails. No scales, no till, no postage meters, no nothing."

The toothpick clamped between his lips rolled and jiggled. "I don't need juice to run an antique, brass cash register." He sighed. "Just customers."

Hannah sympathized. "The utilities could be back

on by midafternoon. Can I order in dry ice or anything to tide you over?''

''Real nice of you to offer, but my daughter's bringing a reefer truck from our store in Sanity. We'll load the perishables in the deli case, then I'm going home to put my feet up and take a nap until it's Miller time.''

Hannah laughed. ''Like Scarlett O'Hara said, 'Tomorrow is another day.' '' She shifted into drive. ''If you do need anything, let me know, okay?''

''I'll do that, and thanks again.''

Carla Forsythe, the boutique's manager, was similarly nonplussed, using the downtime to re-dress the display window and tag new merchandise.

Wiley Viets, the corner newsstand's owner, yammered at Hannah nonstop for five full minutes. ''What do you propose I do with all these papers? Old people can't read in the dark, and they sure as hell won't pay for Tuesday's news on Wednesday!''

Valhalla Springs's ferret-faced purveyor of newspapers, magazines, paperbacks and clothbound bestsellers refused to be mollified. When it became evident he was about to unleash Act Two of his tirade, Hannah turned on a heel and walked out.

''You'll hear from my lawyer about this,'' he yelled after her.

''Oh, that's cost-effective,'' she muttered as she started the Blazer. ''Lose a day's profit, then pay an attorney a hundred and seventy-five an hour to bitch about it.''

With the exception of Hawthorne Street, which she avoided, having no desire to meet Mrs. Hetta Caldwell in the flesh, tenants congregated on sidewalks and driveway aprons as if expecting the Second Coming, or the arrival of an alien spaceship.

A megaphone, better yet, a roof-mounted public address system revered by politicians and evangelists too poor to own their own cable television networks would have spared Hannah the aggravation of repeating the same spiel approximately nine thousand four hundred and ninety-two times.

Just as she turned into the community center's parking lot, half-dollar-size splatters plunked the Blazer's hood, then morphed into a blinding, deafening downpour. Parallel to Valhalla Springs Boulevard, a huge truck, anchored by stabilizer arms, and with its cherry-picker crane aloft, was reduced to a whitish blur.

She had no idea how much an electric co-op's lineman earned per hour, week or year, but it couldn't possibly be enough to hang ten in a plastic bucket suspended less than an arm's length away from a high-voltage power line.

Delbert, of course, would do it for free.

David snickered at the rain-drenched human form dressed in Marlin Andrik's favorite herringbone sport coat.

"Don't even think it," the detective growled from the doorway. Water leaked from his black, soft-side oxfords, marking his trail across the room.

He yanked the visitor's chair away from the desk, peeled off his jacket and hung it on the back. Tie askew, shirtfront damp and bloused above and below his shoulder holster, he looked like an armed and dangerous encyclopedia salesman.

"Coffee?" David asked.

"If I get thirsty, I'll suck on my sleeve." He chafed his hands. "Spring, my ass. More like February out there."

"Did Orr pick up Pete Blessinger?"

"That's partly why I waded over here. The 'bad cop splits before he goes postal' routine. Now Orr's doing the good cop, what-a-friend-you-have-in-me shtick."

"Think it'll work?"

Marlin shrugged. "Pete the Peckerwood is guilty of something. If he doesn't spill to Orr, me walking back in with a ballistics comparison that nails his dick to a tree may start him singing."

David's eyes widened. "You already have a match on the Smith & Wesson from Blessinger's glove box?"

"Only in my dreams does the lab move faster than a friggin' glacier." Marlin grinned. "*You* know that and *I* know that, but Blessinger? Six, seven commercials and voila, the test results are in, and you're toast, baby."

Many law enforcement officers regarded the proliferation of so-called reality TV shows portraying cops in action as a form of industrial espionage. Watching a few changed David's mind. From a professional's perspective, the programs were to actual police work what burlesque was to Broadway.

He said, "After dealing with a major power outage, it'll make Hannah's day to hear Blessinger confessed to Barton's murder when I pick her up for dinner."

"The lights still out in paradise?"

"If her answering machine not working is any indication, yeah."

Marlin's chin rumpled. "So, you're planning a big night on the town, huh?"

"Nope. A quiet evening at my place." David averted his gaze to the window. The rain had slackened to a drizzle. He'd hoped to take a walk up to the knoll after supper and show Hannah the view from his dream house—from where its foundation had been poured, anyway.

They probably ought to rent a movie on their way through town. Let her pick which one. He'd have a fair idea of her mood if a *Lethal Weapon* sequel won out over a chick-flick.

When he looked back, Marlin was nodding slowly, as if agreeing in spirit while mentally tabulating pros and cons. "Sounds like things are…progressing. Except I thought you gave up girls."

"I did." David tried to squelch the lecherous grin tugging at his lips. "Hannah's no girl, amigo. She's all woman."

"Definitely not a tweedledum. Good instincts." The detective's brow corduroyed. "Like her suspicions about Osborn—unless you want to tell me checking her out was your idea."

"You got something?"

"Oh, I got something, all right." His hand fumbled in his jacket pocket for his cigarettes. When David didn't produce the ashtray in his desk drawer, as he did when brainstorming sessions exceeded Marlin's nicotine reserve, he scowled, then crossed his arms like an attorney whose objections have been sustained by the bench one too many times.

"Seems back in the forties, our spinster schoolmarm, alias Edith Faylene Zentnor, did a ten-year stretch at Lansing, Kansas. Accessory to armed robbery, conspiracy to commit, etcetera, etcetera."

"Well, I'll be damned."

"She was just a kid. Barely eighteen. I ran her real name and the aka. It appears during and after her extended Kansas vacation, Zentnor/Osborn kept her nose so clean it must have squeaked when she sneezed."

David's swivel chair made a similar noise as he leaned back in amazement. "She probably paid somebody to match her birth year with a deceased infant's, ordered a copy of the birth certificate and put Edith and her record behind her. Simple enough to do in those days. Not hard now."

"But she never stopped looking over her shoulder," Marlin said. "Besides the social security number she had to have to work, she must have been too scared of blowing her cover to open a bank account, apply for a credit card, start any kind of paper trail."

"Sad," David commented.

Marlin hunched a shoulder. "I toyed with the idea of changing mine back in high school. I mean, Andrik's weird enough without 'Marlin' stapled to it. Perfectly legal, as long you don't do it to duck bill collectors, lawsuits or the long arm of the law."

He rolled his eyes. "I never should have tried the idea out on Ma. Instant coronary. To this day, sometimes she calls up and says, 'Marlin?' like she doesn't recognize my voice, then she says, 'That's still your name, isn't it?'"

David laughed. "Mine waits till family reunions and holidays to zing me and my brothers for every dumb thing we ever did."

"Yeah, and everybody hee-haws like they haven't heard the same crap about two million times."

David said, "Makes you wonder whether Kathleen's—er, Edith's kinfolk disowned her when she got in trouble, or if the new ID let her disown them."

"I'd guess both. Cause and effect."

"If she went up on accessory charges, who was she aiding and abetting?" David asked.

Marlin shook his head. "No details yet. Lansing's

files are computerized, but cross-referencing records that old takes time. The clerk said she'd get back to me a.s.a.p.''

"I hope she does," David said. "Hannah will want the whole—"

"Sher-iff," Heather chirped from the front desk, "a Mrs. Brandon Montgomery is holding for you. She says it's urgent."

"I'm gone." Marlin stood and retrieved his jacket in one motion. "You gonna be here awhile?"

"Well...I kind of hoped to sneak out early."

"Oh, yeah. The big date. Well, if you're gone when Blessinger cracks—or walks—or I hear from Lansing, want me to page you?"

"I hope to shout, I do."

Marlin half turned at the door. "Guess I'll have to think of something to replace 'The Monk,' now, won't I?"

David shot him a "Kiss my butt" look, reached for the telephone, then groaned as the caller's name clicked. Mrs. Brandon Montgomery. He didn't remember her ever referring to herself as Mrs. David Hendrickson.

He took a swig of diet soda, cleared his throat, then depressed the flashing button. "Sheriff Hendrickson."

"Rather formal, aren't we?" his ex-wife drawled. "Or did your secretary neglect to mention who was on the line?"

David didn't correct Heather's job title. He was too busy reminding himself he once loved this spoiled, arrogant woman so much, it almost destroyed him when she left him for "a *real* husband and *far* more satisfying lover" than David would ever be.

"I doubt if you called just to shoot the breeze, Cynthia."

Her laugh had a brittle edge. "Under the circumstances, when Vanessa Rivera asked me to, I could hardly refuse."

David felt the blood drain from his face. From the beginning of their Tulsa Police Academy training, he and Mike Rivera had been best friends. On a whim, David had fixed Mike up with Cynthia's roommate, Vanessa St. James. To David's astonishment and Cynthia's disgust, their meeting sparked the kind of love-at-first-sight people dream of, but doubt ever happens in real life.

"Cut to the chase, Cynthia," he demanded more harshly than he intended. "What's wrong?"

"I'm sorry, I'm—" she sighed "—well, I'm just not very good at this sort of thing." She paused for what seemed like an eon, then said, "Mike was shot in the chest last night. Not on duty—he walked into the middle of a convenience store holdup."

"Oh, Jesus, no."

"Mike came through surgery all right, but he's in intensive care, and Vanessa is—well, it's frightening to see him lying there, hooked up to all that machinery."

David glanced at the wall clock. "Tell her I'll be there by seven—earlier, if I don't get hung up in traffic. Which hospital?"

"No, David, don't come—please. Not yet. Vanessa wanted you to know Mike had been hurt, but told me to remind you, you swore you'd never stand a vigil if something like this happened."

David supported his head with his hand, his mind awhirl with fear, memories and solemn promises made with no thought of ever having to keep them.

"Knights in blue," Mike had called them, although Tulsa's uniforms are green over khaki. "When a warrior falls, the other takes up the gauntlet and goes on. Period. If the day comes I can't stand and look you straight in the eye, leave me the hell alone until I can."

"Same here," David had said. Boys would have pricked their fingertips for a blood oath. Men shook hands.

After he and Cynthia were married, he'd told her of the vow and asked her to respect it. She'd blown it off as a "stupid, macho thing." Vanessa, obviously, had not.

"You couldn't get in to see Mike, anyway," Cynthia said. "Visitation is limited to immediate family, and then, only ten minutes every three hours."

"He'll pull through," David said, as much to bolster his confidence as Cynthia's. "With Vanessa and those two little boys of theirs, he has everything in the world to live for."

Another pause. "You mean you didn't know…?"

Her tone and hesitancy frayed his nerves to the breaking point. "Know *what?*"

"Mike and Vanessa have been separated for months, David. She filed for divorce three weeks ago."

"I don't believe it."

"Well, I'm amazed they lasted as long as they did. It just took Vanessa longer than it did me to understand the difference between 'my husband is a cop' and 'a cop is my husband.' She thought she could live with that shield always being between them, but she couldn't. Few women can."

In his heart, David acknowledged the truth in what Cynthia said. Their marriage had failed for many reasons, but he'd believed Mike and Vanessa had beaten the odds, and he'd been thinking about the two of them a lot lately.

"More water under the same bridge," Cynthia said, bringing him back to the present.

"Yeah. Something like that."

He asked her to give Vanessa his love, exchanged his home and pager numbers for Cynthia's pager and cell-phone numbers, as well as the ICU waiting room's extension.

"Vanessa or I will call if anything changes," she assured. "Mike is listed as critical, but the doctors say, barring complications, he'll be fine."

Physically, maybe, David thought. "Just keep me posted, and hey, I really do appreciate your letting me know."

He sat back and stared through the wall-hung photograph of the Riveras hugging and mugging for the camera at the kegger they'd thrown the night before David moved back to Missouri.

He couldn't imagine his best friend strapped to a gurney in a tangle of tubes, and hoses, and IV's.

He couldn't imagine Mike without Vanessa beside him.

She thought she could live with that shield always being between them, but she couldn't. Few women can.

David's gut snarled into a hard, cold knot. If Mike and Vanessa Rivera couldn't work things out, he couldn't imagine Hannah being in a picture beside him, at all.

19

"Other than some tenants wanting to use the pool for a bathtub, it's been pretty quiet around here," Willard Johnson reported.

Now, there's an idea. Why hadn't she thought of it?

"Well, as far as I'm concerned," Hannah said, "you can post an All Activities Canceled Until Tomorrow sign on the door and take the rest of today off. With pay."

"That won't make the Every-Other-Tuesday Bridge Club very happy," he warned. "Marge Rosenbaum called this morning and said they'd wait awhile, but if the power wasn't on by midafternoon, they'd bring candles."

Hannah surveyed the card tables and folding chairs set up in the community center's main room, giving it the look of an undercapitalized restaurant. "I'll call her and explain why open flames and no water supply aren't a good combination."

Willard hedged, "If you're sure you don't want me to stick around awhile."

She hesitated. "Is the room available tomorrow?"

"It is until two, when the Treasure Hunters' Club meets. Delbert said it isn't a very big group, but they need space to swing their metal detectors around."

Why was she not surprised to hear Delbert was a member?

"Then assume the bridge club will be here in the morning, unless you hear otherwise—from me—in the next few minutes."

Willard said, "I'll put up a sign about that, too. Anything else I can do to help? You can't be having one of your better days."

That did it. A power failure was enough to handle without hauling guilt around like a ball and chain. "As a matter of fact, there is. How about accepting my humble, sincere apology for making a fool of myself yesterday?"

"Don't worry about it. I heard about the attack Sunday night. I've tried a little judo, and being on the receiving end of *shime-waza* isn't fun."

"That's no excuse—"

His head cocked to one side. "Let me get this straight. You apologized, I accepted, and now we're going to argue about it?"

"Bad habit of mine." Hannah laughed. "I'll see you tomorrow, okay?"

The rain had eased to a soft shower before she entered the building, and stopped while she was inside. Slow, deep-throated tolls of thunder and cloud cover hovering just above the trees promised more wouldn't be long in coming.

Hannah breathed in the rich, earthy aroma of a freshly laundered planet and remembered hunkering in a neighbor's root cellar whenever Great-uncle Mort said he "didn't like the way the sky looked over to the west."

Mort wasn't scared of tornadoes, he reminded everyone each spring, but respected their awesome strength.

Even his wife, Lurleen, couldn't muster up a decent argument to that. When purple-black thunderheads rose up like doom on the march and the air went still, Lurleen did, however, say it wasn't respect that sent Mort skedaddling for the 'fraidy-hole.

Two co-op linemen now occupied the parked utility truck's lofted bucket; their torsos veed apart at their waist like the original Siamese twins. Hannah cupped her hands and called, "How's it goin'?"

"Still have problems at the substation," one answered, "but we've about got 'er whipped, here."

On that encouraging note, Hannah drove away, eager to go home and give everyone who called, or dropped by, the impression she wasn't.

Because the day had been anything but normal—though what normal for Valhalla Springs might be, she didn't know yet—it didn't seem particularly odd to see Delbert sitting in his golf cart talking to Elvis.

Delbert spied the Blazer, perked up like a prairie dog, and gestured, "There she is," followed by a "Come here, Hannah" wave.

She shook her head. In her youth, she'd only swooned when Elvis appeared on *Ed Sullivan* to frost her relatives.

Delbert signaled, "Now, and I don't mean maybe."

Pulling crossways in front of his cart, her vehicle half-on and half-off the pavement, she let down the window and said, "I really need to get back to the office."

"Hannah Garvey, this is Jessup Knox, owner of Fort Knox Security."

On closer inspection, other than the hairstyle, the man who shook on their introduction looked less like

Elvis and more like someone who would be named Jessup Knox. "How's it goin', little lady?"

Spoken like a born snake-oil salesman. If reincarnation were possible, his type would return as bottom feeders. "Jes' peachy, big man," she drawled in return. "Any better, and I'd be in a coma."

He laughed. Too loudly.

Delbert said, "Jessup read the stuff you said in the *Examiner* and thought he could help."

She'd lobbed the rolled, rubber-banded newspaper she'd found in the driveway that morning into the houseplant jungle formerly known as her front porch. Assuming Chase Wingate hadn't misquoted her, she said, "Help? With what?"

"Securing these premises against future incidents of felonious criminal activity."

Hannah stared hard at him to keep her eyeballs from rolling completely back in their sockets.

Knox forced his thumbs inside his waistband and rocked on his heels. "Like I was telling Bisbee here, if I were you, I'd close that gate permanent and give tenants electronic key-cards for all accessing and egressing.

"Then I'd install strategically placed videocams connected to a monitor bank. Trust me, with those babies, you'll have yourself an eagle-eyed view of the entire development anytime, day or night."

"Oh, really?" Hannah aimed a sly grin at Delbert. "Which means no one could make a move without me knowing about it, and a camera capturing it on tape. For posterity, as they say."

Knox said, "I guarantee, the zoom lenses on them cameras can tell a tabby cat from a Persian at a hunnert yards."

"Gee, Delbert, did you hear *that?* Maximum surveillance capability."

He banged the golf cart's steering wheel. "By God, if you think I'm gonna live in Alcatraz, you've got another think coming, missy."

"What?" Knox's head wrenched around so fast, his pompadour had to hurry to catch up. "Not two minutes ago you said you'd take my proposal to the residents' board."

"I did, and I will. Then we'll vote against it and adjourn to the bar."

Knox turned back and gave Hannah an oily smile. "Ma'am, in my bidness, I run into this kind of denial pert-near every day. Old geezers, especially, aren't prone to admit even to themselves how afraid they are. Why, it'd be an insult to what little manhood they got left."

Hannah whispered, "Do you want to know what I'm afraid of, Mr. Knox?"

His expression fairly throbbed with sympathy. "I most certainly do, little lady."

"I'm afraid the old geezer sneaking up behind you with that one-wood is going to mistake your head for a Titlist."

Knox jumped onto the golf cart's bumper, springboarded to the asphalt, then made a run for his sport utility vehicle. Delbert chased him, yelling that he had more manhood in his little bitty finger than Knox did in his little bitty dick.

Laughing so hard she could barely steer, Hannah cut a one-eighty onto the boulevard. Residual chortling sputtered and died when she saw IdaClare's Lincoln in her driveway.

Hannah clicked the remote opener's button before

her brain delivered the "No electricity, stupid," message. Having manually raised the door once already and reluctant to invite a double hernia, she abandoned her vehicle to the elements.

When she rounded the front of the cottage, her visitors were standing on either side of the Lincoln's open, back passenger door like a pair of Secret Service agents.

"Get in," IdaClare commanded.

Rosemary tattled, "Junior Duckworth called Ida-Clare a little while ago."

"And we're all going to town to make Kathleen's funeral arrangements," IdaClare finished. "Right this instant."

"Which should have been taken care of Saturday," Rosemary said.

"Or yesterday," IdaClare allowed, "but it can't be delayed another minute. The Duckworths think we've abandoned that poor woman in her hour of need."

Hannah knew better than to remark on the "hour of need" part. She had been derelict—no argument—but a good defense attorney could make a case for countless distractions. If necessary, could plead mental defect. "As soon as—"

"Five minutes are up," IdaClare warned. "Your heinie had better be in this car."

Hannah vaulted the steps, scooped a FedEx mailer from the porch, unlocked the door and sprinted for her bedroom. Toeing off her tennis shoes, she jerked a beige suit from the closet rod, held it at eye level, then rehung it.

It wasn't a beige day. Or teal. Or pink—not *ever* again. A black, button-front jumpsuit with epaulets flut-

tered into view. Slimming. Somber. No panty hose necessary.

Tossing it on the bed, she stripped off her shirt, un-
zipped her Levi's, reached for the phone, dialed, then
wedged the receiver between her ear and shoulder to
wriggle out of her jeans.

"Kinderhook County Sheriff's Department," a
young woman cheeped.

"David Hendrickson, please." Hannah plopped on
the bed to pull off her socks.

"He's not here."

Well, hell. "This is Hannah Garvey at Valhalla
Springs. I really need to reach him. When do you expect him back?"

"I don't know for sure he's coming back." The ad-
mission seemed to distress her. "You want to, you
know, leave a message?"

Hannah slid a leg into the jumpsuit. "It won't do
much good if he's gone for the day, will it?"

There was a digestive pause. By its duration, rapid
assimilation was not the girl's best skill.

Hannah shifted the receiver to insert her free arm in
the jumpsuit's corresponding sleeve. "How about giving me his home number?"

"I don't think I'm allowed to do that."

"It's unlisted?"

"Oh, no, it's in the phone book. Is there anything
else I can do?"

Hannah managed to break the connection without
suggesting an anatomical impossibility.

Gathering a brush, mascara and blusher from the
dark bathroom, she dumped them on the dresser, then
made the mistake of looking in the mirror. Her hair
had taken the initiative to dry itself, and it wasn't

pretty. Then again, this morning's self-inflicted swirly to rinse out the shampoo might be a factor.

Bending from the waist, she brushed the tangled, wavy mass, straightened, then yelped. To hell with makeup. Who'd notice with an atomic frizzball billowing around her head?

Keys, purse and mailer in hand, she ran for the office nook. A whip through the Rolodex to the R's, then Hannah punched Marge's number and prayed she was home.

"Hello?" and "Oh, everyone will be so glad we can play cards tomorrow instead," were Marge's sole contributions to the conversation.

If Hannah hadn't reached for the tablet-size, local phone directory on the credenza, she wouldn't have seen the papers curled over the fax machine's bale. According to the time/date header, they were transmitted at 7:09 a.m., less than five minutes before the electricity failed.

She looked out the window. IdaClare and Rosemary were directing evil-eyed glares from the front seat of the Lincoln, which was idling. The cottage could burst into flames at any second.

Hendrickson was not as popular a surname as Johnson. While the lone D.M.'s phone rang, she speculated on what the "M." stood for.

You know the drill. Speak at the beep or forever hold your peace.

Well, hell—squared. "David, it's Hannah. I'm being kidnapped by IdaClare Clancy. Sorry about dinner, but this was *not* my idea. I'll explain later in gruesome detail."

Cradling the receiver, she exhaled disappointment

along with the fact she'd missed him in more ways than the obvious.

Oh, you do not. You're stressed, you look like the "before" picture in a hair-conditioner ad, IdaClare and Rosemary are furious with you and funeral homes give you the creeps.

Exceeding the deadline by a mere two minutes and nine seconds, Hannah hurled herself into the lap of tufted, genuine-leather luxury. "Wow, a chauffeur and a navigator," she said in a lame attempt at humor.

IdaClare wrenched around. "Just be glad that nice boy with the tool belt opened my garage door, or we'd be afoot." Facing forward, she added, "Buckle up, dear. It's the law."

Turning to insert the belt's metal tongue into the clasp, Hannah glimpsed what appeared to be two pinkish-orange Chia pets snuggled together on a satin pillow. Each wore a faux-diamond collar and a haughty expression.

"Itsy and Bitsy, I presume?" In tandem, the poodles lofted their button snoots and snubbed her like French aristocrats have the bourgeoisie for centuries.

Rosemary flopped down her sun visor. "We shouldn't have been so crabby, Hannah," she said into the lighted mirror. "We know what a strain you've been under."

Addressing Rosemary's reflection, Hannah said, "No, it's me who should apologize. I should have taken care of this long before now."

IdaClare frowned into the rearview mirror. "Well, our investigation is going nowhere fast, too. We tried to worm a confession out of Miriam this morning, but couldn't stand listening to Harve cuss and stomp about no TV to watch."

She slowed to a stop at the gate. "Anything coming your way, Rosemary?"

"No, I don't think so..."

Hannah leaned as far as the shoulder harness allowed in the event Rosemary had overlooked an oncoming vehicle, such as a tanker truck or something equally fatal. She sat back just as IdaClare tromped the gas pedal.

Rather than enter the highway, the Lincoln launched onto it, like a horizontal space shuttle. The poodles' toenails dug into the pillow, but the dogs were otherwise complacent about going from zero to seventy in a blink of their beady eyes.

"I was so disgusted with Harve," IdaClare said, her train of thought unimpaired by centrifugal force, "I called the sheriff to tip him off, but he was out on patrol."

Hannah was thrilled her directive against any more "hot tips" had made such an impact.

"Have you talked to your beau today?" IdaClare asked. "Any news on the Barton case?"

"No, to both." All three, actually, counting "beau."

"Well, darn," Rosemary said. "When we saw you come out with those papers, we thought you had a report."

The mailer's tab Hannah had been surreptitiously peeling back since takeoff came away in her hand. "This is just some stuff I need to review on the way to town." Hint, hint.

"Hope you're a speed reader," Rosemary teased.

"Are you implying I drive too fast?"

"Imply, nothing. You only know two speeds, IdaClare. Snail and bat-out-of-hell."

Hannah tuned them out in deference to Grigsby

Shrader's cover letter. The superintendent was pleased to inform her Beatrice's school board had held an emergency meeting and voted unanimously to offer Kathleen a final resting place in the municipal cemetery and would defray the cost of transporting her remains. And that the new elementary school, due to open next fall, would be named in her honor.

She almost shared the news with IdaClare and Rosemary, but time was of the essence and at a premium. Flipping through photocopied enclosures of commendations, employment records, certifications and miscellanea, her breath caught at the document with a scrolled border and bold, old-English lettering conveying a Bachelor of Science in Education degree to Kathleen Osborn.

There were only two differences between Hannah's college diploma and Kathleen's: the fields of study, and Kathleen had been more precise at trimming off the margin where For Amusement Purposes Only had been stamped.

The flowers hadn't wilted on Caroline Garvey's grave before Hannah was inundated by medical bills, overdue utility payments, the landlord's demands for back rent and funeral expenses. The debt load was so overwhelming for a grieving eighteen-year-old fresh out of high school, she had nightmares of outstretched hands thrusting at her from every direction, the fingers clenching into fists and pummeling her.

Desperate, afraid, alone and determined to pay back every dime rather than allow her mother to be immortalized as ''just another one o' them beggin', borrowin' deadbeat Garveys,'' Hannah had cashed a tiny, term-life insurance policy to finance her diploma-mill credentials and bus fare to Chicago.

Her phony-baloney degree, transcript and résumé were thrown back at her by a dozen personnel managers. Tom Friedlich ignored them and simply asked why Hannah thought she'd be an asset to their up-and-coming advertising agency.

Loyalty, gratitude and fear of discovery had kept her at F&F despite lucrative offers from competing firms. Then, on a Saturday morning that began just like its one thousand three hundred and thirty-nine predecessors, she'd wakened to the fact that all those financial and personal debts had long since been repaid.

Hannah tucked the diploma back inside the mailer, thinking, We did the best we could with what we had, didn't we, Kathleen? Don't worry, your secret is as safe with me as my own.

A road sign flashed by the window. Five miles to Sanity? Ye gods, where was Hendrickson and his stupid radar gun when you needed him?

Using the mailer to support the flimsy fax paper, Hannah squinted at the half-century-old newsprint's blurry typeface.

Business card–size fillers headlined *Lone Gunman Robs Bank* and *Teller's Quick Thinking Foils Heist* were slugged between features that read like ancient history: *Woman Hit By Street Car Dies in Hospital; Truman's Mother, 91, Wants Him to Stay in Senate, Says He'd Rather;* and *Rommel Wounded in Head, Operated On, Danes Report.*

Skimming and rejecting one page after another, her heart skipped at an *Associated Press* wire-service story datelined Lawrence, Kansas, July 21, 1944: *Blue Springs, Mo., Brothers Charged in Bank Robbery, Murder.*

The Lincoln rolled to a stop. Hannah glanced up.

The car ahead of them was waiting to turn onto a side street. She couldn't remember Duckworth's address, but it couldn't be far. Nothing was, in a town of fewer than ten thousand people.

Her eyes hopscotched down the news item, ignoring the extraneous and plucking out the essential five W's.

Farmer's Bank & Savings...Gerald E. Barton, 23...Gilbert N. (Gibb) Barton, 27...bank president forced at gunpoint to open safe...guard killed... manhunt under way for driver of getaway car...Edith Faylene Zentnor, 18...possession of the stolen—

"We're here, Hannah." IdaClare's tone indicated repetition.

Hannah started. Itsy and Bitsy growled and leaped to their feet like pot scrubbers with legs eager to attack a greasy skillet.

"Hush, babies," IdaClare crooned. "You know your aunt Hannah wouldn't harm a hair on your sweet, li'l ol' heads."

Aunt Hannah graced them with a "Don't bet on it" look. Slipping the faxes into the mailer for safekeeping, she laid it on the floorboard, unbuckled her belt and stepped out.

Never trust a porch dog, a Garvey family value, bonged in her mind just as she was about to shut the door. Reaching inside, she whispered, "Or a pair of snotty poodles," then slid the folded mailer into her purse.

Duckworth's Funeral Home occupied a sprawling Victorian mansion built by a founding family who had wanted to show everyone else how rich they were. Two ancient oak trees shaded the lawn, and several wrought-iron settees were arranged in conversational groupings with Please Stay Off the Grass signs staked beside them.

LaVeda Duckworth, a sparrow-like woman who should avoid unrelieved black, said her son, Junior, was out, but his younger brother, Osmond, would meet them in the casket room.

The mortuary's matriarch led them through a maze of rooms and hallways. Jackbooted soldiers couldn't have coaxed a peep out of the padded, celery carpet. Organ Muzak oozed through unseen speakers. Lysol and chemical odors mingled with a cloying floral scent, though the arrangements on every glass-topped table and pedestal were silk.

Focusing on the bilious floor covering, Hannah chanted to herself, I am not claustrophobic. To scream and make a run for the car would be tacky. I'd never find my way out anyway, and would probably end up in the embalming room where I'd suffer a ridiculously convenient, fatal seizure.

Having lost sight of her companions and LaVeda Duckworth, she followed the sound of voices into a large, windowless room where coffins angled this way and that like sports cars in a dealership's showroom.

IdaClare and Rosemary were chatting with a dark-haired, dark-suited man in his mid-thirties standing beside a coffin with a photo mural of a golf course on its outer shell.

"Oh, Ozzie," IdaClare gushed, "I had no idea they made such a thing."

"Art Caskets are new to our line." His palm slid across the gleaming lid. "This one is called The Fairway to Heaven."

Rosemary brought a hand to her cheek as if the *Price Is Right*'s announcer had just bellowed *Come on down*.

"It would be perfect for her, wouldn't it, Hannah?" adding for Ozzie's benefit, "IdaClare has won our club championship so many times, they may bar her from competition."

To his credit, he refrained from licking his chops like the Big Bad Wolf zeroing in on Grandma. "Then it would be a shame to settle for anything less, Mrs. Clancy. Since these are specialty items, a deposit is required to—"

"Mr. Duckworth," Hannah said, "if you don't mind, we're here to finalize the arrangements for Kathleen Osborn."

"Yes, of course," he replied, looking at Hannah as though he could see her in something pine, with nails sticking through the slats.

He gave IdaClare a brochure with his business card stapled to it, then guided them toward two metallic coffins elled in a far corner. Adopting a professional hands-crossed-at-the-crotch stance, he droned, "We suggest a viewing in our chapel at four-thirty tomorrow afternoon, followed by a brief memorial service at five. Particularly when cremation is requested, the bereaved appreciate a private, personal goodbye before the service."

IdaClare and Rosemary sniffled, then IdaClare murmured, "Yes, that would be lovely."

Hannah gripped her purse's shoulder strap, hoped she didn't upset them further, then asked, "Cremations don't usually involve a coffin, do they?"

"Casket," he corrected, indicating the two in the corner. "As we have for other members of the community, Duckworth's will provide, at a nominal fee, either the brushed bronze or silver-finished exclusively for the viewing."

IdaClare hooked a finger at her chin and gazed from one to the other and back again. "I think the silver is more feminine."

"I don't know," Rosemary hedged. "Somehow, bronze seems to suit Kathleen better."

Charging them with the decision-making, Hannah was directed to a telephone to call Reverend Lang and confirm his availability to conduct the service, including an announcement of the Beatrice school board's largesse.

The machine answered David's home number. He was still AWOL from the office, too. Where *was* he? Out lassoing dinner on the hoof?

Two hours crawled by before everyone agreed on everything from hymns, to the urn for Kathleen's ashes, to Ozzie having an itemized statement ready when the trio returned with an outfit for Kathleen to wear.

The group had enlarged to a quintet with the addition of Itsy and Bitsy, whom IdaClare refused to leave in the car, when they arrived at Wal-Mart, her favorite merchandiser.

Drizzle, light fog and temperatures descended before they worked their way up Sanity's retail ladder to Reesa's Fine Fashionables.

When Hannah rejoined IdaClare, Rosemary and the Fur Wads from Hell after another unsuccessful attempt to reach David, she supposed her companions' half-hearted squabble between a clearance-priced gray jersey dress and a pale blue twin set and floral-print skirt was due to fatigue and uglier-by-the-minute weather.

They rallied, however, at the point of sale. IdaClare thrust her platinum American Express card at the clerk. Rosemary butted her away and waved cash at the goggle-eyed employee. Using height to her advantage, Hannah sailed a check over their heads and into the register's drawer.

While Rosemary dawdled around the racks and the clerk snipped tags off the sweater and skirt ensemble, IdaClare hustled Hannah into a back corner of the shop. "Rosemary's hypoglycemic and she's getting shaky. If I suggest having supper in town, she'll give me what-for, but she won't think a thing about it if you do."

Between stops, Hannah had pulled out the faxes, re-read a few lines and shoved them back in the sleeve so many times, the pages were as wrinkled as LaVeda Duckworth's complexion. She wanted to go home, practice not sounding smug, then call David and tell him what she'd discovered so badly *she* was shaking.

On the return trip to the mortuary, Hannah leaned forward to ask, "Is anyone besides me starving? I missed lunch, and a drive-thru burger and fries would sure hit the spot."

IdaClare gave her an adoring glance in the rearview mirror. Rosemary didn't question Hannah's sincerity, which was genuine. Her empty stomach had heard IdaClare mention "supper" and it wanted some.

Instead of fast food, with the emphasis on fast, the driver opted for Riverview Restaurant's "All-You-Can-Eat Seafood Buffet." The entrees were palatable, considering the land miles separating central Missouri from an actual sea. Except IdaClare and Rosemary could have walked to one had the trips between the booth and the steam tables been in a straight line rather than circular.

Rain was falling steadily when the three of them waddled to the car. Finally homebound, Hannah's nerves could have done without the front-seat passengers' bickering about which of them was more night blind, but IdaClare kept the Lincoln below Warp One and between the painted lines.

Cheers erupted when Rosemary pointed at the happy amber glow bathing Valhalla Springs's entry gate. "The electricity is back on!"

Itsy and Bitsy barked and capered like twin dervishes, bounding into and off of Aunt Hannah's lap until she gently clotheslined the front-runner, who yipped in surprise.

"Is everything all right back there?" IdaClare inquired.

"Just dandy," Hannah said, prying her index finger from whichever poodle was auditioning for a starring role in the next *Jaws* sequel.

At the sight of her beloved—though dark—cottage nestled in the trees, Hannah's elation shifted to a mild but earnest panic attack.

Did I turn off the shower this morning? And all the faucets? And while I'm hyperventilating, what about *that stove burner?*

Death-gripping the car door's handle as IdaClare wheeled into the driveway, Hannah said, "Thanks for everything, and don't forget about bridge club in the morning."

Rosemary said, "I'll call Delbert, Leo and Marge about the service for Kathleen. They'll help with a telephone tree."

"Great."

"And I'll print notices for the clubhouse and community center's bulletin boards," IdaClare volunteered.

"Super." Hannah bailed out into the rain. "Good night."

IdaClare called, "We're not moving until you're inside."

Hannah nodded, slammed the door and ran for the cottage. Fumbling for the keyhole, she sneered, "Shrewd move, Einstein. If you left anything on, why couldn't it have been the stupid porch light?"

Tumblers disengaged with a sweet little snick. She waved at the car, whisked inside and locked out the heebie-jeebies as she had a thousand times when her mother had sent her to the store for cigarettes, two long, very dark blocks from their trailer.

She patted the wall in search of the switch plate. Satiny oak panels. Cool polished brass. Her palm grazed the row of plastic toggles, all of them angling...

Down? But the electricity went out a little after seven that morning.

The porch light should still be on from last night.

20

"**B**een waiting a long time for you, Miss Garvey."

The table lamp beside the club chair clicked on. Hannah whirled, then recoiled, the brightness harsh to eyes accustomed to darkness.

Her pulse raced, tripped over itself. Fear intensified the stench of cigarettes left to burn themselves out; the metallic tang coating her tongue; the disbelief paralyzing her body, her brain, her voice.

Light funneling upward from the shade sharpened the planes of the man's face, hollowed his eyes, glinted off his dirty gray hair and the whiskers frosting his cheeks and upper lip.

"Who are you?" She eased backward, groping for the doorknob. "What do you want?"

He stepped into the open. "Drop the purse. Get away from the door." He waggled a long-barreled pistol for emphasis.

Her purse thumped on the floorboards. She angled away from it, and him. "Take it and get out."

A wheezy laugh rattled up his chest. He coughed. His teeth bared and gnashed, as if stanching a jag. "I ain't no goddamned purse snatcher."

"Then who are you?" She hated the mousey pitch, the tremble in her voice.

"The name's Barton. Earl's dear ol' uncle Gibb."

His lips relaxed, then bowed into a sneer. "Seems with him dead, I'm the last of the line."

Facts gleaned from the newspaper articles flitted through Hannah's mind. "What about your brother—er, Gerald, isn't it?"

Surprise devolved to bemusement. "Studied up on us, have you?"

"Earl was an employee here."

"Yeah, and I understand you're sweet on the county sheriff, too." He shrugged. "Baby bro' died at Lansing in—I dunno, '50, maybe '51. Took a bullet when we hit the bank at Lawrence. Healed up okay, but got tuberculosis from it."

"Sorry to hear that."

"I didn't shed no tears." Barton sucked in a breath and flinched, though he tried to hide it. "Gerald always was weak. Followed me around like a damn, dumb puppy."

Hannah knew she had to keep him talking until she conjured a plan of escape, or—please, God—David intercepted her telepathic 911 calls. "It must have been a shock when Earl told you he'd found your long-lost accomplice."

"He didn't." Barton chuckled. "Called me up, mad as hell. Said somebody'd made a movie about the heist and none of us got a dime out of it. Said he was working for the ol' lady that played Edi Fay's part."

A fuzzy, typeset line flashed behind Hannah's eyes: *An interstate manhunt is under way for Edith Faylene Zentnor, 18, of Peculiar, Mo., the driver of the getaway car, who authorities believe is in possession of the stolen money.*

"I take it you didn't believe him?" she asked.

"Told him he and the ol' broad was fulla shit. Found

out when Earl bunked with me last winter that he was dumber than his pa. Kicked him out before he did something to get me busted on a parole violation.''

They both jumped when the phone rang. Hannah started toward the office nook.

''Hold it.'' Barton glanced over his shoulder at the desk, the pistol swinging away as he did. Its barrel and his attention returned to her instantly. ''Let it ring.''

''What if it's one of the friends I went to town with? She'll wonder why I don't answer. She might even come back to make sure—''

''I *said*, let it ring.'' Perspiration sheened his brow.

After the fourth ring, the recorded message began, *Hello, you've reached Valhalla Spri*— A click sounded, then the whir of the tape rewinding.

''Why'd it shut off?''

''It does automatically when the caller hangs up.'' She prayed her attempted bluff didn't turn into a self-fulfilling prophesy. IdaClare probably would have left a message, but Rosemary? Maybe, maybe not.

''If you didn't believe your nephew,'' Hannah asked, ''how did you find out Kathleen Osborn was Edith Zentnor?''

Barton squinted at her, momentarily confused. ''Earl, he, uh, took pictures of her on the sly. Sent me some and the rest to *People* magazine. Figgered he'd pocket a couple hundred on one of them 'Where Are They Now?' stories.''

Hannah thought, Yeah, well, easy come, easy go. ''I wonder why Kathleen didn't think anything of Earl's last name being Barton?''

She didn't realize she'd spoken aloud until Barton said, ''Edi Fay hired him to shovel dirt. 'Earl' was good enough for her. Once he heard about that movie, scared as he was she'd tip off the producer, or studio, or what-fuckin'-ever and keep us from collecting our due, if she'd have asked, Earl woulda given her a phony one.''

Barton advanced toward her. ''Sumbitch killed my golden goose afore I could get a bus ticket down here, too.'' He snickered. ''That's why he's dead. That's what *you're* gonna be, too, if you don't hand over my money.''

The man glaring at her an arm's length away had killed a bank guard in cold blood. He'd murdered his own nephew. He had nothing to gain, but absolutely nothing to lose by killing her.

Hannah stood her ground. ''After wrecking Kathleen's cottage and searching mine, you should know there isn't any money.''

Bluish distended veins in his neck thobbed with his heartbeat. ''I rotted in a goddamned Kansas prison for *fifty-five* years, lady. I ain't got time for no games.''

She hesitated, as fearful of telling the truth as being caught in a lie. Barton was in his seventies and no picture of health, but had the lean, hard body of a middleweight boxer forever hoping to make a comeback.

''When Kathleen, er, Edi Fay…died,'' Hannah said in a calm, measured tone, ''what money she had was in a trust fund. She couldn't withdraw any of it while she was alive, any more than I can now.''

Gibb's face flushed. ''She tried the same bullshit on Earl. Goddamnit, I *know* better. *I* pitched the satchel fulla money into the getaway car.'' He paused, eyes bulging, struggling to refill his lungs. ''Know what she did? The two-timin' slut hit the gas. Left me and Gerald flatfooted in the street.''

''I understand to your way of thinking you were

ripped off. Except Kathleen didn't do it.'' Hannah nodded at her purse. "See that FedEx envelope? The proof is in there, if you care to look.''

"Proof? What kinda proof?''

"Theodore Miller, the president of the bank, opened the safe and filled your satchel, right?''

"I disremember the name, but, yeah. So what?''

"How closely did you watch him?''

"What is this? A stall? Well, it ain't—''

"You wanted proof. I'm trying to give it to you.''

He chuffed. "I watched him as good as I could. Had to keep an eye on the tellers while Gerald put the fear of God in the guard and the customers.''

"Theodore Miller may have put some cash in that bag, Mr. Barton, but most of it was deposit slips, counter checks—whatever he could grab when you weren't looking.''

"If Edi Fay told you that, she's lyin'—*lyin'*, ya hear me? The cops didn't find her till the next day. Never found the money. She stashed it, did her lousy dime-stretch, then fetched it and lived high on the hog—''

"No, she did *not*," Hannah shouted back. "Eight months after you, Gerald, and Kathleen went to prison, Miller was convicted of embezzlement. He used the robbery to cover up his own thefts. He was the one living high on the hog, and he liked it too much to stop.''

Barton hauled back and slapped her. "I was there, bitch. Don't tell *me* how it went down.''

Hannah staggered, reeling from the blow. Don't fall. Don't give him the satisfaction. Shake it off. She licked her lips, tasted blood. Her eyes locked on Barton's. She straightened, jaw clenched, shoulders square.

"Think you're tough, huh?'' He cocked the pistol

and pointed it at her chin. "Ask yourself, what good's that money gonna do you after I blow your pretty face clean off?"

Headlights swept the living room. *David*. Oh, please, let it be David. It had to be him.

A cream puff Edsel's precision-tuned engine purred past the windows, then fell silent. A car door thunked shut.

Barton backpedaled a step. His gaze flicked to the door and back to Hannah. "Real poor timin' for somebody."

Porch risers creaked. Barton's eyes bored into hers. He leveled the gun at her, ready to swing and cut Delbert down through the door the second he thumbed the bell.

Footsteps scraped the planks. Barton pivoted. The gun snapped up into firing position.

"Run, Delbert!" Her kick caught Barton just below the wrist. The pistol boomed like a cannon and flew from his hand.

Hannah cupped her deafened ears. Spent gunpowder seared her eyes, her nostrils.

Snarling like an animal, Barton grabbed a fistful of her hair and threw her to the floor. He pounced on top of her, crushing her chest. Viselike fingers clamped her throat.

She bucked and thrashed. Her knees pounding his back, fists pummeling his arms, his shoulders. Barton's blood-red face, contorted with rage, blurred, began to dissolve into a velvety gray haze.

Elbows jammed against the floorboards, Hannah arched her back, fighting for air. Barton's stranglehold loosened, slipped. She slammed a fist into his temple with all her might. Again. Again.

Mewling, gurgling sounds purled from his throat. Glass shattered. The front door exploded open. Barton groaned and collapsed on top of her.

Howling like a banshee, Delbert grabbed Barton's coat and yanked him off of her. Sprawled on his back, Barton's arms and legs splayed wide, as if boneless. His head lolled, eyes open, fixed, staring into hers.

Footfalls vibrated the floorboards. A metallic *click* was heard. Delbert panted, "Twitch a muscle and I'll kill you with your own gun."

Hannah pried her arm from under Barton's body and rolled away. She could still see his eyes, knew she'd see them behind hers for the rest of her life.

She heard a scuffling sound. Delbert muttered, "Well, I'll be..." His mystified voice trailed away, then he was kneeling beside her, gently pushing her hair back, caressing her cheek.

"Everything's all right, ladybug. He can't hurt you ever again, I promise."

She looked up at Delbert and laid her hand over his dry, coarsened one. "He's dead, isn't he."

Delbert nodded. "Checked under his ear, and a wrist for a pulse. Didn't find one."

A shudder ripped through her. Cold—she was so cold. Bile spilled into her mouth. Grimacing, she swallowed hard, her neck feeling at once swollen twice its size, and wire-thin.

"Think you can make it to the couch?"

"Kitchen," she rasped. "Ice. My throat."

With his help, she struggled to her feet. She was dizzy, disoriented and grimly determined not to look at the man who would have murdered Delbert if she hadn't kicked the gun away.

That's the way she had to think of it. The memory

she must plant in her mind. Like other lies and half truths, some defensive, some out of kindness, if she repeated it enough times, someday she might believe it herself.

Kathleen would understand.

Delbert wrapped the afghan from the rocking chair around her shoulders. Hannah fingered the knotty edges like a string of rosary beads.

Her mother had torn out and reworked the stitches until the yarn separated into curlicued threads. Caroline had tried her best to make it perfect. Hannah treasured its flaws as dearly as her mother had treasured the round-bottomed, purple-and-green clay ashtray her daughter made in fourth grade art class.

"Rosemary called me about the funeral," Delbert said. "Figured I'd come down and ask if you wanted a ride. I half expected Hendrickson to be here. Wasn't thirty seconds later, I was wishing to God he was."

He paused in the breakfast room's doorway to flip on the lights. The French doors looked as if a bear cub had cut its teeth on them. Empty beer bottles, spilled food, food cartons, chip bags and cans with spoon handles impaled in them littered the kitchen counters and floor.

"The son of a bitch had himself quite a picnic."

Hannah couldn't care less. A garbage bag and a gallon of disinfectant would take care of the mess. That Barton had used her mother's candy dish for an ashtray enraged her. The stains and smell would wash out, but it would never, *ever,* be clean again.

Delbert clasped her arm. "C'mon, honeylamb, I'm putting you to bed."

"Uh-uh." Her lower lip stung when she tried to smile. "Just need to sit down. Clear my head."

"Let me get the chair out of your office then. All those at the table are good for is kindling."

Rather than argue, Hannah pulled the afghan tighter around her, shuffled over and sat down. Physical, and consequently, emotional traction were exactly what she needed.

You can't lose it when your chin is up and your spine can't bend.

Great-uncle Mort hadn't taught her that. Life had.

Delbert brought her a lumpy dish towel folded around an ice-cube core. "Okeydoke, now, what else can I get you? Aspirin? No? Well, how 'bout something to drink? Something cold, or—I know, how 'bout a pot of coffee? Does that sound good to you?"

Strangely, it did. Retracting her tongue, Hannah used the tiny pool of saliva that formed to test her swallowing capability. Lesson two, courtesy of Great-aunt Lurleen's bag of pharmaceutical tricks.

"Coffee," she agreed, her voice stronger but gravelly. "First, we have to call David."

Delbert's eyebrows peaked, his expression pensive.

"I know you have," she said.

"Have what?"

"Called 911 too damned many times the past week."

He looked away. "If I'd moved a little faster the other night, much less tonight—"

"Don't even think it, Delbert. Want someone to blame?" She stabbed a finger toward the living room. "Blame *him.*"

He pondered a moment. "I hear what you're saying, but maybe Jessup Knox was right. We can't have bums breaking into houses when folks are gone, then going loco on 'em."

Hannah almost corrected him, then realized she'd spend the next few hours, more likely, days, explaining who Gibb Barton was, why he killed his nephew, why...

Oh, God. I can't. I can't explain any of it without betraying Kathleen. Edith Faylene Zentnor and Kathleen Osborn can't coexist.

With each telling, the grapevine will embellish the story of the beautiful, young, and probably naive getaway car driver, while the quiet, respectable, Nebraska schoolteacher who baked cobblers, sewed stuffed monkeys for sick children and read romance novels by the sackful fades further and further from memory.

Only David can know the truth. No one else. Not even Delbert. Secrets on top of secrets, lies on top of lies.

If it were a perfect world, he'd leave his badge and cop face at the door. He'd shoo everyone else away, and just listen. Wouldn't interrupt with questions or divide his attention between her and taking notes.

And his eyes would stay a soft gray-blue. Not once would they telegraph the fact that, whether in self-defense, or to protect Delbert, she'd killed a man tonight.

Except it wasn't a perfect world. Never has been, never would be. Pain nipped Hannah's backbone as it grated against the chair. "I think you'd better make that call now, Delbert."

Stars glittered in the west where the clouds had peeled away. The goofballs daytime talk shows catered to would say the weather change symbolized good triumphing over evil.

To Delbert, the clearing sky visible through the cam-

ouflage net draping his windshield symbolized the
eighteen holes he could get in before Kathleen's memorial service.

He sipped bourbon-laced coffee from the thermos
bottle's chrome cup. Unlike the soda-pop cans on
wheels they glued together at factories these days, his
Edsel was as cozy as Hannah's cottage.

Which he'd still be in, rather than parked twenty
yards from, if it wasn't for David Hendrickson.

Just when Hannah was about to say how Earl Barton's ex-con of an uncle fit into the scheme of things,
her eyeballs locked with the sheriff's. Delbert didn't
know who hypnotized who, but the next thing he knew,
he was on the exile side of the porch watching a deputy
duct-tape plastic over the hole where the front-door
glass had been.

It was as slick and respectful a heave-ho as Delbert
had ever received, but it put him on the outside looking
in, when he'd wanted very much, and for reasons beyond curiosity, to be where the action was. Most of all,
he'd wanted to be there when Hannah snapped out of
her spooky, controlled stupor.

And that Andrik character could have done with a
little friendly advice, too. Why, anyone who'd caught
Law & Order on the tube could see the detective didn't
know his butt from a Buick about proper investigative
procedures.

Delbert set the cup on the dashboard. His hand
searched for and found the binoculars on the seat. Just
his luck, the infrared jobs he'd ordered from Private
Spy Supply Company hadn't come in yet. They'd be
useless to surveil the cottage's lighted front room, but
who knew how many more of the Barton clan might
be out there in the dark, skulking around?

Thump-thump-thump.

Delbert's posterior parted company with the upholstery. The binoculars parted company with his hands, sailed the length of the neck strap, then boomeranged and clouted him in the nose.

Leo's round face appeared in the passenger window like a grinning, cartoon moon. A pudgy finger pointed down. "The door," he yelled. "It is locked."

Eyes watering, gingerly massaging his wounded proboscis, and cursing with such vehemence a fog billowed up the windshield, Delbert fumbled for the automatic lock button, telling himself a Leo in hand was worth a two-ton idiot thrashing around in the bushes.

The netting complicated the unexpected, unwanted visitor's entrance; a struggle Delbert could have expedited. Instead, he congratulated himself on installing a toggle switch to black out the interior lights, poured himself a refill from the thermos and watched the human drama unfold, refold and contort at stage right.

Huffing, puffing and sweating profusely, Leo finally backed into the seat, causing the Edsel's immediate, fifteen-degree list to starboard.

Delbert warned, "Don't slam the—"

Ka-*whump*. Leo grimaced sheepishly. "Oops."

"Damn it, Schnur. Remind me not to tell you where I'm going next time I do surveillance."

"You did not tell me this time."

"I didn't?" Delbert frowned. "Then how'd you find me?"

It was Leo's turn to look befuddled. "I could not sleep, I take a drive, I see your car, I stop."

So much for his genuine, government-issue, bumper-to-bumper camouflage. That lying jackanapes down at the army/navy surplus store was going to eat his No Cash Refunds sign for breakfast.

While Delbert mentally scripted his irate-consumer speech, Leo borrowed the binoculars for a gander at the cottage. Head bobbing up and down and side to side like a pigeon doing a mating dance, Leo whistled through his dentures. "Hannah's beautiful lawn, it is ruined."

"Mucky as a hog wallow," Delbert agreed. "I told Hendrickson to wait till the ground dried up before calling a tow truck to pull Barton's pickup out of the backyard." He snorted. "Think he'd listen to me? 'Butt out, Bisbee,' he said."

Leo gasped. "The sheriff, he said that to you? 'Butt out'?"

"Well, maybe not in so many words...."

"That is when he asked you to leave, then, eh?"

Delbert squirmed. "Well, no...not exactly that very minute. I kept Hannah company a while longer. Got some crackers down her, so the pill Doc Pennington gave her wouldn't make her sick. You know, stuff like that."

Leo clucked his tongue as he laid the binoculars on the seat. Resting crossed arms on his belly, he aimed an I-don't-have-all-night-so-cut-the-crap glare at Delbert.

It never failed. Teach a buddy how to play poker, give him a couple of tips on reading body language, and sooner or later, he'll use it against you.

"Okay, so Hendrickson had a point. He said he didn't want Barton's truck to be the first thing Hannah saw when she looked out the kitchen window tomorrow morning."

"A kindness, he was doing her, Delbert."

"Tell that to the grass."

"Unfortunate, it is. A catastrophe? No. A little dirt, a little sod, and in a week, maybe two, *whoosh*, the lawn is as good as new."

"Hmmph." Delbert drummed his fingers on the steering wheel. "Would have saved everyone a lot of grief if Hendrickson had found that pickup Barton camped in like a mobile Motel 6 a helluva lot faster."

His best friend exhaled a disapproving sigh. "The sheriff, I am sure, would agree with you."

"Oh, you are, huh?" Delbert stared into the darkness for a long, contemplative moment. "The bone I have to pick isn't with the sheriff, all right? Hendrickson has potential. He just needs a nudge in the right direction now and then."

"Is the bone with me? For knocking on the trunk?"

"Not the smartest thing you've ever done," Delbert said, "but no. This one's mine and mine alone."

He lowered his head, then angled it to look at Leo. "Until a while ago, I thought no starch in your noodle was the worst kind of impotence a man could have."

His heart squeezed, as if an unseen hand was wringing it dry. "That ain't *nothin'* compared to seeing somebody you care about being about two shakes from dead, and you're too old and weak to do a damned thing to help her."

21

David shut the Crown Vic's door a little harder than necessary. Pausing beside it, he allowed himself a moment to feel the sun warm his face.

An oriole's flute had him searching for the colorful, feathered musician; the first he'd heard this year. Robins were the traditional harbinger of spring. David took their appearance as a sign to start listening for the orioles to whistle confirmation.

The old man zipped inside a hooded sleeping bag, snoozing in a chaise lounge on Hannah's porch, looked like a giant cigar with a face at the band end. He blinked, peered up at David, then at the cardboard drink carrier and paper sack. "What's all that?"

"Breakfast."

David set the holder on the porch rail to remove one of the three lidded cups. "You take your coffee black, don't you?"

"Been known to." The sleeping bag's zipper ratcheted downward. Delbert's shoulders, then an arm emerged, a shaky hand targeting the cup. "Thanks."

David fished a napkin and a waxed-paper-wrapped honey bun from the sack. "The cherry danish were tempting, but these just came out of the oven."

Delbert eyed the pastry and its donor. "You delivering for the bakery on the side now?"

"Gee, Bisbee, take it easy on the gratitude, will you? It's getting downright embarrassing."

"Oh, I appreciate it, rightly enough." Delbert wiggled into a sitting position. "I just didn't expect to wake up to breakfast alfresco." With pastry pooching his cheek as if a wisdom tooth had suddenly impacted, he added, "How'd you know I was here?"

"Bill Eustace spotted you about 2:00 a.m. when he pulled through on patrol. He recognized the Edsel from the other night, so he figured it was okay, but called me to make sure."

"Good man." Delbert nodded approval. "Can't be too careful these days."

The drink carrier squealed as David lifted a second cup from it. Steam flued out a hole in the lid embossed with Warning! Contents Are Hot! Evidently, food servers can't be too careful these days, either.

David said, "I was surprised to hear Hannah let you camp on her porch. When I offered to stretch out on the couch, she turned me down so flat my ears rang for an hour."

"Well, I could have told you that, which is why I didn't bother to ask. I hung around till everybody left, went home and gathered my gear, then set up shop."

"Do you think she's still asleep?"

The expert on female behavior paused for a sip of coffee. "She was curled under the covers like a little girl when I checked on her around sunup." He winked. "She snores some, but I've heard worse."

David laughed, knowing Delbert wouldn't be long for this world if Hannah ever found out he'd shared that observation. "Hard as it is for me to admit, under these particular circumstances, I'm glad you have a key."

"I don't. She had the locks changed again."

David frowned. "Then how did you get in? Andrik nailed the deck doors shut, and Hannah locked the back door after us when we left last night."

"That's why I took the porch for picket duty." Delbert gobbled the last bite of pastry in his mouth, then waved a sugary thumb at the front door. "The jamb is too messed up for the dead bolt to hold fast."

"Yeah, I know, but we did double hook the screen."

"About all you could do." Delbert graced him with a smug smile. "Except, like the commercial says, Visa will take you anywhere you want to go."

"Bisbee, I—" David shook his head.

"Aw, don't get your shorts in a bind. You'd have done the same thing, if you'd stayed out here all night, instead of me."

David admitted he would have. To himself.

"Jehosophat, this coffee's hot." Setting his cup down, Delbert struggled to shed his brown thermal cocoon. "Hey, gimme a hand, will ya? The zipper's stuck and I'm roasting alive in this thing."

Energetic cussing on Delbert's part, patience on David's and a coordinated effort from both finally released the sentry from his flannel-lined, subzero-rated hell on earth.

Delbert swung his legs around to sit sidesaddle on the lounge. Dabbing his flushed face with a handkerchief, he said, "Maybe it's a good thing you came along, Hendrickson. A couple more minutes and I'd have been ready to carve."

David chuckled. "Even if you weren't pure gristle, I don't think that would have been a fit ending for a hero."

"Hero, my ass."

"Play it as humble as you care to, Bisbee, but if you hadn't come along when you did last night, Barton would have killed Hannah. No doubt about it."

"Humble has nothing to with it," Delbert said, directing his remarks to the porch planks. "I don't know what kind of Sir Galahad story she fed you, but nothing is the sum total of what I did to help her."

Defeat leavened the older man's voice. His back bowed, and there was a slight palsy in his hands David had never seen before.

"You couldn't be more wrong. You distracted Barton. Gave Hannah a chance to kick his gun away. That's the best I could have hoped to do if I'd been here instead of you."

Delbert looked up. "Nice try, Hendrickson, but—"

"Well, now, I suppose I could have busted the door down and gotten myself shot all to hell while Hannah made a run for it." He shifted his weight. "The only problem is, Barton would have wheeled around and shot her before she put two yards between them."

Delbert reached for his coffee and took a long, slow pull. "I did try to kick the door in, you know. Finally gave up and heaved one of Kathleen's houseplants through the glass, instead."

Lowering his head again, he muttered, "I dunno. Maybe it was better the hand played the way it did."

David stopped himself from restating the facts, swearing on a stack of bibles, or any of the other tactics people resort to rather than let doubt die a natural death.

Lost in their own private thoughts, neither of them moved or spoke. Vehicles braked as they passed by on the boulevard, their drivers' and passengers' curiosity as luminous as their cars' bright red taillights.

Valhalla Springs might set a new record-high temperature before the day was over, with all the hot air, gossip and rumors sure to start flying from here to yonder.

Delbert cleared his throat, stood and returned the cup to the carrier. Smoothing the wild, white tufts of hair with his hands, he crammed a golf cap on his head, then wadded up the sleeping bag, as if it were an anaconda in need of strangling. "Overpriced hunk of junk."

He spun around. "Can a store refuse to give refunds on defective merchandise?"

"It isn't good business," David said, "but it's not illegal."

"Hmmph." Delbert deliberated a moment, then asked, "Had any complaints about Dan Armitage, at the army/navy store?"

David wasn't sure what he was alluding to, but Bisbee alluding to anything made him nervous. "What kind of complaints?"

"Like he's a no-account, sidewinding son of a junk-yard dog that smiles whilst he rickydoos his customers."

David fought so hard to keep a straight face, his jaw stitched. "No, I can't say I've heard any like that."

"Good. Probably means he'll listen to reason." Delbert started for the steps. "Nice talking to you, Hendrickson, but I've got a schedule to keep. 'Preciate it if you'd lug my chair out to the car. Save me a trip."

David folded the chaise flat, then laid it in the Edsel's trunk, which could have held enough lawn furniture for an outdoor rock concert. Delbert shifted the lounger an inch to the right, grunted and closed the lid.

"You'd better tell Hannah I let you in," he advised.

"No sense giving her something to fuss about before you can say boo."

"You don't think bringing coffee and honey buns will get me out of the doghouse, huh?"

"Son, a wise man doesn't get himself *in* the doghouse, if he can help it."

Bisbee surveyed the cottage, his stubbled chin rumpled and a faraway look in his eyes. "Well, I, uh—" He brushed a hand on his trousers and extended it. "See you around...David."

"You bet." He smiled and clasped the older man's hand. "Delbert."

Hannah poked her nose up from the sheet and sniffed. Coffee and yeast and cinnamon. Oh my.

She'd dreamed in color before and some had sound tracks, but she couldn't recall ever smelling one. Delicious. And probably fattening by some sort of metabolic osmosis.

The bracing scent of Aqua Velva drifted into her dream. "Mmm, doughnuts and David. Fantasies don't get any better than this."

"Oh, yes, they do, darlin'."

Her eyelids raised a fraction. Sunlight poured through the mini blinds she'd closed the night before. An indolent breeze sighed through windows she'd shut against the rain. Behind her, a heavy object slewed the mattress.

She turned her head to peer over her shoulder. Reality wore a Kinderhook County Sheriff's Department ball cap, a black T-shirt and a shit-eating grin. It held gooey pastry in one hand and a large paper cup of coffee in the other. "Good mornin'."

Reserving judgment until fully awake, she shoved

the pillows against the headboard. As she skootched into a sitting position, a veritable Mormon Tabernacle Choir of pain sensors howled *Ouch*. Passionately and harmoniously, the crescendo escalated to a screaming high-C.

David's grin evaporated. "Hey, take it easy, sugar."

"I am," she said through gritted teeth. Taking it hard would be simultaneous movement and respiration. Mind over matter. No guts, no glory. Rule Britannia.

Intuitive guy that he was, David transferred ownership of the cup. While the gentleman removed his cap and put his ever-present portable radio on the nightstand, the lady slurped at her coffee, testing its temperature and the soreness of her throat. Wondrous warmth sluiced clear to her tummy.

"Okay," she said. "You can stop looking at me like that now."

"Like what?"

"Like the priest is rushing over to give last rites."

David rolled his eyes. "You don't have to be brave for me."

"I'm not." She reached for the pastry. "I'm being brave for me." Buttery, brown-sugary cinnamon bread sent her taste buds into a swoon, and ordered her tender throat to take its complaints elsewhere.

If hospitals truly wanted to speed patients' recovery, they'd serve comfort food, not tapioca and fruit gelatin. A mush meal never induced anyone to fling off a respirator. Caffeine and sugar were the stuff miracle cures were made of.

Brain function, for instance. "Correct me if I'm wrong, but I seem to recall locking the door behind you and Andrik last night."

"Uh-huh."

"So, how did you get in?"

"Delbert."

She chewed on that, and her breakfast. "And how might he have done that? He doesn't have a key anymore."

For a large, adult male, the sheriff did a decent job of looking like a sheepish ten-year-old boy. "He slipped the hooks on the screen door with a credit card."

"All right, that does it. I'm telling Bob Davies to install a revolving door. Ex-cons, pink-haired ladies, cops, retired postal guys, what have you, come one, come all. If I could cook, I'd give Denny's a run for its money."

"Before you work yourself up into a blue-ribbon snit," David drawled, "you ought to know the old fella slept in a chaise lounge all night, guarding your front door."

She almost dropped her doughnut. "He did? Why?"

"Two reasons, with the first being because he adores you. The second stays between you and me."

Hands and mouth full, Hannah shrugged agreement.

"Numero uno, I think he's worried the woods are crawling with homicidal Bartons. I can't disabuse him of the notion until we decide how to explain last night and keep Kathleen's misspent youth out of it."

Hannah didn't follow, and said as much.

"If Gibb Barton was in jail, confidentiality would be impossible. Since he isn't, I see no reason to deny Kathleen the right to rest in peace."

Dead men tell no tales. Now, there's an irony. If Barton had killed Hannah, the gossips would have had a field day. Ditto, if she hadn't killed him. With nobody left to prosecute...

Oh, God. Stop thinking. Right this minute.

"Hannah? What's wrong?"

"I, uh...never mind." She smiled. "What's the other reason Delbert slept on my porch?"

"Tell me where that funny look came from first."

"The womb."

"I mean it, Hannah."

Great. The slightest hint of a panic attack and up pops Mount Rushmore in the flesh. Well, forget it. A relationship of any kind with someone whose antennae twitched whenever she did was out of the question. Jarrod wouldn't have noticed if she'd had a grand mal seizure, but life was too short to hide everything from angst to minor gas pains.

Amazing, though, how long David could stare at her without blinking. The *Guinness* people should be notified. "You're not going to just let it go, are you?"

"No, ma'am, I'm not. I've seen you happy, nervous, startled, arou—well, lots of things, but pure-de-scared?" He shook his head. "I want to know why."

"Okay, Sheriff. We talked a long time last night about all sorts of things, didn't we?"

"Yes." He'd flinched at the title, his features settling into a wary, glacial mask.

"What we didn't discuss is Gibb Barton's cause of death." She regarded the pastry she held, then laid it aside. Hoisting her cup, she tipped her head as if toasting him and took a sip. Bitter with the sweet.

Confusion chased contemplation around on David's face until understanding took the checkered flag. He divested her of the cup, then clasped her hands in his.

In a voice at once compassionate and firm, he said, "Delbert slept on your porch so anyone else who might try to hurt you had to go through him to do it. Trying and failing to pull off a John Wayne–style rescue wounded a lot more than his pride.

"When we talked on the porch, I told him the God's honest truth. If he'd succeeded, neither of you would be alive to tell about it."

Tears rimmed Hannah's eyes. She hoped with all her heart Delbert believed that. Gibb Barton would not have left any witnesses.

"Now," David continued, "it appears you're paddling the same guilt-stricken boat, but from the opposite end." His hands tightened around hers. "Flat-out, no bullshit, no shadow of doubt whatsoever, you had *nothing to do* with Gibb Barton's death."

The room spun. Barton's yellowed, bloodshot eyes smoldered behind hers. She heard his death rattle, smelled his last fetid breath. "I hit him, David—*hard*. As hard as I could, over and over—"

"Listen to me." He pulled her to him, clasping her hands to his chest. "Barton either had a stroke or a coronary. We won't know which until the postmortem, but I swear to you, those blows you struck absolutely did *not* kill the man."

Hannah wanted to believe him, tried to believe him. But David wasn't *there,* hadn't seen, didn't know—

"To protect Delbert, you kicked the gun out of Barton's hand, isn't that right?"

She nodded.

"Then Barton turned on you, didn't he?"

"Don't, please. I don't want to—"

"He turned on you, didn't he, Hannah?"

"Yes."

"Grabbed your hair and knocked you down, and then what did he do?"

She tried to free her hands. David wouldn't let go.

"Stop it! Leave me *alone*. I already told you what happened—"

"Trust me, Hannah. Tell me again. After Barton knocked you down, what did he do?"

"He choked me. He was on top of me. I couldn't get away. Couldn't breathe."

"And that's when you hit him."

"Yes!" She sobbed and jerked her head away. "No, not then. Everything was going black. His fingers loosened. I—I—could breathe...could fight back again."

David smiled, his thumbs massaging her knuckles. "Think, sugar. Besides proof a guardian angel watches over you, what does that tell you?"

"I don't—" The scene replayed in the same weird slow motion she'd experienced when it had happened. In a voice just louder than a whisper, she said, "Barton was dead *before* I hit him."

"Or within a hair of it," David said. "That's why he let go of you." He eased her back on the pillows. "I'm sorry I had to put you through that, but the 'convincing' had to come from you, not me."

A glorious, feather-light relief skirmished with lingering doubt. "It may take a while longer to make a believer out of my conscience."

He hitched a knee up on the mattress. "Hearing the whole story ought to soothe it considerably."

Hannah smiled. "Give it your best shot—so to speak."

"Your great, good buddy Marlin Andrik used the prints we had on file for Kathleen to track down her prison record, which led to the Barton brothers. Marlin dug a little deeper and found out the surviving brother, Gilbert, was dying of congestive heart failure and had petitioned the Missouri court for parole."

"Missouri? Why? The newspaper clips said the Bartons and Kathleen were incarcerated at Lansing Prison in Kansas."

"They were." David splayed his fingers. "It's a tad complicated, but Missouri, Kansas, and twenty-some others have an interstate compact, which means a native of one state imprisoned in another asks his home court to grant him parole. The petitioner has to meet all kinds of conditions, but if he does, and the court approves, he's their baby.

"Lifers are the healthiest, hardiest population group for their age in the country, but I don't suppose the parole board thought a seventy-one-year-old with a bum ticker posed much of a risk to society."

Only to two or three members of it, anyway, Hannah mused. "When was Gibb Barton released?"

"Last September. I talked to his parole officer yesterday evening. According to him, Barton was a model ex-con. Snake-mean, and not the type you'd show your back to, but he was never a minute late for a check-in."

"Until a few days ago, right?" She aimed a feeble wave at her coffee cup, as though her arm was too short to go the distance. When David delivered it to her, she decided this invalid shtick might be worth milking a while.

David said, "No, Barton wasn't due to check in again until next week. The parole officer didn't know Barton had left town until I called him back this morning."

"So much for his model ex-con." She raised her eyebrows. "Who not only skipped town, he bought a gun somewhere along the way."

"On the street," David said, "or from a registered

dealer doing more business under the counter than over it. Sad to say, it's harder to buy a weapon legally than illegally.''

"Anyone who isn't aware of that hasn't watched TV in the last decade." She sighed. "Barton hated Kathleen, you know. Psychoanalysis isn't my thing, but I think he blamed Gerald and her for screwing up the robbery. When his brother died, Gibb tranferred all the hate to her.''

"Could be. Kathleen being free all these years probably didn't endear her to him, either.''

"True.'' Hannah raked the hair off her face. Jeez, even her hair hurt, thanks to Barton's caveman throw. "Want to know the worst, most sickening part of it all?''

"What?''

"From the minute Kathleen told Earl that stupid movie story of hers, she was a sitting duck. If he hadn't killed her, Gibb would have.''

David nodded. "No quarter given Earl, as ungodly brutal as he was, but well…''

"I know. Gibb would have done worse, and enjoyed it. How that's as abhorrent, if not more so, than what Earl did, I can't explain. It just is.''

Silence descended, as it does when a subject has been verbally exhausted, but lagging thoughts and emotions haven't quite crossed the finish line.

Hannah sensed David had glanced at her, and looked up. Finding him staring into the middle distance above the headboard, she averted her gaze.

Repeated episodes of nonsynchronized eye contact occurred before she fidgeted, a subtler method of communicating "I'm ready to talk again, how about you?''

than invading another's mental space by saying it aloud.

Two squirms and a sniff later, David's smile created doubt whether his musings had been exclusively devoted to murder. Reaching for the ceiling with his left arm, he bent at the waist, winced, then plucked the coffee cup from her hand again.

"Would you mind scooting over? I'm getting a back spasm from sitting crooked."

The "Oh, my aching back" ploy predated original sin by maybe ten, fifteen minutes. Hannah's enlightenment came in 1968, when she was recuperating from the flu. Michael Dean Terhune dropped by after school to deliver her algebra and biology textbooks, sat down on the bed to visit a while, then used sudden sciatica as an excuse to crawl under the covers with her.

Contrary to the rumor he spread afterward, they didn't "do it," but she did learn a few things about her own anatomy, as well as an introduction to male genitalia, which, although fascinating, didn't live up to years of girl talk's giggly expectations.

Still, at any age, snuggling was nice. Warm and comforting and...no, there'll be none of *that*.

Hannah suggested, "Maybe we should just move to the living room."

Mouth pursed, David hunched a shoulder with utter nonchalance, as men do when their bluffs are called. "Fine by me, if you'll unplug the office phone, too. It's rung about every two minutes since I got here."

Come to think of it, the last time she was in the living room, broken glass, dirt and a corpse were elements of the decor.

"I can't unplug it," she said. "It's the only one hooked to the answering machine."

David grinned and made a pushing motion. "Guess we'd better stay in here, then."

Teasing him had been irresistible, but Hannah's earlier fidgets had brought a real and pressing need to the fore. Choosing a sweet smile over puppy-dog eyes, she asked, "Would you mind zapping my coffee in the microwave first?"

Taken aback, his mouth moved, but nothing came out.

"And if it isn't too much trouble, how about pouring it into a mug first, then reheating it." She flashed another smile. "Dishes are in the cabinet, right of the sink. Three minutes on High."

As David's begrudging backside cleared the doorway, she threw back the covers—*ouch*—and swung her legs—*eeyow*—to the floor. Once vertical, gravity's influence on her bladder induced a wide-eyed, arm-waving, headlong rush, like Susan Hayward hurrying along a train station's platform to welcome her lover home from the war.

The call of nature answered, Hannah ran a toothbrush around in her mouth, then smushed and smoothed her hair. Nothing could hide her bruised eye, lower lip and neck, but she dabbed on moisturizer for general principles.

"Get real, Sluggo," she muttered, climbing back into bed. "Men don't make passes at girls who look like roller derby queens."

Balancing a water glass in his palm and carrying a mug by its handle, David reappeared, baby-stepping like one who had never waited tables for a living. He scowled at her, reposed in the same spot she'd been earlier.

"Gosh," she chirped, "I hope I'm not spending my rain check for that steak dinner on all this pampering."

"Truth be known, a phone call from my ex-wife had me convinced we should stick with just being friends. I was going to tell you that last night, if we'd had dinner like we planned."

A familiar, evisceration-in-progress feeling wrenched her insides. Wifey-poo realized she can't live without you, huh? Well, congratulations. May you both be utterly miserable.

"In under two minutes," David continued, "Cynthia told me my best friend had been shot and was in intensive care, then reminded me how crappy it is to be involved with a law enforcement officer."

Huh? Oh, she did, did she? What a heartless, self-centered, vindictive thing to do. David's ex-wife and Jarrod Amberley had a lot in common.

"I'm almost afraid to ask what you mean by 'was' in ICU."

"The doc said Mike could be moved into a regular room this afternoon," he said, setting the steaming cup on the nightstand.

"He must be one tough hombre."

"Yep. Thank God."

"What a difference a day makes."

"Amen to that, but yesterday isn't one I ever want to repeat. Hearing about Mike was bad enough, but I came too close to losing you, too. I knew already, but seeing you in that chair looking like a cross between General McArthur, Whistler's Mother and a lost, little girl drove it home."

How the man could be a linear thinker, and often talk like an oral connect-the-dots game mystified her.

"Sorry, but I guess I'm still a little lost. Drove what home?"

"How much I'm 'in like' with you, Ms. Garvey. Can't say where it'll lead, and the whole idea scares the hell out of me, but I don't want to be 'just friends.'"

While her slack jaw shaped her mouth into a perfect capital "O," her mind scurried about, searching for all those rock-solid reasons why a relationship between a thirty-six-year-old sheriff and a forty-three-year-old operations manager was folly to the nth degree. Apparently, however, that particular lobe of her brain seemed to be on holiday at the moment.

"Lord above, woman. From the look on your face, you'd think I just asked you to donate a kidney."

Hannah threw her head back and laughed. "All right, Hendrickson. I kind of like you, too, okay? Most of the time."

He wiggled his eyebrows. "Wait'll you see my bedside manner." Presenting the water glass he'd held long enough to count as an appendage, he said, "According to the note in the kitchen left by my colleague, Dr. Pennington, you're supposed to take one of these every four hours."

Hannah removed the glass, exposing the pill in David's outstretched palm. "No, I think I'll pass. I don't want to zonk out again." She grinned. "You might take advantage of me."

He chuckled, low and throaty. "When advantage is taken, sugar, it'll be mutual."

His voice shivered through her. Careful. Anything you say can and will be used against you. Hannah snatched the tablet and swallowed it.

"Good girl. Now, since we're 10–7 on the coffee

and the controlled substances, will you please scoot over?''

Hannah patted the coverlet opposite her.

"Nope. Won't work. I sleep on my right side. Stretching out on my left isn't comfortable."

Before she could argue, he whipped back the bed linens, scooped her up, pillows and all, and deposited her gently in the middle of the mattress.

"You ought to wear purple more often," he said, ogling her satin camisole and tap pants.

Feeling a full-body blush zip up from her toes, she yanked the sheet over her. "I thought your back hurt."

"I've bucked hay bales heavier than you."

The bed pitched and yawed with his quest for spinal alignment, then he sighed and said, "Ah, yeah. Much better."

"I'm so happy for you."

He propped his head on a bended arm, then switched to a jaw-in-hand, grunted, and, with obvious dismay, reverted back to the original position.

Hannah slipped a pillow from behind her back and bopped him with it. "You're about as tactful as a freight train, Hendrickson."

After she wriggled and fussed into a single-pillow recline, he snuggled against her, his arm cuddling around her belly. "Now, that's perfect."

And it was. Comforting, even. Her foot at rest on his shin, his thigh pressed to hers, her hip nestled against his—

"Kathleen," she blurted. "What'll we tell everyone. The simpler the better, don't you think?"

"Uh-huh."

The fingers attached to the hand attached to the arm curled around her, massaged her ribs. Nice.

"How about if we say when she told Earl about the movie, he thought she was a rich, retired movie star?"

"'kay."

Heat radiated at her hip, undaunted by the sheet or her lingerie. Nice. Warm. Comforting. The trifecta of snuggling.

"Then Earl told his uncle," she went on, trying not to think about the source of the nice-and-warm or the effect his caress was having in areas nowhere near her midsection, "and they planned to rob her—uh, you know, together."

"So far, so good."

Comfort. Um, oh yes. Definite comfort. "But Earl jumped the gun, so to speak—"

"You mean, took matters into his own hands?" David's own slid under the hem of her camisole.

"Yes…yes, he did, by golly." Languidly, wondrously, the tip of his thumb traced the curving furrow beneath her breast.

She hadn't been this aroused in years. Decades. Ever? Wet, trembling, hungry. Not foreplay. Seduction. She ached to be touched in places she shouldn't let him touch. Ached to touch him in places she shouldn't touch. Not yet.

Next year, maybe. The first time only happens once.

She told herself the slight nudge of her hip was purely unintentional. He nudged back. Hard. Not the nudge, his…*him*.

Raise your hand, just a little, an inch or two, is all. Touch him. You want to. *He* wants you to. Wants you to stroke its thickness, its length, its—

Don't you dare. He's barely at first base, and you're thinking bottom of the ninth, last game of the Series.

She took a deep, ragged breath. "Then Gibb murdered Earl for killing the golden goose."

"Uh-huh."

"And—and Gibb, he thought I had Kathleen's money since I inventoried her cottage."

"Yeah...."

"And came here last night to get it back."

David kissed her neck. "I like it." His lips traveled upward. "Very much." They brushed her cheek. "I think we ought to go with it." Hovering an inch above her, he whispered, "Don't you?"

Arm curling around his neck, she mouthed "Yes," and brought his lips to hers. Tasting sugar, cinnamon and a sweetness all his own, her greedy tongue demanded more. He cupped her breast and she moaned.

Stop. Got to stop before it's too late. You aren't in love with him. He isn't in love with you. He's too young. You're too old.

It's broad daylight, for Christ's sake. He'll see...*everything*.

Desire shuddered through her, his tongue probing, flicking the tip of hers, promising other pleasures awaiting her elsewhere, all in good time.

She read somewhere that every woman owes it to herself to fall for a dangerous man once in her life. Impetuous, remember? *Do it.* Find out how just how dangerous David Hendrickson can be.

Her fingers closed around him. He growled, deep in his throat....

Adam 1–01, this is Baker 2–01. Assistance needed with a 10–24 in progress at the Valhalla Springs Community Center.

David froze. His head snapped up. "Aw, *shit.*"

"You're on duty?" Hannah gasped, unable to leap

from the brink of sweet surrender to disembodied cop speak.

"Twenty-five hours a friggin' day, eight days a friggin' week."

Rolling over on his back, he snatched the handset off the nightstand. "So help me God, Andrik," he yelled into the microphone, "this damn well better be an emergency."

Static crackled for several seconds. *Well, now, you tell me, Sheriff. Despite it being Wednesday, does busting the Every-Other-Tuesday Bridge Club for pot possession constitute an emergency?*

MIRA Books
invites you to turn the page
for an exciting preview of

SOUTH OF SANITY

Join Suzann Ledbetter
as she takes readers back
to the mystery and mayhem in
Valhalla Springs.

Available in paperback
March 2001

1

In less than twenty-four hours, Hannah Garvey had survived as assault with a deadly weapon, almost made love with Kinderhook County Sheriff David Hendrickson and was about to console her boss's sixty-seven-year-old mother who'd been busted for distributing marijuana to members of her bi-weekly bridge club.

Not bad for a Wednesday and it wasn't even noon, yet.

David Hendrickson's hand came to rest on the cruiser's passenger-door handle. His gray-blue eyes flicked from Hannah's bruised neck to her cheek to the puffy shiner she'd camouflaged with liquid make-up—the purplish souvenirs of the previous evening's near-death experience.

"You're as wobbly as a newborn foal," David said. "Will you *please* go back to bed and let me handle this mess at the community center?"

She grinned up at him. "Hypocrite."

"Say what?"

"Funny, how my health wasn't an issue a few minutes ago when you were advancing from first base to second."

His arm tightened around her waist, drawing her snug against his chest where she fit as if her body had been designed for that purpose. "Well, sugar, as I recall, you were doing a mighty fine job of warming up the ol' batter, yourself.''

Dangerous, Hannah warned herself, as she had seconds before Detective Marlin Andrik's radio call stopped her from finding out exactly how dangerous the sheriff could be.

It's safer if I never do, she reasoned. The six-foot-three-inch lawman with the killer grin and ''Aw, shucks'' manner sent her libido screaming into overdrive. But, a solemn vow not to screw up her new life as badly as she had most of her old one nagged her whenever she wasn't in the throes of pure, unadulterated horniness.

Like now, for instance.

''I am this retirement community's operations manager,'' she reminded him, easing from his embrace. ''I can't swear it's part of my job description, but something tells me I ought to be around when my employer's mother is about to be arrested on felony charges.''

David blew out a resigned sigh, then swung the Crown Victoria's door open for her. Sliding into the seat, she turned away so he wouldn't see her wince.

He was right, as he'd been too many times during their short relationship. She should be in bed—alone—popping painkillers like candy. But IdaClare Clancy was in trouble and Hannah knew the irrepressible, pink-haired widow wouldn't have let a little thing like assault and battery get in her way had their situations been reversed.

Enough electronic gadgets and gizmos to delight the Starship Enterprise's navigator arrayed the cruiser's dashboard, floor hump and console. Buttons winked and voices emitted from the police radio. Hannah gave a start when her sandaled heel brushed the cold, smooth barrel of the shotgun jutting from under the seat.

The interior smelled of vinyl cleaner, dust and aftershave. She'd spearheaded advertising campaigns for some of the world's most expensive colognes, but there really *was* something about an Aqua Velva man.

David chuckled as he keyed the ignition. "Never been in a police unit before, huh?"

She smiled. "Not in the front."

His crooked eyebrow begged a question, which she ignored. Keeping the sheriff off-balance was a hell of a lot more fun than spilling secrets like jelly beans from a jar.

Musty, warm blasts from the air-conditioning vents changed to musty, arctic blasts. Locked inside a mobile chest freezer with a man whose metabolism rivaled a polar bear's, Hannah gazed longingly at the late-April, seventy-degree day drifting past the window.

Buttery sunshine enveloped the bowlegged duffers populating the development's golf course. Small boats floated atop the adjacent, spring-fed lake while other anglers tried their luck along its sloped, grassy banks.

In all, three-hundred-and-sixty healthy, moderately wealthy senior citizens lived in Valhalla Springs, a retirement community described as "East of Peculiar and the closest thing to paradise this side of Sanity."

Persnickety types armed with Missouri maps would insist the development was actually east-southeast of Peculiar, a bedroom community near Kansas City, and that the Ozarks terrain surrounding Sanity, the Kinderhook County seat, was too rugged to fit anyone's definition of paradise.

Because three burglaries, two murders and an attempted homicide had occurred during Hannah's brief tenure as operations manager, she took "paradise" with a grain of salt, but admired Jack Clancy, the development's owner, for preserving the land's natural beauty, rather than bulldozing all the trees and naming streets after them.

She silently rejoiced when they turned into the elongated, cedar-sided community center's parking lot. If IdaClare Clancy had run afoul of the law, at least she'd done it where open windows and sliding glass doors promised relief from frostbite.

At ground level, the hub of Valhalla Springs's indoor activities featured a banquet room, six meeting rooms and a commercial-grade kitchen. The basement's swimming pool, weight- and work-out rooms gave tenants no excuse for not getting or staying in shape.

A hand-lettered Closed sign was taped to the door. Hannah made a mental note to clean her office answering machine's heads. They'd need it, poor things, with all the complaints they were sure to record before the center was cleared as a crime scene.

Expecting a cross between a Gray Panther rally and a riot, Hannah wasn't disappointed when she and David entered the building. A platoon of matronly bridge players surrounded Detective Marlin Andrik like magpies converging on a downed wren.

Chin bobbing, mouth working and hands raised in an attempt to stem the tide, the craggy-faced detective was as besieged and beleaguered as a Libertarian at a Democratic National Committee brunch. Hannah didn't blame him for yelling, "Sheriff Hendrickson's here. He's the ranking officer."

The horde pivoted en masse, shaking fingers and fists like a perfectly coifed, heavily perfumed, human tsunami.

David muttered, "Holy Moses," and backpedaled a step.

Wedging a pinkie and thumb between the corners of her lips, Hannah loosed a piercing whistle—a skill learned in childhood and honed by twenty-five years of hailing taxis in Chicago where she'd worked as an advertising account executive at the Friedlich & Friedlich Agency.

The stampede not only halted, invectives were bitten off in midsyllable. Andrik's jaw dropped as if its bone hinges had snapped. David's eyes widened with astonishment.

"If you ladies would please retake your seats," Hannah said, "Detective Andrik and Sheriff Hendrickson will finish their business here as quickly as possible."

Nods and murmured assents accompanied the sea of protest's deployment to its respective tables. Andrik crossed the room as metal folding chairs thumped, rattled and squeaked. "How in the devil did you *do* that?"

Hannah licked her lips in preparation for an encore.

"Not the whistle," he said, "the—" he jerked his head at the tables "—sit down and shut-up part. Those old biddies have been pecking at me nonstop for a half hour."

David said, "She's something else, isn't she?" as if he'd assembled Hannah a la Dr. Frankenstein.

"Before the natives get restless again, Detective," she said, "would you mind telling me where you get off raiding private property without notifying the manager, first?"

"Much less, me," David chimed in.

"I did, soon as I knew I had something. And what'd I get for being thoughtful? My superior hollering 'This by God *better* be an emergency,' into his radio." Andrik cupped his ear. "Still sounds like the ocean in there. May be permanent."

"Would you mind cutting to the chase?" David said.

"Be glad to, boss." Andrik shifted his weight. "I received a tip from a lineman who was out here during yesterday's power outage. He said the pole he was hanging from gave a bird's-eye view of a greenhouse at 2404 Sumac Drive and the healthiest crop of cannabis he'd seen in a coon's age.

"Seeing as how he told us about that pot-patch in the National Forest last fall, it was no sweat getting a search warrant. Mrs. Clancy wasn't home, so I nosed around outside. My informant was dead-on. I rang a couple of doorbells and a neighbor told me Clancy was here playing bridge."

Andrik pulled a zip-top baggie from his sportcoat's pocket. Exhibit A's dried, dull-green leaves rustled softly as he squeezed it. "I guarantee this ain't oregano, children. Neither are the cones Clancy was doling out like party favors when I stopped in to serve the warrant."

Hannah groaned. A few days earlier, IdaClare had mentioned the greenhouse she'd had built without her son's knowledge or consent. When Hannah asked to see it, IdaClare demurred, stammering something about exotic plants requiring unrelieved darkness to bloom.

The evasion tripped Hannah's internal lie detector, but she'd been too preoccupied figuring out why someone had bludgeoned a retired, spinster schoolteacher to death to pursue it.

"What's with the 'Uh-oh' look?" David inquired. "Did you already know about Miz Clancy's secret garden?"

From the moment they met—a roadside interlude that resulted in Hannah paying a five-hundred-and-sixty-dollar fine and court costs for speeding—Hendrickson had demonstrated an uncanny ability to read her mind.

"The greenhouse, I was aware of. What IdaClare was growing in it? Not a clue." Scanning the tables, Hannah added, "Where is she, anyway?"

Andrik poked an elbow at a couch and wing chairs grouped in front of a windowed wall at the room's far end. "Over there with your physical fitness instructor. Maybe you can talk some sense into her. When I tried she waved a 'Bustcard' at me."

"A what?"

David cursed under his breath. "The American Civil Liberties Union prints wallet-size cards listing rights and responsibilities for individuals to use when they're stopped by the police."

Hannah frowned. "So? What's wrong with that?"

"Nothing, except they're advertised as a deterrent to police abuse."

"Could be us law enforcement types are a mite sensitive," Andrik drawled, "but the ninety-nine-point-nine percent of us who don't make a habit of knocking heads together kind of resent the insinuation we're dirtbags with badges."

"I see...." Hannah murmured. And she did.

An involuntary shudder rippled through her. She looked up at David. "Any objections to me talking to IdaClare?"

He consulted Andrik. "All the formalities dispensed with?"

"Duly Mirandized and etcetera-ed, only I don't think the old girl savvies how much trouble she's in."

He scratched a graying sideburn. "If there was ever such a thing as an open-and-shut case, this is it, pard."

IdaClare was clad, as usual, in her favorite color; on this occasion, a pink, light-wool skirt-suit and matching shell. She sat in the high-backed wingchair with her purse in her lap like a patient awaiting a distasteful medical procedure, the hand not stabilizing her pocketbook clasped Willard Johnson's larger, dark one. Willard looked as though he'd slide into a boneless heap on the floor if not for IdaClare's digital anchor.

The physical fitness instructor graced Hannah with a beatific grin. IdaClare took one look at her and gasped. "Your face—those bruises. My stars and garters, child, are you all right?"

"I'm fine," Hannah lied. "What I want to know is, what's wrong with him?"

IdaClare tossed a disgusted look in Willard's direction. "Well, it's his own fault. I told him to help himself to our refreshments, *except* for the brownies on the green tray. But did he listen? Why, he must have eaten a dozen of them before I caught him."

"Better'n my mom's by a mile," Willard slurred, then giggled. "Man, I gotta get her the recipe."

Hannah massaged a temple to ward off the migraine she was due to have any second now. "Don't tell me, let me guess—the brownies on the green tray were spiked with pot."

"Just a teensy pinch or two," IdaClare allowed. "If he hadn't gotten greedy, he'd probably never have noticed." Her thumb caressed Willard's knuckles. "It isn't as if I *poisoned* him or anything."

"But IdaClare..." Hannah's shoulders slumped. She glanced back at the refreshment table. No green tray. Andrik must have confiscated it. Damn. Snorking whacky snacks might reduce the urge to throw something—a tantrum, or perhaps that lovely candlestick lamp through the plate-glass window located so handily behind it.

A majority of the detained card players filed out the door, chins aloft with indignation. Smoke would start rising from the development's telephone wires within minutes.

Marge Rosenbaum, the president of the Every-Other-Tuesday Bridge Club, and the six others still seated at the tables were pictures of serenity, much like Willard, and no doubt for the same reason.

Hannah gazed wistfully at David's broad shoulders, his tapered waist, his sculpted, jeans-clad butt. Her departure from the ad agency had been as impulsive as it had been abrupt. Maybe if she groveled, pled temporary insanity and accepted a pay-cut, Tom and Rob Friedlich would hire her back.

Then again, as Great-uncle Mort Garvey had often said, "It ain't wise to burn your house down just to kill a rat," a homily that actually made sense, as opposed to most in his repertoire. With maturity came the realization that her maternal elder's elevator didn't go all the way to the top, but Socrates had been considered a crackpot in his day, too.

IdaClare clucked her tongue. "I'm truly sorry to have caused such a ruckus, dear. If you never speak to me again, I won't blame you a bit."

Hannah squatted down beside her chair. "I'm not angry—well, not as angry as I am worried. Ye gods, if you're convicted of selling home-grown marijuana—"

"Selling? I've never charged anyone a plug-nickel

for my herbs. It wouldn't be Christian to take advantage of people that way.''

Willard's fist punched the air. "Right on, sister."

Hannah glared at him. "Oh, why don't you take a nap or something?"

Smacking his lips, he murmured, "B'lieve I will." His eyelids drooped like a pair of cheap window shades.

Hannah inquired of IdaClare, "Does Detective Andrik know you don't sell your, uh, herbs?"

"He said he was glad to hear it, not that you could tell by looking at him." She chuffed. "Ever notice how his nostrils pinch? I suspect he was a colicky baby and never entirely recovered."

Hannah tried, but couldn't stifle a laugh at the mental image of Marlin Andrik in miniature burping on his mother's shoulder.

"I know the three of you think I'm a bubble-brained old fool, but I'm not," IdaClare went on, her voice stern and slightly resentful. "I knew exactly what I was doing when I started cultivating my herbs, I'm not one iota sorry I did and if a judge can't find it in his heart to understand why, he can kiss my keister in the middle of the courthouse square at high noon."

A flush mottled her wrinkled, cherubic face. "It's hell getting old, Hannah. I won't bore you with an 'organ recital,' but if I can ease my friends' ailings with a cookie, a poultice, a cup of tea or a pipe, there's no one short of the Almighty Himself who's going to stop me."

The speech and the passion with which it was delivered defeated any argument Hannah might have launched. She glanced at Willard, sprawled and snoring in his chair like a big puppy, then stood. "Do you want to call Jack or would you rather I did?"

IdaClare gnawed a patch of lipstick off her lower lip. Her expression said she'd rather while away her golden years on Riker's Island than confess her sins to her only child. "What do you think he'll say?"

Hannah had known Jack Clancy for years—as a client, then, a cherished friend. A gambler by nature, he'd parlayed a commercial construction-excavation company into one of the county's premier resort development firms.

Essentially, Jack Clancy was a kind, lovable, funny, second-generation Irish teddy bear with nuclear capabilities.

"He'll say a lot of one syllable words," Hannah answered, "and nothing Chase Wingate will be able to quote in next week's edition of the *Sanity Examiner*."

IdaClare flinched. "The boy does take after his father—God rest him—in that respect. Maybe it's best if you talked to him first, dear."

Surprise, surprise. At least Jack couldn't kill the messenger from his St. Louis office, and the distance allowed for a four-hour stay of execution.

Hannah asked, "How about a lawyer?"

IdaClare waved a dismissal. "There's no sense in paying some twit I don't know from Methuselah's grampa to lock the barn door after the horse has run off."

Great-uncle Mort would have loved that one.

"I wish that detective and your sheriff would quit piddling around." IdaClare consulted her watch. "Kathleen Osborn's memorial service is at four, and we are *not* going to miss it."

Before Hannah could refute ownership of the hunky,

thirty-six-year-old county mountie, he called her name and crooked a finger.

Excusing herself, Hannah strode toward the refreshment tables where David and Andrik had poured themselves cups of coffee, then nearly jumped out of her shoes when something *ka-whammed* into the center's front door.

A face attached to a roly-poly, uniformed deputy was squashed against the glass, the mouth open and distorted in a grotesque sneer. After peeling himself from the obstruction, the deputy shook like a sheepdog after a bath, adjusted his hat and gun belt, then pulled the door open in keeping with the directional placard glued beside the handle.

"What's Moody doing here?" David asked.

Andrik cursed. "This is what I get for requesting a patrol unit to help transport our string to the courthouse."

"He's a *deputy?*" Hannah murmured, watching the newcomer smile and fawn over the bridge players like a table-hopping emcee.

"Reserve officer," David said, obviously loath to admit it. "Rudy finally managed to graduate from the academy, but he isn't and never will be on the payroll. Bad example of a fine recruitment program."

"World's worst example," Andrik corrected. He glanced at David. "I'll get Claudina for this."

"After I'm through with her." David added for Hannah's benefit, "Claudina Burkholz is our chief dispatcher. Sending Moody out on calls we're working is her idea of a joke."

The Schmoo in Blue halted and snapped a salute. "I understand we have a 10–15 at this location, sir." He rolled his shoulders back and squinted at Hannah.

"Too bad you're learning the hard way, we have zero tolerance for drug activity in this county."

David groaned. "For Christ's sake, Moody. Leave it to you to pick on the only individual in this room who isn't involved."

The reservist's watery blue eyes tick-tocked between Hannah and the sheriff. "She *isn't?*"

"This is Hannah Garvey, Valhalla Springs's operations manager."

"Oh. Oh, my *gosh.*" Rudy pumped her arm as if expecting to draw water from it. "I'm awful sorry, Ms. Garvey—and about your face, too."

Hannah laughed. Poor guy. Bruises fade, but dumb is usually permanent. "That's okay, Officer Moody."

Rudy's beaming appreciation dissolved into a scowl. "Except if she isn't—I mean—well, sir, who is the 10–15?" He nodded toward Willard Johnson. "Him?"

A buzzer-like noise sounded in Andrik's throat. "Wrong again. At this rate, you don't have a prayer of making it to the Lightning Round."

David gave the detective a curt, "back-off" look. "You're familiar with medicinal marijuana, aren't you Rudy?"

"Why, sure. Groups all over the country are trying to legalize it for folks with cancer and AIDS and such."

"Well, I'm afraid the lady in pink over yonder and those at the tables jumped the gun a trifle."

Rudy's expression resembled a goldfish who'd leaped from its bowl without fully considering the ramifications. "But sir...they're older than my momma."

"Don't let their looks fool ya," Andrik warned. "They're vicious. Every last one of 'em."

David clasped Hannah's arm. "While you two sort

out which of the Apple Dumpling Gang is riding with whom, I'll take Hannah back to her cottage.''

''Oh, no, you won't,'' she protested.

He steered her toward the door. ''Oh, yes, I will. You're as pale as a ghost and there's nothing you can do at the courthouse anyway.''

''I can lend moral support.''

''Nope.''

''Fine,'' she said, shrugging. ''I'll drive myself into Sanity.''

The eyes probing hers were more gray than blue. Not a good omen. ''Why? Just to show me and everybody else how tough you are?''

''No.'' She looked away. ''Okay, I'm lousy at doing what's best for me, especially when someone tells me what's best for me.''

''Is that a fact?'' Grinning, David swung the door open for her.

Hannah looked back. ''What about Willard? He isn't under arrest for anything, is he?''

''No, being slipped a marijuana mickey isn't illegal.''

''Well, I can't just leave him here and he's in no shape to drive.''

''I'll get his keys and lock up, then Moody can drop him off at home on the way to the courthouse.''

''What about his car?'' Hannah indicated a white compact in a shady corner of the lot.

''Call him this evening after he's had time to come back down to earth. Between the two of you, you'll figure out something.''

''You have an answer for everything, don't you, Hendrickson?''

"Sugar, like my daddy always says, I don't even know most of the questions, yet."

As much as she hated to admit it, during the short ride Hannah began to feel borderline wretched.

"You okay?" the sheriff inquired, his tone concerned.

"I will be, as soon as I have a bologna-and-potato-chip sandwich and a nap."

Having seen the reaction before, Hannah knew his curdled expression didn't pertain to the latter. Beyond chocolate, everyone has a personal brand of comfort food. As the only child of an unwed, alcoholic mother, Hannah hadn't had the luxury of being a picky eater. Then again, rich people missed out on trailer-trash delicacies such as refried bean dip and Cheez Whiz on crackers, toasted at 350-degrees for a couple of minutes.

The check-and-balance system. It's what made America great.

One of the fingers curled around the cruiser's steering wheel sprang into point position. David said, "Your nap may have to wait a while."

Bob Davies, the development's Maintenance Department supervisor and an equally blond, burly assistant were repairing the damage wrought on her cottage's front door the previous night. She couldn't hear their hammers, but felt them pound.

David wheeled into the circle drive, shifted into park and laid his arm across the seat back. "I wish I could stay, but I have to get back to the community center."

"I know." She groped for the door handle.

"Remember me telling you about my buddy in Tulsa?"

She nodded. Mike Rivera, his best friend since they

had trained together at the city's police academy, was recovering from a gunshot wound received during a convenience store robbery.

"Well, soon as IdaClare and her girl-gang are booked and bailed out, I'm heading down there to see him." David's browline corduroyed. "Don't know how long I'll be gone. Two, maybe three days."

A soldier shipping out to parts unknown and eminently fatal couldn't have looked more solemn. Hannah clasped her hands to her bosom. "I'll count the hours till your return."

He threw back his head and laughed. "You do beat all I've ever seen, woman." Edging closer, he glanced at the workmen. "Mind if I kiss you goodbye in front of witnesses?"

She hesitated. Past, albeit limited experience had proved the man kissed finer than a fantasy lover. Thorough. Paralyzing. *Dangerous.* She leaned away. "I'm, uh, not keen on public displays of affection."

David studied her a moment. "Second thoughts, huh?"

"Some." Rough estimate, forty-two thousand since their lovemaking had been interrupted that morning.

His lips curved into the lazy grin that banished thoughts of emergency liposuction, chemical peels and breast implants and replaced them with images of how god-like he'd look naked, how much she wanted to see him naked and whether the Crown Victoria's back seat was as spacious as it appeared.

"Will you promise me something, then?" he asked.

Anything. Everything. "Depends on what it is."

"Dinner at my house, the night I get home. The dinner we've already had to postpone twice."

Better judgment and those forty-two thousand second thoughts voted no. "Okay."

"Promise?"

She shivered and blamed it on the car's subzero air-conditioning. "I promise."

Things are heating up...

MARY LYNN BAXTER

SULTRY

Since her mother's tragic suicide, Lindsay Newman has watched her wealthy Mississippi family spin out of control. Tired of being a pawn in men's games, Lindsay is determined to become a rebel in her own life—and Mitch Rawlins ignites that first white-hot spark.

But the Newmans' new groundskeeper isn't interested in playing games with a spoiled rich girl...yet he wants Lindsay more than anything. But, like everyone else in the Newman household, he's got something to hide. Something that could tear Lindsay away from him forever.

"Ms. Baxter's writing...strikes every chord within the female spirit."
—Sandra Brown

On sale mid-June 2000 wherever paperbacks are sold!

MIRA

Visit us at www.mirabooks.com

MMLB588

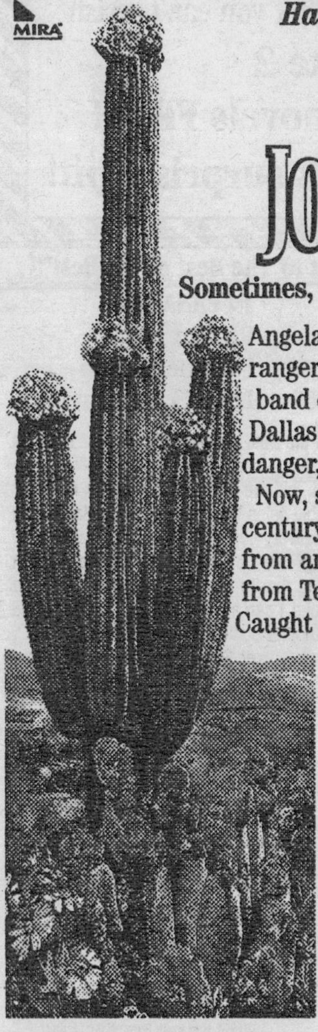

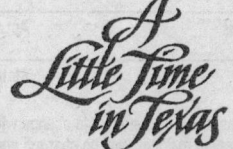